"A love letter to rom-coms in the form of a sweet love story." —NPR

"Kerry Winfrey offers readers a fizzy rom-com with all the humor, heart, and the undercurrent of melancholy of the Nora Ephron rom-coms she pays tribute to within its pages."

—*Entertainment Weekly*

"Kerry Winfrey's feel-good romance is an ideal ode to the genre."

—Oprah.com

"An endearing, klutzy heroine elevates this utterly charming romance [and] the plot's many moving pieces add complexity. Chloe, lovable Uncle Don, and the local coffee shop's colorful characters provide humor and heart in just the right places."

—*Publishers Weekly* (starred review)

"What a total delight it was to read this book! A compelling, heart-warming, hilarious rom-com. I couldn't stop turning the pages!"

—*New York Times* bestselling author Lori Foster

"Winfrey's sweet, hilarious novel is full of klutzy and charming characters, heartwarming moments, and laugh-out-loud one-liners. This quick read is sure to delight readers looking for an escape of everyday life, especially fans of Mary Ann Marlowe and Helena Hunting."

—*Booklist*

"This sweet story is a warm, favorite-sweater-wearing hug for any-one who believes that true love doesn't only happen in the movies."

—kc dyer, author of *Finding Fraser*

**PRAISE FOR**
## *Not Like the Movies*

"The sparkling dialog and hilarious banter in this second in Winfrey's series (after *Waiting for Tom Hanks*) will dazzle readers craving a self-aware rom-com. Perfect for fans of Christina Lauren and Nora Ephron."
*—Library Journal*

"Kerry Winfrey follows up last summer's delicious *Waiting for Tom Hanks* with this deliriously lovely rom-com. . . . Hopeful, heartfelt, and poignantly tender, *Not Like the Movies* is the ideal title for late summer, a simultaneously warm and bittersweet package that feels just like this time of year."
*—Entertainment Weekly*

"Winfrey has built in all of the charming things that make rom-coms addictive: richly developed characters, a deep pool of supportive friends, awkward situations, goofy reactions, missed opportunities, big misunderstandings, and grand gestures. This romance is slow building, but the journey is a delight."
*—BookPage*

"Those who enjoy fast-paced, sparring banter will find much to savor in this sexy story where love may—or may not—conquer all."
*—Shelf Awareness*

# VERY SINCERELY YOURS

## Kerry Winfrey

JOVE
New York

A JOVE BOOK
Published by Berkley
An imprint of Penguin Random House LLC
penguinrandomhouse.com

Library of Congress Cataloging-in-Publication Data

Names: Winfrey, Kerry, author.
Title: Very sincerely yours / Kerry Winfrey.
Description: First edition. | New York: Jove, 2021.
Identifiers: LCCN 2021008030 (print) | LCCN 2021008031 (ebook) |
ISBN 9780593333419 (trade paperback) | ISBN 9780593333426 (ebook)
Classification: LCC PS3623.I6444 V56 2021 (print) |
LCC PS3623.I6444 (ebook) | DDC 813/.6—dc23
LC record available at https://lccn.loc.gov/2021008030
LC ebook record available at https://lccn.loc.gov/2021008031

First Edition: June 2021

Printed in the United States of America
1st Printing

Book design by Ashley Tucker

For everyone who's still figuring it out

# 1

THE NIGHT TEDDY PHILLIPS GOT DUMPED, SHE HAD EXPECTED to get engaged.

It's not that Richard had been too obvious, but there were signs. He was more distracted than usual, looked more nervous when she talked to him. Richard was usually confident, perhaps to a fault, so she found this charming. As if she'd say no! As if she'd say anything other than "Yes, I want to marry you and be with you until death do us part!" after which Richard would pick her up and spin her around.

Richard had asked her that morning if they could talk that night, so she decided to set the mood by making one of his favorite meals: spaghetti and meatballs. Some people might have called Richard a picky eater, but Teddy preferred to think of him as a *selective* eater. Really, why go through all the work of trying out new meals when you knew the five or so things you liked best?

Was she disappointed when she came home from her shift at work to discover that the apartment looked the same as it always had? A bit. But after six years together, she knew not to expect rose petals on the floor or Richard waiting for her by candlelight, down on one knee, asking her to make him the happiest man in the world.

Richard wasn't showy about their relationship, and that was one of the things she liked about him.

But Teddy knew she could create a mood; after all, that was what she did in their relationship. Richard worked long hours as a doctor, and he didn't have time to do things like "decorate the apartment" or "buy coordinating throw pillows" or "prepare his own meals." That was what Teddy did.

A lot of people didn't realize, she thought to herself as she simmered the pork-and-beef meatballs in her special homemade tomato sauce, that being in the background was sometimes just as important as being in the spotlight. Sure, in their relationship, Richard was the one who stood out, the one who had the important job. But being in the shadows wasn't so bad. Someone had to make the shadows cozy; even shadows could use a diffuser or a comfy knit blanket.

And their town house was nothing if not cozy. Teddy was especially proud of the fall tableau she'd created on the mantelpiece of their gas fireplace as soon as she flipped the calendar to September. Pumpkins and a felt leaf garland were involved because, in her opinion, a house wasn't a home unless it was filled with miniature pumpkins in the fall.

Teddy dumped the pasta into the boiling water and set the timer. Humming to herself, she lit candles on the table, then took out her phone to choose some music. This was the first time she'd considered the question: "What music would I like to get engaged to?" She bit her lip, scrolling, and then found a playlist called "Best Music to Play During a Proposal." "Unchained Melody," "Can't Help Falling in Love." . . . Yes, this was perfect.

As the Righteous Brothers started playing, Richard walked through the door with a jingle of keys. Teddy spun around quickly and smiled.

"Um," Richard said, looking around in confusion.

Okay, so this wasn't exactly the reaction Teddy wanted. No matter.

"Hi, you," she said as the timer went off. She grabbed her strainer and carried the pot to the sink. "Just thought I'd make things special for tonight!"

Richard still hadn't moved from the doorway. After Teddy strained the pasta, she crossed the room and closed the door behind him. "How was work today?" she asked.

He blinked. "It was fine. This is just surprising." He sniffed. "Did you make . . . ?"

"Spaghetti!" Teddy said with a smile. "Your favorite!"

Richard frowned at her light gray cardigan. "Don't forget to soak that."

She looked down and saw a splatter of tomato sauce. Richard had once told her that bright colors made her skin look sallow, so now she mostly wore neutrals, and this J.Crew cardigan was one of her favorites. "Oh, shoot," Teddy muttered, then looked back at Richard and smiled. "Anyway, it's almost ready. Want to sit down?"

Richard nodded as Elvis's voice filled the room. "Uh, yeah. Let me go get changed."

A few minutes later, Teddy placed bowls of pasta, glasses of wine, and a loaf of homemade garlic bread on the table as Richard emerged from their room.

He sat down without a word, so Teddy followed suit. He took a bite in silence, so she did the same. *He's probably worried,* she told herself. Asking someone to marry you seemed like it might be a bit nerve-racking, although he *must* already know what her answer was.

Richard speared a meatball with his fork, then cleared his throat. "Teddy, there's something I need to say."

"Yes!" Teddy said brightly.

Richard paused and looked from the meatball to her. "What?"

It finally registered that he hadn't actually asked her anything, let alone proposed. "Sorry," Teddy said. "I . . ."

She sighed. She would have to make this easier for Richard; that was what she did, after all. She made things easier for a partner who worked so hard.

"I know you're nervous," she said, reaching across the table to grab his hand. "I know this is a hard conversation for you."

Relief washed over Richard's face. "You do?"

Teddy nodded enthusiastically. "Of course! You think I haven't noticed the way you've been distant? The way you've been working even more than usual?"

Richard slumped over. "Wow. Have I been that obvious?"

Teddy smiled. "Well, yeah, but it's okay. Because I'm going to answer the question so you don't have to ask it. Yes."

Richard's eyebrows shot up so high that Teddy was afraid they were going to hit his hairline. "Yes?"

She squeezed his hand again. Surely this was the moment he'd get out the ring. "A thousand times yes."

"Whew!" Richard let out a nervous laugh. "I can't tell you how much better this makes me feel. I've been stressing out over this for weeks, wondering how you'd react—"

Teddy shifted in her seat as her smile turned to a frown. "You . . . didn't know?"

Richard's eyes widened. "Of course not. But obviously you could tell something was off, too. Man, this has got to be the easiest breakup I've ever had."

Teddy pulled her hand back. "What?" she whispered.

"Not that there's much of a contest. My high school girlfriend toilet-papered my entire yard when we ended things, and she even used a ladder to reach the really high spots. That toilet paper stayed in the tops of the trees until it rained. Now *that* was a bad breakup."

Teddy stayed silent.

"I mean, to be fair, I *did* cheat on her. But still. It was a bit dramatic."

Teddy looked at the spaghetti sauce, now cold and unappetizing on her plate.

Richard shoveled food into his mouth. "I can't believe how hungry I am now that we got THAT over with. Why is Céline Dion playing?"

Teddy realized, as regret washed over her, that she wouldn't ever be able to listen to "My Heart Will Go On" again without thinking of the time Richard unceremoniously dumped her over a plate of spaghetti. Not that she'd listened to it much since elementary school, anyway, but it was the principle of the thing.

"I can turn it off," Teddy mumbled, pulling her phone out of her pocket.

"I'm so glad you already knew I was going to ask you to move out," Richard said, his mouth full. "But I'm not surprised. You always kinda know what I'm thinking before I do."

"You want me to . . . move out?" Teddy whispered.

Richard shrugged. "One of us has to leave, and it's not like you could afford the town house on what you make at the toy store, you know? So it makes sense."

Teddy nodded. "Right. It makes sense."

"I knew I couldn't be the only one who realized something was off," Richard said, wiping his mouth with his napkin. "And think of it this way: maybe this will be the motivation you finally need to figure out what you want to do with your life."

Teddy recoiled in confusion. "What?"

"Well." Richard chuckled, and Teddy noticed that he had a piece of oregano stuck in his teeth. "It's not like it's some secret that you don't know what you want, Teddy. That's kind of the difference between you and me, isn't it? I've always wanted to do something big, be a doctor, help people. And you . . . well, you've always had a smaller life. I guess we should've known it wouldn't work forever."

Teddy willed herself not to cry. Okay, so she hadn't known what she wanted when she met Richard in college . . . but that was what Richard was *for*, right? *He* was the thing she wanted. She didn't have to worry about figuring out what she should do with her life because she could focus on making Richard's the best it could be. She'd spent years making things as easy as possible for Richard, she thought as she blinked back tears. She should fully commit and make this breakup as easy as possible, too.

"Great dinner, by the way," Richard said, getting up from the table without clearing his plate. "Could probably use more garlic next time, though, don't you think? Oh, and, uh, not to be pushy, but when do you think you're going to leave?"

"Leave?" Teddy asked. Tonight she couldn't stop repeating Richard's words, since she couldn't seem to find any of her own.

"I just think that the sooner you go, the easier it will be," Richard said, wincing. "For both of us."

Teddy stood up and carried their plates to the sink. "Right. I'll leave tonight and come back for my stuff soon."

Teddy knew that she should have probably done something to convince Richard that they should stay together. There must have been something she could say to remind him that they'd been together for years, that they loved each other, that she did nothing but take care of him.

But then . . . that was the problem, wasn't it? Richard didn't want her the way she was; he wanted someone else, someone *more*.

He stood in the middle of the living room, arms crossed. He didn't look devastated or remotely sad. He looked like a man who was about to kick back with a relaxing night of single-camera sitcoms on Netflix.

"Well . . . ," he said, and Teddy thought, *This is it. This is the part where he says it was a mistake, that we should be together, that this doesn't make sense. That we work so well together, that he appreciates me making his life so easy, that he knows he never would've picked out that beautiful area rug he's standing on without me. That he needs me.*

"You need any help?" he asked, the same way he might have asked to help carry some groceries.

This was the end, then. This was the way things were happening, and there wasn't a damn thing she could do to change it.

## 2

IN HER CAR, AS SOON AS THE REALITY OF WHAT HAD HAP-
pened sank in, Teddy burst into tears. She didn't like to cry in front
of Richard, because he was one of those people who got uncomfortable around tears, as if sadness was a contagious disease. But
now, in the comfort of the front seat and as the radio played a com-
mercial for a heating-and-cooling company, she let them fall.

She'd texted her best friends, Eleanor and Kirsten, before she
got in the car and warned them that she was coming over. Even
though she loved them, she didn't see them all that much, since she
was always with Richard. As far as they knew, she and Richard were
the perfect couple, so the breakup would no doubt be as surprising
for them as it had been for Teddy.

So while Eleanor and Kirsten were two of the kindest people
Teddy knew, she didn't know how they'd respond to her showing up
on their doorstep, tearstained and also spaghetti stained. Especially
because she had no idea where she'd be staying until she could figure out how to get her own place. Technically, there was her mother,
although she would probably give Teddy a laminated to-do list of all
the ways she could get her life back on track. She knew Sophia, her
sister, would take her in, but she had two children and a husband.
And then there was her boss, Josie, who was like a second mother

to her . . . but Teddy would feel embarrassed to admit to Josie how low she'd really sunk.

Richard had been her life since the day they'd met at a crowded Starbucks. Teddy had been there because, as a third-year undecided Arts and Sciences major, she was reading *Heart of Darkness* for the third time. For some reason, every lit professor she'd had loved discussing that book. Teddy may have been undecided, but she knew what she *didn't* want: to read *Heart of Darkness* again. And so she'd decided that a caramel macchiato might make the process, if not pleasurable, at least tolerable.

Richard had been in line in front of her. She listened to him order an Americano as she stared at the back of his head and the perfect swirl of his golden hair. She could tell by the way he stood— tall, confident, shoulders back—that he was someone who knew what he wanted. *He* probably wasn't on his third year of being un- decided.

As they waited for their drinks, he got a phone call and walked away from the counter, and then out the door. The barista set down an Americano for Richard, and Teddy watched him outside, pacing as he talked on his phone. He was going to forget his drink, or someone else was going to grab it, Teddy realized. For the first time in a while, she felt a sense of purpose. She'd bring him his coffee.

He hung up the phone as soon as she walked up to him, holding out the cup. "Didn't want you to forget this," she'd said quietly.

He'd looked at her, amused, and Teddy instantly knew she was a goner. Here was someone who, she could tell, needed her. Here was someone she could help. It turned out that Richard, a few years older than her, was studying to become a dermatologist, which seemed so much more important than what she was doing (cur- rently, not much of anything). After a few months of being together, of helping Richard study and quizzing him and making sure he ate balanced meals, Teddy unofficially switched her major to Assisting

Richard. Officially, she ended up graduating with an English degree, more out of convenience than because she had plans to do anything with it. With Richard, she felt *useful*, because unlike the rest of the world, Richard needed her.

Not anymore, it seemed.

Teddy walked up the steps of Eleanor and Kirsten's tiny brick duplex, their porch covered in pumpkins, mums, and a knit throw resting on an Adirondack chair. Before she could knock on the door, it opened.

"Get in here," Kirsten said, ushering Teddy inside and wrapping a blanket around her as if she'd saved her from drowning in an icy pond.

"What are you doing?" Teddy choked out through her sobs. "It's not that cold!"

"Sure, but now you're cozy," Kirsten said. "And being cozy makes everything better."

Eleanor burst through the swinging door to the kitchen, holding one of her beloved vintage teacups. "Oh, honey. What happened?"

Teddy sat down on a pink velvet sofa and started crying harder. "Richard broke up with me."

Eleanor and Kirsten were silent, and Teddy looked back and forth between them. "Did you hear me?" she asked. "The love of my life asked me to move out!"

"Richard?" Eleanor asked at the same time Kirsten asked, "The love of your *life*?"

Eleanor wrapped her arms around Teddy. "Tell us about it."

And so Teddy told them the entire humiliating story, and they winced and gasped at all the right parts.

"And now you can never listen to 'My Heart Will Go On' again," Kirsten said sadly as Teddy finished.

Teddy nodded. "I thought that was one of the worst parts, too."

Teddy looked around, pulling the blanket tighter as if she had come in from a blizzard instead of a slightly chilly fall evening. Eleanor and Kirsten's place had a hominess and lived-in quality that her place—well, Richard's place—didn't, no matter how hard she'd tried to create one. She'd never felt entirely comfortable there, but she already felt that way in Kirsten and Eleanor's apartment. It looked like the home of an artist and a kindergarten teacher, because that's exactly what it was. Each room was painted a different bold color—the living room shone with *Goodnight Moon* green, while the kitchen was clear-sky blue. Kirsten's art decorated the walls, and scribbled crayon drawings from children covered the fridge.

"Thanks for letting me come over," Teddy said, her voice hoarse from all the crying.

Eleanor gave Kirsten an almost imperceptible nod, and Kirsten said, "Okay, it's time."

"Time for what?" Teddy asked as Kirsten grabbed her hand and led her and Eleanor into the kitchen.

Kirsten opened the door to the freezer and Teddy gasped as she realized what she was seeing. "Is this freezer entirely full of ice cream?" she asked.

"Yes," Eleanor said.

"How have you never told me about this?" Teddy asked in wonder.

"You've never needed it before," Eleanor explained.

"We've got local favorites," Kirsten said, pointing to Jeni's and Graeter's. "Your socially conscious classics." She gestured to Ben & Jerry's. "Dairy-free options, and gelato, and rainbow sherbet because Eleanor likes it for some reason."

"Guilty as charged," Eleanor said.

"So there you go, babe," Kirsten said. "Pick your poison."

Teddy had only just stopped crying, but receiving this kindness in the form of ice cream made her start crying again. "Bramble-berry Crisp," Teddy said.

"Flawless choice." Eleanor grabbed the pint from the freezer and handed it to Teddy with a spoon.

The three of them returned to the living room and once again sat down on the velvet couch. Kirsten and Eleanor had lived here for years, but Teddy had been in the apartment only a few times. Typically when they met up, it was for a quick brunch or coffee. Although they always invited her to their elaborately themed movie nights, she declined because she didn't want to miss out on being with Richard in the evenings. How would he feel if she wasn't around to take care of him?

Well, pretty good, apparently. She started to cry harder.

"I don't think I've ever seen a person cry for so long," Kirsten said.

"Teddy," said Eleanor, putting a comforting hand on her back, "where are you staying?"

Teddy shrugged the best she could while shoveling ice cream in her mouth. "Dunno," she said with a full mouth. "I guess I could ask my mom or Sophia. Or Josie."

"Stay here," Eleanor and Kirsten said in unison.

"I can't do that," Teddy said. "I'm already imposing on you guys."

Kirsten gave her a genuine laugh. "Friends can't impose. Especially not after a breakup."

Teddy sighed into her ice cream. "I can sleep on the couch, right?"

Eleanor wrinkled her nose. "Well, maybe not. For one thing, the velvet's not exactly comfortable . . ."

"And for another thing, we definitely found it on the curb last week," Kirsten added. "But you're in luck—we have a guest room!"

Eleanor tilted her head. "Well, technically it's a large closet."

"And even more technically, it used to be my studio. But I got a space somewhere else, so we stuck a bed in there for when Eleanor's sister is in town."

"But," Eleanor said, "Maureen is currently *Eat Pray Love*–ing it all over Europe, so don't worry. The room's yours."

Teddy set her ice cream on the coffee table (which was dark brown and covered with golden giraffes—surely also found on a curb somewhere) and crossed the living room. She peeked in the door of her new room.

It was small, sure. The bed took up almost the entire space, and there wasn't a window. But she felt something she couldn't identify—nausea? excitement?—when she thought about that tiny closet room being hers.

"Are you guys sure?" she asked, surprised that Eleanor and Kirsten were standing beside her and looking in at the room with her. "I mean, this is really nice. I'll do all the chores to make up for the inconvenience. Vacuuming. Laundry. The dishes . . . this spoon! I'll start with washing this spoon."

Eleanor gently took the spoon out of her hand. "We're not asking you to stay here so you can be our housekeeper. We're asking you to stay because you're our friend, and we want to."

"I don't want to bother you," Teddy said softly. She'd spent so long trying to make Richard's life as easy and conflict-free as possible, and now here she was, depositing herself on her friends' doorstep, taking over an entire room of their house, being the biggest imposition possible.

"It would be actually impossible for you to bother us, Teddy," said Kirsten. "You're like one of those weird little animals you see in a viral video where people think it's a stuffed animal because it's so cute but then actually it's a real chipmunk or whatever."

"I'll take that as a compliment," Teddy said, and then, even though she was uncomfortably full of ice cream and her face was still streaked with tears, she realized she was laughing for the first time in a long while.

## 3

IF THERE WAS ONE THING GETTING TEDDY THROUGH THE SUR-
prise breakup from hell, it was children's television. But it wasn't
nostalgia or the annoyingly catchy ukulele theme song of her favorite show that comforted her . . . It was the host.

It wasn't as pathetic as it sounded—or maybe it actually *was* pathetic. Teddy didn't know. All she knew was that, in lieu of an actual
therapist, her therapist was Everett St. James, the host of a local
children's show called *Everett's Place*. Teddy had a surprisingly common fascination with him—an affliction that affected many people
in Columbus, although, to be fair, most of them were moms. Teddy
once stumbled upon a local message board where parents of tod-
dlers discussed looking forward to their child's daily viewing of
*Everett's Place* and had conversations about how much they loved
Everett's hair and his whimsical (yet attractive) sweaters. "After our
seventeenth read of *Guess How Much I Love You*, I practically leapt at
the TV when I saw a human man on-screen," one mom wrote.
"Everett St. James can talk about my feelings anytime," said another parent. "Do you think he's married? He doesn't wear a
ring . . . ," someone posted, but everyone else ignored her. No one
wanted to think about Everett St. James being married. Part of the
fantasy was that he was always available.

While Teddy wasn't a mother, she understood what these message board posters were talking about. She'd found Everett's show years ago when babysitting her niece and had been so distracted by Everett himself that when she finally tore herself away from the screen, she realized that Emma had drawn a picture on the wall, dumped grape juice on the couch, and given the patient family dog a lopsided haircut.

Ever since that day, she'd been watching Everett's show on her own. No one else knew about her habit. It was just her and a message board's worth of sexually and emotionally frustrated moms who needed to project all of their desires onto a broad-shouldered, floppy-haired, sensitive puppeteer.

It was now three days after she had officially left Richard's place (well, after he had officially kicked her out of their place) and Teddy was watching the latest episode on her laptop at work when the bell above the door rang. She quickly slammed her laptop shut as a small girl walked into the shop and gave her an almost imperceptible nod.

From her station behind the counter, Teddy watched the girl in the bright red coat. She trailed her fingers along cabinets, picking up some toys before putting them back disinterestedly. Others she stared at longer, examining them and pulling out an honest-to-God camera, not a phone, to snap a picture.

Weekday mornings were typically a quiet time—even a customer-free time—at Colossal Toys, with most people at work or in school. Why Josie opened the shop so early, Teddy didn't understand. But the girl's presence was especially odd because of her age. Colossal Toys was a vintage toy shop, full of action figures from the eighties and nineties—Teenage Mutant Ninja Turtles and My Little Ponies and Transformers—the shelves so overstuffed that they threatened to topple at any moment. Teddy herself, at nearly thirty years old, hadn't been alive when many of the toys were in their heyday. Any children in the store were usually dragged there by pop-culture-obsessed parents eager to show off original *Alien* action figures to their uninterested offspring.

As if she could feel Teddy's eyes on her, the girl whipped around and leveled a stare at her. "I'm not stealing anything."

Teddy stood up straight and reflexively moved to smooth out the layers of her long brown hair, then remembered that she'd asked a hairstylist yesterday to give her a bob. And so, with a few quick chops, the feature that Richard had complimented most (usually when he was deriding how "unfeminine" he found short hair) was gone.

Teddy pivoted and tucked the edges of her bob behind her ears, chastened by sustained eye contact from a girl whose age was most likely barely in the double digits. "I didn't think you were."

The girl lifted her eyebrows as if waiting for Teddy to state her true intentions, and Teddy found herself unable to say anything. *I'm the adult here,* Teddy told herself. *Get it together. This is a child.*

"Isn't today a school day?" she finally asked.

"My parents don't believe in traditional schooling. I'm allowed to roam the city unsupervised during school hours."

Teddy blinked.

"I'm kidding," the girl said, a small smile breaking through her otherwise serious face. "It's a teacher in-service day."

"Oh," Teddy said, relieved. "I forgot all about those."

"Anyway," the girl said breezily, "feel free to go back to your job. I don't need to be entertained."

Teddy cocked her head to the side, studying the girl. "Do you even know what any of these toys are?"

The girl nodded. "Some of them. My parents are old and I'm an only child. Well, not really. I have a brother, but he's eighteen years older than me, so he's more of a very involved uncle than a brother. My parents distrust most aspects of current popular culture, so I'm more familiar with"—she gestured around the store—"*this* than most of my classmates."

She walked across the store, which took her only a few steps, as it was very small and packed full of toys. "I'm Gretel, by the way."

Teddy held out a hand. "I'm Teddy. What a lovely name."

Gretel rolled her eyes. "As in 'Hansel and.' My parents again. My mom's a literature professor with a concentration in folktales. Where does your name originate? The bear?"

Teddy stifled a smile. "It's short for Theodora. My great-grandmother."

"Oh, candy!"

Gretel's eyes lit up as she saw the large display of vintage candy along the counter (the brands were retro; the candy itself was new). She picked up a packet of Pop Rocks, looking for the first time like an actual child instead of a world-weary middle-aged person shoved into a small body.

"It's on the house," Teddy said, feeling generous and a little protective of Gretel already. It couldn't be easy to have the personality of a precocious kid on a sitcom when you were in school in the real world.

Gretel gave her a small smile, followed by an adultlike nod. "Thank you. I'm headed to the bookstore now, but I'll be back soon. It was nice to meet you."

"And you," Teddy said, returning the nod. "Have a great day!"

The bell on the door chimed as Gretel walked out and a gust of chilly fall air rushed in. Through the window display, Teddy watched Gretel rip open the packet of Pop Rocks, tilt her head back, and dump the whole thing in before walking off.

Teddy was used to seeing all sorts of customers. Colossal Toys was located in the Short North, Columbus's busy arts district. During peak hours, a steady stream of people flowed through—serious collectors, casual browsers, couples on first dates, babies who grabbed Incredible Hulk figurines and hurled them to the ground—and there was no shortage of conversation, which Teddy loved. Teddy considered herself an introvert, but she wasn't shy when it came to one-on-one conversation. She loved it when strangers told her long, involved stories about why they were looking for a specific Conan the Barbarian action figure.

But most of the customers she saw, however gregarious, weren't quite like Gretel. Teddy made a note to mention her to Josie when she came in later, because she knew Josie would get a kick out of her.

Until then, however . . .

Teddy reopened her laptop and started the episode again.

Teddy didn't believe in guilty pleasures as a concept. She figured if you liked something, whether it was the Taco Bell Crunchwrap Supreme or the music of boy bands from the late nineties (okay, so those were both examples from Teddy's life), why feel guilty about it? The world was a tough, cruel place. Why not find joy wherever you could, grab that joy by the metaphorical joy reins, and hold on tight?

That being said, Teddy did feel, if not guilty, then definitely in the neighborhood of weirdish about her love of *Everett's Place*, despite the fact that the message board moms reassured her she wasn't the only one. Given that she worked in a toy store, her obsession with puppet-based entertainment might give the impression that she was a perpetual child.

But there was something about Everett, the titular host and puppeteer, that soothed her. It might've been his large brown eyes and open, honest face that made her feel better about the world. Or maybe it was the way he managed to maintain a conversation with a puppet while responding to a heartfelt letter from a child, which could've been an extremely specific version of the "get you a man who can do both" meme tailor-made for Teddy.

*Everett's Place* was largely about feelings, a favorite topic of both Teddy and preschoolers. Each week, Everett and his crew of puppet friends (an alligator, a raccoon, a sloth, and a llama wearing a particularly sassy hat) explored some predicament that allowed them the chance to examine anger, or jealousy, or love. And then at the end of every episode, Everett and one of the puppets read a letter from a viewer who'd written in with a question. Sometimes they were silly, like the time a boy wondered why he couldn't pee outside like his dog did. And sometimes they were more serious, like the little girl who asked Everett where her grandpa went when he died (that one had made Teddy cry, with Everett and his big brown eyes explaining that the girl's grandpa would always be alive in her memories).

It was all a lot like Mrs. Doubtfire's show in the classic dramedy *Mrs. Doubtfire*, except that instead of Robin Williams dressed as an elderly nanny, this was an attractive man dressed as . . . well, an attractive man.

As the theme song began, the bell above the door jingled, but Teddy didn't bother to close her laptop. "Good morning," she said, offering a wave.

The man grunted at her as he speed-walked to the back of the store, a magazine tucked under his arm. Several days a week, he came in to use the restroom, never speaking to Teddy. Technically, the restroom was for paying customers, and she should've demanded he at least buy a Ring Pop if he wanted to relieve himself on the premises.

But also . . . well, Teddy had a hard time turning people away when they had to perform a basic bodily function. There but for the grace of God go I and all that. And so, since he always kept the restroom clean, she let him stomp past her without saying a word. She didn't know what happened on her mornings off—did he come in? Did Josie or Carlos, the shop's other employee, turn him away?

Teddy didn't know, but she enjoyed the slight mystery it added to her predictable days.

Teddy watched most of the episode without a single customer walking in. She barely noticed time passing until the restroom door flew open and the Mysterious Bathroom Bandit stormed through the shop and out the door.

"Have a great day!" she called as the bell rang.

The episode was almost over, meaning it was time for Teddy's favorite segment—"Letters to Everett." This week's letter, as Everett read to the llama, was from a little boy named Keegan. Everett cleared his throat before he started reading, and Teddy, she admitted, swooned a little bit. There was something about a man who looked like Everett taking a child's feelings seriously. It did things to a lady.

Dear Everett,

All of my friends are good at something. Jayden is good at basketball. Sasha won the spelling bee. Marlon was on *Chopped Junior*. But I'm not good at anything. I'm okay at lots of things (soccer, math, drawing) but not great. How do I find my thing?

Very sincerely yours,
Keegan, age 9

Teddy smiled at the formal sign-off, even as her heart twisted at the child's words.

"Well, Keegan," Everett said, looking straight into the camera (and straight into Teddy's soul), "I bet you're good at lots of things. For starters, this was a pretty good letter. Right, Larry?"

The llama nodded, and Teddy found herself forgetting, as she did every week, that the llama was controlled by a puppeteer's hand and wasn't acting independently.

"I bet you're a good friend, and a good son, and a good student. I can tell that you're kind and generous and helpful. But I know that's not what you're asking. You want to find your thing. Well, you might have already found your thing. It might be one of those things that you told me you're just okay at. Maybe once you spend lots of time practicing soccer, math, or drawing, you might find that you really are great at them.

"But maybe—and this is kinda cool to think about—your thing is out there waiting for you. Maybe your thing is fencing, or singing, or playing the flute. But you won't know unless you try, right? So that's my advice for you, Keegan. Try everything you can. Even—or maybe especially—the things that scare you. Keep your mind and your heart open and be on the lookout, and I know you'll find your thing."

Teddy swallowed hard. "How does he know?" she whispered to the case of original GI Joe figurines beside her.

Of course, Everett didn't know anything about Teddy. It wasn't like he knew she'd stumbled aimlessly through life until hitching her wagon to a man. He wasn't tailoring his message toward an adult woman; he was talking to a child. Also known as his intended audience.

But, oh, how Teddy identified with Keegan. She thought of some of the last words Richard had spoken to her.

*You've always had a smaller life.*

She flinched now, stung by the memory. She looked around the empty store and imagined how she looked sitting here all by herself, hunched over her laptop. Her life *did* feel small, and she wasn't sure that she liked it.

"Hello, hello!"

Teddy quickly closed her laptop as Josie approached from the back of the shop, carrying a large box. Not that Josie would necessarily care that Teddy was watching something, but she didn't think it was respectful to openly watch television when her boss was around, even if her boss was like a second, gentler, much less pressuring mother.

No offense to her own mother or anything.

"Hi, Josie," Teddy said, grabbing the box out of Josie's hands. No matter how often Carlos and Teddy told her to leave the heavy lifting to them, she refused to listen. She was seventy but had the attitude of a petulant seventeen-year-old.

She also had the energy of a seventeen-year-old. She went to Jazzercise three times a week, did an hour of yoga daily, brewed her own beer, had a robust metalworking hobby, and had Teddy over for dinner at least once weekly to demonstrate the skills she learned in cooking classes. Josie was more than twice Teddy's age yet had a significantly more vibrant life, as well as more flexibility and a stronger core.

"I can do it myself," Josie said, but let Teddy take the box and deposit it behind the counter.

"I know you can," Teddy said. "The issue is that you shouldn't."

"Well, look what you did," Josie said as she reached out and ran a hand over Teddy's new hair. "It's lovely."

Teddy beamed. A compliment from Josie always made her feel like she herself was full of sunshine, like Josie's persistent cheerfulness had entered her body through osmosis.

"Thank you," she said, but then watched as Josie's face changed from admiration to understanding.

"Wait," Josie said. "What happened? This isn't any old haircut. This is a breakup haircut."

Teddy stifled a sigh. She knew she'd have to tell Josie about the breakup sooner rather than later—they talked about pretty much everything. But she didn't want the workday to turn into a "Let's

Pity Teddy" party—she knew Josie would feel bad for her, give her one of those patented Concerned Looks she gave to customers who were having bad days, and then Teddy would be expected to explain what had happened.

"Richard and I . . . we broke up," Teddy said as stoically as she could, steeling herself for the hug and the offer of tea. Maybe Josie would invite her over for dinner tonight because she was so concerned about Teddy's mental state.

"Well." Josie patted her on the shoulder, then walked away. "Good riddance, that's what I say."

She made it halfway to the stockroom before Teddy called out, "Um . . . what?"

Josie turned around. "It's about time you dumped that deadweight. Rick the Dick. That's what Carlos and I called him when you weren't around."

Teddy's mouth dropped open. Carlos barely spoke a word to her, and now he was talking to Josie about Teddy's romantic life? "You and Carlos think *I* dumped *Richard*?"

The idea was so preposterous that Teddy almost laughed. She would never have dumped Richard, with his big dreams and his passion and drive and hair that swooped like a Disney prince's.

Josie walked back toward Teddy, eyeing her like she was a rabid animal who might strike. "Are you telling me . . . that the man dumped you?"

"Yes," Teddy said, throwing her hands in the air. "What else did you think happened?"

Josie grabbed a plush Care Bears toy and hit Teddy on the arm with it. "I thought you finally came to your senses and kicked him out on his loser bum."

Teddy rubbed her arm, as if the Care Bear had inflicted damage. "No. I did not. I thought he was going to propose, Josie. I made spaghetti and meatballs for him."

Josie rolled her eyes theatrically. "Oh, Lord. Well, you know what? This is a blessing in disguise. Now you're free and you've got a cute haircut to boot. It's finally time to sleep your way around town."

"I am . . . not going to do that," Teddy muttered.

Josie shook her head. "You think you've got all the time in the world, but let me tell you: you get old enough, and eligible partners are a hell of a lot harder to come across. There aren't a lot of men on the dating apps who are in their seventies, and frankly, I'm not going after the ninety-year-olds. I'm not into cradle robbers."

Teddy crossed her arms and smirked. Josie was, she was pretty sure, exaggerating. She'd been married to the love of her life until he died of a heart attack ten years ago. Colossal Toys had been John's shop, based on John's interest in vintage toys, and Josie had continued running it after his death, bringing in all the toys John kept around the house and making the store more crowded than it was before. Put politely, he had been a collector, although Josie affectionately (and perhaps more accurately) called him a hoarder. Josie often referred to John as her "dream man," and Teddy didn't think she was looking for a replacement.

"Whatever," Teddy said as she shook her head. "Sleeping my way around town, as much fun as that sounds, is the least of my concerns right now. I've got to move the rest of my stuff out of Richard's, figure out a long-term living solution that doesn't involve staying in Eleanor and Kirsten's guest room—slash-closet, and—"

"And figure out what you're gonna do with the rest of your life," Josie said with a pointed nod.

Teddy winced. "I think it's a little late for that. I'm an adult, Josie. The rest of my life is already happening."

Josie waved her off. "You know how many times I've started my life completely over? This is the fun part, sweetie. This is the part where you get to decide what's next, so it's up to you: what are you going to do now?"

And then Josie shuffled off to the stockroom, leaving Teddy alone with the toys.

"What *am* I going to do now?" she asked the empty store.

The toys kept their thoughts to themselves.

## 4

EVERETT'S FIRST MEMORY WAS OF KERMIT THE FROG.

He had been four years old, sitting on the corduroy sofa in his parents' Victorian Village home, watching *The Muppet Show* on a VHS tape they had checked out for him at the library. His parents hadn't cared about the *quantity* of television he watched, but they had distrusted the *quality* of modern entertainment. *Too loud,* they said. *Too crude. Too simplistic. Too . . . well, new.*

And so Everett's first memory wasn't of his own family but of identifying with Kermit the Frog, the sensible guy in a crew full of weirdos. Of Miss Piggy, a misunderstood diva who knew her worth, surrounded by people (or rather, puppets) who needed to get on her level. Of Fozzie Bear telling jokes that Everett would try and fail to tell his friends when he got older. Of Gonzo and his bizarre, frantic energy and semiperverse love of chickens.

*The Muppet Show* might have been made years before Everett was born, but he felt that it had been made for him, like Jim Henson was beaming the weirdness directly into his brain. When Everett was old enough to check out his own movies, he watched episode after episode, racking up enough overdue fines that his parents finally ponied up for the complete DVD collection when it came out. The Muppets were such a part of his life that he assumed the guest hosts of the show were current stars of the late 1990s and went to school talking about Ethel Merman, Jim Nabors, and Bernadette Peters, only to be met with blank looks from his classmates, who then changed the subject to Mark McGwire.

Everett didn't care. He liked living in the wacky world of the Muppets, and soon he'd developed a full-blown obsession with their creator, Jim Henson. Everett learned everything he could about him, watching all of his projects, even the experimental nonpuppet films. He daydreamed about having his own show and made his first puppet (an amateurish but enthusiastic dog) the year he turned ten.

But it wasn't the puppets themselves that held Everett's attention. It was the way Jim Henson used them to communicate a sense of wonder. When he watched the Pigs in Space get into another scrape, Everett laughed, but he also felt a sense of raw *possibility*. A sense of the potential in fabric and imagination. Those puppets could communicate feelings to both children and adults in a way that never felt condescending. *That's what I want to do,* Everett thought, and that desire held steady throughout his entire childhood.

After getting his degree at the Columbus College of Art and Design, Everett threw himself into designing his own show. It was initially a self-made production he put up on YouTube, just Everett and the puppets in front of the camera, with his art school friend Jeremy helping out. But eventually it got noticed, and before long, they had their own show on Saturday mornings, right after the local news.

It's not that it was easy—it wasn't. It had required years of work on something with no guarantee, all while Everett worked at a call center, spending his days asking people if they were happy with their cable provider and his nights pursuing what he loved. But the decision to do it . . . well, that hadn't been hard. In fact, it hadn't been a decision at all.

That was what he couldn't explain to the kids who wrote to him and asked how they could make their own shows, or write their own graphic novels, or follow whatever creative dreams they had. He didn't know what to tell them, because he'd just done it, just woken up every morning knowing exactly what he had to do to make his dream happen, without a worry of failure or rejection. He hadn't even given it a second thought.

Now Everett sat on the floor in his living room, surrounded by pieces of felt and chunks of foam, half-finished sketches covering the rug like freshly fallen snow. He needed to shake it up on the show— things were good, yes, but he couldn't ignore that feeling, the one that started like nausea in the pit of his stomach before turning into a tightness in his chest and finally manifesting as a full-body tingle. It was the "something is missing" feeling. The "there's something more" feeling. The "something needs to change" feeling.

This was the way he'd felt for most of his childhood—like he was working toward something that remained elusive, a cloud on the horizon, forever moving farther away. And then he'd achieved it. A show! A career! Success!

But now, years later, the feeling was back. Something was missing. There was something more. Something needed to change.

And so a new puppet. Nothing against the llama or the bear or any of his other characters—he loved them as if they were people. But much like a long-running sitcom might mix things up by bringing in a wacky neighbor, a new girlfriend, or a previously secret child from a past relationship, he needed to bring something fresh to *Everett's Place*.

"Are you okay?"

Everett jumped, dropping a piece of felt. "What the hell?"

His best friend, Natalie, stood staring at him, arms crossed, her bright orange lipstick shining against her chestnut skin. "I feel like I've walked into an episode of *Hoarders: Weird Puppet Dude* edition."

Everett groaned. "What are you talking about?"

She gestured around. "Uh, you're currently sitting in front of the TV in a pile of what—I'm gonna be honest here—looks like straight-up trash. Your kitchen counter is barely visible under all these empty take-out boxes. And . . . wait." She took a dramatic sniff. "It smells in here. Like a restaurant-dumpster-scented air freshener."

"Okay, okay, okay, I'm a mess. I get it." Everett got off the floor and sat on the couch. At least he'd show Natalie he understood how to use furniture. "How did you get in here?"

She dangled a key in her hand and crossed the room to sit beside him on the couch. "I have a key. Doy. I left my bike helmet here, so I came over to get it. I knocked three times, and when you didn't answer, I got worried that you'd died on the toilet, and I didn't want your parents to have to find you like that. It would be undignified and traumatic. I didn't know I'd walk in and find you"—she wrinkled her nose and gestured toward him—"living in filth and watching *The Jerk* for the hundredth time."

Everett sighed fondly. "Thank you for making sure I wasn't dead on a toilet."

"You'd do the same for me." Natalie bumped him with her shoulder. "You've gotta stop watching this movie. Your crush on Bernadette Peters is getting weird."

"She has big eyes and the voice of an angel. What man could resist her? And anyway, I'm not watching the movie. It's merely background noise while I work."

"I think it might be nice if you found a crush from—I don't know—this century. But whatever. You wanna get dinner with me and Lillian tonight? We're gonna actually go to a restaurant instead of eating while hunched over the kitchen counter like *some* people I know."

Lillian was Natalie's long-term girlfriend and typically the second wheel to Everett's third when he joined them for dinner or movie nights. Everett and Natalie had dated, way back in high school, before Natalie realized that she liked women and that her relationships could consist of much more than the content, companionable dynamic between herself and Everett.

"No, but thanks," Everett said. "I really need to figure out this puppet."

"Ev-er-ett," Natalie said, pronouncing each syllable of his name like it was its own word. "You've gotta take a break. Please don't fashion your life after one of those tech-bro gurus who, like, only eats Soylent and never sees his children and sleeps four hours a night."

"For starters, I don't have kids. And also the take-out boxes prove I eat something other than Soylent."

"You're gonna have a stress-induced heart attack at the age of forty, dude." Natalie got up and crossed the room, then smooshed her bike helmet over her golden curls. "You need to relax once in a while."

But what Natalie didn't understand, and what Everett couldn't possibly explain to her, was that work never stressed him out. Natalie worked in marketing and she loved her job, but she spent zero time thinking about it when she wasn't there. She didn't respond to emails at ten on a Friday night. She didn't spend her weekends visiting the office. In other words, she had a healthy work-life balance and necessary boundaries.

But Everett never wanted boundaries when it came to work.

"Okay," Everett said, staring at one of his sketches, already back in the work zone. "I really can't tonight, but next time, promise."

Even though he wasn't looking at her, he could practically hear Natalie rolling her eyes. "Next time, then. I'm gonna hold you to it. All right, I'm off to have dinner with my girlfriend and enjoy an evening watching terrible reality television, like a normal person who knows how to chill out. Try to get some sleep, okay?"

"I will," Everett said, waving as she shut the door.

The next time he looked at his phone, hours had passed and it was after midnight. He cleaned up all the empty take-out boxes and went to sleep.

## 5

TEDDY, KIRSTEN, AND ELEANOR ALL STARED AT THE LEOPARD-
print chair sitting beside the nonfunctional fireplace.

Richard had insisted that Teddy keep the chair in the basement, on account of it looking "ugly" and "like something a grandma would buy." But Teddy had always kind of loved it. And after a text that morning from him asking her to please get her things out of "the town house" (he still called it that and she still thought of it that way—*the* town house, as if it were the only town house in the world), she'd borrowed Josie's truck, showed up when she knew Richard would be at work, and hauled it out of the town house and into Kirsten and Eleanor's place.

Kirsten tilted her head to the side, like she was examining a painting. "I wouldn't say it . . . matches with anything."

"Leopard is a neutral," Teddy insisted.

"It's certainly cheerful!" Eleanor gave her a bright smile.

Kirsten narrowed her eyes. "Is it, though? It makes me think about dead animals. Not cheerful."

"It isn't *real* leopard," Teddy reminded them. But then her shoulders slumped. "I knew I should've left it on the curb. Richard always said it was awful, and he was probably right."

Kirsten and Eleanor looked at each other, and Teddy couldn't miss the entire conversation that took place in one glance.

"Keep it," they said in unison.

"It looks great," Kirsten said. "Cosmopolitan!"

"Chic!" Eleanor added.

"Sophisticated."

"Unique!"

"Okay, you're overdoing it," Teddy said, shaking her head. "I know you're only feeling sorry for me, but I'll accept your pity if it means I get to keep the chair in here."

"Can we please address what's sitting on the chair?" Kirsten asked, holding up a throw pillow that read *IT'S FALL, Y'ALL!* "I know for a fact that this wasn't in our apartment this morning."

Teddy raised her hand. "I also took that from the town house. I bought quite a bit of seasonal décor and I thought you guys might appreciate it more than Richard did."

Kirsten held the pillow out in front of herself. "I like it because it's true. It *is* fall, y'all."

"Right now I'm really enjoying the thought of Richard sitting in discomfort on a throw-pillow-less couch," Eleanor said, staring off into space as if she was picturing the scene.

"Well, now I feel bad," Teddy said.

"Don't feel bad," Kirsten said, putting the pillow back on the chair. "Not to be a gender essentialist, but I don't think men care about throw pillows. They're content to live in throw-pillow-less squalor."

Teddy smiled, grateful that they were trying to make her feel better . . . and grateful for their friendship, in general.

Kirsten, Eleanor, and Teddy had been friends since they met at a Jens Lekman show in college at the Wexner Center shortly before Teddy met Richard. It turned out that "Swedish pop music in an art museum" was one of the few places their interests overlapped, and if it weren't for that concert, they never would have met. Kirsten went out only if it was for an art-adjacent reason, Eleanor loved pop music but hated being out late on school nights, and Teddy almost never went anywhere by herself. That night, however, she felt like she would crawl out of her skin if she had to spend one more night at home. She went to the concert, where, even if she was technically alone, she could be surrounded by other people who liked the same music she did.

And so all three of them had ended up there, wearing the exact same argyle-print ModCloth dress. None of them looked the same in it—Kirsten was tiny and pale with a blond pixie cut, Eleanor was plus-size and Korean with long black hair and blunt bangs, and Teddy was sized somewhere in between them with brown hair that rolled past her shoulders in waves. When they spotted one another, it had been like one of those movie moments, all long glances and slow smiles and being drawn together across the room as if by magic.

They discovered that even if they didn't have much in common other than the music and the dresses, they were deeply in friend love with one another.

Teddy had met and started spending the bulk of her time with Richard soon after that, and so she'd missed out on doing most things with Eleanor and Kirsten. But now that she was here, she thought maybe she would feel like an equal part of their relationship again, that maybe she could turn the isosceles triangle of their friendship into an equilateral triangle.

"This is the first time all of us have been under one roof," Eleanor said, eyes wide, jolting Teddy back to the present. "That reminds me: we need to have a pajama-movie night."

"We're all in our pajamas right now," Teddy said.

"Yeah, but this isn't planned. Pajama-movie nights are a production. We have themes and snacks and decorations," Eleanor clarified.

"You guys don't need to do anything special on my account," Teddy said, shaking her head.

"But we're so glad you're here," Kirsten said, "because we hated Richard."

"Kirsten," Eleanor said, her voice a low warning.

"It's true. He treated you like garbage." She pronounced the word *gar-BAJ*, like it was French or something.

"He didn't treat me like gar*bage*," Teddy muttered, mimicking Kirsten's pronunciation. "Not all the time, anyway. Not at the beginning."

"Well, we're way past the beginning now, and that dude sucked. What was it he used to say, when he asked you to read aloud his textbooks to him like you were a human audiobook?"

Teddy swallowed hard. Kirsten had been so horrified by this detail that Teddy had stopped telling the girls anything about her relationship (which, of course, had only made her even more isolated). "Behind every good doctor, there's a good woman."

"Riiiiiight," Kirsten said slowly.

"That wasn't very kind," Eleanor pointed out, sounding like she was talking to one of her kindergartners. Teddy almost expected her to say, *That's not how we treat our girlfriends, is it?*

"And what did he say when you wanted to hang out with us?" Kirsten asked.

"He liked it when I was at home! And I liked being there! I liked being around when he needed me." Teddy crossed her arms.

Kirsten nodded, lips pursed. "And did he ever take your needs into account? Did he ever prioritize your interests? Did he ever give one single solitary shit about what you wanted, or was it the 'Richard Show,' twenty-four seven?"

Teddy sighed. She couldn't possibly explain to them that she'd been happy to do whatever Richard wanted because it took the pressure off her. Richard wasn't cruel, but she couldn't deny that he'd been happy with her only when she was serving him.

Well, until he wasn't, anyway.

"And listen," Kirsten continued. "I understand that his job is important. I respect the field of dermatology—I myself had a precancerous mole frozen off last week. But my dermatologist is a kind and professional person who doesn't act like she's Sandra Oh performing surgery in the first season of *Grey's Anatomy*."

"Love Sandra Oh," Eleanor murmured.

"The first season *is* great," Teddy agreed.

"Sandra Oh's greatness is not under scrutiny here. We're talking about Richard," Kirsten said, crossing her arms and staring at Teddy.

Teddy looked toward Eleanor for help, but Eleanor winced.

"He was kind of . . . well, a *dick*," Eleanor whispered, and Kirsten whooped.

"Why does everyone keep saying that?" Teddy protested.

"We're not saying this to make you feel bad, Teddy. We're saying, *Good for you*. You're free of that loser. No longer must you cook the same five bland meals. No longer are you shackled to his demands. Now you get to do what you want. And look at you! You have a breakup bob!"

Teddy smiled bashfully. "I do."

"And it looks amazing," Eleanor said, placing a hand on Teddy's arm.

"Forget Richard," Kirsten said. "Seriously. That guy doesn't exist. From now on all you care about is Teddy. It's time to focus on *you*. You've spent years taking care of him, but now it's Teddy time. Oh, I like that. *Teddy Time*."

"That sounds like a picture book," Eleanor said, nodding in approval.

"Or like a lingerie moment," Kirsten mused.

"What the heck is Teddy Time?" Teddy asked, confused. She sat down on the pink couch, trying not to think about what ancient bodily fluids might be embedded in the velvet.

Kirsten and Eleanor sat down on either side of her. "Teddy Time is a chance for you to focus on yourself," Kirsten said. "Figure out what you enjoy when you're not busy making food for a grumpy dermatologist."

Teddy couldn't help but laugh, even if the entire concept of Teddy Time didn't really make all that much sense. Then she wrapped her arms around Kirsten and Eleanor, all three of them squished into an awkward hug on the curb sofa. "I love you guys. Thank you."

"You don't need to thank us," Eleanor said into her armpit. "But never get back together with Richard."

They all laughed, but Teddy felt a tiny pinprick of nausea start in her belly. Richard wouldn't ever want her back, because a man like him should be with a woman who had more *direction*.

She shouldn't want him back. She knew that. But what she wanted was that sense of certainty, knowing the answer to any question in any situation. But now that she couldn't hide behind someone else's desires anymore, it was up to her to figure out her own life. To figure out what *she* wanted.

Maybe Kirsten was right. Maybe Teddy Time was the answer.

The oven timer went off, making everyone jump.

"Is someone cooking something? Is that what that smell is?" Eleanor asked, sniffing the air. "I assumed it was our neighbor. Or, like, a fragrant ghost."

"I made dinner for you!" Teddy called, running into the kitchen. "It's a pot roast. It's been in there for a while."

She pulled it out of the oven and returned to the living room, where Eleanor and Kirsten were staring at her, eyebrows raised.

"Do you . . . not like pot roast?" Teddy asked nervously. "I can make something else. And I made French bread, too, so if you don't like the roast, at least you can have that."

"Why did you make us dinner, Teddy?" Kirsten asked suspiciously.

Teddy started to sweat. "Because you guys are being so nice, and I wanted to say thank you, and I figured you'd be hungry, so—"

"And why have you been washing the dishes all week, even though the chore wheel clearly states it's my turn?" Eleanor asked.

Teddy threw her hands in the air. "I wanted to show how much I appreciate everything you're doing for me."

"You did every chore on the chore wheel," Kirsten said. "That's not the way chore wheels work, you know."

"Do you think we don't notice the way you've been vacuuming, and bringing in extra throw pillows that you've stolen from your ex, and mopping the kitchen floor?" Eleanor asked gently.

"We are morally *opposed* to mopping," Kirsten said.

"Teddy," Eleanor said, "what are you doing?"

Teddy swallowed. "I'm making things comfortable for you guys. You took me in, and I like doing all this stuff, and—"

"No one likes mopping," Kirsten said with a headshake.

"Sweetie," Eleanor said, "you don't have to pay us back by making us food. That's not how this works. I don't know what Richard did to make you believe you had to earn his affection, but that's not the way real relationships work, whether they're romantic or friendship."

"This is your place, too," Kirsten said. "You can just . . . exist here, you know? You don't have to be a one-woman chore wheel."

"Okay." Teddy nodded as an unfamiliar feeling washed over her. It was happiness, she realized. Just plain happiness that she got to be here with her two best friends who loved her exactly the way she was.

"That being said . . . that pot roast smells amazing. Can we eat it now?" Kirsten asked.

After the three of them had demolished the entire pot roast and most of a loaf of French bread along with a bottle of wine, Eleanor said, "We're not saying you should never cook for us. I mean, we like to cook for movie night."

"But we don't want you to feel like you have to," Kirsten said, taking a sip of her wine. "We already love you, Teddy. You don't have to convince us."

"Okay," she said with a relieved smile. "And I'll think about the whole Teddy Time thing. Maybe I have some undiscovered passions, after all."

"All right, then," Kirsten said, a cautious smile on her face. "Speaking of passions, I'm going to attend to mine right now. I'm working on some oxidation art."

"What's oxidation art?" Teddy asked.

"It's where she pees on canvases!" Eleanor said brightly.

"Don't worry." Kirsten stood up. "I do it in my room. Well, I do now. I used to do it in the studio."

Teddy nodded, trying not to cringe.

Eleanor smiled as she stood up. "Don't even think about doing the dishes. It's my turn—so says the chore wheel, and we must defer to its wisdom. Will you be okay for the rest of the night?"

"Yes," Teddy answered, but then thought about it. She'd spent the past few days staring into space instead of sleeping, wondering what Richard was doing as she lay in bed alone. Maybe she could spend tonight not thinking about him *or* cleaning Kirsten and Eleanor's apartment. Maybe this could be one of the very first evenings of her brand-new, terrifying, wide-open life. Day one of figuring out who Theodora Phillips really was.

"I'm going to do whatever I want," she said.

Eleanor gave her a thumbs-up and a smile, and Kirsten said, "Hell yeah!"

Teddy walked into her bedroom/studio/closet and shut the

door, sniffing the air a few times (no pee smell). She hadn't lied to her friends; she was going to do what she wanted tonight.

But what she wanted right now was to see someone she could count on, someone who could comfort her, someone who understood her.

She pulled her laptop out from under the bed (storage space in the bedroom/closet was lacking), snuggled under the blankets, and started watching the latest episode of *Everett's Place*.

## 6

EVERETT PULLED HIS JACKET TIGHTER AGAINST THE OCTOBER wind and climbed the stone steps of his parents' brick Victorian Village home, which was larger than the home of two professors had any right to be. His parents had purchased it with an inheritance before Everett was born, and so his childhood had been spent in this magical storybook house, one that had a literal turret, even if it was slightly tumbledown.

Once upon a time, the turret had been Everett's room, the place where he read vintage Hardy Boys books late into the night (with a bedside lamp illuminated, because his parents weren't the type to get mad at late-night reading and necessitate the covert under-the-blankets flashlight method). Now it was his sister's room, and Everett had no idea what she did up there. Hatched plans to take over the world probably.

Everett turned the doorknob and stepped inside. Despite the house's slightly imposing exterior (see: *brick, hulking size, turret*), the inside was cozy, with lots of small rooms full of wood accents that made everything dark but comforting. Everett slipped his shoes off before he stepped onto the threadbare (his mother would have said *well loved*) rug that had been there as long as he could remember. The air smelled of onions, garlic, and something he couldn't place, which meant his father was cooking. When Dad cooked, he tried new recipes—things he'd read about on food blogs or in the *New York Times*, or had at local restaurants and attempted to re-create at home.

When Everett's mother cooked, it was largely vegetarian chicken nuggets. This had also been true when Everett was a child, long before health and climate concerns made vegetarian options hip and commonplace. Back then vegetarian chicken nuggets were seen as incredibly gross, at best, to every kid who came over.

His sister appeared silently in front of him, which would've startled him if he weren't used to her by now.

"Hello, Gretel," Everett said. "How are you?"

Gretel was a full eighteen years younger than him, a late-in-life child for his parents, but he still spoke to her as if she were his sophisticated aunt. That was the type of response Gretel's presence demanded.

"You're late," Gretel said flatly. "The falafel's getting cold."

"Falafel?" Everett asked, his voice tinged with hope, but Gretel was already walking toward the dining room.

Everett hung his coat in the hall closet and followed her to the table, where both of his parents already sat.

"Everett!" they said in unison, joy in their voices.

There was a reason Everett had dinner at his family's home so often. He knew that most people his age only hung out with their families out of obligation, but his reason was simple. He liked them.

"Hey, guys," he said, sitting down on an antique wooden chair that creaked with displeasure. Everett had always been tall, with a body type best described as "sturdy," so since he'd been in high school, it had seemed like only a matter of time before he broke one of these delicate chairs.

His dad, who was built like him but with flyaway gray hair and a matching beard, smiled back. "It's falafel night."

His mother, who was a full two feet shorter than both of them, clapped her hands. "Falafel night, indeed!"

"I'd long resigned myself to a life of only eating falafel in restaurants," his dad said, gearing up for one of his patented monologues. Everett had always wondered if his dad became a professor simply so he'd have a captive audience.

"Who am I to attempt deep-frying at home? The oil. The mess. The work. But today I wanted falafel, and I thought to myself, 'Dave, what sort of example are you setting for your children? That you shouldn't take a chance? That you shouldn't risk an oil-splatter burn on your forearm? That you shouldn't make your own pita?'"

"Am I correct in assuming that the oil-splatter burn wasn't purely hypothetical?" Everett asked.

He caught Gretel rolling her eyes as his dad cheerfully held up his arm, which sported a bandage. "No risk, no reward—that's what I always say. Let's eat."

Dinner was delicious, especially when compared to what Everett usually ate: frozen pizza while working at home, fast food while working at the studio, vending machine snacks that his producer, Astrid, pelted at his head when he forgot to eat and got snappy.

"This is amazing," Everett's mother said, throwing her hands in the air. "The best thing I've ever eaten. You know I hate hyperbole—"

"That's one of your most defining characteristics, dear," Everett's dad said with a solemn nod.

"But this might be literally the best falafel I've eaten in my entire life."

"You know why I think that is?" Everett asked, pasting a thoughtful look on his face. "Because it's made with love."

Everyone pretended to gag, Gretel so convincingly that Everett started to worry she'd throw up on her plate.

"Mom's right," Everett said when everyone was done gagging. "This is fantastic."

"It is," Gretel agreed, wiping her face with her cloth napkin.

"So!" Everett's dad said with a subject-changing handclap, after absorbing his required amount of praise. "Everett, what's happening in the world of public television puppetry?"

"Yes, do tell," his mother said, leaning forward.

Everett looked at Gretel, who mouthed *Do tell*, then crossed her eyes. He ignored her.

"I'm working on a new character," Everett said. "I need another girl puppet."

His mother nodded. "Your puppets do skew male."

"I believe the term is 'sausage party,'" his father said, patting his mother's hand.

Everett wrinkled his nose and avoided making eye contact with Gretel. "Regardless, I'm working on a new puppet, but she isn't feeling real yet. Something's missing."

"So you're at the fun part," his mother said, eyes gleaming. "The part where you're uncovering the idea."

"Sure, the fun part. Also known as the part where I have no clue what I'm doing, no clue if it will work out, no clue if I'll ever have another idea again for the rest of my life, no clue if I'm a washed-up has-been who will spend his remaining days chasing an original thought that will never come."

"Also known as the creative process," his dad said with a smile.

"You say this every time," Gretel said.

Everett turned to look at her as she shoved a piece of pita into her mouth. "What?"

"Every time you start something new. You walk around all spacey, moaning about how you're never going to make anything new ever again, and then guess what."

She paused, and everyone waited.

"You always do."

"This is why I say you're my smartest daughter," Everett's mom said, then looked him in the eyes. "She's right. You'll be fine."

"Gretel!" his father boomed. "What did you get up to on this fine day?"

Everett knew that the prevailing parenting logic in this day and age valued protection and security over freedom, and people didn't let their young children roam unsupervised. But Everett's parents were—in case this fact has not already been established—*different*. For them, it was always the 1970s, and they let Gretel go where she wanted as long as it was on foot. It was also important to note that Gretel, being Gretel, was almost constitutionally unable to make a bad decision and despised most strangers, so there were limited worries about her running off with one.

"Much like Everett, I'm working on a new project, although I'm feeling significantly less tortured about mine," Gretel said. Everett suppressed an eye roll.

Everett's dad's smile shone beneath his mustache.

"I'm making a comic about my childhood," she said.

"You're twelve," Everett said.

Gretel raised her eyebrows. "And?"

Everett held up his hands in surrender. "Point taken."

"I'm currently in the research stage," Gretel said, and Everett watched his parents beam. No two people loved research more.

"I visited a vintage toy store today," Gretel continued. "Colossal Toys. They have a lot of old stuff . . . *Star Wars*. GI Joes. Barbies."

Everett's mind flashed briefly to what he'd been working on last night. He'd emailed some ideas to Astrid, and he fought back the strong urge to pull his phone out of his pocket to check for a response.

"Everett?" his mother asked, and he realized they were all staring at him.

"Stop thinking about your own work for two seconds and answer our question," Gretel said, frowning.

"What was the question?" he asked.

His mother smiled patiently, long used to his distractibility.

"What was that cartoon you and Gretel used to watch when she was a baby? The one with the tiny man who rode a fox?"

*"David the Gnome,"* Everett said without hesitation, and Gretel pulled out a notebook and scribbled something down.

"Is that really going in your graphic novel?" Everett asked. "An old cartoon we used to watch?"

"Perhaps," Gretel said with a sigh.

"But here's the real question: what are you going to write about your dear old pops?" Everett's dad leaned back in his chair, his hands behind his head and his elbows splayed out.

"Absolutely nothing at all," Gretel said, but she was smiling.

Everett's dad pointed to his bandage. "You guys wanna see my gnarly burn?"

"NO!" everyone else shouted in unison.

"For God's sake, Dave," Everett's mother muttered.

"This is, actually, going in the book," Gretel said, her pencil scratching across her notebook.

Everett smiled and took another bite of falafel.

## 7

AT ONE POINT IN HER LIFE, BELIEVE IT OR NOT, TEDDY HAD
been a daredevil.

She didn't remember using the training wheels on her bike—
from the moment she started riding, all she wanted was to fly down
a hill, hands up, no inhibitions. She climbed trees and fell out of
them. She was the first to put her hand up in class, whether or not
she knew the answer to the question. She would go anywhere, do
anything, regardless of whether her parents wanted her to. In fact,
as any rebellious child knows, sometimes it was the mere fact that
they didn't want her to do something that made her try in the first
place.

It was one of those days, though, that had changed her life. She
was going to the movies with her best friend, Vicki, a girl whom
Teddy loved but also slightly judged for not having her joie de vivre.
Vicki never wanted to do anything, Teddy had moaned to her sister,
Sophia, that morning.

Sophia had smirked into her cereal bowl. "Not everybody can
be hell on wheels, Teddy."

And that was what Teddy felt like that day, riding her bike to the
three-screen movie theater to meet up with Vicki, the wind blowing
her hair and her feet pedaling harder, faster. She was twelve years

old, she was hell on wheels, and she was going to see a movie she wasn't permitted to watch.

Her parents and Vicki both thought she was going to see a movie about missing dogs who were trying to find their way back to their family. And this was, technically, true. But then she and Vicki were going to sneak into a horror movie that was playing on another screen. Of course, Vicki didn't know this yet, but she'd go along with what Teddy wanted. She always did.

When the movie was almost over, Teddy leaned over to Vicki and whispered, "Okay, I have a plan. Let's go."

Vicki slowly turned to look at her, tears streaming down her face. "What?"

Teddy tried to tamp down her impatience. "*Come on*. We're sneaking into the movie next door."

"*Blood Sacrifice?*" Vicki squealed, and Teddy shushed her. The last thing they needed right now was someone complaining about them to an usher.

"But that's an R-rated movie," Vicki said, her tone of voice as scandalized as if Teddy had suggested they commit their own blood sacrifice. "We're not even allowed to see PG-13 movies by ourselves. And this movie isn't over! I want to know how it ends!"

Teddy rolled her eyes. "I mean, how do you think it ends? The animals find their way home."

Vicki's mouth dropped open. "Did you ruin the ending for me?"

Finally, unable to hide her frustration any longer, Teddy grabbed Vicki's hand. "Come with me."

The two of them ducked and shuffled down the aisle, spilling popcorn as they went. "Teddy!" Vicki hissed as dogs barked onscreen. "Do you really think we should be doing this?"

They reached the theater doors, and Teddy peeked her head out into the hallway. No one was watching. Without giving Vicki another chance to balk, she grabbed her hand and pulled her into the next theater, where *Blood Sacrifice* was in progress. Both the movie and one of the actual sacrifices, if all the blood on-screen was to be believed.

The girls took their seats, and Vicki slouched down. "I can't believe we did that and— Oh! What happened to that guy's eye?"

"It's all fake," Teddy said, happily shoving popcorn into her mouth.

"I don't know how you can eat at a time like this," Vicki muttered before someone shushed them, and they watched the rest of the movie in silence.

When it was over, Teddy deposited her empty popcorn container in the trash can, said her goodbyes to a visibly shaken Vicki, and walked out to unlock her bike. As she rode the few blocks home, she felt exhilarated. Someday, she'd be old enough to see whatever gruesome, gory, disgusting movies she wanted without sneaking into them. Someday, she'd be able to do whatever she wanted. The thought filled her with a happy sort of anxiousness, a bubble in her stomach that rose to her heart and made her feel like she was flying.

And then, without knowing what was happening, she truly *was* flying. Over the handlebars, through the air, onto the pavement. Her helmet slammed onto the ground and her knees skidded through gravel. But the worst parts were the smash-pop of her arm as it struck the road and the searing pain that roared through her.

"Oh, no," Teddy muttered. She was only twelve, but she knew this wasn't good. Arms weren't supposed to feel or look like this. She picked up her bike with her one working arm and dragged it beside her. Luckily, this had all happened a few houses away from hers, and no one had been outside to witness her spectacular crash.

She dropped her bike in the front yard and pulled herself up the steps, but stopped outside the door when she heard her parents through the open windows.

They were yelling at each other as usual.

"She was supposed to be home an hour ago!" her mother said, a thin, frantic note in her voice. "Should I call someone? I should call someone."

Teddy already knew who "she" was. Sophia didn't do anything to warrant yelling.

"Didn't I tell you," came her father's voice, "that she was too young to be riding around the city by herself?"

"She rides within a three-block radius—" her mother started, but her father cut her off.

"This is a slippery slope. Do you understand? From day one, that girl hasn't listened to anything anyone told her. If you let her keep running around town like that—"

"Then what?" her mother said dryly. "She'll end up pregnant?"

Teddy held her breath.

"Maybe if she had a father who actually—I don't know—did some parenting, then we wouldn't be in this situation."

"What situation?" her father asked. "Is me being miserable a situation for you? I can't stand this. I can't do this anymore. I—"

Teddy opened the door. "I'm home," she attempted to say brightly, but her mother's eyes widened when she saw her.

"Teddy!" she cried, running across the room. She grabbed Teddy and pulled her into her chest. "What happened?"

"Wrecked my bike," Teddy tried to say nonchalantly, but she started crying. Not just because her mom was pressing against her arm (which she would later learn was, indeed, broken), but because she suddenly didn't want to be hell on wheels. She didn't want to be a grown-up who decided what to do. She didn't want to hear her parents arguing or know that her dad was miserable with them. All she wanted was a hug from her mom.

"I'm getting blood on your shirt," she said through her sobs.

"I don't care about my shirt," her mother said, leaning down to inspect her face. "Thank God you had your helmet on. Oh, honey. We're going to the hospital."

Teddy instinctively looked toward her dad to see if he was going, too, but he wasn't standing there anymore, and Teddy's mom didn't call out for him.

In the car, Nelly's "Hot in Herre" played on the radio as they drove in silence. Teddy's mom put on the blinker at a stoplight and reached out to grab Teddy's hand. She squeezed it, and Teddy knew what was coming: words of wisdom, an emotional speech, a declaration of love that she'd remember for the rest of her life.

Her mom gave her a tiny smile, then looked back at the road as the light turned green and Nelly instructed everyone to take off all their clothes. "Your dad's an asshole," she said, hitting the gas.

THAT MONDAY AT school, everyone knew three things:

1. Teddy's dad had moved out.
2. Teddy had broken her arm.
3. Vicki wasn't Teddy's best friend anymore.

"I told Ashley P. what you did," Vicki whispered to her before Science class started. "You know her dad owns the theater? He could have you arrested."

Teddy thought about pointing out that Vicki had been there, too, that although she was an unwilling accomplice, she was an accomplice all the same. But Teddy couldn't help focusing on a more pressing fact. "He couldn't have me arrested."

"You'd go to jail for the rest of your life," Vicki said smugly, sitting back in her chair, and even though, logically, Teddy knew that most twelve-year-olds didn't get life in prison for sneaking into an

R-rated movie, she still felt that nervous, "pee your pants" feeling she got when she was in trouble.

"Really?" she asked.

"Oh." Vicki leaned over again. "And I told the girls about that gross movie you made me watch. We all think it's disgusting."

*The girls? We?* Vicki was a "we" with Ashley P. now, and probably Ashley M. and Ashley T., too. Apparently Vicki and the Ashleys had gotten together to discuss all the things that Teddy had done wrong.

Teddy thought that this might be a temporary situation, but she sat alone at lunch. And when she came home, her dad was still gone. And Teddy knew, no matter what anyone told her, that it was all because she'd decided to sneak into that movie.

In her dad's absence, her mom stepped up. She started working longer hours at multiple jobs, leaving Sophia in charge. Their lives were scheduled down to the minute, and the idea of biking to the movie theater by herself and doing something against the rules no longer sounded fun. It sounded dangerous. Teddy stayed at home and read more, climbing the maple tree in the backyard not to jump out of it, but instead to read comforting books in its branches. She sped through the YA classics and soon moved on to adult classics, reading Toni Morrison and Carson McCullers and Shirley Jackson far before she understood their words. All she knew was that the words were on paper. Static. Safe. Sometimes they were challenging or confusing, but they would never get her in trouble.

Her dad sent cards and even visited for one awkward birthday party where he and Teddy's mom stood side by side, arms crossed, like two people who didn't know each other. But they'd all moved on. Their family unit no longer needed him, and he didn't need them, either. Eventually he remarried, had a baby, and started over.

So Teddy let her mom take control. She let Sophia take control. After a week of watching Vicki and the Ashleys from across the cafeteria, she started eating her lunch in a sympathetic teacher's classroom. While Mrs. McBride graded papers, Teddy came up with a plan. From now on she'd stop making decisions on her own—especially ones that would affect other people. She'd go along with what everyone else wanted, stop causing trouble, and maybe this would all get better. Maybe the guilt from breaking up her family would fade. Maybe she'd even make friends again.

And so instead of forging her own life, Teddy became Sophia's shorter, almost identical shadow. Teddy's mother referred to her, with a smile, as Tagalong Teddy because of the way she followed Sophia everywhere. Teddy didn't mind. Maybe being a tagalong was better than being hell on wheels, anyway. At least tagalongs didn't get broken arms or cause arguments.

She liked Sophia's friends, the way they always knew exactly which movies you were supposed to watch (the ones with cute, floppy-haired boys—*not* the ones with blood sacrifices), which nail polish you were supposed to wear, and how to dress so you fit in. Sophia never cared that Teddy crashed all her sleepovers; in fact, she seemed to like it, as if having a little sister who looked up to her made her feel cool.

Teddy remembered one night when it was just the two of them at home. Their mom was working the night shift at one of her many jobs—Teddy lost track of where she was at any given time. Teddy woke up with a start, covered in sweat, certain that someone had broken in to kidnap her and Sophia. Too nervous to go downstairs and check, she'd crept into Sophia's room.

"Soph?" she'd whispered. "Are you awake?"

"Teddy?" Sophia asked, her voice thick and groggy with sleep. "Is everything okay?"

"I had a bad dream," Teddy said, suddenly feeling ridiculous, like a stupid little kid. Maybe she *was* a stupid little kid. Who else would wake up their older sister to complain about a nightmare? "Sorry. I'll go back to bed."

"Come here." Sophia scooted over and patted the bed. "You can sleep here."

Teddy slid into the bed in relief. She tried to take up as little space in Sophia's twin bed as possible, holding her body still so Sophia wouldn't change her mind and tell her to go back to her own room. She studied the lines of Sophia's face, almost exactly like hers but still somehow different. Sophia had the face of someone who wasn't afraid of everything. She had the face of someone who knew what she wanted.

"You don't have to be scared," Sophia said without opening her eyes. "There's nothing to be afraid of. I'll always be here."

Teddy had smiled then, feeling a sense of comfort she hadn't felt since she broke her arm and her dad left. He might be gone, and her mother might be at work, but at least she had one other person. At least she had Sophia.

But then Sophia had gone to college, and the occasional phone calls dwindled to almost never. Her visits home weren't the same; she spent most of her time on the computer doing work or chatting with her roommate. Teddy told herself that this was normal, that it was what happened when people grew up—they grew apart.

But that didn't stop her from missing Sophia or from wondering what had happened to her always being there.

# 8

"EVERETT," SAID LARRY THE LLAMA, "YOU HAVE A LETTER."

Everett looked at the camera in surprise, then back at the llama. "Larry, did you know this is my favorite time of day?"

"You tell me every day, Ev," said Larry.

"You know there's nothing I love more than hearing from our friends at home," Everett continued.

"I know," said Larry. "Are you gonna take this letter? I'm getting a little bit tired of holding it in my mouth."

"Sorry!" Everett said, grabbing the letter. "Who's it from?"

"I don't know," Larry said with the closest thing a puppet llama could get to a shrug. "I don't know how to read."

Everett laughed, a real laugh, because that hadn't been what Jeremy and he had rehearsed. "Right, right, of course. Okay, let's read today's letter."

Everett opened the letter and started reading.

Dear Everett,

Are you married? Do you have a family? Do they ever get mad at you? Sometimes my mom gets mad at me when I do

things I'm not supposed to. Sometimes I get mad at my mom
when she tells me not to do things. Sometimes I want to yell,
but my mom says I shouldn't.

Angel, age 4

Everett put the letter down and looked into the camera.

"Angel, I'm not married, but I do have a mom, a dad, and a sister. I don't live in their house with them because I live in my own
home, but I see them a lot. And even though we love one another,
we still get mad at one another sometimes. Did you know that just
because you love someone, it doesn't mean you never get mad at
them, or sad because of something they did, or frustrated because
of something they said? Sometimes the people we love can hurt us,
or annoy us, or even make us cry. And sometimes we can hurt the
people we love, even if we don't mean to.

"I know what you mean when you say you want to yell. Sometimes, I want to yell, too. Actually, I'm going to try it right now. Will
you try it with me? Let's count. One, two, three . . ."

Everett yelled, a guttural roar that made Larry cover his ears.

"What's wrong, Larry?" Everett asked.

"I didn't like that," Larry said. "It scared me when you yelled. It
was loud."

Everett nodded, then looked at the camera. "That might be how
your mom feels when you yell, Angel. Maybe it scares her, too. So
it's a good idea to find other ways to express your anger. You
shouldn't ignore it or hide it, but yelling isn't always the best way to
let it out. You could try using words to explain your feelings to your
mom or anyone else you're angry with. My favorite thing to do
when I'm angry is make something. You might want to draw a picture and put your feelings on the paper, or maybe make a big, angry

finger painting with whatever colors you want. Or it might help to take a bike ride, or run around your house, or jump as high as you can. Sometimes anger feels better when we're moving.

"But the most important thing to remember is that just because someone's angry at you, it doesn't mean they love you any less. Even when I'm angry at my little sister, I still love her more than anyone in the world. And I know that even when my parents got angry with me when I was a kid, they still loved me. We can be mad, but it's our responsibility to treat everyone with kindness, even when we don't feel our best, and to say we're sorry if we hurt someone we love.

"Thanks for trusting me with your words, Angel. I hope you can talk about this with your mom. And remember . . . even when they're big, or scary, or overwhelming, it's okay to feel your feelings, and it's okay to talk about them."

"Cut!"

Everett instantly relaxed from his on-camera posture, and Jeremy stood up from behind the couch.

"Aw, shit, man," he said, wiping his eyes with the hand that wasn't in Larry. "How do you do that? I know what you're going to say and I still cry every time."

"Believe it or not, my goal isn't to make you sob with each episode," Everett said, folding his letter from Angel.

"This isn't a sob. It's more of a sniffle," Jeremy said, looking at Larry for confirmation. Larry nodded.

Everett stood up and put a hand on Jeremy's shoulder. "It's okay to feel your feelings, dude."

"I know, I know," Jeremy said, and then he and Larry walked out of the living room set that made up *Everett's Place*.

"Great job, Ev."

Everett jumped and turned to see Astrid standing behind him, ever-present clipboard in her hands. "You think so?" he asked.

She wrote something down and then looked up at him, eyebrows raised. "You can't possibly be fishing for compliments. You did good. You always do good."

"I wouldn't mind hearing 'Damn, you continue to push children's entertainment to new heights.'"

Astrid frowned. "After we get through this next episode, I'll be sure to schedule a parade in your honor."

Everett's mouth dropped open. "Was that . . . a joke?"

Astrid stared at him, unblinking.

Everett put a hand on his heart. "I can't believe this. Astrid Vargas is out here making jokes. At my expense, yes, but still. I can't believe how far we've come."

"Take a break," Astrid called over her shoulder as she walked away. "Wardrobe change and be back here in twenty."

Everett headed toward his office/supply closet to put on a fun sweater (sometimes clothing companies sent him things, which he loved because the last thing he wanted to do in his free time was attempt to find whimsical yet adult clothing). He smiled, waved at everyone he passed, and took a minute to think, as he did each day, about how lucky he was to be living his dream. He was working with people he loved, making a show he cared about, pursuing the thing he'd been obsessed with since childhood. While he didn't have an inflated sense of self-importance—he was well aware that he wasn't conducting open-heart surgery or anything—he could go to sleep every night knowing that he'd made a difference in the lives of the kids and parents who watched the show, even if that only meant one moment of peace or laughter.

He stepped into his office, closed the door, pulled off his button-down, and yanked a sweater covered in cats over his head. He looked at himself in the small mirror Astrid had installed, and as he fixed his hair, he stopped for a moment and stared at his reflection.

It was back. The feeling that something—he didn't know what—was missing. The feeling that he wasn't where he was supposed to be, even though, as far as he knew, he was *exactly* where he was supposed to be.

Everett shook his head and stared at himself in the mirror, waiting for the feeling to pass. He waited. And waited.

It didn't pass.

He frowned at himself. "Buck up, you idiot," he told himself, which made him feel like a fraud, because he would absolutely destroy someone who told any of his child viewers something like that.

He decided to try a different approach. "It's okay to feel your feelings," he told his reflection, which only made him frown further. Because how the hell was he supposed to feel a feeling if he didn't know what it was?

## 9

AS AN ADULT, TEDDY WASN'T DELUSIONAL. SHE KNEW, LOGI-cally, that her parents had faced down years of discord and animosity and made the correct decision to separate. She knew that her dad simply wasn't a good parent and that his move to California was no big loss. California could have him.

But years and years of avoiding making her own decisions had worn a groove into her brain, like the way sitting on one couch cushion leaves behind a butt imprint that you roll into whenever you watch television. After a while, Teddy forgot how to decide things for herself or who "herself" even was. She made friends after Vicki, but she kept everything on the surface level—there were people she had lunch with, people she studied with, and people she occasionally went shopping with, but no one was ever allowed to get too deep. The last thing she needed was full-scale ostracizing again.

When she got to college (OSU, of course, because that was where her mother thought she should go), with its sprawling campus, tens of thousands of students, and classes on virtually anything she could ever want to learn, she panicked. She stared at everyone else striding purposefully across campus and wondered how they *knew*. How did they have so much confidence in what they wanted?

Teddy would think back to that little girl, hell on wheels, and wonder what she would've done. But at this point, Teddy didn't know anymore. Thinking about herself as a child was like thinking about a stranger.

Of course, things fell into place when she met Richard. Suddenly, she had a purpose—Richard's purpose. And as long as she did what he wanted, she'd never have to make another decision again.

Today, she winced as she cradled an apple crisp and walked up her mother's porch stairs, the same ones she'd walked up with her broken arm all those years ago. But this time, her wince wasn't because of the physical pain; it was because she was here for dinner (an extremely early dinner, because Sophia and Craig liked to start their children's bedtime routines no later than six thirty p.m.) and knew she'd have to tell her mom and sister about her breakup, and probably hear them lament what a great guy Richard was and how Teddy was a fool to let him go.

She gave a courtesy knock and walked in to find Sophia standing in the foyer, staring blankly into space.

"Hi," Sophia said in a whisper. "We're still potty training Liam and I needed a moment of peace and quiet by myself and— Oh, your hair."

Sophia stepped toward her sister with sympathy in her eyes and wrapped her in a hug.

"Does it look that bad?" Teddy asked, her voice muffled in Sophia's shoulder. It had been so long since her sister had hugged her that it should've felt awkward, but it didn't; she relaxed into the hug, feeling like they were little girls sharing a bed again.

"No, you look hot," Sophia said, pulling back to study Teddy's face. "You know who you look like? What's that French movie with the cute girl who runs around Paris helping people? And there's, like, accordion music?"

"Are you trying to say I look like Amélie?" Teddy asked. "Because I don't."

"You kind of do."

"My bangs are way longer," Teddy protested, but Sophia cut in.

"Okay, fine. Listen, I haven't seen a movie in like . . . five years. All I'm saying is, your haircut is cute, but if it means what I think it means, I'm sorry."

"Mommy?"

Liam was now standing in the foyer, wearing a T-shirt but no pants or underwear.

"I have to potty," he said.

"Where's my husband," Sophia muttered, then screamed, "CRAIG? WHERE ARE YOU?" so loud that Teddy jumped.

Sophia waited a second, then sighed and grabbed Liam's hand. "Okay, let's get you to the potty."

"I'll be . . . in the kitchen," Teddy said to Sophia's retreating back, but her sister was already focusing on Liam. It wasn't like Teddy thought that here, in her mother's foyer next to her pantsless nephew, was where she and Sophia were finally going to reconnect and have a real conversation, but she felt disappointed all the same.

Teddy wandered into the kitchen, where her mom was plating a huge salad. "Hey, honey, could you grab me a—" her mom started.

And then she turned around and stopped midsentence. "Your hair!"

"Okay, why does everyone keep saying it like that?" Teddy asked. "It's not like I showed up with a face tattoo of a curse word. It's not that shocking."

"No. Of course not." Her mom smiled thinly. She didn't ask where Richard was, Teddy realized, because Richard rarely came with her to family dinners. He was always, of course, too busy.

"Grab me the salad tongs, will you?" her mother asked. "Oh,

did you bring a dessert? So nice, Teddy. Everything's ready. Let's go sit down."

"Sure." Teddy put the apple crisp on the kitchen counter. She wasn't fazed by her mother's rapid-fire, scattershot way of speaking— as usual, her mother had about one million things on her mind and felt the need to say them all at once. Teddy found the tongs in the same drawer they'd been in since she could remember and followed her mother into the dining room, where Sophia, Craig, and the kids were seated. Liam was, by this point, wearing pants.

"Your hair is short," Emma said bluntly.

"Sure is," said Teddy.

"Okay, let's eat!" her mother said, clapping her hands.

Everyone passed around the dishes, and for a moment, things were quiet. And then Teddy broke the silence with "Richard and I broke up."

For a moment, no one said anything. And then Craig, with his fork halfway to his mouth, asked, "But we didn't like that guy, right?"

"Craig!" Sophia barked.

Craig looked to Teddy's mom for support. "Right? I mean, he never came over here. He made fun of my job—"

"He made fun of your job?" Teddy asked. Craig had owned his own auto-repair shop since before he and Sophia met.

Craig waved her off and took another bite. "Something about how it must be fun and how he wished he could have a job where he didn't have to think so hard," he said with his mouth full. "Let me tell you, there is nothing less fun than trying to repair a family's minivan when they have to leave for Myrtle Beach at six a.m. to-morrow. Which is what I did today. Do you know how many pan-icked phone calls we had to deal with?"

Sophia put a hand on his arm. "Not the point right now, babe. Teddy, how are you?"

The simple question made Teddy's eyes fill with tears. "I'm okay, I guess. I'm staying with Eleanor and Kirsten."

"He was grumpy," Emma said before taking a sip of chocolate milk. "I don't like him." And then her eyes brightened. "Your new boyfriend should be Cookie Monster! I like *him*."

"Cookie Monster is very . . . enthusiastic," Teddy agreed. "I'm not really looking for a new boyfriend, but thank you, Emma."

"Okay," Teddy's mom said, wiping her hands on a napkin and chewing. "Obviously, it's time for you to go back to school."

"Obviously?" Teddy asked.

"You go to night school or take classes online, and you don't have to make any changes with your job. Haven't you always wanted a business degree?"

"Have I?" Teddy asked, genuinely curious. She didn't remember ever saying anything about wanting an MBA, but maybe this was some sort of childhood dream she'd forgotten. Maybe all small children talked about how they wanted business degrees.

"I think your main focus should be finding a place of your own," Sophia said, shaking her head. "Everyone should live on their own at least once in their life. You know, to really understand yourself, and know what it's like to be alone, and . . . Emma. Do not eat those peas with your hands. That's what forks are for."

"Well, I don't plan on living with Kirsten and Eleanor forever . . . ," Teddy started.

"Great. Now there are peas all over the floor." Sophia sighed.

"All I'm saying is, you'll feel better with a business degree. I'll send you some links to apply, okay?" her mom said.

"I have to poop!" Liam wailed. "Moooom!"

From under the table, Sophia asked, "Craig? Can you take him to the potty?"

"Honey, I'm eating dinner," Craig said, looking at his plate forlornly.

"What do you think I'm doing?" Sophia asked as her hand popped up to deposit more peas from the floor. "Playing tennis?"

Teddy hoped that Craig and Liam's exit would naturally change the subject, but she wasn't so lucky. Her mother had seized onto this topic and wouldn't let it go until she had Teddy's entire life planned out, including what type of burial she'd like.

As both Sophia and her mother stared at her, Teddy realized she'd spaced out while they were talking. Sometimes it was easy for her to do that—let them figure out what was happening and then go along with it.

"What?" she asked innocently, taking another bite. "Great salad, by the way."

"Thank you," her mother said. "The beets are from the farmers market, and you know you can't work at the toy store forever."

The food in Teddy's mouth suddenly tasted less like farmers market beets and more like cardboard. She heard Richard's voice in her head. *You've always had a smaller life.*

"What's wrong with Colossal Toys?" Teddy asked, even though she knew what her mom would say.

She made a noise that was half cough, half secondhand embarrassment. "You can barely live on that money. It's important to be able to take care of yourself. Trust me."

She didn't have to mention the second job she'd taken after Teddy's dad left or the fact that she probably hadn't slept a full night since then. "I take care of myself," Teddy said.

"Yeah, but you're staying with your friends right now," Sophia said. "Trust *me*. A place of your own. It matters."

"I pooped!" Liam said, walking back into the room, Craig trailing behind him. "And Dad wiped my butt."

"Did you wash your hands?" Sophia asked.

"Yep," Craig said.

"Not you," Sophia said slowly. "Liam."

"I washed my hands!" Liam yelled.

"You know I'm only saying this because I care," her mom said, patting Teddy's hand. "I want the best possible life for you, and that means being able to support yourself. Maybe you could be a lawyer, like Sophia!"

Teddy wrinkled her nose.

Sophia shook her head. "Don't go to law school. *Don't* do it."

"I have to potty again!" Liam yelled.

"You *just* went!" Sophia said.

"Don't you want what Sophia has?" Teddy's mother asked. "A house of her own, enough money to send Liam and Emma to fancy music lessons? I wish I could've sent you two to music lessons. Maybe you would've become talented musicians."

"But that time I pooped. Now I have to pee again!" Liam said, sliding off his chair.

"I knew he shouldn't have had so much juice," Sophia muttered.

"Mom, I was *very* bad at the recorder in music class," Teddy reminded her. "That thing sounded like a goose honking when I played it. I don't think a lack of formal music education is why I don't have a career as a musician."

"All recorders sound like geese honking, and we're not going to be able to come up with a plan for your future at this moment," her mother said, gesturing vaguely at the family to encompass all the bathroom talk. "But check your email later. I'll figure it out."

Teddy took another bite of food and stifled a sigh. Her mother would figure it out; she always did. But this time, Teddy knew she needed to figure it out herself.

## 10

AFTER DINNER ENDED AND THEY SAID THEIR GOODBYES, TEDDY got into her car feeling heavy, and not because she was full of meat loaf (between the poop and the advice, she'd barely been able to eat). She felt bogged down under the weight of her mother's expectations and Sophia's opinions.

She wished she could talk about it with Sophia—really talk about it—but it wasn't like she could say she was scared and crawl into her sister's twin bed again. People used the phrase "grew apart" so casually, as if it was a natural thing that happened. And maybe it was for some people, but for Teddy, it felt more like a dramatic, earth-shattering crack, yet another way her family had broken.

Teddy loved her family. Really. But sometimes hanging out with her mom was like mainlining fifteen different advice columns at once, and all of the questions were about your life, only you didn't remember ever actually asking for advice.

She didn't want to feel like a teenager again, but she also didn't know what the hell she was supposed to do.

Should she go back to school? Get another job? Move out of Eleanor and Kirsten's place? But she had no idea what she'd go to school for, and she liked her job. She liked the warmth of the shop, being around Josie, her friendships with the regular customers.

And although she knew it couldn't last forever, she loved living with Eleanor and Kirsten.

But clearly Teddy needed to do something. Her family was right; her life was a mess. Her breathing grew shallow as she drove, the streetlamps lighting her way in the dark of the early-fall evening. Hadn't it just been summer? Hadn't it been light at nine p.m. yesterday? And here it was, six p.m. and the streetlamps were on. Time was moving too fast, moments were slipping away, Teddy was almost thirty, and she had no idea what she was doing with her life. . . .

Her car beeped to let her know she'd received a text message. She pressed the PLAY button and the robot voice read:

> Kirsten says: Pajama-movie night starts in one hour. We made a bunch of chicken drumsticks and if you don't get here soon I'm going to eat them all.

Teddy smiled. They were watching *The Birds* (Kirsten and Eleanor were working their way through the Alfred Hitchcock oeuvre) and apparently chicken legs passed for themed refreshments. They were birds, after all, although presumably the titular birds were more flight-worthy.

The car beeped again, and Teddy pressed PLAY, assuming it was Kirsten adding more snack details.

> Richard says: Sitting here eating a protein bar. I miss your dinners. Crying emoji.

Teddy stopped breathing. Typically she thought it was charming that the car described emojis, but now she was too annoyed to be amused. *Crying emoji?* Her entire life had been a crying emoji since their breakup, and now Richard was using one in a text?

She pictured him sitting at his island—*their* island—protein bar wrapper crinkling as he ate in a lonely apartment where there was certainly no milk in the fridge. Was he eating protein bars for every meal? That wasn't nutritionally sound.

This wasn't about what Eleanor and Kirsten said, that she was taking care of someone to prove her worth. This was simple concern for his health—what was she supposed to do, let him starve? Only a truly cruel person would do that, and Teddy wasn't cruel.

She put her blinker on and headed toward the store.

IT FELT STRANGE to ring the doorbell at what was her home— well, what had been her home until recently—but of course she'd given Richard her keys back.

He pulled open the door of the town house, looking confused at first, but then she held up the grocery bags in her hands.

"I come bearing dinner," she said, and he smiled.

He sat on the couch, computer on his lap, as she bustled around the kitchen. She didn't feel awkward at all as they fell into their accustomed roles. In fact, she felt comfortable for the first time in weeks, opening these familiar cabinets and using these familiar pans, everything exactly where she had left it. Even in the refrigerator, which held several now-moldy containers of berries she'd purchased before moving out.

"You really need to clean this thing," she said lightly, tossing them into the garbage.

"I know, I know," Richard said from the couch. "This is what's happened to me since you left. I'm living a disgusting bachelor lifestyle."

*I didn't leave,* Teddy stopped herself from saying. *You kicked me out.*

She looked toward the mantelpiece to see what Richard had done with it since she'd removed the mini pumpkin tableau, but there was nothing at all on that mantel, and no throw pillows on the couch to replace the ones she'd taken. There wasn't a single seasonal candle in sight. Teddy shuddered.

Dinner was quick but satisfying—steaks with a salad of kale, red onion, and pomegranate seeds, plus a loaf of crusty bread she'd picked up. Since she hadn't been able to eat much at her mom's, what with the constant conversation about her failure of a life, she found she was hungry again, and she snuck a piece of bread into her mouth.

She hummed to herself as she pulled down the plates and bowls she was used to eating from, the same ones she'd picked out years ago. Of course Richard didn't pay attention to things like plates or anything that made a house a home. He would have used old sheets to cover the windows if she hadn't been there to pick out curtains.

"Everything's ready!" she said brightly, plating his steak and salad.

"Oh, thanks, Teddy," he said, standing up off the couch and stretching, then crossing the room to the island. "This looks amazing. You're amazing."

Teddy beamed.

"What's that?" he asked, poking at the kale.

"A salad," Teddy said with a smile.

"Always trying to get me to eat vegetables," Richard groaned, but he grinned as he said it. Teddy blushed; it felt like an inside joke, like an acknowledgment that he really did appreciate how she'd taken care of him all these years.

As she started to put her own steak on a plate, Richard carried his back to the couch and reopened his laptop. He shoveled the food into his mouth, not looking at her, already forgetting she was there.

Teddy's mouth went dry and her face got hot. She blinked quickly, willing the tears to stay put.

Richard hadn't invited her over to have dinner *with him*—he hadn't invited her over at all. No, he'd expressed a need—*I'm hungry*—and she'd decided she had to be the one to fill it. Just like always. She didn't know what to do with her life after dinner at her mom's and so she looked to Richard to tell her what to do. She went for what she knew, what was easy: being Richard's wife.

But she wasn't Richard's wife, and she wouldn't ever be.

She looked down at her plate, no longer hungry. She stuck the steak in the nearly empty fridge, and as she closed it, her gaze caught on their bedroom—now Richard's bedroom, where an unmade bed stared back at her like a wide, unblinking, judgmental eye.

For God's sake, he couldn't even make the bed on his own?

She looked again at Richard, who was still staring at his laptop. He had a splotch of vinaigrette on his shirt. As if he felt her eyes on him, he looked up, then tilted his head. "Your hair," he said.

Self-consciously, Teddy ran her fingers along the ends of her bob. "Yes?"

He smiled at her, and with his voice full of condescension, like he was speaking to a child who'd had an accident, he said, "You know I always liked you with long hair."

Her hand dropped to her side. One thought ran through her mind, and this time she said it out loud.

"This was a huge mistake."

EVERETT HADN'T PLANNED ON STAYING IN COLUMBUS FOR college. In true Everett St. James fashion, he'd chosen the college he wanted when he was ten years old and had never wavered—he would go to the University of Connecticut and major in puppetry. Some nights before bed, he flipped through the college brochure and imagined his life there—taking classes on marionette performance, constructing his own puppets, and learning about costumes and design and sets. Finally, the thing he loved would be his entire life.

But then Gretel happened. When his parents sat him down on their old striped sofa with stuffing poking through the holes, he'd thought they were kidding about his mother being pregnant. In fact, he'd laughed, sure this was part of some elaborate practical joke his parents were playing, despite the reality that neither of them had ever been capable of telling any sort of joke (his dad was always rushing to the punch line, so desperate to get to the laugh that he screwed up the timing entirely; this was why Everett got his comedic training from television).

It became clear that they weren't joking when Everett saw his mother in a hospital bed holding a tiny, squirming human, and that was when he knew he wasn't going anywhere. The first time he held Gretel in his arms, he didn't care about his years of dreaming and planning and memorizing the brochure. She was his sister, this little baby, and she needed him.

It turned out she did need him in more than a metaphorical sense—because his parents had had what was referred to as a "geriatric" pregnancy (a term his mother objected to, even if it was medically accurate), they didn't have as much energy as when they'd had Everett at the age of twenty-two.

Everett enrolled in film and video classes at the Columbus College of Art and Design because there was no puppetry major. It wasn't his original dream, of course, but he hardly cared. He studied art, he focused on puppetry when he wasn't in school, and every other second of the day was taken up by being Gretel's live-in babysitter. He pushed her stroller through Goodale Park, took her to story time at the Columbus Metropolitan Library, and became an expert in changing poop-filled diapers.

Although Everett already knew he wanted his own show, it was Gretel who convinced him that the show should be centered toward young children's feelings (well, as much as someone who could barely talk could convince someone of anything). Everett had pictured himself doing an irreverent, child-friendly but grown-up-oriented program, but as he created new puppets and roped Jeremy into working with him, he realized that entertaining Gretel was far more satisfying than entertaining adults could ever be. For starters, Gretel was an unflinchingly honest critic. If she didn't like something, she gave it a raspberry or simply toddled away and started doing something else. Children couldn't lie to preserve someone else's dignity the way adults did, and that authenticity pushed Everett to work harder.

But as it turned out, it wasn't just the jokes and silliness that he loved about performing—what really mattered was helping Gretel process her emotions. And as a toddler, she had a lot of them. She constantly screeched in joy or yelled in frustration, and Everett understood. How bewildering it must have been to feel so out of control, so unable to understand the world around you. But with puppets, he and Jeremy could talk through what was happening and help Gretel accept whatever emotions she had.

If Jeremy thought it was weird to spend his free time at his friend's house putting on puppet shows for his friend's young sister, he didn't say so, and soon Everett and he were working out a way to expand their audience beyond one child. The very first episode of *Everett's Place* (Jeremy was more than fine with Everett's name being in the title, as he preferred to appear on-screen only when it was absolutely necessary and even then required bribery in the form of food and beer) was filmed in Everett's house, in his turret bedroom. Everett made his own music and built his own puppets, while Jeremy filmed, did some puppetry, and occasionally gave Everett input on design.

They put the show up on YouTube and didn't expect much. But as parents discovered it and their small children became obsessed with it, their following grew. And by the time they graduated from CCAD, they had an offer from a local television station—suddenly, they had a real set to construct, professional equipment, and, most important, a much larger audience.

Ever since then, Everett had been doing the same thing five episodes a week: talking to children about their feelings, helping them work through family drama or friendship issues. And he loved it. Because while Gretel, as a twelve-going-on-forty-year-old, didn't share her emotions with Everett anymore, he still had that knack for talking to kids, for getting on their level and relating to them in a way that most adults simply couldn't.

Everett felt a responsibility to the kids he spoke to—he never wanted to let them down or phone it in, not when they trusted him to be honest in their conversations. That was how he thought of each episode—like a conversation with a kid on a topic like anger, or fear, or death, or jealousy. Childhood was a confusing and often overwhelming landscape, and although he couldn't fix all of the problems his viewers brought to him, he always wanted at least to provide a map to figure the way out.

Which was why this new puppet was a massive pain in the ass. Someone needed to give him a map to figure it out, but unfortunately, no one had volunteered.

Everett was spending yet another night on his living room floor, alone, thinking. It wasn't that he didn't like working by himself, but sometimes he wanted someone to bounce an idea off of. He could call Jeremy, he realized, and Jeremy would tell him what to do.

The phone rang a few times before Jeremy picked up. "Everett?" he asked, the sound of voices and glasses clinking in the background.

"Is this a bad time?" Everett asked.

"Well, Tess and I are at dinner," Jeremy said, not unpleasantly.

"Oh, shit." Everett glanced at his watch. "Sorry. I had no idea it was dinnertime."

"Is everything okay?" Jeremy asked.

Everett sighed. "I'm thinking about the new puppet, and I wondered if you had any thoughts—"

"Everett," Jeremy said gently, "I'm out on a date night with my wife and I've had exactly two beers and I'm trying very hard not to have thoughts on anything except what we're going to do tonight while our kids are at their grandparents'. I'm definitely not thinking about work."

"Right, right." Everett ran a hand over his face. "I'm sorry I called."

Jeremy laughed. "Don't be sorry! But why don't you go out? See some friends? Not me, no offense. I already told you what tonight is about."

"Yep, not interested in cockblocking your date with your wife," Everett said with a sigh.

"At least go get some sleep or something," Jeremy said.

"Will do, Jeremy," Everett said. "See you next week."

After they hung up, Everett sprawled on the floor. Surprisingly enough, nothing seemed easier from this vantage point, so he sat back up. Of course he wasn't upset that Jeremy was out enjoying life. But it did make him wonder—what was wrong with him that he was at home by himself on a beautiful fall evening when maybe he should be . . . at a bar? He didn't even know how to complete that sentence, because he didn't know what normal people did instead of working every night. He felt it again, that familiar "something is missing" feeling taking over his body, squeezing the breath out of his chest and making his heart beat faster.

But there was one thing that always made that feeling go away: work. And he knew that once he figured out this puppet and wrote a few new episodes, everything would be better. He'd feel better. He had to.

He took a deep breath and got back to work.

## 12

"I'M SORRY," TEDDY SAID THE SECOND SHE BURST THROUGH the door, tears running down her face, a McDonald's bag in hand.

The room was dark, and on-screen Tippi Hedren screamed as birds dove from the sky. Eleanor and Kirsten turned to look at her, and Kirsten dropped a drumstick from her mouth.

"Teddy!" Eleanor shouted, standing up and running toward her. "What's wrong? Are you okay?"

Teddy took a deep breath and then, through heaving sobs, said, "I made dinner for Richard!"

"You made *dinner*?" Kirsten asked as she paused the movie and turned on the lights.

Teddy wiped her eyes. "Steak and salad."

"I don't think the 'what' is important," Eleanor said patiently, putting an arm around her. "Let's focus on how."

They guided Teddy toward the couch, and as she cried, Teddy told them what had happened. "And I missed pajama-movie night! I'm the worst friend in the world."

"Listen, pajama-movie night *is* important," Kirsten said. "It's one of the highlights of my week. But ultimately, we were eating chicken while watching bird attacks. We can repeat the experience, I promise."

Eleanor handed Teddy a tissue, and Teddy wiped her nose. "I

know. But it's the principle of the thing. I never want to cook dinner for him again."

"Can I ask . . . why are you clutching a McDonald's bag like it's a sack of treasure?" Eleanor asked gently.

Teddy sighed and opened the bag. "I don't know. This is my third dinner, although I didn't really eat the one at Richard's on account of . . ."

"On account of he's Rick the Dick," Kirsten said.

"Right," Teddy said. "But I don't know, I drove away from the town house and a force greater than me compelled me to go through the McDonald's drive-thru. It was like I wasn't in control."

"God works in mysterious ways, and She knew you needed a Quarter Pounder with Cheese," Eleanor said.

"Amen," Kirsten added, rubbing Teddy's shoulder comfortingly. "You deserve all the processed, sodium-filled goodness you can get."

"Oh, also." Teddy bent down to grab another bag, which had fallen onto the floor. "Before McDonald's, I went to Bath and Body Works."

"Was there a candle sale?" Eleanor asked with an edge of frantic excitement to her voice.

"I sure hope so," Kirsten said, "because if you pay full price for a three-wick candle, you're a damn fool."

"Oh, there was a sale," Teddy said. "I was at Richard's and I got depressed about the lack of seasonal décor, and then I was like, well, maybe we need a pecan-pumpkin waffle candle—"

Eleanor nodded. "Yes, we do. Keep going."

"And then I remembered that we're almost out of soap and there was a sale on that, so long story short, I hope you like autumnal scents and foaming antibacterial hand soap."

"I *adore* both of those things," Kirsten said.

"I think it's time we put Project: Teddy Time into effect," Eleanor said firmly, then reached over to the coffee table and grabbed her planner.

"Do you always have your planner with you?" Teddy asked, her mouth full of french fries.

"Organization doesn't happen by accident," Eleanor said, flipping through the pages. She uncapped her pen and, in her perfect teacher's penmanship, wrote *TEDDY TIME* on one of her blank pages. "Are you familiar with Eleanor Roosevelt?"

"Am I familiar with . . . the wife of President Franklin Roosevelt?" Teddy asked. "Yes. I've heard the name a few times."

"Well, she's my namesake. My parents were weirdly obsessed with her. I don't know—it was a whole thing. The point is, I grew up hearing her words all the time, and you know what? That woman was a lot of things—assumed closeted lesbian, boss bitch, and also a one-woman quote factory."

"Okay," Teddy said tentatively as she reached into the bag for another fry. Kirsten held out a hand, so Teddy gave her one, too.

"And the thing she said that my parents were most fond of was this: do one thing every day that scares you."

Eleanor paused dramatically as Kirsten and Teddy chewed.

"Turns out she probably didn't actually say that, at least not in such a Pinterest-graphic-worthy way, but the point remains: you, Teddy, are going to do one thing every day that scares you."

"You want me to take inspiration from a misattributed quote?" Teddy asked.

"Every day," Eleanor said firmly, ignoring her question. "You try one new thing. You make one new plan. One thing you never would have, or could have, done with Richard. One step, big or small, outside of your comfort zone. How do you expect to find your passion if you don't have a plan, Teddy? *This* is your plan." She paused and smiled. "Sound good?"

"Whoa," Teddy said. "I didn't know you could be so . . . authoritative."

"She means bossy," Kirsten said with a grin.

Eleanor flipped her hair over her shoulder. "Different students require different tactics to succeed!"

"Okay," Teddy said slowly, thinking of Everett's response to the little boy named Keegan. Wasn't that what he'd said? That Keegan should try new things, especially the things that scared him?

"This would never work for me," Kirsten said, leaning back against the throw pillows. "Nothing scares me."

"Except for possums," Eleanor reminded her.

Kirsten shuddered. "Their faces! Their teeth! Well, I guess I'd have to confront a possum."

Teddy shook her head. "I'm not scared of possums. But I am scared of . . . a lot of other things. Like everything, maybe? Life without Richard, that's what scares me. This sounds like a bad idea."

Teddy thought about all the decisions she'd avoided throughout her life. Going with the flow, along for the ride. Tagalong Teddy wouldn't ever do anything that scared her . . . well, not unless a bunch of other people were doing it, too. If everyone around her was jumping off a bridge, then Teddy would definitely do it. No question.

Eleanor smiled gently. "That means this is a great idea. Let's take some classes! I love classes. Oh! One of my coworkers also teaches over at Sew to Speak. Do you know how to sew?"

"I've never tried," Teddy said. "It looks hard."

"Well, now's your chance!" Kirsten said. "Line dancing! Skydiving! Getting a regrettable tattoo! Hitchhiking across the country and almost getting murdered and then writing a memoir about the experience! You're doing it all."

"I'm not doing any of *those* things," Teddy said matter-of-factly. "But sewing sounds nice."

"You're gonna *Eat Pray Love* your way all over the world! It's time for you to say yes to life!" Kirsten said, ramping up.

Teddy placed a hand on Kirsten's shoulder. "I don't have the time for a pasta-based spiritual journey, but if life ever asks me a question, I promise I'll answer in the affirmative."

Kirsten sighed. "I suppose that's good enough for me."

"This is exciting," Eleanor said, wiggling her eyebrows as she closed her planner. "I haven't been this jazzed about a project since I decided to reupholster the cushions on our kitchen chairs."

"High praise," Kirsten said. "She loves to reupholster."

"You're not doing this by yourself, Teddy," Eleanor said, putting an arm around her. "You have a life outside of making dinner for Richard, and we're going to help you figure out what it is."

Teddy brushed away a tear, embarrassed. "I'm an adult woman. I shouldn't be figuring this stuff out now."

"There's no time limit on dreams," Kirsten said, putting an arm around her other side so that Teddy was the filling in a warm, cozy best friend sandwich. "Colonel Sanders didn't become a chef until he was forty, and look at what that man accomplished."

Teddy snort-laughed through her tears. "Well, I don't plan to start a successful chain of fried-chicken restaurants, but thank you. And thanks for being so nice to me even though I missed pajama-movie night."

Kirsten waved her off. "We'll plan another one."

"And we're going to have an official tea time to fully map out your plan," Eleanor said. "This is merely brainstorming. Think about all the things that scare you, and we'll make up a full list over scones."

Teddy nodded. Somehow, talking about this with Eleanor and Kirsten felt different from when her mom and Sophia told her what to do—it probably had something to do with how Eleanor called it Teddy's plan. She was the one who was in charge; no one else could have Teddy Time for her.

And after all, this was what Everett St. James had recommended, and who did she trust more than a television host she'd never actually met?

"I think I'm going to go to sleep," Teddy said, disentangling herself from their hug. "I'll see you in the morning, okay?"

In her room, tucked into bed, Teddy rewatched Keegan's episode of *Everett's Place*. Once again, Everett told Keegan that he should keep searching for his passion, keep trying new things, keep looking for what lit him up. Basically, he was telling Keegan to have Teddy Time, if not in so many words.

*This is right,* Teddy thought. She had to try to do the things that scared her, like Eleanor and Everett said.

But upon this viewing, Teddy focused on something she'd never paid attention to before: the words that flashed on the screen as the show ended.

*Have a question for Everett? Email him at Everett@Everettsplace .com. Parental permission required. All emails become property of the show.*

She opened her email.

It wasn't that she thought Everett would respond. Well, honestly, she hoped he would. Sort of. She knew the show wasn't meant as a puppet version of Oprah's *Super Soul Sunday* and that she wasn't the target audience. But in that moment, thinking about that disastrous dinner at Richard's and Teddy Time and her family's plan for her and the fact that she related to a nine-year-old, she figured that emailing Everett might make her feel a little better, even if she was flinging her words into the abyss.

**Dear Everett,**

She shivered. Even typing his name, like they were old friends, gave her a little thrill. She really needed to get ahold of herself.

I need your help. You see, I watched you tell Keegan how he could find his "thing"—that is, the thing he's really good at, the way his friends are good at their respective things. And it's not that you didn't give him good advice—you did, and I'm sure Keegan is destined to live a long, passion-filled life once he discovers his love of the flute.

But, and not to sound too solipsistic here, what about me? What about a woman who's aging out of her twenties and recently got an ill-advised breakup bob? Is it too late for me to discover my thing? What if I had a chance to find my thing when I was, say, 23, and I missed it? Am I doomed to live the rest of my life thing-less?

Teddy exhaled. This email to Everett felt very, very scary. She kept typing.

Help me, Everett St. James. You're my only hope.

Very sincerely yours,
Theodora

PS: Do adults often write to you? Am I the first? Maybe I should be ashamed, but I had a very rough night that involved a Quarter Pounder with Cheese and I'm feeling vulnerable (and slightly nauseated) right now.

She clicked SEND, then pulled the blankets over her head. Day one of her Teddy Time plan was officially in the books, and maybe it was the nerves or the fast food, but it kind of made her want to throw up.

## 13

EVERETT COULDN'T SLEEP.

This wasn't unusual for him, at least not when he was on the verge of a creative breakthrough. People thought his job was easy. You talked to some kids, made a puppet say a few words—no big deal, right? But the thing was, someone had to make those puppets. Someone had to write those words. That someone was Everett, and the idea that he might be letting a kid somewhere down by half-assing his job kept him up at night.

Or, more accurately, kept him up in the morning, seeing as it was four a.m.

He ate a bowl of cereal (responsible, joy-free Raisin Bran, because even though he worked in children's entertainment he still understood the value of a fiber-rich breakfast) and by five a.m., he was letting himself into the studio.

This was his favorite time of day to be there. Most of the lights were off and it was silent, giving the whole place an almost eerily calm vibe that it never had during the day when he was filming.

But as he walked down the hallway toward the studio, he could hear the squeaky wheels of the custodian's bucket rolling along.

"Tom!" Everett called. "It's me! Not an early-morning robber who's looking to steal the set pieces of an iconic local children's show!"

Tom poked his head around the corner. "Whew," he said. "Good. All I have is my mop to defend me."

"You really ought to consider Mace," Everett said, his eyebrows knit in concern. "You're working around valuables."

Tom nodded, then continued squeaking down the hall. "I'll let you know if anyone tries to carry out that ugly sofa."

"The sofa's not ugly!" Everett called as Tom kept walking away. "It's endearing! Families love it! Kids love it!"

Tom ignored him, so Everett opened the doors and walked onto the set, which was empty and quiet. His producer, Astrid, wasn't rushing around and peppering him with a million questions. Jeremy wasn't there for him to bounce ideas off of. Without the lights and people around it, the sofa in question looked like a zoo exhibit missing its animals.

"I love you just the way you are," he muttered, running one hand along the couch. "Never change."

Everett walked into his "office," which was more of a storage closet for the show where he went to be alone, and pulled out his laptop. It was ultimately his job to choose which kids' emails to answer on the show, but Astrid forwarded him the ones that she thought might be good picks, weeding out the junk emails or obvious jokes from teenagers with burner email addresses like WEED BONER69@gmail.com.

So he wasn't exactly sure how an email from a woman named Theodora made its way through Astrid's screening process. Theodora was apparently an adult, for starters, and as such, her question wasn't broadly applicable to his audience of four- to nine-year-olds.

He gnawed on his bottom lip as he read through the email and couldn't help smiling. *You're my only hope.* A *Star Wars* reference. An extremely obvious *Star Wars* reference, but a reference all the same.

One of Everett's favorite episodes of *The Muppet Show* guest-starred Mark Hamill, who ended up singing "When You Wish upon a Star" with all of the Muppets, including Miss Piggy dressed as Princess Leia.

He shook his head. *Focus.*

*Theodora.* She sounded cute. Then again, Everett tended to think that most women were cute. Natalie was always making fun of his millions of celebrity crushes.

A granola bar smacked him on the head, jolting him out of his mental wanderings.

He turned toward the source. "What the hell's a breakup bob?"

Astrid crossed the room, picked up the granola bar from where it had bounced off his head, and handed it to him. "First off, why are you here so early? And secondly, I know you didn't eat breakfast and I don't want to deal with you being a petulant baby because you don't know how to feed yourself, so here."

Everett tore the wrapper open. "I ate a bowl of cereal at home, but I'll accept this."

"A breakup bob is exactly what it sounds like. A haircut a woman gets when she goes through a breakup." She thought about it for a minute. "I suppose a man could get one, but most don't have hair long enough for a proper bob."

"Maybe men do a breakup head shave," Everett mused; then his eyes widened. "So she's single."

Astrid gave him a no-nonsense headshake. If her essence were distilled into one gesture, it would be a no-nonsense headshake. "No. Nuh-uh. No way. I thought I deleted that email."

"What email?" Everett muttered, already looking at his computer again.

Astrid sighed. "I absolutely did not intend to forward you that one. The last thing you need is a cute girl to get obsessed with. You're already distracted enough as it is."

"She *does* sound cute, doesn't she?" Everett rotated the chair to look at Astrid, who leaned against the doorframe, arms crossed. She narrowed her eyes.

"Why are you here so early?" he asked.

"I already got in my morning run, so I figured, why the hell not come into work?"

"This is why we work well together. You act like you can't stand me, but we're actually the same, me and you." Everett paused. "Except for the running. I'm never going to start running. Hey, have *you* ever gotten a breakup bob?"

She pursed her lips. "No. People think a bob is an easy hairstyle, but it's actually a lot of work. Can't put a bob in a ponytail. Can't put it in a bun. There's nowhere to hide with a bob. Frankly, it's an impractical hairstyle with great marketing."

Everett blinked. "Okay."

Astrid frowned, then started to walk away. "Eat," she called over her shoulder.

Everett chewed and began typing his response.

## 14

TEDDY LOOKED AT HERSELF IN THE MIRROR AND SIGHED. WOM-en's magazines and cute pictures of celebrities on gossip blogs had lied to her. This bob wasn't easy. It wasn't chic. It didn't even look *good*. It was like the left side and the right side of her head were dressed up for costume parties with entirely different themes. The left was smooth and sleek, while the right side had a cowlick sticking out at an odd angle.

Whatever. Richard loved long hair, and honestly, screw him. She'd have to make this unflattering bob work somehow, damn it.

"Off to work!" Eleanor called.

Teddy poked her head out of the bathroom. "Have fun molding young minds! Don't forget to grab one of the pumpkin muffins I made, but just because I thought we could all use muffins and not because I'm trying to prove my worth!"

"Got one. Thank you!" Eleanor said as the door shut behind her.

Kirsten and her boyfriend wandered out of the kitchen, the boyfriend holding a mixing bowl full of cereal. He'd stayed over last night, and Teddy had tried to ignore the noises. She made a mental note to invest in some headphones. Some heavy-duty noise-canceling headphones. Maybe the kind air traffic controllers wore.

While Teddy might have been uncomfortable with the volume

of his lovemaking, she couldn't be mad at his cereal consumption, because he'd brought his own box. He was courteous like that.

They all called him the Viking, because that was a nickname Kirsten had given him when they'd started dating (in the way that all women must give nicknames to potential suitors, as foretold by the prophecy in *Sex and the City*). But the nickname stuck, and although they all knew his real name was Dwayne, they still called him the Viking. Even Kirsten. Even, as Teddy unfortunately knew, during amorous moments.

"What are you guys up to today?" Teddy asked.

"Work," the Viking said. He worked in construction (hence the muscular physique that partly earned him his nickname, along with his impressive hair).

"I'm working on some commissions," Kirsten said with a smile, patting the Viking on the arm as he drained the milk from his cereal bowl. In addition to her own avant-garde pee-related work, Kirsten also did more conventional artwork at the request of many Columbus residents. She painted landscapes, animal portraits, whatever people asked for, and even though the ideas weren't hers, she seemed genuinely happy while she did it. Teddy wondered wistfully what that must be like, to know that what you did not only made you happy but made other people happy, as well.

"Bye, babe," Kirsten said as the Viking leaned in for a kiss so loud that Teddy considered putting her fingers in her ears. She felt like she was in a sound effects booth and someone was stirring a plate of fettuccine Alfredo.

As Kirsten shut the door behind him, Teddy decided to be bold and broach the topic of last night. It wasn't that she wanted to. Did anyone ever really want to ask their friend to stop getting lucky quite so loudly? But the sheer awkwardness of the conversation was enough to scare her, and so she figured it counted for today's item.

*Do one thing every day that scares you: talk to your roommate about how her sex life is negatively impacting your sleep.* Check!

"Hey, Kirsten?" Teddy's voice came out with a squeak, so she coughed to clear her throat. "Can I talk to you about something?"

"What's up?"

"Um, so, I'm not sure if you know this, and I'm not saying it's a huge deal, but . . ." She paused, then said the rest of the words in a rush. "Icouldn'tsleeplastnightbecauseyouandtheVikingwerehaving sexsoloudly."

"Oh, were we loud?" Kirsten asked, her eyebrows knit in concern. "I didn't realize." She looked contemplative for a moment. "I guess I don't know my own strength."

"I'm not sure strength has anything to do with it," Teddy said gently.

"Oh, believe me, it does," Kirsten said, and Teddy declined to follow up on that statement.

"Teddy!" Kirsten said, stepping closer and then poking Teddy on her cheek. "You're blushing!"

Teddy covered her cheeks with her hands. "Am I?"

Kirsten placed her hand over her heart. "Were you uncomfortable talking to me about my vigorous sex life?"

"A little."

Kirsten opened her mouth in shock. "Well, Teddy, we haven't even drawn up the official plan for Teddy Time, and look at you. Already doing things that scare you. Kudos."

Teddy smiled. "Thank you. And sorry for . . . you know."

Kirsten shook her head dramatically. "No, no, no. From now on I'll tell the Viking to keep it down. No matter how good—"

"No." Teddy held up her hands. She'd heard enough. "I know I'm the newest roommate here and maybe I don't have the standing to make rules, but I think our friendship needs some boundaries.

Like maybe we know exactly where we are in one another's cycles, but I don't know what you say when you orgasm."

Kirsten nodded, looking thoughtful. "I guess that's fair."

Teddy smiled. "I've got to go get ready for work."

In her room, she grabbed her phone to check the weather but saw that her email was glowing with a little red notification. Her heart skipped a beat. She knew it was probably an email from Old Navy telling her about yet another deal on denim (there was always a deal on denim; at this point, it would have been more noteworthy if there *wasn't* a deal on denim), but she allowed herself a moment of excitement. Maybe it was Everett St. James saying, *Yes, let's be best friends. Yes, let me solve all your problems. Yes, I see you and understand you in a way that no one else ever has.*

She took a breath and opened her email.

It was from Everett St. James.

She fell back on the bed without meaning to. It was as if her body simply lost the capability to stand up. If you had asked Teddy about it later, she would have told you that she died for a moment, left her body, hovered near the ceiling watching the scene below, and then entered her body again in time to read the email. Sure, that exact situation seemed improbable or even perhaps impossible, but the sheer euphoric excitement she experienced was too much to be contained in her earthly form.

She scanned the email once quickly, then read it again slowly, her heart thumping out an alarmingly fast beat as she imagined the words in Everett's voice.

Dear Theodora,

Thank you very much for your email. It's not often that I get emails from adult women . . . at least not emails that don't immediately have to be forwarded to local law enforcement.

Teddy sat up and smiled, crossing her legs under her on the bed.

You say you're worried about finding your "thing." Understandable. But might I suggest that you've already found your thing and don't know it? For example, you made a *Star Wars* reference and wrote an email with impeccable spelling, which is something most of my email correspondents don't do (possibly because they're still learning to read). Perhaps your thing is sending perfect emails that brighten the days of their recipients.

Teddy pressed her lips together, imagining Everett, his huge body crammed into a desk chair somewhere, smiling as he read her email. Smiling! Because of her!

I discovered my thing (which I hope you've guessed is puppetry) when I was four years old. Sometimes it helps to think back to what made us happy when we were young, before we met people who told us our dreams were silly or unrealistic. What lit up your heart when you were a kid? Maybe that's your thing.

As Pablo Picasso once said (according to Google, anyway, which I can only assume would never lie to me): "Every child is an artist. The problem is how to remain an artist once they grow up."

On the other hand, maybe you and Keegan both need to take flute lessons. Only time will tell.

Yours eternally,
Everett

PS: I asked my producer to explain the concept of the breakup bob, but I still don't fully understand. Is it bad? Is it good? Should I get one?

Teddy put her hand over her mouth to stifle a laugh (the walls in the house were thin, as she knew all too well, and she didn't want Kirsten to ask what she was laughing at, lest she have to explain she was emailing a children's TV host). Everett was *funny*. She knew that, of course, but now she knew he was funny in a nonpuppet context. Not everyone could send a good email, after all. It took skill to be charming in such a flat medium.

Teddy had heard the rule that you weren't supposed to text a man back immediately if you were dating. You know, to suffuse yourself with an air of mystery and all that.

But this was a situation she didn't know the rules for. When attempting to develop an email friendship with a cute stranger whom you'd watched for hours upon hours, how soon was too soon?

She put her phone down. She didn't need to respond right away, and anyway, this wasn't her most pressing concern. Teddy had enough self-awareness to realize that she was using Everett's email as a distraction from her real-life circumstances: recently dumped, no career trajectory, passionless, and living in a room that might have recently been peed in.

It didn't sound great when she laid out all the details like that.

But today was a new day, and she was out here having potentially awkward conversations with her roommate! She would trust Future Teddy to craft a perfectly composed, perfectly charming, perfectly witty, perfectly *perfect* email to Everett tonight after work.

**15**

Dear Everett,

When I was a kid, I loved riding my bike as fast as it could go, until I broke my arm, ended my parents' marriage, and became the outcast of my middle school.

Scratch that. Too pathetic.

Dear Everett,

When I was a kid, I loved watching gory movies because it was fun to be scared. But then I realized that life itself is terrifying, and why should I voluntarily put myself into a scary situation?

Nope. Way too honest.

Dear Everett,

Sometimes when I watch your show, I feel like you would truly understand me, if we knew each other in real life. Like

you would let me be myself, or find myself, instead of pushing me to be the person you think I should be. Also, you have
extremely attractive hands and they've been the subject of
several erotic daydreams.

Wow, no. Too "Call the authorities. This woman's going to appear outside your front door."

"Are you okay, dear?"

Teddy blinked a few times and stood up straight. "What's that?"

Josie peered at her over her glasses. "You were staring into space
and muttering to yourself."

Teddy shook her head a few times, like a dog shaking off water.
"Sorry. I'm . . ."

Well, she'd been mentally composing an email to Everett
St. James, which wasn't something she could explain to Josie right
now. Not without a lot of backstory, anyway.

Josie patted her on the shoulder. "Scares the customers, you
know. The muttering."

Teddy smiled. "Right."

Carlos was in the back corner talking about LEGO with a customer. Josie and Teddy watched him as he smiled, gestured wildly,
and nodded in agreement at something the customer said.

"Why doesn't Carlos talk to me like that?" Teddy asked, frowning. "I'm always asking him how his weekend went and all I get are
monosyllabic responses. I think he hates me."

Or maybe, she wondered, Carlos was just like her. Maybe he had
someone telling him that his life was small, someone who made
him feel like what he had to say didn't matter. Maybe, Teddy
thought, she should try to be Carlos's friend.

Josie waved her off. "I think you'd have to take an original Darth
Vader action figure out of the packaging to make Carlos hate you.
Carlos and I talk all the time. He just takes a little time to warm up

to people, and he mostly likes to talk about toys—no one knows about this stuff like him."

"Hey," Teddy said, mock-offended, "I know quite a bit about the world of vintage toys, thank you very much."

Josie lightly swatted her on the arm. "Yeah, but you're here for the paycheck and the sparkling conversation with yours truly. Carlos lives and breathes this stuff. Look at him over there, convincing that customer that they simply have to buy a LEGO pirate ship."

Teddy knew this was meant to be a compliment to Carlos, not a dig at her, but it still smarted. Of course it wasn't her passion. She didn't even *have* a passion. Not vintage toys or metalworking or Jazzercise or . . .

"Josie," Teddy said, turning to face Josie with such intensity that Josie stumbled backward and bumped into the register. "Can I come with you to Jazzercise some time?"

Josie stared at her, confused. "But I've been asking you to come to Jazzercise for years."

"I know," Teddy acknowledged.

"And you always say no, on account of you 'don't like to move your body in front of people.'"

Teddy nodded.

"That was a direct quote," Josie reminded her.

"True."

"You also said, 'I have the coordination of a college girl wearing one high heel at one a.m. on High Street.'"

Teddy frowned. She didn't remember saying that, but she must have, because that was the description of a real girl she'd seen once, years ago, leaning on her girlfriends. She often wondered about her. Did she ever find her other shoe, or was it still missing, waiting for its owner to sober up and come back for it? It made her feel sad to think about, like when she saw a lonely, waterlogged stuffed animal on the side of the street.

"Okay, okay, okay, I said a lot of things about Jazzercise and my disinterest in it," Teddy said with a wave of her hands, wiping the chalkboard clean. "But I may have reacted too hastily. Because now I would very much like to try it."

Teddy didn't really want to try Jazzercise. In fact, she was terrified of entering a room full of women in workout gear and dancing to popular music. It all sounded horrifying and embarrassing and a situation in which there might be a hidden camera recording her for the express purpose of putting the video on Twitter, after which it would go viral and spawn a bunch of news stories and Halloween costumes ("Jazzercise Girl," they'd call her).

"I would love nothing more than to bring you to Jazzercise," Josie said. "But what's gotten into you? Did your doctor tell you to get more physical activity? Because you're quite sedentary. And your posture. Yeesh." Josie grimaced.

Teddy hesitated. She wasn't planning on telling anyone about Teddy Time. She could only imagine telling her family about this and what her mother would say. *Teddy, it's not that difficult. Just follow each step of my ten-step plan, the one I concocted without any input from you.*

But this wasn't her mother. This was Josie, and Josie wouldn't pressure her.

"I'm trying to do one thing every day that scares me," Teddy explained. "It's something we all came up with together, Eleanor and Kirsten and me. It's because I spent so much time not doing what I wanted, or not even knowing what I wanted, because of . . . well . . ."

"Rick the Dick," Josie said, shaking her head as if she'd gotten a surprise taste of something rotten.

Teddy couldn't help but let out a tiny laugh. "Okay, I get it. You don't like Richard."

Josie widened her eyes. "It's not that I don't like him. It's that I want to drop him into a volcano."

Teddy lowered her head into her hands.

Josie waved a hand. "Teddy, the man was the pits. He was a looker, sure, but you can't coast on looks forever, believe me."

"Oh, now, Josie, you're still beautiful—" Teddy said, but Josie cut her off.

"I wasn't talking about myself. But most men? Well, no matter how cute they are in their twenties, you'd better mentally prepare yourself for the day they're red-faced and alcohol bloated and wearing stained clothing."

"Thank you for the advice," Teddy said with a nod. "I'll file it away for future use."

"All I'm saying is that Richard didn't treat you right, but I never said anything because what's the point? People have to make their own decisions, even if their slightly older but much wiser boss tells them the truth. But now that you two are for sure done . . ." She trailed off, raising her eyebrows.

"We're done."

"Then, okay, he was the human embodiment of spoiled milk," Josie said, throwing her hands in the air.

Teddy sighed. "Well, as terrible as you think he was, I was *happy* to follow him around, because I had no idea what I should actually do. But now he's not here, and I am. So I'm trying things myself."

Josie's face exploded into one of her giant Josie Smiles—Teddy often thought that someone should bottle and sell that joy. You could make millions.

"You and your friends are smart girls," she said. "This is exactly what you need. The best way to get over a terrible man is by getting into bed with a new one, but this sounds like the second best way."

Teddy's mouth fell open in shock. "Josie! What are you talking about? You haven't been with anyone since John died!"

"Ah." Josie patted Teddy's hands. "But John wasn't a terrible man. He was a fantastic one. And besides, who says I haven't been with a man? You meet a lot of men with a hobby like metalworking."

"Josie McNealy," Teddy said in wonder, "you're full of surprises."

"So are you, my dear," Josie said, turning to look at her again. "Jazzercise is tonight at seven p.m. Think you can make it?"

Teddy grimaced. "Carlos is closing, so I guess so."

She started to panic. It was finally starting to hit her that she was going to an exercise class. Most of her experience with exercise involved (a) kids in elementary school gym class making fun of her for her terrible kickball performance, (b) passing out while running a mile in high school, and (c) doing a yoga video on YouTube when Richard walked in and laughed at her "terrible form." In retrospect, what did he know about yoga? He was a dermatologist, not a fitness instructor. But still, it had left a mark.

"What do I wear?" asked Teddy, because sometimes the best way to manage anxiety was by making sure one had the right outfit.

Josie waved her off. "Whatever you want. Find some fun leggings. We're not too serious over at Jazzercise."

"Fun leggings," Teddy said, nodding, as if that was a thing she owned. Maybe she had time to run by a store after work. She made a mental note to google "fun leggings store." "Sure."

"Teddy," Josie said, squeezing her shoulder, "we're all a big family at Jazzercise. One big happy, sweaty family. Everyone's gonna be glad to see you, and no one's gonna judge you."

Teddy nodded, but she wasn't so sure.

The customer left, and Carlos came back up to the counter. He didn't make eye contact with Teddy or Josie as he unlocked the display case behind the counter and put the pirate ship back in.

"See you tonight at seven," Josie said, and then to Carlos, "You wanna join us for Jazzercise tonight, sweet pea?"

Carlos smiled at Josie. *Carlos never smiles at me,* Teddy thought jealously. "I'm good. Thanks," he said, then opened a comic book and started reading as he leaned on the counter.

"Your loss!" Josie called as she walked to the back room.

"Carlos," Teddy said so loudly that Carlos actually jumped, "how was your weekend?"

Carlos looked back at his comic book. "Mmmm," he said noncommittally.

Teddy frowned. She was going to befriend Carlos if it was the last thing she did. "I brought in some pumpkin muffins. Would you like one?"

Carlos shook his head without looking up. "No, thank you."

The bell above the door rang and the Mysterious Bathroom Bandit came stomping in, newspaper under his arm.

"Hello!" Teddy said with a smile, and he grunted as he walked past her. Carlos kept reading.

As the bathroom door slammed, Teddy turned to Carlos. "Are you familiar with the Mysterious Bathroom Bandit? He comes in here most mornings to use the bathroom. He's borderline rude and I don't know what his deal is, but he doesn't make a mess, so I don't stop him."

Carlos stopped reading and looked up, meeting Teddy's eyes for the first time that day. *This is it,* Teddy thought. *Finally, a real conversation, one where Carlos and I will become actual friends who have a fun inside joke about a regular, and I'll be assured that he doesn't hate me.*

"Can't say that I've noticed," Carlos said, then returned to his comic book.

Teddy slumped over the counter, deflated. After a few minutes had passed, the Mysterious Bathroom Bandit opened the bathroom door and stalked back through the shop.

"Thanks for stopping in! Great to catch up!" Teddy called after him, and he gave his typical grunt in response.

Teddy sighed. She was starting to take all this rejection a bit personally.

**16**

Dear Everett,

Thank you for responding. I'll admit, I hoped for a response but didn't expect one, given the whole "I'm an adult woman and not a child" thing.

And thank you for your advice to think about what I loved doing as a child. Most of what I remember from my childhood involves books. I spent a lot of time sitting in the maple tree in our backyard while reading and rereading library copies of the entire Alice series by Phyllis Reynolds Naylor.

I'm not sure that interest really translates to a career, but then again, it's also probably too late to become a career flutist. Maybe I should spend more time reading about the trials and tribulations of adolescent girls. Maybe I should find a new maple tree (something tells me my mom would balk if I showed up at her house and started reading in her tree). You've given me a lot of things to think about.

In the spirit of complete transparency, I should tell you that I've started a new project to find my "thing." Do you know the famous quote "Do one thing every day that scares you"? A lot of people think Eleanor Roosevelt said it, but it sounds like it's kind of a Pablo Picasso situation. Whoever said it, it's behind my project. With the help of my roommates, I'm doing one thing every day that scares me.

And also, I must admit, my project is more than a little bit inspired by you and the advice you gave Keegan. Do you remember when you told him he should try new things, even and especially the things that scared him? Maybe you don't remember saying that, because it's probably second nature to you. But it isn't to me, and I couldn't stop thinking about it. So now . . . I'm doing it.

Tonight I attended a Jazzercise class with my boss. Are you familiar with the phenomenon of Jazzercise? I spent the last hour wearing pizza-print leggings (I borrowed them from my roommate and they barely fit) while dancing to a playlist largely dedicated to the Jonas Brothers. I regret to report that I now feel great. I guess endorphins are real, and also I might like the Jonas Brothers now. There are a lot of changes happening in my life, and frankly, I'm scared.

But even though I'm scared of my newfound love for athletic wear and the JoBros (that's what I call them now that I'm a fan), I'm still glad I went. Because here's the thing: I was pretty miserable when my boyfriend dumped me. And although I'm feeling better every day, sometimes I still feel like everyone I encounter can see the word REJECT stamped on my forehead, like they can tell I'm damaged goods before I even open my mouth. But it's hard to be sad when I'm scared, and it's hard to be sad *or* scared when one of the Jonas Brothers is crooning about how he's a sucker for me.

I'm sorry. I know that's a lot for an email, especially because I sort of know you and you have no idea who I am. But it's late and I'm tired, emotional, and drunk on Jazzercise.

Thank you again for writing back to me. I know you must be busy, what with your show and all.

Yours till Niagara Falls,
Theodora

PS: I don't recommend a breakup bob. Have you ever been dumped? Because if so, you should consider literally any other haircut. It looks terrible and I hate it, but that's the problem with rash hair decisions. You have to accept your mistakes and live with them for months.

PPS: I just googled it, and it turns out flute players are sometimes called flautists. Who knew? Flautists, presumably.

It took Teddy hours to compose her email to Everett, but only one and a half minutes to regret it. When the enormity of what she'd told Everett finally sank in, Teddy actually, literally smacked herself on the forehead. Imagine telling a beautiful, sensitive man that you're damaged goods. Or that your hair looked bad. She was never going to Jazzercise again; clearly it had adverse effects on her mental function.

But it was too late. The email was out there, floating through . . . cyberspace? Teddy didn't really know what happened with emails, but she knew one thing: she had said what she was feeling to a man for the first time in forever, and now he was never going to email her again.

# 17

"EVERETT."

Everett looked up from his laptop, startled, to see Astrid and Jeremy staring at him. Astrid looked annoyed, while Jeremy looked curious.

"Why do I keep finding you smiling at your laptop?" Astrid asked, walking over to look at his screen. "This is uncomfortable. What are you doing?"

"Are you watching game shows on there?" Jeremy asked. "They always make me laugh. *Family Feud*, man."

"Which host?" Everett asked. "We talkin' current Steve Harvey run? Or are you going back to Richard Karn?"

Jeremy shook his head. "Steve Harvey's the GOAT, but don't sleep on Louie Anderson."

Everett nodded, impressed. "Good picks."

Astrid snapped her fingers, but Everett knew her well enough to know that she was holding back a smile.

"Let's focus on Everett and whatever strange thing he's got going on. Oh, no," Astrid said, finally looking at his screen. "Is this another email? You're smiling like this over *email*?"

Jeremy peered over his shoulder. "Well, well, well," he said, rubbing his hands together. "Looks like our pal Everett has a lady friend."

"More like lady acquaintance," Everett clarified. "Lady associate?"

"That sounds like an escort," Jeremy said. "*Is* she an escort?"

Astrid narrowed her eyes. "Do escorts typically write lengthy emails? Serious question. I wouldn't know."

"She's my pen pal," Everett said. "I guess. This is only her second email to me."

"Nice," Jeremy said, nodding. "That's how I met my wife. We started messaging on Myspace, and look at us now."

"Still on Myspace?" Astrid asked, an eyebrow raised.

"No. Married for seven years," Jeremy said. "All I'm saying is, words can be romantic. She fell in love with my messages long before we met in person."

"Whoa, whoa, whoa," Everett said, closing his laptop. "Who said anything about love?"

"Yeah," said Astrid with a smug smile. "We all know Everett doesn't do relationships, because that would mean spending time on something that isn't work. He's content to have an unrequited crush on young Carol Kane."

"Or, frankly, old Carol Kane. At any age, that woman can get it. Her sense of comedic timing is great, and she's got those big eyes," Everett said, deflecting the insult. He had zero desire to talk about the fact that it had been years since his last serious relationship, and look how that had turned out. He had his reasons for focusing on work.

Astrid sighed. "Okay, as great as it's been making fun of Everett . . . and to clarify, I find that deeply enjoyable . . . maybe it's time to—I don't know—do our jobs? Everett, why aren't you dressed?"

Technically Everett was dressed, in jeans and a T-shirt, but what Astrid meant was that he wasn't in costume. Not that he wore a superhero costume or anything, but he did have a look for the show. One that (he hoped) said *I'm a professional adult, but I'm fun. I'm educational, but I'm creative. Kids like me, but I'm not a kid.*

He pulled on the navy blue cardigan he'd thrown over the back of his chair. "Done. Dressed. Let's do this."

Astrid rolled her eyes. "This is why women write you emails. Because you dress like hot Mr. Rogers. Why don't you wear a red cardigan and make the homage more obvious?"

Everett bristled. "I would never. The man is a legend, and it would be disrespectful to invite the comparison."

Astrid shook her head and followed Jeremy out the door to set. Everett drummed his fingers on his laptop, thinking about reading through the email one more time, but decided against it.

Astrid poked her head back in the room. "Hey, before I forget.... I have to talk to you about something later. Not related to your love life, thankfully."

"Can't you tell me now?" Everett asked.

"Nope!" Her voice carried as she walked down the hall. "Later!"

Everett sighed, his mind running through the possible bad news it could be. Was he fired? Doubtful. The show had his name in the title. Was the show canceled? Astrid was in way too good a mood for that to be happening. Budget cuts? Possible. Probable, even.

He sighed again. Okay, he'd read the email one more time.

AFTER FILMING ENDED for the day, Astrid caught Everett while he was still sitting on the couch. "Hey, you have a second?" she asked.

Everett looked around them. They weren't alone—people were still walking around set, even though no one was paying any attention to them. "How much are they cutting it?"

Astrid coughed. "What?"

"The budget," Everett said.

"Oh. Oh!" Astrid barked out a laugh. "You thought this was *bad* news. Wow. Okay."

Everett sat still for a moment as Astrid laughed. "Uh, Astrid? Filling me in right now would be great."

She wiped her eyes. "Right. Okay, well, this is the opposite of bad news. I got a call from the Imagination Network—"

"You what?" Everett cut her off. The Imagination Network was the biggest children's production studio in the country, a place so out of his reach that he'd never dreamed he might be able to work with them.

"Yeah. They saw the show, and Everett . . . they liked it. They *really* liked it. In fact, they want to meet with you."

"They want. To meet. With me?" Everett sounded the words out slowly, like they were a language he was just learning.

Astrid nodded. "Yep."

"About . . . the show."

"No, about your illustrious burlesque career. Yes, about the show!" Astrid took a sip out of her thermos, which Everett knew was full of herbal tea. Astrid never needed caffeine; she was permanently in the state that most people could achieve only via coffee. The only thing she ever needed from a beverage was the ability to calm down.

"I can't even focus on how you made another joke because holy *shit*," Everett said slowly, sprawling back on the couch.

"My thoughts exactly," Astrid said.

"So . . . what's happening? Are they coming here? Do we have a phone call?"

"They're gonna come here to talk to you," Astrid said. "And provided things go well, they'll fly you out to see their studios after that."

Everett exhaled.

"Ev," Astrid said, meeting his eyes, "this is a big deal."

"I know," Everett said, looking back at her. If this worked out—if the Imagination Network liked him, liked the show, wanted to work with him—then all of this would be worth it. The fact that he was unable to sustain a real romantic relationship. The fact that he always turned Natalie down when she wanted to hang out. The fact that he was a thirty-year-old man who spent 95 percent of his social time with his family. If his nonstop focus on work paid off, instead of flaming out in a few years when some better show came along and parents and kids grew tired of him, then he wouldn't have that persistent voice in his ear whispering, *Something is missing.* This *was* the something.

Although Everett clearly idolized the classics, the Imagination Network was responsible for most of the innovative children's programming happening right now, at this moment. Their shows were never flashy, trendy, or focused on selling kids some shit they didn't need. They wanted to help kids grow, not turn them into consumers. And their focus was on *all* kids, specifically low-income children who might not have access to preschool or fancy after-school programs. Everett cared about every kid, but he knew that working with the Imagination Network would help him reach the kids who really *needed* programs like his, shows that helped them work through their feelings and told them that it was okay to ask questions, be confused, even be angry sometimes. His heartbeat quickened as he thought about what it would mean for the show, for the kids, if *Everett's Place* had a national audience. This was what he'd been working toward ever since that day Jeremy and he had started making the show in his parents' attic.

And then he thought about how he and Astrid had been working together for so long, how she was the one who kept them all on schedule, how the show would never be what it was without her, how *he* would never be anything without her, and all of a sudden, he was overcome with gratitude.

"Come here," he said, leaning forward to envelop Astrid in a hug.

"Okay," she said into his shoulder. She stiffly patted him on the back. "Uh, thanks."

He leaned back. "Thanks for making this a great show, Astrid."

She looked at him and he thought, for a moment, that he could see some sort of tenderness in her eyes. But then she frowned and said, "Good news makes you emotional, huh? Go hug Jeremy, you weirdo."

**18**

Dear Theodora,

First, I should address one thing: nothing is too personal to email about. You're talking to someone who sees the innermost thoughts of small children every day, and they rarely have a filter. This email is barely personal when compared to the things a four-year-old will tell you about their toilet habits.

Have I ever been dumped? Oh, have I. Prepare to regret asking this question, because I'm about to give you far more information than you wanted.

I had a girlfriend once (sorry, I didn't mean for this to sound like I'm an ancient sea captain looking out to the ocean while smoking a pipe and recounting his lost love). Her name was Elissa, and she was great—funny and smart and supportive. My family loved her. I loved her. She thought we were going to get married, but I . . . well, I wanted to get married. Theoretically. Someday. But in a practical sense, in a sense where we got engaged and picked a date and—I don't know—tried a bunch of cakes (my knowledge of wedding planning is limited)? I didn't care. She tried to talk to me, but I was never 100 percent there, because I was always 100 percent with the show. Eventually, she broke up with me because she said I'd never be married to her while I was married to my work.

The worst part of it was, she wasn't cruel about it. She was sad, and so was I, because I loved her. But I didn't love her the right way, and that's the part that makes me wonder if there's something fundamentally wrong with me. Like maybe I'm too much of a fuckup to accept love. And if so, maybe I'm a fraud for doing a children's show about feelings.

But there's the real heart of it. I understand kids. I understand their feelings. Other adults? Or, God forbid, myself? Not always.

Well, let's assume you're no longer worried that your email was too personal. You know I've never told anyone any of this? Even my family and friends don't know why we broke up.

Theodora, take it from me, someone who might, in fact, be a bad person and/or a robot who doesn't know how to fully love: you're not damaged goods. You're not a reject. I don't even know you, and I know you're an incredibly special person who is willing to take a chance to make her life better. Not everyone can do that. That takes guts.

On a slightly jazzier note: up until this point, I thought that Jazzercise was merely the stuff of myth. I certainly didn't know it was still happening, let alone so close to home. Is it weird that I'm intrigued? What would happen if I attended a class? Are men allowed at Jazzercise? Do I need to break the

Jazzercise glass ceiling, or would my presence as a large man be tainting a safe, jazzy, male-free space?

I hope you gain so much strength through Jazzercise that you're able to drop-kick your shitty ex in the face.

Keep me updated about your project.

Jazzily,
Everett

Teddy read the email once, twice, and then a third time. She had the sudden urge to clutch her laptop to her chest, like she was a woman holding a wartime soldier's letter in an old movie.

In all the years with Richard, he'd never been this honest with her. Never made her feel this good. Certainly never been this emotional.

Everett St. James was in touch with his feelings, and it was *extremely* hot.

Eleanor popped her head in as Teddy fanned herself with her hand.

"Sorry," she said. "Do we need to turn down the heat?"

"What?" Teddy asked, startled.

"You're all sweaty and fanning yourself," Eleanor said. "If we're keeping it too warm, let us know! Anyway, we're ready to go to the teahouse now if you are."

Apparently, the Cambridge Tea House was where Kirsten and Eleanor discussed all official roommate business, which was as wide-ranging as what kind of cake to get for Kirsten's birthday celebration (ice cream, obviously) to whether they should get a pet (they'd decided on a goldfish). And now, as they sat at their table, they were discussing how, exactly, Teddy would change her entire life by con-

fronting her fears, a decision that was at least marginally more important than what cake to choose (but only marginally, because Kirsten
really loved cake).

"I can't believe I've never been here before," Teddy said, taking
in their surroundings as they sipped their tea. The teahouse, which
was in a building with a pointed roof that evoked a cottage, was
decorated in red and gold. All around them sat families and friend
groups sharing pots of tea and tiered trays of finger sandwiches.
Also, Teddy noted hungrily, scones.

"You'll love it," Eleanor assured Teddy. "I mean, what's not to
like about scones with jam?"

Kirsten held up a hand. "With cream. Always with cream. You're
gonna have to be the tiebreaker here, Teddy."

"I think I'll go with both," Teddy said, and the girls nodded
appreciatively.

"I like the way you think, woman," Kirsten said, and Teddy
attempted to study the menu but zoned out as she thought about
Everett's email. Her entire body flushed, like she was a teapot in one
of the cute little teapot cozies she saw on the next table. Sure, she'd
always admired Everett on the show, but now she knew he was more
than an extremely attractive, sensitive man with beautiful eyes and
touchable hair (not to mention the hands again). Now she knew he
was smart. Funny. Reassuring. Remarkably self-aware. Not one of
those guys who referred to his exes as "crazy."

"Teddy?"

Teddy jolted and sloshed tea out of her cup.

Eleanor laughed. "What is up with you today? I mean, generally
you have the vibe of a woodland creature, but right now your vibe
is like 'woodland creature who's being hunted.'"

"You can share it with us. The teahouse is a safe space," Kirsten
said.

Teddy shook her head. She wasn't about to tell the girls about

Everett. They'd let her stay in their pee studio but maybe they didn't want to know about her clandestine correspondence with a puppeteer. They'd probably think she was a stalker and kick her out, and then she'd have to go live with her mother and get a business degree.

"I don't know the first thing about business," Teddy accidentally muttered out loud.

"Most woodland creatures don't," Eleanor said with a smile. "So we usually get the afternoon tea—it comes with finger sandwiches and a scone on those fun little tiered trays."

"Yes." Teddy nodded. "I need that tiered tray."

She thought about what Richard used to tell her, especially on nights when the girls invited her to hang out with them and Richard wanted her to go to yet another night out with his friends. "They aren't good friends," he'd say, leaning toward her as if he were letting her in on a secret. "Come on . . . Kirsten is an 'artist'? And Eleanor teaches kids, but she dresses like one, too. Is that really who you want to hang out with?"

Teddy had bristled. She loved the way Eleanor dressed, all bright colors and printed tights. She wished she had the courage to dress like that, instead of in the basic dark skinny jeans and sweaters she usually wore. And she loved Kirsten's art.

But she hadn't said that to Richard. Kirsten and Eleanor would be fine without her, and so she put off every invitation with a texted excuse and a few sad-faced emojis. And eventually, her social circle narrowed to include Richard, Richard's friends, who mostly shared inside jokes about school and work, and that was it.

But now that the tiered tray of teatime delights was coming her way, Teddy realized it seemed unlikely that two people who weren't good friends would (a) let her live with them, (b) invite her to hang out with them constantly, and (c) devote their limited free time to helping her sort out her directionless life.

Teddy was starting to realize that, in this and many other areas, Richard might have been wrong.

As soon as they ordered, Eleanor pulled out her planner.

"I can't believe you went to Jazzercise," Kirsten said. "Look at you, taking the bull by the horns."

Teddy shrugged. "What can I say? The spirit moved me. And then the up-tempo beat of the Jazzercise soundtrack moved me. Josie is in good shape for someone in her seventies, by the way. I couldn't keep up with her—she was grapevining and lunging all over the place."

Eleanor clicked her pen. "Okay, so obviously you've been doing great with finding things that scare you, and Teddy Time allows for spontaneity. But a list helps."

"'A List Helps: The Eleanor Cho Story,'" Kirsten said.

Eleanor waved her pen. "Stop it, you. I make lesson plans for five-year-olds. Don't mock my organizational skills."

Teddy smiled.

Eleanor turned her chair to face Teddy. "Writing things down makes them real, and it makes your plans more likely to actually happen."

"Like a bucket list!" Kirsten said. "Except that you're not dying. Well, presumably not soon, anyway."

Eleanor opened up her notebook and the three of them started to list things Teddy could do. Some of them were things that she didn't want to do, but knew she needed to, like go to a restaurant by herself, without the security blanket of Richard or a friend. Have a real conversation with her sister for maybe the first time since before her bike accident.

Kirsten started saying things, and Eleanor started writing them down before Teddy could process them. Teddy heard her mention karaoke and wrinkled her nose but didn't have time to object before they'd moved on to Teddy taking a sewing class with Eleanor.

"Go on a date," Eleanor said as she wrote. Then she specified, "A non-Richard date."

"What if I don't want to go on a date?" Teddy asked, and then silently asked, *What if I'd rather sit in my room and read emails from a man I don't know?*

"But does it scare you?" Eleanor pointed her pen at Teddy.

"Yes," Teddy admitted.

"Onto the list it goes!" Eleanor said. "Remember, this is simply a list of options. Who knows how long you'll want to keep doing this before you decide you don't need it? Eventually, you won't be afraid of things anymore."

"I don't know," Teddy said, taking a sip. "I can't imagine I'll ever be fearless."

For a moment, she saw herself on her tiny bike, felt that wind in her hair. *Hell on wheels.* "Can we add 'ride a bike'?" Teddy asked.

Eleanor stopped writing. "It's your list! We can add anything you want. But are you really scared of bicycles?"

"A relatively nonthreatening mode of transportation," Kirsten said.

Teddy nodded. "I had . . . an accident once. When I was a kid. I broke my arm and I never got on one again."

"All right!" Eleanor said. "Riding a bike it is!"

They added more things to the list until it took up two pages. Two entire pages of things Teddy could do to change her life, fix her problems, find her passion.

"This is really scary," Teddy said, clutching her tiny teacup with both hands.

"That's how you know it's the right thing to do," Kirsten said as the servers brought out their scones and finger sandwiches.

Teddy's phone buzzed, and her tea sloshed out of the cup when she saw Richard's name on her screen. At first, she felt that familiar comfort/panic she always felt when he texted her—the sense that whatever he said would be a clear directive, but also the knowledge that she'd have to drop whatever she was doing to make it happen.

But this time, she thought about Everett's latest email and how he called Richard her shitty ex-boyfriend. He kind of was, wasn't he?

Her mouth went dry and she had to take a sip of oolong before she could whisper, "I came up with another item for my list. I think I want to tell Richard no."

"Gimme, gimme, gimme," Eleanor said, making grabby hands across the table. Teddy handed her the phone and Eleanor read the text out loud. "'Hey, babe. Wondered if you wanted to come over tonight? Miss you.'"

"'Babe'?!" Kirsten said, offended.

"It's only 'babe,'" Teddy muttered. "It's not like he called me the c-word or something."

Eleanor sputtered and almost spit out her tea sandwich. "I mean, yeah, okay, but that's a pretty low standard."

"Richard having the gall to refer to you as babe is too much, and I will not stand for it," Kirsten said, raising her voice. "He might as *well* be calling you the c-word."

Someone loudly coughed, and the three of them looked at the next table, where a father sat with a small boy and girl, the three of them wearing crowns and enjoying the restaurant's princess-prince tea. The little boy took a drink of his chocolate milk.

"Sorry," Kirsten said, inexplicably doing a half bow at the table. But then, to the girls, she muttered, "That dude needs to chill. It's not like I actually *said* the c-word. Listen, we know Richard never liked us."

"That's not true! He . . . he liked you guys," Teddy tried to protest, but her voice trailed off and she wasn't very convincing.

Kirsten spoke more quietly, chastened by the table next to them. "Come on, Teddy. He kept you isolated in that town house. It was weird, right?"

Teddy sighed. "I know it's easy to blame Richard for everything. But I kept myself isolated, too, you know. It was easier."

Kirsten gave Teddy a serious look. "Listen, I know this might be hard to hear, but do you think you were Richard's girlfriend, or do you think you were his unpaid personal assistant?"

Teddy sat back in her chair. Kirsten was right—this was hard to hear. She thought about all the meals she'd cooked, the floors she'd vacuumed, the bathrooms she'd cleaned. The appointments she'd scheduled, the moods she'd managed, the exams she'd helped him study for.

"When you put it that way . . . I guess unpaid personal assistant," she said, defeated.

Eleanor waved her hands. "You know what? We're gonna respond to him. Do you trust me?"

"Do I . . . ," Teddy faltered.

Eleanor leaned forward and grabbed her hand. "I said . . . *do you trust me*, Teddy?"

"Yes," Teddy said with a nod.

"Okay." Eleanor sat back, tapped out a quick text, then handed her phone back. "Done."

Teddy looked at the screen and read the text out loud. "'No.' That's . . . it?"

"You said you'd tell him no."

Teddy felt her heart drop into her chest and then to her knees. What would Richard say? What would he think? What if he really did need her? She'd never, ever said no to him, or really anyone else, before. She'd even gone along with him asking her to move out, willingly removing her things from his place simply because he'd requested it. The thought that Richard was at his place right now sitting on his couch, staring at his phone, and feeling annoyed filled her with terror.

A small giggle escaped her throat. And then a bigger one. And then she was full-on laughing, the kind of laugh that sent tears rolling down her cheeks.

Eleanor and Kirsten exchanged a look. The dad at the next table stared at her. The little girl in the princess crown asked, "Is she okay, Daddy?"

"I'm fine," Teddy said to the girl, attempting to find composure. "It's just . . . Have you ever been so terrified to do something, and then you do it and it's okay? It's better than okay. It feels amazing. Do you know that feeling?"

The dad shot her a look. "Eat your sandwich, sweetie," he said to his daughter.

"You're scaring the children," Eleanor said. "And us. What's happening?"

Kirsten waved a hand at Teddy, her eyebrows knit in concern. "Is this . . . your pent-up emotions finally coming to the surface?"

Teddy nodded. "I think so." She wiped a tear off her face. "I'll be right back."

She weaved through the tables, careful to avoid the children she might have traumatized, and found her way to the bathroom. She splashed some water on her face and took a good look at herself in the mirror. She knew the woman staring back at her—Theodora Phillips, hiding in the background.

But now there was something in her reflection that she didn't recognize. A glint in her eyes, a smile on her lips, a flush in her cheeks—this woman in the mirror was a mysterious person, and Teddy wanted to get to know her.

"Let's do this," she said to her reflection.

Teddy went back to the table and focused on being a good friend. She asked Eleanor how work was going and heard a story all about a kid who wouldn't stop eating Elmer's Glue, which was nontoxic but was still not exactly designed to be eaten. She asked Kirsten about her latest artwork, a giant painting of lilies that Kirsten said was "turning out a bit more vaginal than I expected, but sometimes art surprises you." And as the three of them talked and laughed, Teddy realized that there was no place else she'd rather be at that exact moment than at the teahouse, ordering another pot of oolong with her favorite people.

19

Dear Everett,

At this point, I'm no longer Jazzercise-curious. I'm not a casual attendee; no, I've been to Jazzercise two more times, and you know what? I'm a convert. If getting a cardio and strength workout while the Maroon 5 song "Moves like Jagger" plays is wrong, then . . . well, maybe I don't want to be right. And I'm sorry for getting that certified earworm stuck in your head.

As much as I'd love to encourage your enthusiasm in the world of Jazzercise, I do think your presence would make things a bit awkward. Mostly for me. I don't look my best while performing a chassé, and I don't want to be judged.

Thank you for your kind words about my breakup (I know it's odd to refer to "I hope you drop-kick your shitty ex in the face" as kind words, but in this context, I think they were). I'm sorry to hear about your breakup. How long ago was it?

And for the record, I don't think you're a robot or someone who doesn't know how to love. I've seen your show, after all. A robot couldn't talk to children about their feelings that way.

Well, maybe a really advanced robot could, but let's assume the technology isn't there yet.

An update on my project: while I may not have kicked my ex in the face (gotta get through a few more classes before I'm strong enough), I did take a big step. I told him no when he asked me for something. The truth is, as much as I wanted to believe I was in a real relationship, I might have been more of a housekeeper/personal chef/human calendar than a girlfriend. Which is likely why I'm faced with the whole "I have no idea what I'm doing with my life even though I'm almost thirty" problem. Aren't thirty-year-olds supposed to know what they're doing?

At this point, I'm halfway considering training to become a Jazzercise instructor. I promise in my next email I won't talk about Jazzercise at all.

Too jazzy for my own good,
Theodora

Everett found himself whistling—whistling!—as he walked down the sidewalk toward his parents' house. He raised a hand in greeting at an elderly woman walking her dog, smiled at an open-mouthed child who clearly recognized him, dodged a group of teenagers who couldn't have cared less that he was attempting to walk around them. Theodora was right—he wasn't a robot! Could a robot make a show for children about their feelings? No. It could not!

All of the porches were decorated with mums, pumpkins, and the occasional skull and/or oversized spider. It was fall, and soon it would be Halloween, and Everett felt good.

He walked up the stairs of his parents' porch, past their own mums and pumpkins. It wasn't unusual for him to show up unannounced; their house had kind of an open-door policy.

Fortunately or unfortunately, that open-door policy also extended to their students, who occasionally came over for help with essays, answers to questions about their assignments, or a quiet place to read when the library was crowded. Everett had become so used to this as a child that it was somewhat comforting to walk into the foyer and see a random early-twentysomething sitting in a ratty armchair.

The man looked up at Everett expectantly, and Everett found himself in the position of introducing himself to a stranger in his parents' house.

"Hi, I'm Everett," he said, holding out a hand. "Miranda and Dave's son."

The man's face broke into a huge smile and he stood up, dropping his book on the floor. "Everett! I'm Rob. Oh, our class has heard so much about you!"

"All good things, I hope," Everett said.

"Sometimes!" Rob said brightly.

Everett frowned. "Uh, do you know where my family is?"

"Miranda's around here somewhere. Dave's in the kitchen—it's pancake night! And the little one . . ." He trailed off.

Everett stifled a smile.

"She's sort of terrifying, you know?" Rob said, sitting back down. "I think she went to her room. I tried to ask her a question about *Frozen* and she . . ."

"Did she fix you with a withering glare?" Everett supplied.

Rob pointed at him. "Yes. That is exactly how I would describe it."

"Sounds like Gretel. Nice to meet you," Everett said as he headed up the wooden stairs, lined with a faded now-beige runner.

"See you at dinner!" Rob called.

Everett hadn't been in Gretel's room in ages (it was the kind of place you needed an invitation to get in, and he wasn't on the list), but he climbed the second (dark, foreboding, creaky) set of stairs up to the turret.

He knocked on the door three times, then waited for a response.

Eventually, he heard Gretel's voice. "Yes?" she asked skeptically. How a child could sound skeptical in one word and through a door, Everett didn't know, but Gretel managed it.

"It's me."

"You're going to have to be more specific."

He sighed. "It's Everett. Your brother. You know, tall, good-looking, beautiful hair—"

The door swung open and Everett looked down to see Gretel's bored expression. "Ugh. Stop."

"So, uh, what's going on?" Everett asked.

"Why are you in my room?" Gretel asked, eyes narrowed.

Everett tilted his head. "Technically I'm not in your room, because you haven't invited me in yet. Kinda rude, frankly. Maybe Mom and Dad should send you to charm school."

Gretel rolled her eyes and stepped back, allowing Everett to walk in. He let out a childlike "Whoa" as he took in his surroundings.

It was a small room and shaped like, well, a turret, but Gretel had packed it to the gills. Bookshelves took up half the wall under the windows, and they appeared to be stacked two books deep. Twinkle lights hung from the ceiling, shining in the dusk. Glow-in-the-dark stars were stuck on the ceiling, a detail so mundane that Everett could almost pretend his sister was any other twelve-year-old. Her bed, of course, was neatly made, and he could see the indent of where she'd been sitting, right next to a stack of books.

"Wow," he said, turning around to take everything in. "It looks . . . different than it did the last time I was in here."

"You mean when I was a toddler?" Gretel asked dryly, sitting back down on the bed. "Yes, there's no longer a changing table."

Everett shook his head while looking at her. "They grow up and learn how to control their own bladders so fast."

Gretel wrinkled her nose. "Did you come up here to talk to me about childhood incontinence?"

"No, actually," Everett said, bending down to look at the book-shelf. Classics. Essay collections. Poetry. He could feel Gretel cringe as he pulled out a book. "I'm putting it back carefully." He looked at her as he slid the book back onto the shelf.

"Ev!" she shrieked, jumping off the bed. "You're not even look-ing at what you're doing. These are alphabetized."

She grabbed the book, and he put his hands in the air. "Sorry. Wow. Didn't realize you had a system."

"Everybody has a system," she huffed, her arms crossed.

"Okay, well . . . have you heard of the Alice series? By, um . . ."

Everett started to pull his phone out of his pocket to look at Theodora's email, but Gretel asked, "Phyllis Reynolds Naylor? Yes, I know it."

Everett paused. "Really?"

"Mom gave me the whole series when I turned eight."

Right. Of course their parents were behind Gretel reading young adult literature from the eighties and nineties.

"Why?" Gretel asked, confusion splashed across her small face. "Do you . . . want to read them?"

"Yes." Everett nodded.

"Really?" Gretel asked, staring at him.

"Yes. An, uh . . . a friend of mine recommended them."

Gretel narrowed her eyes. "Oooookay," she said slowly. "The en-tirety of the series would be way too much for you to carry out of here, but"—she leaned over her bookshelf and pulled out a few—"here are the first six books."

"Thanks!" Everett said, easily holding three slim, tattered paperbacks in each hand. With his head, he gestured toward the stack of books on her bed. "What are you reading?"

"Gene Luen Yang, Lynda Barry, and Jerry Craft. Graphic novel research," she said, sitting back down on her creaky bed. At the first squeak, a black shape squeezed out from under the bed and rubbed against Everett's leg.

"Sassafras!" Everett said, bending down to greet the cat with a pet. Sassafras purred in response, so he picked her up. Sassafras loved attention from Everett, a fact that annoyed Gretel to no end.

"You don't even live here," she said, pouting. "Why does she like you so much?"

Everett put Sassafras down, at which point she jumped on the bed. Gretel pet her possessively.

"Just the effect I have on the ladies, I guess."

Gretel groaned.

"And on that note, I'm out of here." Everett held up the books. "Thanks for these."

"Hey!" Gretel called when he was halfway down the stairs. He turned to see her silhouetted in the doorway, still holding Sassafras.

"Yeah?" Everett asked.

"What girl are you trying to impress?"

Everett scoffed. "Who says I'm trying to impress a girl? Maybe I'm broadening my horizons."

"Well, whoever she is," Gretel called after him as he kept walking, "she has good taste."

Everett smiled without looking back. As he started down the second staircase, he heard, "Not staying for dinner, man?"

He startled but thankfully stopped himself from tripping down the stairs. "Rob. Wow. I, uh . . . wasn't expecting you to still be there."

Rob looked back at him, not offering an explanation.

"No, I have to get home now. But thanks for the offer," Everett said, before realizing he was thanking a stranger for inviting him to dinner at his own parents' house.

"No problem," Rob said with a smile. "I'll let Miranda know you stopped by."

Everett nodded. "Go ahead and do that."

And then he walked onto the porch and shut the door. The night had turned cold, but in that pleasant early-fall way that people liked to describe as "crisp." You could wear a jacket, but you didn't need a hat. Couples walked down the street with their dogs, headed for Goodale Park, and parents trailed kids on scooters. As if to complete the picture, a single leaf twirled down from the sky and landed at Everett's feet.

As he picked up the leaf and spun it around, a rogue feeling shocked him. Something he wasn't sure he'd experienced ever, or at least not recently. He was struck with the sudden desire to share this moment with someone, to be one half of one of the couples walking down the street, to be holding on to both a hand and a leash, to point out his observations about this night to another human being, instead of saving them in his head with hopes of using them on some episode of the show that discussed seasons.

He shook his head and walked down the stone steps. These emails. They were doing things to him.

**20**

Dear Theodora,

You have my word that I would never, ever judge your chassé. Mostly because I don't know what that is. To be honest, it sounds too inappropriate for what is technically my work email, so I'll change the subject.

Regarding the "shouldn't thirty-year-olds have their lives figured out?" question: well, that's hard for me to say. After all, you're talking to a freak of nature who's been interested in puppetry since the tender age of four. I realize that's not necessarily normal.

The breakup happened four years ago, which seems both like a lifetime away and like yesterday. She's married with a kid now, and honestly, I'm happy that she finally got what she wanted, even if it wasn't with me.

Good job telling your shitty ex no. So what else is happening on the "do one thing every day that scares you" front? Have you skydived yet? Bungee jumped? Watched *Human Centipede*?

Of note: I'm halfway through the second Alice book. I am scandalized that Pamela's bikini top fell off at the beach.

In rapture, sort of,
Everett

Teddy flushed. She couldn't stop flushing, because this email was one giant recipe for a full-body flush. She knew Everett's sign-off was a reference to the book he was reading (*Alice in Rapture, Sort Of*), but . . . he was reading the Alice books? He was reading an (admittedly genius) series of books aimed at preteen girls in the eighties and nineties just because she'd mentioned them once? She pictured Everett sitting in a chair, his big fingers turning those tiny paperback pages.

It wasn't an altogether bad image. She smiled, then frowned.

Before the emails, she would have said she had a crush on Everett St. James the way someone might have said they had a crush on Chris Evans, in the way where they simply enjoyed watching him on-screen and spent little time considering his personal life.

But that was not how she felt now. Now she had a living, breathing crush on Everett St. James, the real kind, the kind where she imagined him reading her favorite childhood books, smiled at his emails, and wondered what he was doing at any given moment. Everett St. James, the man who no doubt had plenty of women (and not only married moms, although who knew? Maybe married moms were his thing!) at his disposal. Everett St. James, who'd known what he wanted to do since he was four years old. Everett St. James, who certainly couldn't ever be attracted to a woman who didn't know what she wanted, even if he was very kindly humoring her via email.

*No,* Teddy thought, *there's no way this is going to end well.*

She closed her email and opened a tab to watch the latest episode of Everett's show. She didn't know how far in advance they were filmed; had he made this since they'd been talking? Or, rather, emailing? Was the Everett on-screen aware of who she was, even if he didn't really know her?

She was smiling as Everett talked to an owl puppet when Kirsten walked by her open door.

Teddy slammed her laptop shut, and Kirsten tilted her head. "Oh, Teddy, no need to hide anything here."

"I'm not hiding anything," Teddy said, sitting up straight.

"I'm not going to judge whatever weird porn you were watching with the door open," Kirsten said. "This is a judgment-free zone."

"I wasn't watching—" Teddy started.

"I'm just glad you're happy," Kirsten said before Teddy could explain. "Eleanor? You ready?"

Eleanor breezed past Kirsten and into the room. With the three of them there, even with Teddy sitting on the bed, the room was pretty much at capacity.

"Why are you wearing your sparkly skirt?" Teddy asked, pointing to Eleanor's sequin-covered silver miniskirt that she'd paired with maroon tights and a denim jacket. "Are you going on a date or something?"

Teddy hadn't been living with the girls long, but she already knew that the sparkly skirt was Eleanor's "going out" attire.

Eleanor shook her head as if she was offended. "No. Well, maybe a friend date. We're going to karaoke!"

"I can't do that," Teddy said immediately.

Eleanor and Kirsten looked at each other and then back at Teddy. "What do you mean, you can't? Are you, like, physically unable to sing?" Kirsten asked.

"Is this a vocal cord issue?" Eleanor asked with concern.

By all accounts, Teddy Time was going swimmingly. Teddy mentally ticked off the list. Emailing Everett? Check. Going to Jazzercise?

Check. Confronting the fact that she'd actually loved Jazzercise? Big check. Having a conversation with Kirsten about her and the Viking's sex life? Check, check, and check.

She was doing it! She was moving out of her comfort zone, and she had the sore calves to prove it! But this . . . this was perhaps a bridge too far.

"I'm not a karaoke person," Teddy said firmly.

"Untrue!" Eleanor said, a finger in the air as if she were bringing up an important point. "That's because everyone is a karaoke person."

"There are two types of people," Kirsten said. "Those who love karaoke and those who don't know they love it yet."

She and Eleanor nodded in sync.

"Okay, no, you're not getting it," Teddy said, frustrated. "I can't sing. Like, I *really* can't sing. Once I was singing in the shower and Richard popped his head in and asked me to stop because he said I was so off-key, it was making it hard to study."

Eleanor narrowed her eyes.

"I'm serious, you guys. When I sing, dogs howl. Glass shatters. Randy Jackson shows up and says, 'That's gonna be a no from me, dawg.'"

"Teddy!" Kirsten grabbed her shoulders. "That's the absolute beauty of karaoke! You don't have to be a good singer! In fact, it's better if you aren't. Everyone else kinda hates the great singers. Who are they showing off for?"

"We're not good singers, either," Eleanor said.

Kirsten lifted a shoulder and muttered, "Eh, speak for yourself."

Eleanor gave Kirsten a quick side-eye and a laugh. "I mean, we are not *classically trained*. We're not belting out the high notes on Mariah Carey songs. We just . . . have fun! If you pick a good song, and the vibe in the room is right, everyone starts singing along with you, and you look over that sea of faces, all of them singing the words right back to you. . . ."

"And it's almost a religious experience," Kirsten said. "Trust us. You're gonna love it."

This wasn't scary. This was *terrifying*. Teddy had spent years hiding, metaphorically and kind of literally. And now she was supposed to put herself on an actual stage with a microphone? It was absurd.

Reading the hesitation on Teddy's face, Kirsten asked, "What would Eleanor Roosevelt say if she walked in to this room right now?"

"Well," Teddy said, "she's dead, so probably not much."

"In that case, what would zombie Eleanor Roosevelt say?" Kirsten raised her eyebrows.

"Something unintelligible about eating brains?" Teddy asked. "I don't know. I don't watch a lot of zombie movies."

"Not the point!" Eleanor said. "The point is, you're trying to do things that scare you. Nothing changes if *you* don't make any changes! Dreams only work if you do! I have memorized *all* the posters in the teachers' lounge and I won't stop quoting them until you agree to go out with us!"

"She'll keep doing this all night," Kirsten said. "Come on, Teddy. Eleanor Roosevelt didn't sacrifice herself so you could *not* go to karaoke."

"How exactly do you think Eleanor Roosevelt died?" Teddy asked.

"TEAMWORK MAKES THE DREAM WORK!" Eleanor shouted, surprising everyone, including herself. "Sorry. That was louder than I intended."

Teddy bit her lip. She knew she had to do this. Not only because of the plan, and not only because the entire point of her life right now was to get out of her comfort zone even when (especially when!) it scared her.

No, she had to do this because Eleanor and Kirsten were asking. Because she'd blown them off for years, missing out on birthday parties, nights out, movie marathons, and late-night gossip sessions. She'd missed out on everything because she'd put her eggs in one

Richard-shaped basket. They were inviting her, and so she had to go. She needed them to know that she was here now, all in on their friendship, ready to be around for the long haul.

"We're not going to make you do this all alone," Eleanor said. "We can do a song together. It will be fun!"

All three of them onstage together. Okay. She could do this.

Teddy smiled. "You're right. It will be fun."

Eleanor and Kirsten cheered for approximately one half second, then went off to find their purses and coats. It was almost like they'd known she'd agree to go.

"Ghost of Eleanor Roosevelt, give me strength," Teddy muttered. And although she wasn't remotely sure where that prayer was going, she did feel a sense of certainty and calm overtake her. Tonight was going to be a good night.

# 21

"YOU PROMISED YOU'D GO OUT NEXT TIME," NATALIE SAID, standing in his kitchen. "Well, guess what, bro. It's next time."

Everett groaned. "But I actually meant the time after next time."

Natalie shook her head. "Everett St. James, I swear to all that is holy, you are the worst friend in the world."

Everett looked up from where he was sitting on the floor, once again surrounded by puppetry supplies and sketches. "Am I the worst friend in the world? Or am I kind of . . . the best?"

Natalie pretended to think about it. "Nope. The worst. All I ask is that you go out with me tonight, on the anniversary of the day we met and began this historic friendship . . ."

Everett sat up straighter. "It's the anniversary of the day we met?"

Natalie gave him a slow smile. "I have no idea what day we met, Everett. I was trying to get your full attention and it worked."

Everett slumped back down and focused on his sketches again. "Fuck you."

Natalie cupped her hands around her mouth and said, "Booooo!"

"I have a lot of work to do," Everett said, frowning at Natalie.

"You always have a lot of work to do. So does everyone else. But you know what's good for that big ol' creative brain knocking around in your head? Some downtime. Come to karaoke, sing "Islands in the Stream" with me, have a few drinks, and give your moneymakers a break." She wiggled her hands in the air.

Everett looked at Natalie, at his puppet supplies, and at Natalie again.

"Come on. Spend the evening with your best friend and also her girlfriend and two of their friends."

"Wait. I'm not the third wheel this time? I'm the fifth wheel?"

Natalie tilted her head. "I prefer to think of you as a spare tire."

"Oh, my God," Everett muttered.

"What? Spare tires are important! If you get a flat, you're gonna wish you had one!"

"You know what? Fine," Everett said, letting the paper in his hand fall to the floor as he stood up. "Let's go. But only because I want to completely dominate karaoke and not because I care about your friendship at all."

"I'll take it!" Natalie said, grinning.

"Can't believe this," Everett said, sliding his wallet in his back pocket. "A spare tire."

"You know, my bad for caring about your mental health," Natalie said as she walked out the door. "Sorry I'm a good friend."

Everett fought a smile as he followed her out the door. He could still feel work calling him, but he willed himself to let it go for a few hours. Natalie was right—a mental break was good. After all, didn't people always get their best ideas in the shower? Maybe he'd crack the code to this new puppet when he was onstage. Stranger things had happened.

He sighed as he locked the door. He really hoped tonight was bearable.

# 22

TEDDY HADN'T BEEN TO A BAR FOR QUITE A WHILE, AND WHEN she had, it had been with Richard's friends, who tended not to go to the sorts of places with karaoke. They went to bars with a lot of leather, jazzy music, expensive cocktails, and air that still hung heavy with cigarette smoke from thirty years ago.

This bar was . . . not that.

Ahead of her, Kirsten and Eleanor jostled their way to the bar, glancing over their shoulders to make sure she was still following.

Eleanor had a conversation with the bartender that Teddy couldn't hear; then Eleanor turned around. "Okay, I ordered us drinks," she said.

"What did you get us?" Teddy asked apprehensively.

"Oh, you'll see." She wiggled her eyebrows.

A moment later, the bartender slid three tall glasses across the bar and they each grabbed one.

Teddy took a sip and coughed. "Eleanor, what is *in* this?"

"Whenever we come here, we ask the bartender to pour whatever they want into a glass and stick an umbrella in it. We call it the Mysterious Umbrella."

Kirsten took a large gulp. "Different every time . . . yet always delicious."

"Not sure that's the word I'd use," Teddy mumbled, but took another sip to be polite (to whom, she wasn't sure).

"Let's go look at the songbook!" Eleanor cried. At the moment, a middle-aged man was onstage gripping the microphone with both hands and warbling along to Kate Bush's "Wuthering Heights," which seemed like a bizarre choice to Teddy, but then again, what did she know? She was a karaoke virgin.

Kirsten followed her glance and said, "That's Brian. He always does that song. No idea why, but it really brings the house down."

Teddy looked around as she took another sip and realized that Kirsten was right. People were swaying back and forth, some with their eyes closed as they mouthed the words, some waving their phones like lighters.

"Hmmm," Teddy said, nodding along. She felt her body begin to sway to the music, without her permission. Perhaps the Mysterious Umbrella was working. She adjusted the dress Kirsten and Eleanor had insisted she wear. It actually belonged to Kirsten, so it was a bit short and skintight . . . and also fire-engine red, a color Teddy categorically did not wear. But the girls had been insistent that she looked hot, and so she'd worn it (although she'd compromised by wearing black tights underneath because, after all, it was about thirty-five degrees).

They found themselves in front of the songbook, and Eleanor flipped through it quickly, as if she knew what she was looking for.

"Found it!" she said.

Teddy and Kirsten leaned over her shoulder to see her finger pointing at the words "BENATAR, PAT: 'WE BELONG.'"

Kirsten made a noise of appreciation. "A classic."

"I don't know that song," Teddy said, starting to feel the panic grow in her stomach, overriding the calming effects of the Mysterious Umbrella.

Eleanor tilted her head. "Well, first of all, everyone knows this song. Even if you think you don't know it, it's embedded in your bones."

"We're all born with knowledge of this song," Kirsten agreed.

"Not me!" Teddy said, her voice precariously close to a shriek.

"But most important, we're all going to be up there together," Eleanor said. "Also, they put the words on the screen. You can't get that lost."

"Don't underestimate me," Teddy mumbled, struggling to find the straw with her mouth. "I think I might be drunk."

Eleanor smiled serenely. "It's a fast-acting drink."

Kirsten got them each another drink as they waited for their turn to sing.

"Is this one . . . stronger?" Teddy asked, wrinkling her nose.

Eleanor took a sip. "The magic of the Mysterious Umbrella is that it's never the same drink twice."

A lanky guy was dancing onstage to INXS's "Need You Tonight." "I love this song!" Teddy said, despite the fact that she'd thought of the song maybe once in the past twenty years. "Or . . . wait. I'm just drunk."

"It's an amazing song, *and* you're getting blitzed," Kirsten said. "Those facts are not mutually exclusive."

"We're up!" Eleanor said, and Teddy glided behind her to the stage. Somehow she wasn't holding her drink anymore as the three of them crowded around a microphone. She felt her frazzled nerves for a moment, but then Kirsten squeezed her hand, the opening notes started, and . . . the girls were right. She did know this song. She knew these words deep in her bones, and she didn't have to look at the screen to know what she should sing next (which was good, because the words were very blurry; someone should get that screen checked). The music poured out of her, she and Kirsten and Eleanor were harmonizing like they were a girl group that did only Pat Benatar covers, and the crowd was feeding their energy right back to them. They *did* belong to the light! *And* the thunder! She and Eleanor and Kirsten belonged *together*, damn it!

Teddy found herself pointing to Wuthering Heights Brian, who was standing right in front of the stage and belting along. He pointed back at her. They were best friends now. She heard his voice inside her; she saw his face everywhere, et cetera.

She looked at Eleanor and Kirsten, and they smiled back at her. They all put their arms around one another and she leaned her head on Eleanor's shoulder. The girls had been right—this was fun. Teddy felt so grateful to be snuggled in between them now, to be with her favorite people in the entire world, to feel so warm and welcome and light. She didn't even care that she was wearing a bright, bold dress that practically demanded people look at her. She wasn't worried about how her voice sounded, or how she looked, or whether her eyeliner was on her cheeks. Everything was perfect.

She let her eyes roam over the crowd, at everyone out enjoying their nights with their own best friends, at the mix of people in the room, when her eyes snagged on someone.

The rumpled brown hair. The big hand gripping a glass. The brown eyes that were . . . that, oh God, were staring directly at her.

Everett St. James was in this bar, and he was watching her sing a Pat Benatar song.

# 23

EVERETT WAS THE FIFTH WHEEL ON A LESBIAN DOUBLE DATE, he was drinking his second mai tai, and onstage, someone was singing "Need You Tonight" by INXS.

Okay, so maybe Natalie was right about the whole "leaving the house and seeing other people" thing. This was a legitimately great night.

"I love this song," Everett said to everyone and no one.

"Ev." Natalie leaned across the other couple, Tanya and Meaghan. "How are you drunk already? You're a giant and this is your second drink."

Everett downed the rest of the mai tai. "I'm a cheap date. So sue me."

"Also." Lillian put a hand on his shoulder. "Why are you drinking mai tais?"

Everett took the umbrella out of his drink and stuck it in Lillian's hair. "Because they taste amazing."

She wrinkled her nose and looked at Natalie, who laughed.

"Okay, listen," Natalie said. "You're going to talk to a woman tonight."

Everett opened his mouth, and Natalie cut him off. "No, not us. A woman who actually wants to make out with you."

Everett started to talk again and Natalie cut him off again. "And a woman who isn't on the computer."

Everett slumped down, defeated. "I need another mai tai."

"'Need' is perhaps not the right term, but I'm driving tonight, so whatever," Lillian said. "Go get your mai tai on."

On his way to the bar, Everett stopped to flip through the songbook and signed himself up to sing, vaguely registering the beginning notes of Pat Benatar's "We Belong." He sang along under his breath as he waited for his drink, then nodded his thanks to the bartender as he slipped a few dollars into the tip jar.

He found Natalie, Lillian, Tanya, and Meaghan at their table and sat down, singing, "Weeeeee belong!" in a falsetto.

"Wouldn't have pegged you for a Benatar fan," Lillian said.

Natalie shook her head. "I absolutely would have. Hey, check out these girls. They're all cute."

Everett looked at the stage, at the three women singing into one microphone. They *were* all cute. One of them had long hair and bangs and glasses; another one had short hair, although when he tried to make out more personal features their faces kind of blended together.

But then he looked at the girl in the middle. She was pointing at a man in the crowd, giving the song the reverence it deserved. She closed her eyes, as if the song's lyrics were really moving her, as if she, too, belonged to the sound of the words she'd fallen under. She had on a bright red dress, like she was a traffic light telling him to stop and pay attention.

"I love this song," Everett said, staring directly at the girl.

"Oh!" said Natalie, taking the situation in. She waved a hand in front of Everett's face, and he didn't blink. "Here we go. Which girl are you into?"

"Is that a breakup bob?" Everett asked, pointing to the girl in the middle.

Natalie and Lillian looked at each other. "How do you know about breakup bobs?" Lillian asked.

"My friend in the computer told me," Everett muttered, keeping his eyes on the stage. He took another sip of his drink. "Do you think that haircut means she's single?"

Natalie rubbed her hands together gleefully. "Hell yes. All right, Ev. You're gonna talk to this girl."

Everett shrugged. "Okay."

He liked to say he wasn't the type of man who approached random women in bars, but the truth was, he wasn't the type of man who was often in bars, nor was he the type of man who really had to approach women. At the risk of sounding arrogant, women usually approached him—that was one of the nice things about being a semipublic local figure. And anyway, it felt weird to be the one initiating conversations with strange women. It seemed like that was a one-way ticket to being the subject of message board threads with titles like "Children's Show Creep Slides into Women's DMs."

But Everett never had a problem talking to anyone, whether it was a puppet or a cute girl. He was willing to accept a brush-off with cheerful acceptance, so there was nothing to lose. And right now he had the courage of two and a half mai tais under his belt.

"Love the confidence, Ev," Lillian said, slapping him on the shoulder.

Just then the girl's eyes met Everett's, and they locked in place. He felt, for a moment, like there was some sort of force field between them, some sort of magnetic pull or mystical attraction or Pat Benatar–sanctioned connection.

As he watched her, her eyes widened and she suddenly slid out from under her friends' arms, then ran off the stage. Her friends looked at each other; then the blond one said, "Give it up for Pat Benatar, everybody!" and then they, too, left the stage.

"Huh," said Natalie. "Well, that was weird."

"Am I wrong," Tanya asked, "or did she take one look at you and then run offstage?"

Everett nodded. "That appears to be what happened."

A woman onstage started belting out Adele's "Someone like You," and the mood was considerably dimmer than it had been during "We Belong."

Everett looked at his mai tai. "I don't think this is working anymore."

"It's this bummer of a song." Natalie sighed. "Like, don't pick an iconic vocalist's slow jam, you know? You'll never live up to the challenge and nobody wants to hear this downer while they're drinking."

"Oh!" Everett said. "I forgot to tell you. I signed up to sing a Prince song. A slow one!"

The women all turned to look at him.

"Truly, every time I think you couldn't be weirder, you blow through all my expectations," Natalie said, slowly shaking her head.

"Well, after you're done butchering a classic by a legend, why don't you say hi to that woman you scared?" Lillian suggested.

"When you put it like that, I'm not so sure it's a good idea," Everett said, taking another sip.

"I think they're calling your name!" Meaghan said. "You're up!"

Everett knocked back the rest of his drink. "Let's do this," he muttered as he made his way to the stage.

## 24

"WHAT HAPPENED UP THERE?" KIRSTEN ASKED.

Teddy shook her head and held on to her glass of water. Seeing Everett in the crowd had immediately sobered her up. What was worse, he was looking directly at her, directly into her soul, as if he knew she was the one he'd been emailing all this time.

But he couldn't know. So why had he been staring at her like that?

"I told you guys I was scared," Teddy muttered into her drink.

"But it was going so well!" Eleanor said, putting an arm around her. "You were killing it up there!"

"Wuthering Heights Brian was loving the energy," Kirsten agreed.

"I think maybe we should go home," Teddy said.

"Can we wait a minute?" Kirsten asked. "I put an order in for fried pickles."

Eleanor clapped. "Fried pickles!"

Teddy wrinkled her nose. "Why does a pickle need to be fried?"

For a moment, all she could hear was a woman maiming an Adele song.

"Teddy," Kirsten said, placing a hand on her arm gently as if she were asking a delicate question, "have you . . . never had a deep-fried pickle?"

Teddy shook her head. "I mean, fried food upsets Richard's stomach, so . . ."

Kirsten shot a look at Eleanor, then exhaled with determination. "Okay. This is fine. We're gonna fix this."

As if they sensed their moment, the fried pickles appeared on the bar. They each grabbed one, but before Teddy could take a bite, Kirsten said, "Wait! A toast."

"A toast!" Eleanor agreed.

"To what?" Teddy asked.

"To . . . new things! Doing what scares us! Obliterating comfort zones! Deep-fried foods!"

"To deep-fried foods!" Teddy and Eleanor repeated, and then they all took a bite.

"Oh, no," Eleanor said, opening her mouth.

"Hot," Teddy said, sucking in a breath.

"Burning!" Kirsten shouted.

Teddy downed her water.

"Okay," Kirsten said, fanning her mouth. "I forgot how hot those suckers get."

"I think I burned the roof of my mouth," Eleanor said sadly.

"But it was worth it," Teddy said, grabbing another fried pickle and staring at it in wonder. "This is so good."

A few slow piano notes played through the bar, and the girls turned to see who was onstage. Teddy dropped her pickle.

"Five-second rule!" Kirsten said.

"Kirsten, *no!*" Eleanor shouted. "No more eating things off bar floors."

"Oh, no," Teddy said.

Everett St. James was onstage and he was singing "The Beautiful Ones" by Prince, also known as one of the classic slow jams from the *Purple Rain* soundtrack.

"That's the guy from the TV show!" Eleanor said, following Teddy's gaze. "My kids love him."

"He's rocking the hell out of that falsetto," Kirsten said with admiration. "But can I say that this is a supremely weird choice for karaoke? It's, like, slow but . . . also strangely sexual?"

"I love it," Teddy said, her voice coming out low. She coughed. "I mean . . . I love this song."

"Really?" Kirsten asked. "Because I have never once heard you talk about Prince."

Teddy shook her head. "We listen to this album all the time at the store. It's Josie's favorite. She especially loves the track about the woman masturbating in a hotel lobby, which I always tell her is inappropriate to play when there are children in the store."

"Huh," Eleanor said, nodding in appreciation. "Oh, he's doing the spoken-word breakdown. He has a very soothing voice!"

"The crowd is loving this," Kirsten said approvingly, and she was right. The crowd *was* loving it. People were waving their hands, and while no one would ever confuse a tall white puppeteer with Prince, the fact remained that Everett had really committed to this song.

Teddy bit her lip as Everett got down on his knees to screech out a particularly intense part of the song.

"Okay, I get it," Kirsten said. "This guy has something about him."

"A certain . . . je ne sais quoi, you might say," Eleanor agreed.

"And he has nice hands," Kirsten said. "Look at him up there gripping that microphone. Have I ever told you that the first thing that attracted me to the Viking was his hands?"

"You have told me this," Eleanor said, sipping her drink. "Often and at length."

Kirsten sighed fondly. "Sometimes I watch him holding a glass and I'm like, damn. Wish I was that glass."

"Everett has very nice hands," Teddy said, but so quiet that neither of her friends heard her.

The song ended, and Everett dropped the mic and jumped off the stage. People patted him on the back, and Teddy assumed this was it; he'd go back to his group of friends and head off into the night, and she would be able to continue her crush on him from afar.

But he didn't head back to his table. In fact, he locked eyes with Teddy and moved straight toward her. The rest of the crowd turned blurry and faded and Everett was the only thing she could see. He was the color in a black-and-white room and he was headed right toward her.

"Holy crap," Teddy muttered.

And then he was there. She'd known he was tall, and she knew from a lifetime of being in her own body that she was relatively short, but she was unprepared for the physical feeling of him standing directly in front of her. He took up all the space in the room, swallowed up all her attention and still asked for more, blocked the sun and *was* the sun all at the same time. He was Everett St. James, and he was looking at her.

"Hi," he said, his wide, guileless smile, the same one he used for puppets and children, on his face.

"Mmmph," Teddy said.

"I loved the song," he said. "Pat Benatar rules."

There were several things Teddy could have said. Maybe *I loved your song, too.* Or *I like your show.* Or even, if she was feeling bold, *We've been sharing our innermost thoughts via email for a while now.*

But what she actually said was "I'm sorry, I have to go throw up." And then she turned and fled.


"PLEASE TELL US what happened back there."

Teddy was in the backseat of the Viking's car with Eleanor,

while Kirsten twisted around in the front seat to talk to them. The Viking had been kind enough to pick them up after Kirsten and Eleanor decided Teddy was too much of a puke risk for an Uber.

He turned up the local metal station, and Kirsten reached over to turn it down. "Not now, babe," she said gently. "Teddy's having a crisis."

"Sometimes Pantera helps," the Viking muttered, but he didn't turn the radio back up.

"I'm not having a crisis," Teddy said to her lap.

"Teddy, a man talked to you, and you said you had to puke and then ran away. That sounds like a crisis to me," Kirsten said.

"In her defense, she did have to puke," Eleanor said.

"I really did," Teddy mumbled.

"Oh, I know. I was there," Kirsten said. "But, like . . . what was up with you and that guy?"

Teddy sighed, looked out the window, then glanced back and forth between her two best friends (and also the Viking, who occasionally looked at her with concern in the rearview mirror). If she couldn't tell the two people she loved most in the world and also one of their boyfriends about her bizarre, secret Internet pen pal relationship, then who could she tell?

So she told them.

She told them the whole story, about how she had emailed Everett in a fit of despair and it had scared her, but over time emailing a strange man she knew only from TV became less scary and more . . . comforting. Easier. Like talking to a friend. Like he *was* a friend now.

"Huh." Eleanor tapped her chin. "Well, this is an interesting development."

"This is great," Kirsten said. "He's cute. And he's tall. And he seems nice."

"Caring," Eleanor added.

"Good with kids," Kirsten said.

"Gentle," the Viking added.

They all looked at him. "What?" he asked. "I watch TV, too."

If tonight hadn't happened, maybe Teddy never would have told everyone about Everett. It wasn't that she thought they'd make fun of her, but . . . Well, okay, she kind of thought they might. After all, there was a part of it that was odd or at least unexpected. But she should've known her friends would never make her feel bad about something that mattered to her, even if the night did end with her vomiting in an alley.

"But he would never be into me. I mean, not me, me. The me in email, maybe. But ME?"

Eleanor scrutinized her. "You're still drunk. How? You puked so much."

"I mean . . ." Teddy sighed and looked out the window at the lights of the restaurants and shops as the Viking's Honda Accord inched down the crowded street. A lit-up plastic jack-o'-lantern winked back at her from a bar window. "He was there with someone. With a girl. With four girls. He's probably in a polygamous relationship. And he's probably happy in his polygamous relationship with his four girlfriends. I bet he doesn't even have time for a fifth girlfriend. Not that I want to be his fifth girlfriend. I want to be his only girlfriend. Or wait. I don't wait to be his girlfriend at all! I just . . . Oh, forget it."

She slumped against the side of the car, the window cold against her cheek, the slight bounce of the car rocking her to sleep.

"Wait!" Kirsten screeched so suddenly that everyone jumped, except for the Viking, who was apparently used to Kirsten yelling while he drove.

"What's wrong?" Teddy asked, panicked.

"Pull in over there!" Kirsten frantically gestured across the street.

"Taco Bell?" Eleanor asked.

Kirsten smiled back at them. "This calls for Crunchwrap Supremes. Teddy, this dude is *smoking*. And he's good with kids. And he's gonna be so into you as soon as you tell him who you are."

"Celebratory Crunchwrap Supremes!" Eleanor cheered. "The perfect drunchies!"

Teddy wrinkled her nose. "What's a drunchie?"

"You sweet, innocent child," Kirsten said with a headshake. "Drunk munchies. Drunchies. Something to shove down the ol' gullet and soak up all the alcohol and questionable decisions. And trust me, the Taco Bell menu is scientifically designed to be perfect drunchies."

As the Viking pulled into the drive-thru, Teddy couldn't help but smile, even as she wondered if Taco Bell was actually the wisest decision right now. But whatever. Her friends remembered her ideal Taco Bell order and didn't flinch when she puked and were happy when she was happy.

She might have mortally embarrassed herself in front of Everett St. James, but things weren't so bad after all.

# 25

"SO?" NATALIE ASKED, EYES WIDE. "HOW'D IT GO?"

Everett looked down at the four women staring at him. Lillian took a sip of her beer.

He frowned and sat down. "I think I struck out."

Natalie narrowed her eyes. "You think? What does that mean?"

Everett rubbed his neck. "Well, I said hi, and she told me she had to puke."

Natalie stared at him.

"And then she ran away," Everett added.

Natalie and Lillian exchanged a glance.

"Seems bad, right?" Everett asked.

"Here." Natalie handed him her beer. "I haven't had a drink of this yet, and you need it more than I do."

Everett took a sip, then sighed. "Have I lost it? Did I ever even have it? I thought women liked me."

Lillian lifted a shoulder. "Kinda sounds like you drove this one to nausea."

Natalie elbowed her. "Not helpful. Are you sure there wasn't something else going on? I mean, I've seen you around women. They love you, and they typically keep control of their bodily functions."

"I guess my string of successful female interactions had to come to an end sometime," Everett said, taking another drink. "Now women find me disgusting. I'll just have to get used to the idea of dying alone. Can I have another beer?"

"On it," Lillian said as she headed to the bar.

Natalie scooted over to take her place and put an arm around Everett. "Okay, so Puke Girl aside, aren't you glad you came out tonight?"

Everett raised his eyebrows. "Listen to what you just said."

"I mean, you killed it at karaoke. Pretty sure Prince himself, in the afterlife, put a hand to his ear and was like 'Uh, what's that? Some big white dude is absolutely doing my song justice?'"

"I don't think that's what happened," Everett muttered to his empty bottle.

"And you got drunk," Natalie said. "Isn't that nice? Didn't you enjoy that mai tai buzz?"

"I'm only a happy drunk for a while," Everett said, peeling the paper off the bottle. "Now I'm tired and annoyed."

The unmistakable piano notes of "Wuthering Heights" started and Everett's eyes shot to the stage. "Is he seriously doing this song again?"

"Oh, hell yes," Lillian said, sitting down beside Natalie and handing Everett his beer without taking her eyes off the stage. "I love this song."

Natalie shook her head in wonder. "The people want what the people want, and what they want is Wuthering Heights Brian."

Everett sighed. What *he* wanted was to be at home, on the couch, working. Sketching. Writing. Answering emails from kids. Writing notes to share with Jeremy next week. Because at least there, he was in control. When he was working, he knew that if he gave it enough time, something would happen. He'd have that breakthrough and figure out what the show was missing, and then everything would be perfect again.

He also, he realized, wanted to be emailing Theodora and telling her about how terrible tonight had gone. He wanted to tell her the honest truth about how he felt and get her honest answers back. He wanted to talk to someone who knew him, and the strange thing was, he felt like she did. He wanted to finish his most recent Alice book, which was all about Alice and her friends taking an eventful train ride to Chicago, and ask Theodora about her thoughts on it, and also ask her why it was that girls always read books about boys but no one ever made sure boys read books about girls. It seemed wrong somehow.

He looked down at his beer, already half empty. This wasn't gonna make things perfect.

But then he looked over at Natalie and Lillian. Lillian loudly "woo"-ed for Wuthering Heights Brian, and Natalie clapped. The lights from the karaoke stage reflected in her eyes, and for a moment, he saw High School Natalie, the one who had been his best friend then just as she was his best friend now. And as much as he kinda sucked as a friend sometimes, as much as he turned her down when she asked him to come out and have fun, he knew he owed her one night of being present and hanging out with her girlfriend and doing what she wanted to do.

She turned. "Why are you staring at me like that? Maybe we should cut you off."

"Hey," Everett said. "After this, do you want to do our song?"

Natalie's eyes widened. "You mean . . ."

Everett nodded. "'Islands,' dude."

At their high school prom after-party (where they'd been each other's dates, despite the fact that they'd been broken up for a year, because who the hell else were they going to go with?), there'd been karaoke at a bowling alley. They'd done a daring rendition of Kenny Rogers and Dolly Parton's "Islands in the Stream," and while it hadn't exactly brought down the house (it seemed to confuse most of their classmates, who were more into Morris Monroe's admittedly great version of BTO's "Takin' Care of Business"), it had prompted their chaperone and chemistry teacher, Mr. Allen, to give them a standing ovation. And that guy usually got excited only about electron configurations.

Natalie pumped her arm. "I am not nearly drunk enough, but why not? Our usual parts?"

Everett scoffed. "Um, yes. Obviously, I'm Dolly."

Natalie smiled at him. "I love you. Forget about that girl. Let's go do Dolly and Kenny proud."

Everett smiled at his best friend, and then he followed the latter part of her command. They really did kill it with "Islands in the Stream"; they always did.

But the first part? Forgetting about that girl? Well, that one was a little harder.

## 26

COLOSSAL TOYS WAS FAR TOO BUSY THE NEXT MORNING.
Unbelievably, the Crunchwrap Supreme, Cinnamon Twists, and
large Mountain Dew had done nothing to ward off the hangover to
end all hangovers, and now Teddy stood behind the counter with a
splitting headache and slight nausea.

But the thing about retail was that you still had to be perky,
even when you were trying to decide if you never wanted Taco Bell
again or if you actually needed more Taco Bell.

Since it was a weekend, both Carlos and Josie were in the store.
Beside Teddy, Carlos talked animatedly about Teenage Mutant
Ninja Turtles to a fiftysomething woman who then bought a still-
in-the-box Raphael action figure. Teddy was half-listening to their
conversation when she saw the girl in the red coat walk in.

"Gretel!" she said, then realized she was using way too much
enthusiasm for a child she'd met once. But she'd genuinely enjoyed
talking to Gretel last time, and seeing her cut through the fog of
discomfort Teddy was feeling.

Gretel waved with her whole hand. "Hi there. How's the vintage toy biz treating you?"

"Quite well, actually," Teddy said.

Gretel narrowed her eyes and gave Teddy a once-over. "You
look, as my father would say, a bit green around the gills."

"Well," Teddy said, looking down. Damn, nothing got past a child. "I had some bad Taco Bell last night."

"That would be all Taco Bell," Gretel said.

Teddy opened her mouth in faux shock. "I won't stand for this inflammatory anti–Taco Bell rhetoric. Crunchwrap Supremes are the perfect drunchies, which is a word I just learned last night, and it means food you eat when you're . . ." Teddy trailed off and started to blush as she remembered that she was talking to a child. Perhaps she shouldn't have been so enthusiastic about showing off her new vocabulary.

Gretel gave her one of those withering looks that only a kid can give a clueless adult. "I've seen a television show before, you know. And I have an older brother. Although he's kind of a nerd. I think he mostly eats fast food at work, and 'wunchies' isn't even half as catchy."

"Well, then," Teddy said with a prim smile, "it sounds like your brother is setting a good example."

Gretel wrinkled her nose. "He's definitely not. I like your dress."

Teddy glanced down at her outfit, a rainbow-striped number with a red cardigan on top. She'd gone shopping with Eleanor and picked out clothing that didn't blend in, like the sweaters and jeans she was so used to wearing. Now her outfits stood out and actually inspired compliments. And although karaoke the night before had ended not so much in a blaze of glory as in a blaze of humiliation, she'd still enjoyed the experience of having all eyes on her in her red dress. *Do one thing every day that scares you: wear clothing that people notice.* "Oh, thanks," she said.

Gretel smiled, and Teddy couldn't help but feel a sense of kinship with her. "I'm gonna go look around," Gretel said. "This is actually a research trip."

"Research?" Teddy asked. "For what?"

"I'm writing a comic about my life," Gretel said breezily. "Some people, like my brother, think I'm too young, but I don't think you're ever too young to write your first memoir."

"I agree," Teddy said with a nod. "Tell your brother he's absolutely wrong. I'd love to read your memoir."

"Thanks," Gretel said as she started to walk away. "I'll see you later. Will you be here during HighBall?"

What with her entire life being uprooted and all, Teddy had forgotten about HighBall. Every year around Halloween, the Short North shut down to hold a huge costume party, one that attracted tens of thousands of visitors. People went all out, dressing up in elaborate costumes and, perhaps more notably, drinking in the street. It was always a highlight of the year, seeing the sorts of costumes that came into the shop.

"Yeah, I'm working that night," Teddy said.

"Great. I'll see you then," Gretel said, heading down an aisle. "Maybe I'll convince my brother to come, if he's not being an asocial weirdo."

HighBall was technically an all-ages event, although it certainly wasn't geared toward children (see: the drinking in the street), but Teddy wasn't really surprised that Gretel would be there. She seemed to move through the world with her own set of rules.

While Teddy had been talking to Gretel, most of the browsers had left, so now there were only a few people wandering around the store. Carlos was back to rearranging the display case under the counter, so Teddy took a moment to check her email on her phone. Not that she was expecting anything from anyone in particular . . .

She had one email from Everett St. James.

Dear Theodora,

Do you ever feel like you're in a television show about your own life? I know that I make a television show with my own name in the title, but that's not what I mean.

Sometimes, it feels like things are happening to me purely to make an audience laugh, as if God is a benevolent showrunner who doesn't want to torture me so much as put me through minor humiliations for a chuckle.

Take last night, for example. My best friend invited me out for karaoke with her friends. I'm not really a karaoke man—my job gives me plenty of attention, and I'd rather spend my free time at home. But I went for my friend, and while I was there, I kind of hit on someone (well, not hit on . . . more like talked to), and she told me she had to puke.

There's really only one way for a guy to take a brush-off like that, and now I have to shoulder the burden of knowing that my presence made an innocent woman vomit.

It's actually better if I pretend it's a sitcom plot, instead of my life.

But enough about me. What scary things have you done lately? Eat a ghost pepper? Wrestle a pig? Maybe those things aren't scary for you. Maybe you love spicy food and pigs. Even after all these emails, there are so many things we don't know about each other.

For the record, I am anti–ghost peppers but very much pro-pig (the animals, not wrestling them, but why rule anything out?).

Peppers and pigs,
Everett

Teddy stared at her phone as her armpits started to tingle. She was sweating. Everett was talking about her. He remembered her. Well, sort of. He remembered the her she was last night, not the her she was right now, and . . . Oh, this was all confusing. Having a secret identity was far more complicated than movies made it seem.

"You're doing it again."

Teddy jumped and turned to see Josie staring at her and holding a cardboard box full of new (well, old but new to them) toys. "What?"

Josie tilted her head. "You know what. The whole 'dreamily staring into space' thing. Remember, it scares the customers?" Her eyes widened as she had a sudden realization. "Wait. Did you take my advice? Is there a new fella in the picture?"

"No!" Teddy tossed her phone on the counter with a clatter as if it was damning evidence. "There is no fella. I mean, no man. I am one hundred percent focused on my own self-improvement and I have no interest in a relationship."

"Who said anything about a relationship? Anyway, you're not very convincing. I can see the way you keep staring at your phone. Go ahead and read your romantic texts."

"We don't text," Teddy said, then realized she'd given herself away. "It's . . . I'm in an email-only relationship right now. I mean, it's not a relationship. An email-only . . . flirtation? Maybe not even that. A friendship. I guess that's what people call it."

Josie put down the box and looked at her skeptically. "You've got a man emailing you? Oh, honey. How did you two meet?"

Teddy opened and closed her mouth a few times as she considered what to say. "We . . . haven't, really. Well, technically we met last night, but he doesn't know it. I emailed him first. It's . . . it's a bit of a complicated situation."

"Huh." Josie nodded slowly. "Sounds like it."

"How much is this?"

They turned to see Gretel holding up a Care Bear.

Josie waved her off. "That thing's been here forever. Give me five dollars and it's yours."

"Sold." Gretel slipped a hand into the pocket of her red coat and pulled out her wallet, then handed a five-dollar bill to Teddy.

"Is that for research purposes?" Teddy asked. "It seems like it was . . . before your time."

Gretel looked at her like she'd said something bizarre. "No, it's cute." She held it up. "See?"

Teddy nodded. Right. Gretel was twelve years old, despite the fact that she carried a wallet.

Gretel held the Care Bear in front of her face and observed it. "I'm going to put this on my bed. Hopefully Sassafras won't destroy it. She's my cat, and she has a lot of pent-up nervous energy. What she needs is more enrichment."

"You know, you can find playlists for cats," Josie said, and both Teddy and Gretel looked at her in confusion. "I'm serious! Some animal specialist put together music that's meant to calm cats down. Or—I don't know—maybe it wasn't an animal specialist. Maybe it was some random guy who's trying to make a buck."

"Thank you," Gretel said seriously. "I'm going to try it with Sassafras."

"Report back!" Josie said cheerfully, then headed toward her office as Gretel walked out the door with her stuffed animal, giving them a wave over her shoulder.

With Josie back in her office, the shop was quiet, other than the sound of Carlos rearranging the LEGO cabinet.

"Hey, Carlos," Teddy said. Sure, Carlos had resolutely ignored her during her last conversation attempt, but she wouldn't stop trying. "What's your go-to karaoke song?"

Carlos paused for a moment, shook his head, and went back to the LEGOs.

Teddy sighed. "Watch anything good on TV last night?"

"Nope," Carlos said, adjusting a LEGO pirate ship.

Suddenly, Teddy had an idea. If she wanted Carlos to be her friend, she shouldn't expect him to come to her turf. Perhaps she would have to come to Carlos. As Josie had said, Carlos mostly liked to talk about the toys.

"So what's the deal with the pirate ship?" she asked, stepping out from behind the counter.

He looked at her. "The deal?"

"Yeah, I mean . . . is it old?"

Carlos nodded. "Very. In terms of LEGO, that is."

Teddy smiled cautiously. This might be the most that Carlos had ever said to her, so she had to tread lightly. "And, uh . . . what makes it special?"

"Special?" Carlos asked slowly.

"Yeah, I see you, you know, paying extra attention to it. Dusting it. Explaining it to customers. What's the story behind it?"

For a moment, Carlos didn't say anything, and Teddy worried that he'd give her another monosyllabic answer. But then, as if her question had flipped a switch, something changed in his posture; he went from rigid and focused to relaxed and engaged. "Well, there are a lot of things that make it special, but specifically, this pirate ship is from 1989 and has cannons that actually shoot round bricks. In later years, LEGO used two different types of nonfunctional cannons—one with the old cannon mold that could still move but didn't have a spring, and another mold that was a solid piece. But that's specific to the US. In Europe—"

Teddy nodded eagerly, trying to keep up as Carlos kept talking. *Convince Carlos to be my friend.* Check.

## 27

Dear Everett,

I didn't eat a ghost pepper this weekend, but the roof of my mouth is still burned from my first-ever fried pickle, which seems like kind of the same thing.

I'm sorry your weekend wasn't the best. Mine wasn't the greatest ever, either. I'm supposed to be facing my fears and trying new things and finding my passion, but I had a chance to be bold this weekend and I let it pass me by. I had a chance to do something that scared me, and instead I ran away. I hope I get a chance someday to make up for it.

This week I'm going to a sewing class with one of my best friends. She's a kindergarten teacher and she can do every crafty thing under the sun, so I'm sure it will be easy for her. And as for me? Well, my fifth-grade art teacher once told me that not all of us were "blessed with artistic ability" and that I probably had other things I was good at. This was after I painted an (admittedly very . . . abstract, to say the least) portrait of Shaquille O'Neal for an assignment where we were supposed to paint a hero. The weirdest thing is, I didn't (and don't) care about basketball. I think I heard some other kids talking about how great Shaq was and decided to run with it. So not only did I paint a very poor portrait of Shaquille O'Neal, but I didn't really even like him that much in the first place (no offense to Shaq, who seems like a great person). I feel like there's some sort of lesson there.

But the difference between the old me and the new me is that I'm determined to try something new, even if I do totally suck at it.

Anyway, I'm sorry a woman ran away from you and puked. That's not a sentence I thought I'd ever type to Everett St. James, but here we are. Here's hoping the rest of your week is better.

In Shaq we trust,
Theodora

Everett was mad.

This was a familiar anger, the kind he felt whenever an adult was dismissive of a child. It was something he was used to feeling—when he saw a parent insult their kid in public, when he heard any-one laughing at a child's honest question, whenever someone put down the dreams and desires and plans of a tiny person who trusted them. He felt a fury that coursed through his body and turned his hands to fists.

Because this was the core belief of his show, of his work, of his life: children deserved respect. They deserved to be listened to, be-lieved, and accepted. All children deserved the space and time to explore their interests, hobbies, and passions, and he was unfortunately aware that there were so many well-meaning adults in the world who could crunch a child's self-esteem under their heel without even knowing it.

And that was what had happened to Theodora back when she was only a kid and barely knew who she was. Someone had told her she wasn't creative, and she'd believed it. And here she was, years later, still carrying around that erroneous belief, still thinking she couldn't do anything artistic because she hadn't been "blessed."

Everett knew, of course, that was bullshit. Everyone was creative. Just like that possibly Picasso quote he'd told Theodora about in his first email, everyone starts out an artist. But sometimes people encountered parents or teachers or other authority figures who stomped all over their dreams before they even had a chance to explore them.

This was what Everett had always loved about his heroes, Mr. Rogers and Jim Henson. They both had an openness, a willingness to let the children in their presence be themselves. They didn't force kids into being a certain way; they let them ask whatever wacky questions or say whatever awkward things came into their heads. They let kids be kids. And that was all he hoped he could do with his show.

"They're here."

He looked up and saw Astrid standing in front of him, looking more high-strung than usual. She'd twisted her long hair into a tight bun and she was way more dressed up than usual.

"Should I have worn something else?" Everett asked, gesturing to his outfit of black jeans and a plaid button-down over a Ted Leo and the Pharmacists T-shirt.

"No, no, no," Astrid said, waving a hand at him. "This is fine. They should see you how you are. That's kind of the point."

And then two men and one woman walked into the room, all of them in suits. Everett took a deep breath, stood up, and shook their hands.

**28**

Dear Theodora,

This weekend I had mozzarella sticks, also known as the fried pickle's slightly drunker cousin. My best friend's girlfriend got them for me as a pity gift at the bar. Fun fact: it's actually impossible to eat mozzarella sticks without burning 75 percent of the roof of your mouth. But that doesn't stop me from eating them at every opportunity.

Theodora, I know we don't really know each other, but I hope I'm not overstepping any boundaries by saying that you're entirely too hard on yourself. Whatever bold choice you didn't make—I bet it's okay. In fact, I know it's okay. I have a belief that, as long as you keep trying and pushing and working toward your goal, something will happen, even if it doesn't happen the exact way you thought it would.

For example, I was dead set on majoring in puppetry in college (yes, that's a thing you can major in, and as you might guess, I had to explain that constantly to curious adults who asked what I wanted to go to college for). But I ended up staying here in Columbus when my little sister was born, and that turned out better than I ever could have imagined. I figured out that kids are awesome and hilarious and so, so weird, and that shaped my career in ways that might not have happened if I'd gone away to school like I planned.

So I guess what I'm saying is: it's okay. Whatever you did or didn't do, it's okay, and you'll figure it out, because you're Theodora (fill in your last name here, please), damn it, and you get things done!

There. Was that enough of a pep talk for you?

And no disrespect to your teacher, but they sucked. You're artistic because everyone's artistic. You have to let yourself express it, and it won't be long until you're sewing . . . Well, I don't actually know what you make in an intro-to-sewing class.

Yours till the mozzarella stick cools,
Everett

PS: You didn't think I was going to forget about that portrait of Shaq, did you? I need proof.

Teddy read Everett's email approximately fifteen times before she and Eleanor left for their sewing class. His words felt like the best kind of hug. Of course she and Everett didn't really know each other, but he believed in her. He knew she could do difficult things, or even sometimes fail to do difficult things, but that she'd get it right next time. Sure, he didn't know that the situation in which she chickened out was actually that email, that she hadn't told him they'd met at the karaoke bar. But no matter. Everett St. James believed in her.

"I'm Theodora Phillips, damn it, and I get things done!" she said out loud to her empty room.

"Love the enthusiasm!" called Eleanor from the hallway. Teddy always forgot how thin these walls were (the Viking's sleepover last night was nearly silent, aside from some loud bumps and shushes from Kirsten).

"You ready?" Eleanor asked, poking her head in.

Teddy shut her laptop. "You bet."


IT WASN'T THAT Teddy expected a sewing class to be an adversarial experience, but she came in with her guard up. Maybe this would be like that elementary school art class. Maybe her teacher would hold up her pillowcase as an example of "what you shouldn't do," much like her unfortunately lumpy Shaq portrait. Presumably her pillow wouldn't be a poor representation of an NBA star, but she still worried her stitches would be bad enough to deserve public mockery.

There were only a few other people in the class, and each of them was set up in front of a gleaming white sewing machine. The teacher explained that a pillowcase was a great project for absolute beginners, since it was basically sewing a rectangle, but it would teach them the skills they'd need to sew anything else.

Their first task was picking out the fabric, so Teddy roamed the warm, well-lit sewing space, running her hand across the bolts. There were so many colors and patterns that she felt overwhelmed, and she almost asked Eleanor what she was going to pick. She craned her neck to spot Eleanor on the other side of the store, humming to herself as she picked up some yellow-and-green printed fabric and held it up.

But no. Teddy could do this on her own. She'd sung karaoke,

she'd befriended Carlos, and she was fully capable of choosing her own fabric.

"This isn't a life-or-death decision," she muttered to herself.

"It's really not."

She looked up to see her teacher standing beside her. She smiled gently. "If you don't like what you make, you can always make another one."

Teddy nodded. "Very good point." She bent down and picked up an orange-and-red floral print.

"Beautiful choice," the teacher said, then called over her shoulder as she walked away, "Red is definitely your color."

Teddy looked down at what she was wearing—a red jumper over a white collared blouse. She and Eleanor had found it while vintage shopping at Flower Child, and she liked to think about the jumper's previous life. Maybe it had belonged to some other person who was starting over, someone who was finally discovering who they really were.

After spending so many years in gray cardigans with Richard, Teddy could hardly believe that she'd become someone who had a color, and that color was red. She was still getting used to people seeing her, to trying to be seen, but she was discovering that she liked it.

Teddy brought her fabric back to her machine and tried her best to follow along with the teacher's clear instructions. Eleanor was, of course, humming right along—her pillowcase looked beautiful. Showroom perfect, really. If there were ever a pillowcase art show at the Columbus Museum of Art, Eleanor's would be on display. Teddy's, meanwhile . . . well, her seams were crooked. She still wasn't sure about the fabric. It seemed . . . wrong, somehow.

Teddy swallowed the ball of anxiety in her throat as the teacher walked slowly around the room, inspecting each person's work and pointing out areas they might want to focus on. Teddy's breath quickened as her teacher approached, and although it wasn't really possible to use a sewing machine frantically, she felt as if her stitches had a slightly manic edge to them.

The teacher bent down to say something to Eleanor, and Teddy could feel herself sweating. Here it came. She was next, and this was the moment of truth.

Teddy sat motionless as the teacher finished talking to Eleanor and moved on to Teddy's station.

She peered over Teddy's shoulder as Teddy held her breath.

"Looks great!" she said.

"Wait," Teddy said as the teacher walked away. "That's it?"

She stopped and turned around.

"You mean you're not going to hold up my pillowcase and tell the class that it's an example of what not to do?" Teddy asked.

The teacher paused and pursed her lips. "No?"

"Oh." Teddy turned back to her pillowcase, suddenly feeling lighter than she had all evening. She laughed. "Okay!"

She spent the rest of the class lost in the whirr of the machine.

THE CLASS WENT so well that Teddy and Eleanor ended up splitting the cost of a sewing machine and bringing one home. They named him Scott.

The next evening, with Everett's latest email in mind, Teddy visited her mom. She wanted to find the lumpy portrait of Shaq, which she knew was somewhere at her mother's house, because her mother never got rid of anything from Teddy's and Sophia's childhood. Somewhere in the basement, there was definitely a creepy jar full of their baby teeth. Teddy made a note to tell Kirsten about it; it would probably be great for some of her more experimental work, or at the very least for Halloween decorations.

Teddy's old bedroom had been completely redecorated and was now a guest room with tan walls and Target-sourced artwork on the walls. Teddy supposed this was probably more soothing to her mom's guests than the giant *Titanic* poster she'd hung above her bed in elementary school so she could sleep under the watchful gaze of Leo and Kate.

The closet, however, was where most of Teddy's things lived. Boxes of old grade cards, stories she'd scribbled when she didn't know how to spell much of anything, reports she'd written on elephants. She knew if she dug around enough, she'd find Shaq in all his slightly misshapen glory.

"What are you looking for, again?" her mother asked from the bedroom doorway, where she leaned against the frame with her arms crossed.

"Just . . . an old picture I made when I was a kid," Teddy said from the closet. "It's kind of hard to explain, but I need to see it."

"Ooooh-kay," her mom said in a singsong voice. "So how are things going?"

"Good," Teddy said, riffling through a box of poetry from fourth grade. Wow, she'd written a lot of haiku about pandas.

"What's happening on the job front?" Her mom's voice carried into the closet, slightly muffled.

Teddy paused, elbow deep in a bin full of papers. "Uh . . . not much," she said, glancing at an eighth-grade report card. *Teddy is clever and extraordinarily bright, but reluctant to speak up in class.* Some things never changed, apparently.

"Did you check out the links I sent you?" her mom asked eagerly. "You can take classes online or at night, so you don't have to quit your job to get an MBA."

"Mmm," Teddy said noncommittally.

"There's always law school like Sophia."

Teddy frowned.

Her mother's voice grew wistful. "I'm so glad she's a lawyer. That was my dream job when you two were little. I wanted to be Ally McBeal, wearing those tiny skirts, surrounded by drama."

"Yes!" Teddy hissed.

"So you do want to be a lawyer?"

Teddy emerged from the closet, a drawing in hand. "I found it! This is the portrait I made of Shaquille O'Neal!"

Her mom tilted her head, studying it. "Is that who that is? Huh. I figured that was one of your teachers."

Teddy held the picture protectively to her chest. "He's wearing a jersey, Mom. I know it doesn't look much like Shaq—"

"It sure doesn't."

"But," Teddy continued with an edge to her voice, "I wanted to show it to a friend."

Her mom shrugged. "Okay. I made you a sandwich. You want some lemonade?"

Teddy smiled. "Sure, Mom."

"You know," her mom said, looking around, "if you get tired of living with your friends, you can always move back here. We can fix up your room, and don't make that face."

Teddy realized she was wrinkling her nose. "No, sorry. I don't mean—"

Her mom rolled her eyes. "Come eat your sandwich and I'll show you the website for the online college program I think you'll like."

As Teddy followed her mother downstairs, she couldn't help but smile. Yes, her mom was kind of a control freak who didn't seem to understand that Teddy had her own life, but she did everything out of love and an attempt to make Teddy happy. It might have been a misguided and overblown attempt, but it was an attempt all the same. But this time, Teddy knew she couldn't simply go along with someone else's plan—she had to figure things out herself.

But a sandwich? Well, she could at least let her mother do that much for her.

## 29

Dear Everett,

Thank you for the kind words in your last email. We may be mere pen pals, but that pep talk made my whole day. I was nervous about the sewing class, but it was actually . . . kind of great? Better than great, even. I made a functional pillow-case and no one told me it was terrible, so I consider that a victory. My friend and I ended up buying a sewing machine and we spent last night making more pillowcases, so many that our third roommate asked what we were planning on doing with all the pillows, so I guess it's time to learn to make something else.

I spent so long thinking that making things wasn't for me. Sure, I know how to cook some basics, but that was always utilitarian. I make something. Then I eat it. Sewing isn't nec-essary for me. It's probably cheaper to go to Target and buy a pillowcase than it is for me to make one, but it's fun. Even more than that, my brain shuts off when I'm doing it. It's like sewing puts me in a meditative trance, the way that real meditation doesn't. I'm not great at it (clearly; I've made a few pillowcases, not my own wardrobe), but it's fun. It's been so long since I did something purely because it was enjoyable.

It actually does make me feel better to know that your life hasn't been a straight line toward success. It's easy to look at someone like you and think, "Well, Everett St. James has always known what he wanted to do and nothing has ever thrown him off course." I bet you're so glad you stayed home to see your sister grow up. She's probably a wonderful young woman now, having you as an example/big brother.

At your request, I've included my Shaquille O'Neal portrait. Don't laugh. I know I can't see you through the computer screen, but I'll be able to feel it if you do.

Wearing thimbles on my fingers,
Theodora

Theodora might have told him not to laugh, but Everett hadn't signed a contract. As soon as he opened the attachment, his tiny chuckle turned into a full-blown laugh attack. Shaq, if you could call him that, stared back at him with uneven eyes and a grimace that was surely meant to be a smile. He looked absolutely nothing like the famous basketball player.

"Oh, my God, I love this woman," he muttered, wiping a tear off his face. Then, even though he was in his apartment alone, he corrected himself. "I mean, I don't know her. The 'love' was hyperbolic. I think she's wonderful and hilarious."

He wondered, not for the first time, what Theodora looked like. With such an old-fashioned name, he imagined her with big curly hair and sunglasses that took up half her face, like a seventies singer-songwriter. But when he really tried to imagine her face, he couldn't see anything. She was a blank, a blinking cursor in his mind. He spent so much time wondering about her, and he didn't even know what color her eyes were.

Before he could stop himself, Everett typed out a quick email.

**Theodora,**

**I'm going to print out this portrait of Shaq and hang it on my studio wall. I love him.**

**Should we meet?**

**Hopefully,**
**Everett St. James**

Then he looked at the time—shit. He was supposed to be at his parents' place ten minutes ago, and it was pasta night. Gretel was going to be pissed if the gnocchi got cold on his account.

**GRETEL OPENED THE** door before Everett had gotten all the way up the stairs; clearly she'd been watching out the window.

"The start time of the meal is the time we're supposed to eat. It isn't a suggestion," she said, closing the door after he walked in.

"Gretel." Everett's mom walked into the foyer and swatted her with a dish towel. "Give Everett a break. He's working hard."

"So are you and Dad. So am I. And yet we manage to make it to the table on time," Gretel said, then walked toward the kitchen.

"She's really something else," Everett's mom said, holding out her cheek for a kiss.

Everett leaned in and kissed her, then gave her a hug. "She's right, though. I shouldn't be late. I'm sorry."

"You're fine," his mother said, pulling away and looking up at him. "You gave your father a chance to have a Manhattan and tell Gretel more stories from his childhood."

"Oh, her favorite topic," Everett said with a smile.

"She might roll her eyes, but I think she secretly loves it."

He walked into the kitchen and his dad, as always, roared, "Everett!" as if Everett were returning from war, not coming over at least once a week like he always did.

"Hi, Dad," Everett said, sitting down at his usual seat. "Sorry I'm late."

"Not a problem," his dad said, waving him off. "It gave me more time to talk to my favorite daughter."

Gretel turned to Everett. "Did you know that Dad once met Keith Richards at a gas station? Or at least a man who looked like Keith Richards?"

Everett arranged his facial features into an expression of shock. "No! I had no idea! He certainly hasn't told us about this one billion times!"

"Okay, okay." Their dad groaned. "Let an old man remember the good times."

"Like when you saw a random dude in a leather jacket buying a six-pack at a gas station. Golden memories," Everett said, accepting the bowl his mom passed to him.

"Oh, your mother helped out with dinner tonight!" their dad said, then gave them a stern look that clearly communicated *so be nice about it, even if it's inedible.*

"Garlic knots!" Everett's mother said proudly. "But I think there was something wrong with the yeast. The dough was supposed to double and, well . . . it didn't."

Everett took one from the towel-lined basket, and it fell onto his plate with a clatter. "I'm sure they're great."

Gretel took one gingerly. "Can't wait to try it, Mom."

"So, Everett," his dad said, taking five garlic knots and passing the basket back to his wife, "how's work?"

Everett felt his eyes light up. "Big news, actually. Do you guys know the Imagination Network?"

"You mean the company you've been obsessed with forever?" Gretel asked. "Yeah. We've heard of them."

"What do you know about forever? You're twelve," Everett said, then continued. "Anyway, we had a meeting with them this week. They came here from New York, and they're . . . well, they're interested in the show."

"Of course they are!" his mom said, beaming.

"They'd be lucky to have your show," his dad said.

Gretel, though, stared at him. Everett stared back. "What?" he asked. "Why are you looking at me like that?"

"Does that mean you'd have to move to New York?" she asked, her voice sounding more like a typical child than a twelve-year-old-going-on-forty.

"Well, yeah, I guess," Everett said. "I hadn't really thought about it, but that's where their studios are, so . . . yeah, I'd move to New York."

"Hmm," Gretel said, concentrating on her food. "The gnocchi is great." And then, quickly, "Oh, and so are the garlic knots."

Everett picked one up and took a bite. Well, attempted to take a bite. The toughness of the knots required a bit of gnawing.

"Delicious," Everett's dad said with a full mouth.

His mom sighed, then smiled. "You're all a bunch of liars."

They sat in silence, chewing heavily.

"Terrible liars," she said. "These things are garbage."

His dad started to laugh, and Everett started to laugh, and then even Gretel started to laugh.

"Mom, they're terrible," Everett said. "But we love you."

"Thank you for being honest," she said, and then she started laughing, too.

After dinner, Everett helped his dad clean up and then said goodbye to his mom, who was reading in her favorite armchair by the fireplace. It was, like everything else in their home, slightly rumpled and almost obscenely cozy. She had a tattered quilt that used to be her mother's slung over her lap, and Sassafras sat on her feet, licking a paw.

"Where did Gretel go? I haven't told her bye," Everett said.

His mom slipped a bookmark into her book. "Hmm . . . not sure. She said something about doing her homework, but you know that usually takes her about five minutes."

"Right. I'll go find her. Love you." He leaned forward to kiss his mom on her cheek and walked into the foyer. He was about to go upstairs when he heard a strange sound. He stood still for a moment and listened. Was it . . . sniffling?

Quietly, he walked toward the half bath and pushed open the door. Gretel was on the floor. "Go away," she said brusquely through her tears.

"Gretel!" Everett said. "What's wrong? Did you . . . hurt yourself?"

He tried to think of a time he'd seen Gretel cry. When she was a baby, of course. She had cried constantly because she resented not being in charge of her own life. She was basically born wanting to drive a car and open a bank account.

"Did you . . . read a sad book?" he asked gently.

"No!" she yelled, and then more quietly asked, "You're not really going to leave, are you?"

"Well, yeah, I have to get home—"

"No, for your job. Are you really going to move to New York?" She looked up at him, eyes wet.

"Oh!" he said, then squatted down and hugged her. "Gretel, nothing will change if I move."

"Except that everything will change," she grumbled. "Can you come over once a week if you're in another state?"

"Well, no . . ."

"Will you be able to come to my band concerts? I'm going to start playing the French horn next year."

"Maybe Mom can hold up the phone and I can watch through FaceTime," Everett suggested.

"FaceTime isn't the same!" Gretel wailed, burying her face in his shoulder.

Everett exhaled. He hadn't expected this. Obviously he knew that he and Gretel spent a lot of time together, had always spent a lot of time together since the day she was born, all pink and wrinkled and angry-looking. But he didn't know she liked it. Most of the time, she acted annoyed with him, and he didn't mind because being annoying was part of the older-brother contract.

But this . . . well, this was a surprise. Gretel wanted him around.

"Hey," he said, "nothing's decided yet. We've had one meeting, and I still have to go there and check out their offices. Let's not worry about it, because it might not happen."

Gretel wiped her eyes. "It'll happen. Your show's great, and everyone loves you."

"Hold on," Everett said, handing her a tissue. "Can you say that again? I want to record it."

Gretel punched him in the arm. "I hate you."

"Not what I heard," Everett said, and they both stood up. "I promise you'll be the first person I tell if I get any news about the show, and even if I do move—which isn't guaranteed—we'll work something out, okay? I'm not going to disappear."

Gretel sighed, then shook herself off. "Pretend you never saw this."

Everett smiled. "I'm never gonna forget. Come here. Hug."

"Nooooo," Gretel whined as Everett wrapped her in his huge

arms. She was still so little—sometimes he forgot that. She was just a kid who wanted her family, like so many of the kids who wrote to him.

He knew he needed something more, something different, and moving the show to NYC and making it bigger and better would certainly be that. But could he leave all this? The coziness of his family's house, the weekly dinner with his aging parents, and his little sister?

Right now, as he hugged Gretel and she tried not to start crying again, he didn't really want to think about it.

## 30

"HE THINKS WE SHOULD MEET!" TEDDY SHRIEKED.

"Oh, fun! You can finally go on a real date!" Eleanor said from the sewing machine, which they'd set up at a table in the corner of the living room. Scott's comforting hum was keeping Teddy company as she idly scrolled through her phone before pajama-movie night started.

"No, no, no," Teddy said, standing up and pacing. "This is bad. This is so bad."

Eleanor stopped sewing. "You don't want to meet him?"

Teddy threw her hands in the air. "Of course not!"

Eleanor furrowed her brow. "Then why are you emailing him?"

"Nothing I'm doing makes sense to me!" Teddy yelled.

Kirsten walked in, wearing pajamas. "Why is there so much yelling going on in here?" she asked, curious but unperturbed.

"Because Teddy won't meet Everett St. James," Eleanor said, returning to her sewing. And then, in a singsong voice, she said, "And it's tearing her apart!"

"It is," Teddy said miserably. "I just . . . I can't meet him. Does that make sense?"

"No!" Kirsten said. "It makes zero sense. Why are you emailing him if you don't want to meet him?"

Teddy sat back down and slumped into the couch cushions. "I don't know!" she wailed. "Weren't you apprehensive when you met the Viking?"

"Not at all," Kirsten said, sitting down beside her. "He was sitting in the European art section of the Columbus Museum of Art and I sat down beside him and said, 'Listen, do you want to go get milkshakes?'"

Teddy thought about it. "And that worked?"

"Of course it did. Who doesn't want a milkshake?"

"The lactose intolerant," Eleanor said, not looking up from the sewing machine.

"I can't do that, though," Teddy said. "This works over email because he doesn't know me. He can't see me. If he actually meets me and finds out I'm not nearly as witty in person as I am over email, he won't like me and then I'll never be able to watch his show again because it will only remind me of my shame and how Everett St. James thinks I'm a big loser." She took a breath.

"Or," Kirsten said, tilting her head, "maybe . . . and hear me out . . . maybe you guys get along, since you've been getting along pretty well online?"

"Also, didn't he approach you at karaoke?" Eleanor asked, looking up. "So clearly he thinks you're cute. Oh, shit. I need to pay attention. Scott does *not* thrive on neglect." She stuck her tongue out and kept sewing.

"I like things the way they are now," Teddy admitted. "I email him. He emails me. I look forward to our conversations. It's comfortable and easy and I don't have to worry about anything."

"Hmmm," Kirsten said, tapping her chin and pretending to think. "Sounds like you think meeting Everett would be . . . scary."

"No." Teddy pointed at her. "It's not on the list. I like the sense of comfort I have now. It's safe."

"Safety sucks!" Eleanor yelled, then stood up, yanked her project off the machine, and held it up. "Look, pants!"

Eleanor had indeed sewn a pair of pajama pants out of a cute raindrop-printed flannel.

"Did you make pajamas for pajama-movie night?" Teddy asked. "They look *great*."

"I told you," Kirsten said proudly as Eleanor tugged the pants on under her dress. "We take themes seriously around here."

"They fit!" Eleanor said.

Tonight their movie was *Singin' in the Rain*, which Teddy had never seen but Kirsten swore was one of the greatest films ever made. For their snacks, they had sandwiches and milk, because that was what Gene Kelly, Debbie Reynolds, and Donald O'Connor ate before busting into a song-and-dance number.

"I need to go put on pajamas," Teddy said, walking into her room. But as soon as she shut the door, she pulled the email up on her phone.

**Should we meet?**

There was no way to respond *Nah, I'm good, thanks*. And Teddy couldn't bring herself to say yes, because apparently she wasn't as bold as Kirsten and Eleanor thought she was. She knew she *should* say yes. She *wanted* to say yes. But hiding from Everett just felt so damn comfortable.

She closed the email without responding.

## 31

EVERETT SIGHED. "THERE'S NOTHING HERE, NAT."

"Then maybe you should actually plan ahead for once," Natalie said, flipping through several packages of wigs. "What's wrong with being prepared?"

"But this is the fun part!" Everett insisted. He'd never been that into Halloween, since his job involved a fair degree of transformation. Not that he wore a costume, per se, but changing himself into Television Everett was enough. He didn't want to spend weeks creating a persona for Halloween.

So instead, he liked to go to Walmart on the morning he needed a costume and choose from whatever was left. This had led to some memorable past costumes, including Princess Leia (but without the hair, because someone had taken it and so the costume was 50 percent off) and something vaguely tigerlike (he'd found a children's tiger face paint kit and pleaded with Natalie to do it, even though she repeatedly told him she wasn't an artist, and the result had been both abstract and terrifying).

He usually found the chaos of it inspiring, but today his plan had backfired terribly. All that was left were children's costumes and wigs.

"What the hell am I supposed to be?" he asked. "A big guy in a wig?"

"Oooh," Natalie said, picking up a pumpkin costume. "This is cute."

Everett grabbed it from her and looked at the size. "This is for five-year-olds."

She pulled it out of his hands. "So I'll wear it with leggings. Whatever. I'll make it work."

"Yeah, well, not all of us can be tiny pumpkins," Everett grumbled.

Natalie tugged at the sleeve of his T-shirt. "Hey. Don't you have a red cardigan at home?"

Everett closed his eyes. "Yes, Natalie."

"Maybe it's time to be Mr. Rogers," she said. "Come on. Dress pants. Dress shoes. The cardigan. I know you have a Daniel Striped Tiger somewhere."

"On a shelf in my apartment, yes. It's a collectible, not a prop."

Natalie gestured toward the open shelves. "Well, what are your other options? Tiny train? Tiny elephant? Tiny Dorothy from *The Wizard of Oz*?"

Everett grimaced. "I'm imagining wearing any of these in public, and every scenario ends with me getting arrested for public exposure and/or being a total creep."

Natalie shrugged. "I mean, it's supposed to be cold tonight. Why not be comfortable in your cardigan and pay homage to a hero?"

Everett sighed. "Fine, but I don't feel great about it. Let's go."

"Wait. First I have to go grab a bag of Twix," Natalie said.

"Why?" Everett asked. "You don't get trick-or-treaters at your apartment."

Natalie scowled at him. "These aren't for trick-or-treaters. These are for me."

## 32

IT WAS THE FIRST NIGHT OF HIGHBALL, WHICH ALWAYS GUAR-
anteed a completely bonkers but absolutely fun evening at the shop.
The date changed each year, mostly dependent on the Ohio State
University football schedule (because even street drinking couldn't
convince central Ohioans to abandon a college football game). This
year, HighBall happened just a few days before Halloween.

In years past, Teddy had always been one half of the comforting tradition known as the couples costume. She was the egg to
Richard's bacon. The Rocky to his Bullwinkle. The outlet to his
plug. She was, of course, the one who had come up with these
ideas, but there was security in being one half of a costume. By
yourself, you would look silly—an egg wandering the streets alone.
But together? Everyone knew what you were supposed to be, and
everyone knew you had bacon who loved you. No one was looking
at you by yourself—instead, they were looking at the two of you
together.

Now she was on her own, and she wasn't even going to bother
coming up with a solo costume. But then Kirsten had insisted
Teddy wear one of her old costumes.

"What is this?" Teddy had asked, pulling the stretchy red fabric
out of the box.

"A sexy devil!" Kirsten had said gleefully. "It's going to look amazing on you."

It looked more skintight than amazing, but it came with a mask, so Teddy decided to go with it. And so here she was, wearing what was basically a bodysuit, but at least she was behind a counter and no one could tell it was her (well, except for the regular customers, who weren't exactly fooled by the top half of her face being covered).

"Did you know there's a Cajun food truck out there?" Josie asked her after she sold a My Little Pony to a man in a startlingly realistic adult-sized Chucky costume. "Carlos was eating some crawfish mac and cheese and it looked amazing. I'm thinking about going to get some."

Teddy smiled. "If you think you guys can handle it here, I'll go grab it for you."

"You're a sweetheart," Josie said, patting her on the arm. "Where would I be without you?"

"Certainly not in close proximity to mac and cheese," Teddy said, then frowned. "I can't believe I'm voluntarily walking the street in a costume that looks like it was poured onto my body."

"Pssh." Josie waved a hand at her. "If I looked like you, I'd walk around in nothing but high heels. Actually, did I ever tell you that's how I met John?"

"You're full of baloney," Teddy said. "I know you two met in high school."

"You don't know how I dressed in high school," Josie pointed out.

Teddy laughed. "Okay, fine, I'm going. I'll be back in two shakes of a sexy devil's tail with all the mac and cheese you could ever want."

"My hero!" Josie called behind her as she walked out the front door.

Teddy smiled at the scene greeting her. It was early, but the street was already bustling with people in costume having fun. She started walking down the street, narrowly avoiding crashing into the cast of *The Golden Girls*, enjoying the surprisingly mild weather. In October, you never knew what the weather gods would bring down upon HighBall—it could be warm, or snowing, or so rainy that the entire weekend (and everyone's elaborate hairdos) would be ruined. Teddy was still smiling to herself when she saw him.

Richard.

And then she saw that there was someone beside him. A female someone. A someone who was holding his hand.

Teddy stopped. She stopped walking, breathing, or thinking. She simply stared at Richard, who laughed at something this mysterious blond woman said as she gazed up at him in adoration. They were dressed as superheroes (Teddy didn't know which ones), both of them in latex.

Richard looked . . . happy. Certainly not like he missed Teddy. And more than that, he looked *the same*, not as if he was wasting away without his girlfriend to make him meals or keep his apartment clean.

That was when Teddy realized they were headed right toward her, although luckily they hadn't seen her. She looked down at herself and remembered that she was one big, bright, eye-catching sexy devil. Richard's superhero companion looked casually sexy, all "Oh, this? I'm a crime fighter, but being sexy is merely a side effect that I can't help." Teddy looked desperate, like she was trying to pick up drunk men who had no imagination.

"Damn it," she muttered, then ran to a trash can and ducked down. Or, rather, she tried to duck down, but the skintight costume made movement difficult. Slowly, she lowered herself to the ground and watched as they walked past.

She exhaled in relief, then realized that someone was standing beside her.

"We could see you from the window," Josie said, arms crossed. "Me and Carlos and all the customers. We got worried when you ducked behind a trash can. Everything okay?"

"I saw Richard," Teddy said. "He . . . he has a new girlfriend."

"Oh, honey," Josie said, instantly changing from worry to sympathy. "Come here. I'm gonna hug you even though you were leaning against that disgusting trash can."

Teddy got up and put an arm around Josie. "His new girlfriend's a superhero."

"I'm sure she's a regular woman just like you."

"No, I mean, they're dressed as superheroes," Teddy said. "And he looked . . . happy."

Josie sighed as Teddy leaned her head on her shoulder. "Well . . . screw Rick the Dick."

Teddy started giggling, which then turned into a full-on laugh. "Josie, you have *got* to stop calling him that."

"Maybe he's got to stop being a dick. That's another solution."

Teddy wiped her eyes. "I've gotta get your mac and cheese."

"Forget about it. Thinking about Richard killed my appetite."

Teddy smiled, even though her heart felt a bit bruised. Richard had moved on. She thought he would be lost without her, and it turned out he wasn't lost at all. He was thriving with his new superhero girlfriend. He was already one half of a new couples costume, while she was a lone sexy devil working at the shop, dreaming small.

Teddy shook herself off as they walked into the store. She smiled at the next customer in line and decided that if Richard could move on, then she could, too.

## 33

EVERETT WAS SUPPOSED TO MEET UP WITH NATALIE AND LIL-
lian later, but for now he was Gretel's chaperone for the early hours
of HighBall. Their parents might let her travel solo on foot during
daylight hours, but they drew the line when there were intoxicated
adults in costumes roaming those same streets.

Not that Everett was upset about it. After Gretel's unexpected
outburst the other day at dinner, he was happy to spend time with
her and, hopefully, show her that their relationship wasn't so fragile
that it couldn't survive distance. He was her big brother, and he'd
always be there for her.

Gretel was dressed as Totoro from the Hayao Miyazaki film *My
Neighbor Totoro*, and Everett was wearing his red cardigan and holding his Daniel Striped Tiger re-creation in one hand. When Gretel
saw him, she'd frowned and said, "Kinda obvious, isn't it?" She'd
spent several evenings turning a gray onesie into Totoro by sewing
on ears, eyes, whiskers, and a disturbingly large smile, and she
seemed disappointed by the lack of craft involved in his costume.
But she wasn't too embarrassed to be seen with him, so he guessed
it was okay.

"So what first? A beer?" Everett asked as they walked down the
street.

Gretel gave him an exasperated look. "Have you been to Colossal Toys?"

Everett thought about it. "Not for years. Why?"

"Come on. I go there all the time. I'm basically a regular." Gretel grabbed his hand and pulled him through a crowd of what Everett initially thought were extremely committed zombies, then realized were drunk dudes splattered in fake blood (at least, he hoped it was fake blood).

The store was crowded, full of people dressed as Rainbow Brite, Pee-wee Herman, Wayne and Garth, and a group of Teenage Mutant Ninja Turtles. The pop-culture costumes really congregated in Colossal Toys, apparently.

Gretel jostled her way through the crowd while Everett got distracted by a *Fraggle Rock* plush toy. "Oh, I need this," he muttered to himself, grabbing it off the rack. "Gobo, you're coming home with me, my dude."

He figured he should probably keep track of Gretel, so he gently nudged his way through the crowd. "Excuse me," he muttered, then saw Gretel talking animatedly to a devil behind the register. Well, it was a woman dressed as a devil, and as Gretel gestured wildly, Everett realized that he couldn't take his eyes off her. There was something about her, and yes, part of that something was definitely the fact that her costume was basically a second skin, but there was something else, too. A feeling, even as he watched her smile at Gretel from across the room, that he knew her somehow. A feeling of comfort. Of home.

"I'm very sorry, Pee-wee, but I'm going to need you to move," Everett said, pushing on the man's shoulder a bit more forcefully until he finally stepped aside.

"I can't believe you designed this yourself," the devil woman was saying. "The ears are especially impressive."

Gretel beamed back at her. "I watched the movie five times in a row to really study Totoro."

"Not that it was a chore for her," Everett broke in. "She loves that movie."

As the devil woman turned to look at him, the smile fell off her face and her cheeks grew almost as red as her costume.

Gretel sighed. "Teddy, this is Everett St. James, my brother. Everett, this is Teddy Phillips, my friend." She leaned over to him and whispered, "Don't be weird."

"I won't be," Everett whispered back, although he knew Teddy could hear everything they were saying.

"This is . . . your brother?" the woman named Teddy asked quietly, giving the question far more gravity than it needed.

"Unfortunately, yes. He's dressed as Mr. Rogers because he also hosts a puppet-based children's show and I guess his imagination is temporarily impaired," Gretel said.

"Hi there," Everett said, holding out a hand, less because he cared about a proper formal introduction and more because he couldn't go even a second longer without touching Teddy's skin. She stared back at his hand and then finally gave him hers. He held it for a few seconds more than he really needed to, memorizing the feeling of her fingers, soft and smooth, and letting his mind wander to wonder what the rest of her skin felt like.

*Inappropriate train of thought while my kid sister stands beside me,* he reminded himself.

But there it was again. That feeling of home, the feeling that they must have met before, although he couldn't place her. It must have been the mask covering the top half of her face. He'd always made fun of the idea that Superman's coworkers didn't recognize him as Clark Kent without his glasses, but he truly couldn't figure out who this woman was.

"Do we know each other?" he asked, and finally, she spoke.

"No," she said, her voice like warm maple syrup. "I don't believe we do."

"Well," he said, now feeling like his entire body was made of warm maple syrup, "it's very nice to meet you, Teddy."

Her smile was a bit shaky. "It's very nice to meet you, too, Everett."

They stood there, smiling at each other. Everett felt like he should say something, but this seemed better, somehow. Maybe he could skip the rest of HighBall and simply stare at Teddy for the remainder of the evening.

But Gretel's voice snapped him out of it. "Everett. Staring is rude."

Everett shook his head. "Right. Can I . . . buy this?"

Teddy's smile widened. "That's what I'm here for."

He shoved Gobo at her.

"Did you see the Muppets glasses we have?" she asked, gesturing to the case behind her.

"Uh, yeah, actually . . . I have those already."

"He has multiple sets," Gretel said, leaning forward as if she were telling Teddy a particularly scandalous secret.

"Okay," Everett said with a laugh as he put an arm around Gretel and squeezed her shoulder hard enough to, he hoped, communicate that she needed to stop talking. This woman might not recognize him from TV, and she might actually think he was a normal person, one who didn't own more than one set of Muppets glasses from the 1980s (because what if one *broke*?).

Teddy bit her lip as she placed Gobo into a bag. "Well, I can see why you'd want to have a backup set. They're very nice glasses, and what if one broke?"

Everett felt his mouth drop open. Gretel reached up and pushed it closed. "You're still being weird," she hissed.

Everett couldn't stop his eyes from roaming over every inch of Teddy's face. He knew that he knew her, but how? He rarely left the house unless he was at work, and she clearly wasn't Jeremy, Astrid, or Tom, none of whom would ever dress as a sexy devil.

He gave Teddy his credit card and kept watching her. She handed it back to him, then gave him a bag. "Here you go!" she said brightly, her big eyes looking back at him from underneath her mask. "I like the costume, by the way."

Gretel scoffed. "He literally just pulled a cardigan out of his closet."

"Well." Teddy gestured to herself. "I'm wearing one of my roommate's old costumes, so I'm not really in a place to judge. Not my most creative year, but I'm used to coming up with couples costumes, and, um . . ."

Her face got red again as she trailed off.

"So you're saying there's not a Mr. Devil around here somewhere," Everett said, leaning against the counter.

Teddy pressed her lips together, looking as if she was trying not to laugh. "No. There isn't."

"This can't be happening," Gretel muttered.

Suddenly, Prince's "Take Me with U" started playing. Everett looked toward the ceiling, as if questioning the speakers. "This isn't very spooky," he said.

"It's certainly no 'Monster Mash,'" Teddy said. "But my boss loves Prince, so she put him on the HighBall playlist."

Prince. Something caught in Everett's mind. A memory. A song. A face. And then it dawned on him. . . .

"Karaoke!" Everett shouted. The man working at the other cash register looked at him in alarm.

"Sorry," Everett said to him. "Didn't mean for that to come out so loud. I just realized . . . you're Karaoke Girl."

"What?" Teddy asked, her warm maple syrup voice suddenly high and squeaky.

"Wait," Gretel said, disappointment on her face. "Don't tell me you guys know each other. Ugh. Teddy, you can do better."

"This is blatant disrespect and I'm going to take you home,"

Everett told Gretel, and then to Teddy, "You were at karaoke that
night, weren't you? You sang 'We Belong' and then told me you had
to throw up?"

"Um . . . ," she said, glancing toward her coworker, who was now
openly watching them and ignoring the customer in front of him.

"Oh. No. Sorry. I mean . . . that probably wasn't you. Just . . .
some other girl who looked a little bit like you, but now that I . . ."
He squinted and tilted his head. "Yeah, now that I look at you, I can
see that I'm wrong. Clearly not you."

Teddy sighed and, with a little laugh, said, "Okay, okay, okay! It
was me. I'm Karaoke Puke Girl."

"Oh." Everett felt a smile spread across his face.

"Not my best night," she said, still looking at him from underneath that mask.

"It was . . . actually not that bad for me, now that I'm thinking
about it," Everett said, leaning against the counter. Behind him,
someone cleared their throat. Everett turned around to see an impa-
tient SpongeBob SquarePants staring at him. Quietly, Everett said,
"Listen, SpongeBob, can you give me a second? Long story but I'm
reconnecting with someone."

"I don't care," SpongeBob said, but Everett didn't hear him, because in the process of turning around, he'd noticed that Gretel was
no longer standing beside him.

"Oh, no. Gretel?"

Teddy frowned and peered around the store. "She was just here."

"Shit," Everett said, glancing between the front door and Teddy.
"I have to go find her but I . . . um . . . I'll see you later, okay?"

He ran toward the front of the shop, heart pounding, wondering where Gretel could've gone. As he opened the door, he heard a
woman say, "Theodora, could I bother you to refill the toilet paper?
I think someone took it—one can only assume to use as a make-
shift mummy costume."

Everett stopped, the door half open. Theodora. Teddy. Teddy could have been short for Theodora, couldn't it? And how many Theodoras were there, really? Non-elderly Theodoras, that is.

He turned slowly to look at her and found her staring at him, mouth in a perfect "O," looking as if he'd caught her doing something she wasn't supposed to do.

"It's you," he said, too quietly for her to hear.

"What?" the older woman asked. "Did that guy steal something?"

"Uh, excuse me," said one of the Teenage Mutant Ninja Turtles, and Everett realized he was blocking the door. And then he remembered that he had no idea where Gretel had gone. Damn those tiny fast legs!

"Shit," he muttered, and then, to the TMNT, "Sorry, Raphael." He ran out into the street, looking for his twelve-year-old sister, lost among the crowd.

"I'm Michelangelo," the TMNT called, offended, but Everett barely heard him.

## 34

"OH, NO, JOSIE. OH, NO," TEDDY SAID.

"Seriously, what's going on over here?" Josie said, a smile plastered on her face for the customer who was buying a puzzle. "Who was that guy? He was cute. Like Mr. Rogers but, you know, sexy."

Teddy groaned. "That's my pen pal. Everett St. James. Apparently he's Gretel's *brother.*"

Josie whistled—actually whistled—and said, "Well, damn, Theodora. I don't know why you're not chasing after him."

"Because I don't want him to know who I am!" Teddy sputtered frantically. "We had a perfectly charming conversation, and oh, he's so cute, but at no point did I mention that we've been emailing for weeks. At no point was I like 'Oh, by the way, I know your full romantic history and you've seen a terrible painting I made of Shaq.' And also I've been building a friendship with his little sister, so he's going to think I'm some sort of stalker even though that was entirely coincidental! Our emails are keeping me going right now, and now he knows how weird I am and he's going to stop emailing me! I was dumped by half of a latex-wearing crime-fighting duo! I have so little to look forward to, Josie!"

Teddy stopped, panting.

Josie's eyes traveled over Teddy's face. "Why don't you go home for the night, sweetie?"

"Tonight?" Teddy balked. "But it's HighBall! This is one of our busiest nights!"

Josie patted her on the shoulder, already decided. "What you need is a cup of tea and a good night's sleep. I know I say this a lot, but you're gonna scare the customers. Also, I think you tore your costume when you were rolling around behind that trash can."

Teddy let out a frustrated sigh as she looked at the rapidly expanding hole on her upper thigh. Soon, this costume was going to be a public-indecency risk.

And then she glanced toward the door. After Everett's sudden departure, she was afraid he might be back, and the last thing she wanted was to have a longer conversation with him. She could still feel the way his strong hand had felt holding hers, the way his eyes had run over her face, the way that, even in the store, while Prince played and Everett's sister and a bunch of Teenage Mutant Ninja Turtles looked on, she'd felt like they had a connection.

If he came back tonight, she was afraid that whatever she said would make it worse. He might ask her why she hadn't mentioned that she was his secret email pen pal and she might threaten to puke again. Or maybe he wouldn't come back—maybe their relationship wasn't even special. Maybe he had email pen pals all over town.

"Fine," she told Josie, then leaned over and gave her a quick kiss on the cheek. "And thank you."

"Just come back tomorrow your usual perky, nonfrantic self," Josie said. "Shoo. Get outta here."

Teddy fled toward the back of the store, grateful for a boss who was a true friend. Maybe no one else understood why she still worked here, but she knew.

35

"GRETEL!" EVERETT CALLED INTO THE CROWD. "GRETEL, WHERE are you?"

"Bro, are you supposed to be Hansel?" asked a man wearing orange braids that stuck out.

Everett, momentarily distracted from his search, stopped. "I'm . . . no. I'm Mr. Rogers. Who are you, Pippi Longstocking?"

The man threw up his hands. "I'm the Wendy's logo! What the hell? Why do people keep asking me if I'm Pippi Longstocking? I don't know what that is and it sounds weird as shit!"

Everett didn't have time to explain children's entertainment to this profane stranger. He waved him off and kept searching the crowd.

Logically, he knew Gretel was safe. She hadn't gone far and she could handle herself in most situations. But still, the idea that she was so little and he didn't know where she was . . . it made him feel like his own heart was walking around outside of his body, possibly interacting with a sketchy adult.

"Gretel!" he shouted again.

"What?"

He frantically looked for the source of that small voice; then his eyes settled on her a few feet away from him.

"Gretel! Where did you come from? Where did you go?" Everett was so relieved to hear her that he didn't even stop to acknowledge that he'd quoted the song "Cotton Eye Joe."

"I had to get out of line for the Cajun food truck because *someone* wouldn't stop yelling my name and it was freaking people out," she said, looking irritated. But she returned his hug.

"Okay, listen. New rule when we're in crowds, especially crowds full of people who are progressively getting drunker: do not run off by yourself," Everett said, wiping a hand over his forehead.

"Not even if there are alligator bites to be had?" Gretel asked.

"Not even then!" Everett yelled, then took a deep breath. "I was worried, okay? And that girl in the shop—"

"No!" Gretel pointed at him, looking surprisingly threatening in her cute costume. "I saw the way you two were looking at each other. You are not allowed to hit on my friend Teddy."

"Well, you can't really tell me who to hit on, because I'm an adult and you're a child," Everett muttered. "But . . . what's her deal? Is her full name really Theodora?"

"Yes?" Gretel said slowly.

"Wow," Everett said on an exhale. "This is . . . Wow."

"Do you know other words?" Gretel asked.

"I've been emailing her," Everett said. "I think, anyway. I mean, how many Theodoras can there really be in one city?"

"Probably a lot of elderly ones."

"But how many young ones?" Everett asked.

"Wait. Why have you been emailing Teddy?" Gretel asked. "This is odd."

"I do *not* have time to explain it right now," Everett said. "I have to get back to the store and see her. I need to . . . I don't know. Ask her out? What are you supposed to do when you accidentally meet someone you've been corresponding with? Oh, and also technically we did meet once already, and she ran away from me."

Gretel stared at him. "Are you seriously asking your twelve-year-old sister for dating advice?"

Everett nodded. "Fair point. Guess I've gotta figure this out myself."

"Go ask her out, man!"

Everett and Gretel turned to see the man dressed as Wendy giving them a thumbs-up.

Gretel looked back at Everett. "Who is this guy, and why has he been listening to our conversation?"

"Could you mind your own business, Wendy?" Everett asked.

"Fine," he muttered, walking away. But then he turned around. "Aren't you that guy from television?"

Everett winced. Of course, the one time he was borderline rude to a drunk man in the street, he'd be recognized. "Um, yeah. Listen, I'm sorry. . . ."

"Damn." The man dressed as Wendy shook his head in wonder. "Wait till I tell my mom I met Mr. Rogers."

Before Everett could correct him, he shuffled off into the crowd.

"I hope he's going home to get some sleep," Gretel said with a mixture of condescension and concern. "His cognitive skills are seriously impaired."

But the more Everett thought about it, the more the drunken human embodiment of the Wendy's mascot was right. Maybe he *should* just ask her out. And anyway, there were probably worse fast-food mascots to get romantic advice from. The Burger King, for example. Ronald McDonald, for sure.

"What are you thinking about?" Gretel asked. "You're doing that annoying thing you do when you're lost in thought. You're staring off into the distance and kind of muttering to yourself."

"I'm just thinking! This is how I think! Why are you so judgmental?" Everett sighed. "I've gotta go talk to her. Come with me."

"No!" Gretel literally put her foot down, stomping on the street.

"I am getting the alligator bites that I came here for because I've never had alligator and this is a *life experience!*"

Everett rolled his eyes. "Okay. Fine. I'm going to miss out on talking to the woman of my dreams because you couldn't wait to eat fried food and call it a 'life experience.'"

"How can she be the woman of your dreams when she never guest-starred on *The Muppet Show* and sang a duet with Kermit the Frog?" Gretel asked dryly.

"I have other dream women!" Everett snapped. "Go get your food!"

By the time Gretel had waited in line, paid, and walked away victorious with alligator bites, minutes had passed. Minutes that Everett wasn't speaking to Theodora/Teddy and figuring out if their connection extended past email into real life. Which it obviously would; he was too much of an idealist to think otherwise.

"Ev," Gretel whined, "I can't keep up with you. Your legs are too long, and I'm going to drop my food."

Everett slowed his stride a little. "Want me to pick you up?"

"No!" Gretel said in horror.

"You could ride on my shoulders, like you used to when you were a toddler," he suggested, which only earned him an eye roll.

By that time, they were at Colossal Toys, so Everett took a deep breath and opened the door. The store was packed, full of both people and toys, and he couldn't tell if Teddy was still there. Seriously, the aisles were uncomfortably narrow; wasn't this a fire hazard? He muttered, "Excuse me," to a couple dressed as Jim and Pam from *The Office* and attempted to see around someone dressed as Dark Helmet from *Spaceballs*, but the oversized helmet blocked his view of the register.

Finally, he made his way through the crowded aisles to the counter. "Do you want to go out sometime?" he asked, out of breath, slapping his hands on the counter.

"That's a very nice offer, honey, but you're a bit young for me," said a woman with frizzy gray hair piled on top of her head.

"You're not Theodora," Everett said.

"The words I love to hear from a man." The woman put the glasses hanging on a chain around her neck on her eyes. "Oh! It's you! The Mysterious Email Man!"

"Is that what she calls me?" Everett asked.

The woman laughed. "No. But that's what I call you. I'm Josie."

She held out her hand and Everett shook it. "I'm Everett. But maybe you already knew that."

"I did." She nodded in a way that was both comforting and a little mocking. Everett decided he liked Josie.

"You're not dressed up," he said.

Josie shook her head. "Halloween is amateur hour, and I'm not an amateur."

Everett nodded. "Got it. Is Theodora around?"

"She had to go home," Josie said. Everett thought she might offer some other information, but she stared back at him and let the silence between them grow. He got the feeling she was the type of woman who wasn't uncomfortable with silence.

"Okay, then," Everett said, tapping a hand on the counter. "In that case, I'll be off."

"It was nice to meet you, Everett," Josie said with a genuinely warm smile. "You should go ahead and email her."

Everett stepped out of the way as another customer plopped their merchandise on the counter and Josie turned her attention away from him. She was right. He should send Theodora another email—after all, that was how they'd been communicating up until now. *Why not ask her to—I don't know—get a burger somewhere? Or, wait. Is she a vegetarian?* He didn't even know. There were so many gaps in their communication. He'd have to find out.

"Are we done here?" Gretel asked. "There's no food allowed in the shop so I had to shove the rest of it in my mouth, and I almost choked. Not that you noticed."

"You didn't almost choke," Everett said. "Come on. You got what you came to HighBall for. Let's get you home."

Gretel whined a bit, but Everett knew she'd be content as soon as she got up in her turret bedroom with her twinkle lights and her books. And then he'd go back out with Natalie and Lillian, get a little bit drunk in the street, and maybe eventually email Theodora. Or Teddy. Or whatever he was supposed to call her.

**36**

Dear Theodora, who I now know is also Teddy,

Should I keep calling you Theodora? Do you prefer Teddy? I don't want to be rude. What I do want is to see you sometime, in a situation with no karaoke and no masks and also without my sister (who I love, but come on).

Do you want to go out sometime?

Awaiting your reply,
Everett

PS: I know that's not a very clever sign-off, but I just got back from HighBall and I am drunk and also I've eaten far too many alligator bites. Please excuse any typos.

Even when he was drunk, he didn't make typos. Ugh. He was perfect.

Teddy shook her head. No, she knew he wasn't perfect. He had plenty of bad habits—maybe he didn't clean the sink after he shaved, leaving tiny little prickly hairs everywhere. Maybe he wore his shoes inside the house, which everyone knew was disgusting (Teddy had once read an article that said "every inch of sidewalk has been peed on" and now she couldn't get it out of her head). Maybe he smelled bad.

She wrinkled her nose. That ought to be enough to stop her from thinking about him.

But as it turned out, it wasn't. She didn't even care what he smelled like; she liked him, and she wanted to keep knowing him, but she was terrified.

She closed her laptop and didn't respond for one day. Two days. Then three days. He didn't email her again; he probably assumed she didn't like him, which was so far from the truth it made her want to laugh, but she couldn't stop thinking about his perfectly earnest face when they'd "met" at Colossal Toys. He hadn't known who she was yet but he'd trained those deep brown eyes on her, looking at her like she was the only person in the shop. If those eyes ever looked at her like she was boring, or disappointing, or not enough, she didn't know what she'd do.

So of course she didn't respond. Who could blame her? She was barely holding it together.

But then, one morning when she was the only person working, the bell above the door jingled and Everett walked right in.

The second she saw him, the word "Oh" quietly left Teddy's lips and floated out into the shop. At this point she'd met him in person twice, and she still couldn't quite believe he was real. Real and right in front of her.

"I promise I'm not going to bother you if you say no," Everett said in lieu of hello. "At this point you've run away from me twice, although I think that was situational and not because of me. And you didn't respond to my email. And when I put it like that, actually it's starting to sound like maybe I should get out of here and leave you the hell alone. I mean, that's a lot of rejection, when I think about it."

"No," Teddy said.

"What?" Everett asked.

Teddy cleared her throat. "No, don't leave."

Everett smiled, and Teddy's heart broke into a million pieces that she'd have to sweep up off the shop floor later. He had the best smile she'd ever seen in her life, like a baby animal and a classic Hollywood leading man combined. Like she wanted to hug him and grow old with him and also have sex with him. It was a smile that contained multitudes.

"Okay, then. So, Theodora . . . or Teddy . . . Wait. What should I call you?"

"Either one is fine," she said. "But pretty much everyone aside from Josie calls me Teddy."

Everett smiled again. "Teddy it is, then. Teddy, do you want to hang out sometime? Without your friends or my friends or my sister, someplace where we can talk about anything except Jazzercise because we said we were done with that topic—"

"Yes."

"What?" Everett asked. "Yes?"

Teddy smiled, despite the unease currently roiling in her stomach. She said she was going to do one thing every day that scared her, and right now, more than skydiving or bungee jumping or getting a tattoo, what scared her most was going out with Everett St. James. And now that he was standing directly in front of her, staring at her with those expressive eyes and that mouth she desperately wanted to kiss and those hands she desperately wanted to hold, she was both calm and terrified.

"Yes," Teddy repeated. "Let's hang out."

"Great." Everett smiled. "So, uh, do you want to go eat somewhere, or . . ."

"Do you have a bike?" Teddy asked.

Everett held completely still for a moment. "A bike?"

Teddy nodded. "I want to learn how to ride a bike. Well, relearn, I guess. It's been a while, because I have a bicycle fear. It's on my list."

She loved that she didn't have to explain the idea of her list to Everett, because he already knew. He already knew so many things about her. Maybe all friendships/relationships/dates should start with several long, personally revealing emails, for convenience's sake.

"Yeah," Everett said, running his hand through his hair. "My best friend will probably let me borrow hers. I have one, in storage at my parents' house, but it's too big for you, I'm sure. But I think Natalie's about your size."

"Okay," Teddy said. "Could you do tomorrow evening around five thirty? And you don't mind? Being there for my first bike ride in years?"

Everett smiled and leaned forward until his face was maybe half a foot from hers. He decidedly did *not* smell bad—he smelled like a bed she wanted to climb into.

"Theodora Teddy Phillips," he said, "it would be my honor to help you relearn how to ride a bike."

Teddy couldn't help it; she felt a smile bloom across her face like a field of wildflowers. She was a cliché screen saver picture and she didn't even care.

"And you know what they say," Everett said, leaning back. Teddy had to fight the urge to tell him to lean closer. "You don't forget how to ride a bike. It's ingrained in you, presumably like your knowledge of Jazzercise footwork."

Teddy pressed her lips together. "I actually have to relearn the steps with every class. I'm terrible at Jazzercise."

"We said we weren't going to talk about Jazzercise anymore," Everett said, walking backward toward the door without taking those big brown eyes off of her. He bumped into a rack of novelty socks and jumped. "Okay, sorry," he said, grabbing the rack and righting it. "I . . . Oh, no. Great. I've showed you what a lumbering oaf I am. This didn't come across in the emails."

Teddy smiled (she could not stop smiling! Her face was going to break!). She liked this lumbering oaf. "You don't have to worry about the socks. They're not fragile."

"Right," Everett said, bumping into the door. They couldn't stop looking at each other. This was ridiculous; it was like the shop was a Magic Eye picture and Teddy kept staring at the center to see Everett St. James appear.

"Wait," Teddy said as he pushed the door open, still looking at her. "Where are we meeting?"

"I'll pick you up," Everett said, holding the door open with one arm.

"But you don't know where I live."

Everett smiled again, and it made Teddy want to shiver. "Why don't you email me?" he asked.

This was the part where a very different kind of man would wink. A man who had a different kind of charm, maybe even a bit of smarm. But Everett was not the winking type, which was one of the things Teddy could already tell she liked quite a bit about him. Instead, he held up a hand in a wave, and then he was gone.

Teddy stared at the door and put her hand on her chest, feeling for her heartbeat to make sure she was still alive. "Everett St. James," she said, needing to hear his name out loud. He was no longer a person on a screen, words in an email, thoughts in her head. He was a real man, one she'd be seeing tomorrow.

"Oh, shit," she said, realizing what she'd agreed to. She was going to ride a bike with Everett St. James tomorrow.

**37**

Dear Teddy,

I would like to clarify one thing before tonight: I do own drinking glasses that aren't Muppets themed and from the 1980s. In fact, usually I drink out of perfectly normal adult glasses.

Mostly because the Muppets glasses are collectibles and I don't want to break them.

Do you have a specific place you want to ride? A trail? The sidewalk? A street? The Tour de France (may be difficult logistically, since you aren't registered and it isn't occurring right now but I think I could figure something out)?

Drinking out of a basic, boring clear glass,
Everett

Dear Everett,

My roommates' favorite mug is one that has a picture of a dachshund and says "DON'T SQUISH THE WEEN," so I'm not really in a place to judge anyone for their choice of drink ware. Seriously, we all fight over that mug, but this morning I won.

As tempting as the Tour de France is, I wouldn't want to show anyone up. Likewise, I don't want to be hit by a car on the road or a fast jogger on the trail, so let's try a parking lot. I know a good, particularly empty one that's usually only occupied by teenagers attempting to practice for their driver's test by maneuvering around orange cones.

Drinking out of an inappropriate mug,
Teddy

. . . . . . . .

Dear Teddy,

Thank you for including a picture of the mug. It's adorable, perhaps made even more so by the juxtaposition of the horrific sentiment.

A parking lot it is! And this way, no matter what happens on your bike, at least you'll be able to heckle teenagers who don't know how to drive yet.

I'm assuming you know how to drive a car or I'm going to look like a huge asshole,
Everett

Dear Everett,

I do know how to drive a car. You'd think that would be scarier than riding a bike, but what can I say? I like to do things a little bit differently, i.e., I like to let a childhood fear of bicycles follow me into adulthood.

Uniquely,
Teddy

· · · · · · · ·

Dear Teddy,

Well, prepare to conquer that fear. Should I see if I can affix training wheels to the bike? You know, for safety/reassurance purposes?

Helpfully,
Everett

· · · · · · · ·

Dear Everett,

Please don't. The teens will point and laugh. I need them to think I'm cool.

Pulling down my sunglasses,
Teddy

Dear Teddy,

See you tonight. I can't wait.

Everett

**38**

"WOW, THIS IS VERY 'GO BIG OR GO HOME' OF YOU," KIRSTEN said, nodding approvingly. "You're meeting your Internet crush *and* conquering your fear of bicycles."

"What's the deal with the bike fear, anyway?" Eleanor called from the bathroom, where she was doing her hair.

"Did you once have a traumatic experience on two wheels?" Kirsten asked, leaning forward from her seat on the sofa. It was officially Halloween, and she was dressed as a tiger, complete with yet another skintight costume, ears, and drawn-on whiskers. Even though the only people seeing their costumes would be the children coming to their door, Kirsten had said it was still important to dress up, insisting that it was disrespectful not to.

"Something like that," Teddy said. She wasn't ready to explain the entire situation to her friends, and anyway, she was getting ready to go out with Everett. She didn't have time to explain the story of the last time she was a carefree person who did whatever she wanted and then ended up destroying her parents' marriage and breaking her arm.

"What about this?" she asked, twirling around in the outfit

she'd chosen: a cardigan over a short-sleeved button-down with tiny red flowers, a full skirt that went past her knees, and thick tights because it was, after all, October.

Eleanor stuck her head out of the bathroom, hands in her hair. "You're going to look like Audrey Hepburn on a bike! I love it!"

Kirsten tilted her head. "I hope that skirt doesn't get tangled in the bike wheels."

Eleanor waved her off. "Google 'Audrey Hepburn on a bike.' You'll see a bunch of pictures, none of which are Audrey on the ground after a skirt-related bike crash."

"Well, that's good enough for me," Teddy said.

Her phone buzzed, and she felt her stomach drop. Anxiety and excitement were so close together, it was like they were the same feeling. She couldn't tell if she was terrified or thrilled or . . .

> Waiting outside. Your neighbor is staring at me suspiciously. I think she's afraid I'm about to ask her for candy.

Terrified *and* thrilled. Both of them, all at once, swirling in her body like a slightly nauseating cocktail.

> Also it's weird to text you. But emailing you to say I was here felt weirder.

"He's here, isn't he?" Kirsten asked. "Because you're staring at your phone with a look of what is either wide-eyed horror or wide-eyed excitement."

Teddy's head jerked up. "This is a date, right?"

Eleanor stepped out of the bathroom, wearing a collared dress covered in suns, moons, and stars. "Uh, yeah. He asked you out. This is a date."

"What is this costume?" Kirsten asked. "You said you'd be going as something we'd recognize."

Eleanor spun around. "I'm Ms. Frizzle, obviously. Of *The Magic School Bus* fame?"

"Ohhhh," Teddy and Kirsten said appreciatively.

Eleanor sighed. "You guys aren't the only ones who didn't recognize the costume—none of my students did when I wore it to our class Halloween party, on account of they're five and they don't watch television from *my* youth."

Teddy smiled. She knew Gretel would probably get the reference. And then thinking of Gretel reminded her that Everett was waiting outside, and suddenly, she felt hot. She fanned her face with her phone. "I haven't been on a date since . . . well, since Richard and I started dating. And that barely counted, because I kind of started going over to his place and then we were together. But I don't know how to do this! I've never dated! I—"

"Whoa, whoa, whoa." Kirsten stood up and crossed the room, then put her hands on Teddy's shoulders. "Do what I did on my first date with the Viking. Tell him he has frosting on his mouth and ask if you can lick it off."

"But why would he have frosting on his mouth?" Teddy asked, panicked. "Are we going to a bakery?"

"Absolutely do not say that!" Eleanor shouted, shaking with laughter. "Kirsten is kidding!"

"I mean, that's literally what happened, but sure, I'm kidding. It's a joke! Don't do that!" Kirsten shook her finger at Teddy.

"Be yourself, Teddy," Eleanor said soothingly, putting an arm around her. "Be your normal, charming self. We love you. Everyone loves you. He will, too."

"Okay," Teddy whispered. "But what if he . . . doesn't?"

"He will," Eleanor said firmly as Kirsten nodded.

Teddy sighed and rested her head on Eleanor's shoulder. "You're very comforting as Ms. Frizzle, you know. How can I be a full-fledged grown-up and just figuring out something that most people learn at sixteen?"

"What did we tell you?" Eleanor said gently. "There's no time limit on dreams. Don't make Kirsten repeat that Colonel Sanders anecdote again."

"Maybe I should stay here and hand out candy with you guys," Teddy said quickly. "That sounds like a fun tradition I'd love to be part of."

"Nope." Eleanor steered Teddy toward the door, grabbing her purse and handing it to her. "You're going out with your puppeteer crush and you're gonna have a great time."

She opened the door and all but pushed Teddy out.

"Don't forget the frosting trick!" Kirsten called as Eleanor shut the door.

Teddy stood on the porch, blinking in the early-evening fall sunlight like a confused baby animal who'd just been born. She wasn't sure she could do this. Go on a date? Who thought that was a good idea?

"Hey."

She turned to her right to see Everett leaning against the wall, smiling that Everett St. James smile at her. And now she knew: it didn't just look that way on TV. In person, it made her feel lit up from the inside, like a glowing jack-o'-lantern (but with better teeth).

"Hey," she said softly.

"What was that about frosting?" he asked.

"Oh, you heard that?" Teddy exhaled. "That's my roommate. It was encouraging in context, but don't worry about it."

"Okay! So," he said, pushing himself off the wall, "you ready to ride a bike?"

"I was born ready," Teddy said.

---

TEDDY DIRECTED EVERETT to the parking lot of a nearby high school. It turned out her cardigan, while cute, was no match for the autumn chill, so Everett loaned her his jacket, and Teddy was so distracted by how it smelled—spicy and sweet and perfectly warm— that she could barely focus. As they parked, children in costumes flooded the streets, their chatter and shrieks floating through the air as they ran down the sidewalk dressed as lions and superheroes and unicorns. Dead leaves scuttled across the parking lot, and Teddy happily realized that she couldn't have picked a more perfect fall evening for a date with Everett if she'd tried.

"Okay," Everett said, pulling the bike out of the back of his car like it weighed no more than a child's tricycle. "What do you think?"

Teddy was a few steps away from Everett, so she slowly closed the gap between them. She ran her hand over the bike, appreciating it as if it were a sports car. "This is good," she said.

Everett smiled. Across the street, children yelled, "Trick or treat!" at someone's front door.

"I only hope the elementary school children don't laugh at me," Teddy said.

"Just tell them you're dressed as 'a woman who doesn't know how to ride a bike.' Oh, that reminds me!" Everett turned around, grabbed something out of the backseat, then held up a helmet. "Safety first."

Teddy looked at it skeptically. "Am I really going to be fast enough to require a helmet?"

Everett gave her a faux-disproving look. "Teddy. Who do you think you're talking to? Reminding children of safety rules is, literally, part of my job. We did an entire episode about helmets, and at no point did I say, 'If you're a cute girl who plans on riding very slowly in a high school parking lot, no helmets are needed.' And besides, you're setting an example for the children. They're always watching."

Teddy was so caught up on how it felt to hear him say her name that she barely even noticed he'd called her cute. He could've said anything at that point and she would've swooned. *Teddy, you have spinach in your teeth.*

She quickly ran her tongue over her teeth. Okay, maybe not that.

She realized Everett was still holding out the helmet and looking at her, so she grabbed it and put it on. "Helmet. Got it. I care about safety, Mr. St. James."

Everett groaned. "Please don't call me that. The kids don't call me that. Mr. St. James is my father."

"Noted," Teddy said with a smile.

She placed her hands on the bike handles and squeezed the grips, then lifted one leg over the frame and sat. It wasn't a perfect fit, but she didn't want to adjust a strange woman's bicycle, so she decided to make it work.

"It's just like riding a bike," she muttered to herself, pushing one pedal, then the other. And then she was moving . . . well, gliding at a low speed through the parking lot. The wind might not have been whipping her hair back, but it was certainly caressing it gently.

Everett clapped from the car. "You're Lance Armstrong right now! I wish I could think of someone who never got in trouble for doping, but cycling isn't really my sport," he called.

Teddy laughed, reaching the curb. She attempted to turn around but realized she hadn't given herself enough space; she was about to hit a parked car. She panicked, put one foot down, then tilted to the side.

"Teddy!" Everett shouted, and from her new vantage point on the ground, she saw his vintage-y-looking white-and-red sneakers running toward her. She looked up to see his face, surrounded by the gray clouds in the air.

"Are you okay?" he asked, kneeling beside her. He quickly ran his hands over her arms, like he was checking for an injury, and her entire body shivered.

"I'm fine," she said. "I fell off a bike. This happens a lot to children when they're learning."

"Yeah, but they're closer to the ground," Everett said, appraising her skeptically. "I don't know how injured you can get when you roll off a tricycle."

"What *is* your sport?" she asked.

"What?"

"You said cycling isn't really your sport. So what is? We've never talked about it."

Everett smiled then, his big, easy grin. "Basketball. It's indoors, it's fast-paced, and it has Shaq. Or had, anyway. I don't know if you know this about me, but I'm a huge Shaq fan. I can show you a really amazing portrait of him, if you'd like. It's by this fantastic local artist who's learning to ride a bike."

"She sounds great," Teddy said, trying to keep her smile from taking over her whole face. Weren't you supposed to show some sort of restraint on a first date instead of staring at a man with complete adoration?

"What about you?"

Teddy frowned. "My sport? I prefer a more intense competition. More cutthroat. Brutal."

Everett's brow furrowed. "Hockey?"

"*Kids Baking Championship* on Food Network," Teddy said. "Sometimes they have to make cupcakes that look like mashed potatoes, and I think that's the only true way to judge an athlete's skill."

Everett laughed, loud and unselfconscious, and Teddy suddenly felt her breath leave her body. It was like the air had been knocked out of her, but not by the fall—by Everett's presence, his nearness, the fact that she'd made him laugh.

And then Teddy realized she was still basically lying on the ground, so she sat up. "Thanks for caring," she said.

Everett picked up the bike, then held out a hand for her and pulled her up. "What do you mean, thanks for caring?"

She thought about all the times Richard had rolled his eyes when she'd tried something new, sighed at her whenever she messed something up, made her feel like of course she couldn't do anything right. If she'd fallen off a bike around him, he would've laughed and assumed she'd pick herself back up.

And perhaps it went without saying that he didn't care about *Kids Baking Championship*. She never would've watched it around him—he watched prestige television where terrible men made horrible decisions. It's not that she didn't like those shows, too, but sometimes a person just needed to watch Valerie Bertinelli comfort a small child whose custard had curdled.

"I mean . . . don't worry about it." Teddy brushed herself off as a raindrop hit her nose. "Is that . . . ?"

Another raindrop on her arm, and then another on her cheek. Suddenly raindrops were pelting them, the big, fat kind, and a burst of lightning flashed in the air. "Uh-oh," Everett said, looking up.

Children squealed with delight, running down the sidewalk with their parents, bags full of hard-earned candy clutched to their chests.

"We should probably get in the car," Everett said. "I mean, I've always heard you shouldn't stand outside when there's lightning. Especially not if you're holding what is essentially a big piece of metal."

"That does seem to be the conventional wisdom," Teddy said, watching a father lift a tiny werewolf onto his shoulders. Everett carried the bike to the car and shoved it in the back, then opened Teddy's door for her and she slid in.

Her bangs were wet and she knew they were going to dry in some unflattering, unpredictable way. Her skirt had parking lot dirt on it and she was pretty sure she had gravel embedded in her knee. But when Everett St. James walked around the car and sat in the driver's seat, there was nowhere she'd have rather been.

"So," Everett said, drumming his hands on the steering wheel, "bike riding is out. Where to now?"

## 39

"ARE YOU SURE THIS IS WHAT YOU WANT TO DO?" EVERETT asked, unlocking the door to the station. "I mean, visiting my place of work seems like a very boring date. Especially because it's after hours, and nothing is going on right now."

Teddy took a deep breath, wondering if she should tell Everett the truth. On the one hand, it felt bad to start a . . . *whatever* they were starting without telling him that she'd been watching his show regularly, and that it was sometimes the only bright spot in her day. But on the other hand, that was a little over-the-top, right? What if he thought she was some obsessed fan who was going to chain herself to the *Everett's Place* sofa and refuse to leave?

"It's not boring," she said in a rush, "because I love the show. I've seen every episode."

Everett paused, the door partially open. "Every episode?"

Teddy nodded. "I don't have a kid or anything. I mean, I have a niece and a nephew, and that's how I started watching, but I kept going on my own. Now they prefer to watch *PJ Masks*, anyway."

Everett shrugged. "Who can blame them?"

Teddy clapped a hand over her mouth. "I'm sorry. That was rude," she said, her words muffled.

Everett laughed. "I think I'd have to be a pretty big narcissist to care that children enjoy watching a show about kids who fight crime in their pajamas."

A loud beeping sound filled the air and Teddy moved her hands to her ears. "Oh, shit," Everett shouted over the sound. He ducked inside, pulling Teddy with him, and pressed a few buttons. The beeping stopped.

"Sorry," he said. "The alarm. I didn't notice I was holding the door open."

"It's okay," Teddy said. In the absence of the alarm, the silence was so loud, and she couldn't help but realize she was standing so close to Everett, his hand still clasped around her elbow from where he'd pulled her through the door.

"I didn't mean to scare you," he said softly, looking down at her. She kept forgetting how tall he was—that was something you didn't notice when you saw a man next to puppets.

"It's okay," she said again, then grimaced. She had to show him she knew other words. "Thanks for taking me here. Is it . . . I mean, is it weird that I asked?"

Everett smiled and started walking down a dimly lit hallway, unfortunately removing his hand from her arm as he did so. "It might be weirder on my part. I don't, like, bring every woman I meet here. Not that I'm meeting tons of women," he added in a rush.

Now it was Teddy's turn to smile. "I get it. I wasn't under the impression that you were a monk because you host a children's program. I mean, I've seen the message boards."

Everett groaned. "You looked at the mom boards?"

Teddy nodded, eyes wide. "Those moms love you. And they would like to do some very PG-13 things on that couch."

Everett's face flushed, and Teddy found this almost impossibly charming. "No offense to the moms, but let's just say I deeply wish I didn't know those discussions existed." He fumbled with the keys to open the studio. They stepped through the door and he flipped a switch, bathing the room in light.

And then there it was. Everett's place, and also *Everett's Place*. "Here it is . . . where the magic happens," he said wryly.

"Whoa," she said quietly, looking around. Of course it looked different from this angle. There were cameras, for starters, which obviously weren't visible on the show. Cords snaked across the ground and equipment was everywhere.

But right in the middle of it was a room that felt more real to her than anywhere she'd ever lived. The plaid-papered walls with framed children's artwork, the bookshelf full of picture books, the lamp Everett turned off at the end of every episode . . . and, of course, the couch. The one where Everett sat when he talked to the camera and, by extension, to Teddy. The one where he held conversations with puppets and read letters from children and dispensed advice that never felt like teaching so much as it felt like understanding.

"Is it okay if I . . ." Teddy gestured toward the set.

Everett nodded. "Sure! Go ahead, look around."

Teddy stepped into the living room, and a surreal feeling washed over her. "I can't believe I'm here," she whispered, pulling a book off the bookshelf before putting it back in exactly the same place. "I'm sorry. I shouldn't be touching anything."

"You can touch things," Everett said. He was standing by a camera, giving Teddy the strange feeling that she was performing on a stage, like she was being watched and recorded. "I don't mind if things aren't in the exact same place from episode to episode. I like it to look lived in, you know? Like this is really my living room."

"Is this what your real place looks like?" Teddy asked, studying a crayon scribble that looked sort of like a dog. Or a cat. Or a possum.

"Uh . . . no." She heard Everett's heavy footfalls, and then he was standing directly beside her. "My place is more basic. It's really just a space where I work, eat, and sleep."

Teddy nodded. "Who drew this? You?"

Everett smiled the lopsided grin he did when he really thought something was funny—Teddy had seen it so many times on the show, when one of the puppets puppeteered by someone else said something that seemed to surprise him. "Believe it or not, my work is slightly more sophisticated. No, this is something Gretel did when she was a kid."

"That's sweet," Teddy murmured. "You two seem like you have a really close relationship."

"We do," Everett said. "I was basically an adult when she was born, so it always kind of felt like she was partially my own kid. This picture, though . . . not so sweet, actually. It's supposed to be a raccoon that was terrorizing our neighborhood one summer. She was obsessed with it."

"I can see why," Teddy said, leaning in. "It's disturbing."

"Oh, no, she wasn't scared," Everett said. "She thought we should adopt it. You know, keep it in our home. But it had rabies, and she was forced to give up her plan to convince our parents."

Teddy laughed. "She's great."

"She is," Everett agreed. "She's also occasionally terrifying."

They were standing close together, so close that their arms were almost touching. Being near Everett while on the set of the show that had kept her afloat was almost too much sensation, so Teddy took a step away. She pointed toward the couch. "May I?"

"Only if you promise not to give any details about the couch's texture to the mom message boards," Everett said.

"You know I can't promise that," Teddy said, sitting down. "And anyway, I think we both know they don't need any help creating extremely vivid fantasies."

Teddy looked out at the cameras. This was what Everett saw whenever he filmed. This was what he saw whenever she saw him, when they were staring at each other without even knowing it.

"Kind of makes it all seem a little less interesting when you see the behind-the-scenes stuff, huh?" Everett asked, sitting down beside her.

Teddy shook her head vigorously. "Not at all. If anything, this makes it better. Seeing what you see . . ." She could feel herself blush. "There were some days . . . some hard days . . . where seeing the show, seeing you, was all that I looked forward to."

Everett watched her, so she kept going.

"When I was with my ex . . . Richard was his name. When I was with Richard, I didn't ever feel like he was really listening to me when I talked. Or like he valued what I said. It seemed like I was some sort of instrumentation for him, like a hood ornament on the BMW of his life. And when I saw your show for the first time, I couldn't get over the way you talked to kids. Like they mattered. Like you saw them all for the people they were, not for the people you thought they should be."

Everett reached out and grabbed her hand. "That's the goal," he said softly.

Teddy took a sharp breath in, then kept going. She reminded herself that Everett already knew so much about her through their emails and that she could be honest with him.

"I don't want to make myself sound pathetic, because I'm working on it now and trying to figure out what I want my life to be. But sometimes it's hard to forget that I spent so much time with someone who made me feel like nothing I said or did was important. And the worst part is, sometimes I think he was right, because I don't know what I want to do, and everything I say seems like it comes out wrong."

She smiled sheepishly. "Like now. God, I can't stop talking. I'm sorry."

Everett shook his head slowly. "No."

When he didn't say anything else, Teddy asked, "No?"

"I don't think that's true. Everything you say isn't wrong," Everett said, never taking his eyes off hers. "I think everything you say sounds just right, Teddy."

Teddy looked down at their hands, where his thumb rubbed slowly and gently over her palm. She could hardly believe that Everett St. James's hands, the ones she'd stared at on TV all this time, were now holding hers.

"Maybe we haven't known each other very long," Everett said, and Teddy met his eyes again. "But with our emails, I feel like we know each other pretty well. And based on what I know . . . well, I like you quite a bit, Theodora Phillips."

"I like you quite a bit, too, Everett St. James," Teddy said, her voice coming out in a whisper.

Everett leaned toward her and she had a brief flash of terror. A moment of *I can't possibly kiss Everett St. James, television star and man of my dreams.* What if he didn't live up to her expectations? What if he thought she was a bad kisser? What if they'd gotten along so well through words but realized quickly that they had no sexual chemistry and would have to pivot back to platonic pen pals and pretend that was enough? What if . . .

But this was the new Teddy, she reminded herself, and this time, she did things that scared her. She didn't run away, she didn't hide behind someone else, she made her own decisions, and damn it, she decided that she was going to kiss the ever-loving daylights out of Everett St. James on this couch.

The second his lips touched hers, she knew all of her worries were meaningless. This was the free fall after jumping out of the airplane, the feeling of floating, floating, floating through the clouds. Everett placed a hand on her cheek, so softly, and Teddy felt like she was something fragile and special, something that deserved to be looked at and displayed instead of hidden away.

Teddy pulled back suddenly and studied Everett, who looked at her in alarm. "I've never felt like this before," she said simply. "Isn't that funny? That I'm almost thirty years old and there's still a brand-new feeling? I thought I'd felt them all already, but this is new. This feels special." She paused. "Maybe I shouldn't have said that."

"No." Everett smiled back at her, his face inches from hers. "You should have. It's special, Teddy. You're special."

They kissed again, and Teddy could feel his lips smiling against hers, and she closed her eyes tight to memorize this moment. She knew she liked Everett on his show, and she liked Everett in his emails, but finding out that she liked Everett so much, this much, in person filled her with so much joy that she never wanted to forget it.

# 40

"YOU'RE IN A GOOD MOOD," NATALIE SAID, LOOKING AT HIM suspiciously.

Everett took a bite of the eggs Benedict she'd made. About once a week, he and Natalie tried to get together for brunch. They used to go out, but Natalie had recently proclaimed she was too old and tired to wait in line for pancakes, and so now they got together at her apartment and each contributed something. Natalie always made a dish, while Everett typically got a box of donuts from the Little Donut Factory. They might not have been homemade, but in his defense, they were very good donuts.

And anyway, Natalie's apartment was bright and airy, full of plants on the shelves and in the corners and in baskets hanging from the ceiling, so they might as well have been in some hip brunch spot.

"I hung out with Teddy this week," he said.

"Teddy?" Natalie asked. "Fill me in. Is this Email Girl?"

Everett explained the entire story to Natalie, and her eyes grew wider as he got to each detail.

"Wait," said Lillian, who'd walked in during the story, as she grabbed a pink sprinkled donut. "Are you telling me she's the woman you talked to at karaoke?"

"One and the same," Everett said with his mouth full.

"This is unbelievable," Natalie said. "Oh, so *this* is why you're so happy. You got laid."

"Nope!" Everett said with a smile.

"No one has ever been so cheerful about not getting laid," Natalie said. "You're scaring me, Ev."

"It will all happen in due time. We kissed," Everett said. "And it was amazing. *She's* amazing. She's beautiful and she's funny and she understands the show and—"

"Of course he brings it back to the show," Natalie muttered to Lillian.

Lillian elbowed her. "Shush. Let the man emote. We need to encourage straight men to share their feelings; that would solve, like, ninety percent of the world's problems."

"See, Lillian gets it," Everett said.

Natalie pointed at him. "This is Everett we're talking about. His entire career is built on feelings."

Everett took another bite. "I like her. That's all. She's . . ." He paused. "She's really lovely."

"Sounds like someone's in looooove!" Lillian called out, grabbing a chocolate-iced donut.

"Just be careful, Ev," Natalie said, narrowing her eyes.

Everett stopped chewing. "What's that supposed to mean?"

Natalie looked at her plate. "It means I know how you are. I know you get obsessed and you run those obsessions into the ground. The way I see it, this goes one of two ways. You fall head over heels for her—"

"Which kind of looks like it's already happening," Lillian pointed out.

"Orrrrr you return to your safe, comfortable obsession—work— and hurt this poor girl's feelings when you duck your head back into the sand and she has to beg you to spend time with her."

"I'm not going to do that," Everett said. "Do you think I do that?"

Natalie and Lillian exchanged a quick glance, but it wasn't quick enough for Everett to miss it. "What?" he asked.

"You work a lot, Ev. You know that," Natalie said, pushing her food around with a fork and not meeting his eye. "Forget it. I shouldn't have said anything."

"I work a perfectly normal amount."

Natalie tilted her head, as if weighing whether she should keep going. "Your work tends to consume you. It's like the rest of the world falls away and you're on a different planet."

Everett nodded; that was what he liked about work. "I don't see why that's a problem."

"It's not a problem," Natalie said. "Most of the time. But sometimes you can forget about people, even if you care about them. Remember the surprise party you threw for my birthday last year?"

"Of course."

"That was so thoughtful and well planned," Natalie said. "You even got my mom there, and that lady hates to leave her house. I was truly surprised, and I felt so loved, and that was classic Ev."

"Right," Everett said. "That was a good party!"

"But . . . you were also an hour late," Natalie said. "To the party you organized."

Beside her, Lillian winced. Everett shot her a betrayed look, and she mouthed, *Sorry*.

"I didn't think you noticed that," Everett muttered. "I was tied up with something. It's hard to turn work off, you know?"

Natalie nodded. "I know, dude. But sometimes the people in your life need you to turn it off. Unless you want to be one of those eccentric geniuses who's been divorced fifteen times and lives in a giant mansion full of regret."

Everett shook his head. His parents had gotten married when

they were in college, and they'd stayed married for over thirty years. That was what he wanted: to do it once and get it right and know that the person he was with was the perfect fit. To build a family full of creativity and weirdness and obsession, to have a house full of fun and memories and tattered old furniture. He didn't know why he couldn't skip all the in-between stuff and get there. It would be so much easier to focus on work that way.

"I'm not going to live in a regret mansion," he said. "And I'm sorry about your party."

"You should be sorry you missed it," Lillian said. "Natalie's mom got sooo drunk."

"No, I was there in plenty of time to see Jill wasted," Everett said. "She was hilarious."

"Ugh," Natalie said. "Don't remind me again how much moms love you. I'm pretty sure mine has a crush on you and I don't want to think about it."

"I don't know," Everett said, pretending to contemplate it. "Jill's a confident, independent woman. I appreciate that."

"Ew, stop!"

Everett's eyes lit up. "I could be your stepdad!"

"EVERETT!" Natalie shouted as Lillian dissolved in laughter.

As Everett laughed, he pushed down the tiny stinging feeling that Natalie might be right. Maybe it was bad to spend so much time focused on work, even though it was often one of the few things in life that felt absolutely, perfectly, 100 percent right.

But now, he thought as he smiled to himself, he had something else that felt 100 percent right. He had Teddy.

41

Dear Teddy,

Just a quick note to say that, after much contemplation, I decided to print out your portrait of Shaq and hang it in my office (which is also a storage room).

Please see photo attached.

Gazing adoringly at Shaq,
Everett

. . . . . . . .

Dear Everett,

Thank you for supporting my art, although seeing it hung up on a wall really highlights the . . . shall we say, imperfections of the piece? I hope that Shaq himself never sees it or that, if he does, he isn't offended by a very lumpy depiction of his head.

And I have to ask . . . since you're in this picture, who's taking it?

Officially an artist,
Teddy

. . . . . . . .

Dear Teddy,

I asked my producer, Astrid, to take it. I'm not saying she fully understood what she was doing, but she went along with it.

Have you thought about turning this into a series? Maybe including other basketball greats? Jordan, Kobe, LeBron? I think it would make a great exhibition.

Your new agent,
Everett

. . . . . . . .

Dear Everett,

Only if that exhibition remains in the dark supply closet you call an office.

I didn't think it was possible for me to be more embarrassed than I was when I sent you that picture, but it turns out I can be! Knowing that your producer also saw it is mortifying.

But I suppose I can be convinced to create more paintings if the price is right.

A total sellout,
Teddy

. . . . . . . .

Dear Teddy,

What are you doing tomorrow afternoon? It's the perfect time to go to the zoo. Kids are in school, it's cold so no one else wants to be there, and you get a front-row seat to see the Mexican wolves running around.

Don't leave the wolves and me hanging,
Everett

. . . . . . .

Dear Everett,

Well, I wouldn't want to disappoint the wolves. They do need the company.

See you tomorrow,
Teddy

# 42

TEDDY ENDED UP HAVING A WONDERFUL AFTERNOON AT THE zoo with Everett. They had the place to themselves, and it turned out that the reptile house was a surprisingly romantic spot for a make-out session (it was probably the dim lighting and the sense of contained danger created by all the snakes behind glass).

It was a relatively quick date, though, because Teddy had dinner plans with Josie that evening. Josie lived in a beautiful old house in German Village, one that was small but full of windows and surrounded by lush gardens, which of course were all dead in the fall. When Teddy let herself in, Josie's three dogs bounded toward her. She'd stopped ringing the doorbell when Josie claimed it excited them, but Teddy didn't really see the difference—either way they jumped all over her.

Not that she minded. "Oh, hi, Ralph," she said, scratching the black-and-white mutt under his chin. Three tails thumped a comforting rhythm on the hardwood floor. "Maybe I need a dog."

"Most people do," Josie said, handing Teddy a glass of red wine. "But why stop at one when you can have three? That's my motto."

"Hear, hear," Teddy said, clinking glasses with Josie before taking a sip. Josie's wine was always fantastic, like everything in Josie's life. Teddy walked to the dining room table, passing through the slightly cluttered but not messy living room. There were piles of books on every surface, an abundance of throw pillows, and a crackling fire in the fireplace. The local classical station, Classical 101, played quietly through the speakers like it did every time she came over. And as she sat down at the table, she saw the beautiful cloth napkins Josie always set out.

Teddy sighed with pleasure. "I hope someday I have a house exactly like this one," she said wistfully as Josie sat down across from her.

Josie waved her off. "You mean a house covered in dog hair and full of book stacks that threaten to crush you at any moment? Here, have some wine-braised short ribs."

Teddy gladly took some, adding some mashed sweet potatoes flecked with nutmeg and a green salad topped with pepitas and feta. "You're such a good cook," Teddy said as she took her first bite.

"That's because I've had a whole lifetime to practice. Trust me, there were plenty of dud meals along the way. I once made a brisket that chipped John's tooth."

Teddy smiled as she chewed. "It's nice to know you haven't always been perfect."

Josie laughed. "Please. My life has been nothing but a series of humiliations and failures that eventually led to accidental success. Speaking of success, how are things going with your cute new fella?"

Teddy swallowed. "The fella is good. We made out at the zoo today."

Josie raised her eyebrows. "That's it? Making out?"

Teddy frowned and took another bite. "I think they have rules about going further than that at the zoo. It's a family establishment."

Josie smiled. "We both know I didn't mean at the zoo, but that's fine. A lady never kisses and tells. And anyway, I didn't ask you over here to grill you on your love life."

Josie's hands played with her napkin, and Teddy suddenly panicked. "Josie?" she asked, throat dry. "Is everything okay?"

Josie laughed. "Yes. I wanted to ask you something."

Teddy took a nervous sip of wine.

"You know, although I obviously don't look a day past thirty-
five, I'm not quite as young as I used to be."

"Rubbish," Teddy said. "You have the spirit of a teenager."

"And the bones of a seventy-year-old," Josie said. "It's becoming increasingly clear that I can't run the shop forever, nor do I want
to. I want time to finally read that ever-increasing book stack and to
work more on my welding. And to work more on getting Herbert
from welding class to pay attention to me."

Teddy was now so uneasy, she couldn't focus on Josie's lustful
welding comments. She felt dizzy and she didn't think it was only
because of the wine. "What are you saying? Are you closing the
shop?"

Josie shook her head vigorously, her messy gray bun bouncing.
"Absolutely not. But I wondered if you might like to take over."

She said it so casually, as if she was inquiring whether Teddy
might like to box up some of the leftover short ribs, that Teddy almost didn't realize what she'd asked.

"But . . . you run the shop," Teddy said slowly.

"Right." Josie smiled gently. "But perhaps it's time for me to
retire now, while I still have my health. Maybe I could finally do all
that traveling I've been talking about. You know, *Eat Pray Love*?"

"Why does everyone reference that book so often?" Teddy muttered.

"I prefer the movie," Josie said with a wave of her hand. "I've
always felt like I have a lot in common with that Julia Roberts.
Great hair, great teeth."

Teddy shook her head, eyes closed. "But, Josie . . . how could I take over the shop? I don't know the first thing about running a business."

"Well, neither did I when I started," Josie said. "But I learned, and you could, too. You're the perfect person to do it. You're incredibly responsible, you never take a day off, and I happen to like you quite a bit."

Teddy couldn't stop herself from beaming. Praise from Josie, although it was generously and frequently doled out, still made her feel like a dog having its ears scratched.

But . . . being the one in charge? "What about Carlos?"

"I thought about Carlos," Josie said, "but he's so young. I can't imagine he wants to saddle himself with a store."

"I don't know. This all sounds like too much."

Josie looked at Teddy for a moment, then threw her napkin on the table. "Didn't you say you wanted to do things that scared you? And haven't you been taking chances, learning new things, meeting new people?"

Teddy nodded.

"Take some time to think about it. Whether you tell me yes or no, I won't be hurt. But promise me that you won't turn this down because you're scared, okay?"

Teddy nodded again as she thought about it. Could she really own the business? If she ran Colossal Toys, no one could accuse her of wanting a small life or not having passion. You couldn't run a business if you weren't passionate about it, could you? And okay, so maybe she wouldn't describe her feelings toward vintage toys as "passionate" at the moment, but she could start at "vague interest" and move up to "passion," right?

But most important, if she had this job, then no one . . . not Richard, not her mom . . . could ever make her feel like she needed their help again. She'd be the one in charge.

Teddy bit her lip, thinking about the way she'd felt lately. Since she'd stood up there onstage at karaoke and looked out into the crowd, a little bit afraid but doing it, anyway. Since she'd gone out with Everett, even though she was terrified that he wouldn't like the real her, the one who wasn't sitting behind a computer screen and meticulously composing banter-y emails. She felt strong now, and bold, and . . . happy. She felt like a different person from the one she'd been with Richard, from the one she'd been for a very long time now.

"Okay," Teddy promised, looking up to meet Josie's gaze. "I'll think about it."

# 43

AFTER SHE LEFT JOSIE'S, TEDDY THOUGHT ABOUT GOING HOME and immediately telling the girls about her latest work development, but she needed a few minutes to herself.

She decided to check another item off her Teddy Time list by visiting a restaurant by herself. The restaurant in question was a place she'd been wanting to try forever but that Richard would never go to on account of the name was "too girlie": the Butterfly Café. She'd heard they had great pie, and she knew some dessert would help her think about Josie's proposition.

She kept her car parked in front of Josie's and walked down the brick sidewalk and into the café. Instantly, she knew she'd come to the right place—the walls were a bright yet soothing blue, and the air smelled like cumin, cinnamon, and peppers. A woman with blond milkmaid braids and bright pink lipstick was cleaning a table. *I'll bet she's never tried to hide behind anyone in her life,* Teddy thought.

"Oh, sorry," Teddy said. "Are you closed?"

"Almost!" the woman chirped. "But I can get you something quick!"

"I just want dessert," Teddy said, taking in the restaurant. No one was there except for one man in a baseball cap sitting beside the window.

"Perfect!" the hostess said, then escorted her right away to a small table, tucked in the corner against the exposed brick wall, right next to a framed painting of a multicolored bouquet.

"My name's Chloe, and I'll be taking care of you!" The woman frowned. "I mean . . . ugh, I hate it when people say that. 'I'll be taking care of you today.' But I will! Whatever you need! As long as it's food related!" She took a breath.

"I like your apron," Teddy said, pointing to the purple apron covered with embroidered flowers.

"Thanks!" Chloe smiled, taking out her notepad. "So what can I get you?"

Teddy stared at the menu, where the items all ran together. This was so much easier when she was with someone and could order what they told her to, or when they were at one of the few places Richard liked where she'd already memorized the menu (and where she ordered something Richard wanted, anyway, so he could steal a few bites off her plate).

But she was a new Teddy now. Bold. Sophisticated. Possibly a future small-business owner. She could take a chance.

And strangely enough, she already felt comfortable around Chloe, who seemed happy, secure, and like she had her life all figured out. "Surprise me," Teddy said.

Chloe looked up from her notepad. "You want me to bring you something random?"

Teddy nodded. "Yes. Is that . . . weird?"

Chloe smiled wide. "Sure, but I love it! This is a challenge, and I accept."

She stuck the notepad back into her apron pocket and headed to the kitchen without another word.

As a soundtrack of smooth and jazzy music played, Teddy pulled her laptop out of her bag and opened it up on the table, then typed "owning a business" into the search bar.

And "small-business taxes."

And "small-business failure rate."

And "how do I know if I really want to be a small-business owner because honestly it seems pretty stressful."

The last one didn't return many results, but as Teddy scrolled through her findings, her heart sank.

"Maybe I should try searching 'what if I want to take over my beloved boss's business primarily for emotional reasons, but I don't know much about business and don't particularly care to learn,'" Teddy muttered.

"Hey, now, no work allowed in the Butterfly Café!"

Teddy quickly snapped her laptop shut.

Chloe widened her eyes and set a glass down on the table. "I was kidding! Sort of. I'm trying to create, you know, a chill vibe here, one where people feel comfortable hanging out and talking, not where you feel like you have to be another cog in the capitalist machine."

"I wasn't working. I was . . . researching. I have a big decision to make." She took a sip of her drink.

"Ooh, a big decision!" Chloe wiggled her eyebrows and, to Teddy's surprise, pulled out the chair across from her and sat down. "I love big decisions. Tell me more."

Teddy nodded. Sure, she'd tell this complete stranger what was going on; it seemed less risky than talking about it with someone she knew. "Well, my boss just asked me to take over her business. And I love my boss. I mean, I respect her, I idolize her, I want to be her. So of course it would make sense to take over her store."

Chloe gestured around them. "Sure. Small businesses are the backbone of society."

"Did you know," called the man in the corner wearing a baseball cap, "that for every dollar you spend at a small business, sixty-seven cents goes back into the community?"

Chloe turned to look at him. "Yes, Gary, I did know that, because I wrote it on the sign by the window. But thank you for reminding me."

Gary tipped his hat at them and went back to his book.

"So what's the issue?" Chloe asked.

Teddy sighed. "I don't know the first thing about running a business. Business ownership has never been a dream of mine, you know? But I don't even know what my dream is. Maybe I do want to run a business. Maybe the problem is that I just didn't believe in myself enough before to even consider that I could run a business. But now my life's starting to get back on track. I'm not with Richard anymore, I'm doing things that scare me, I've started dating Everett, and I didn't even tell you I started sewing!"

"Okay, wow, a lot to unpack here," Chloe said, placing her hands on the table. "I don't know who Richard is, but I hate him. Boo. He sucks."

Teddy nodded. "Everyone hates him."

"Great. So what about this Everett guy? Is he your boyfriend?"

Teddy thought about it. "No. Or maybe not yet. We made out at the zoo, if that matters."

"A promising step," Chloe said thoughtfully.

"Hey, are you planning on picking up this order or what?" came a voice from the kitchen. They looked over to see a man pointing to the plate in the window between the kitchen and the café.

"Nick, I am busy having an emotional discussion with a customer!" Chloe yelled, and the man gave her an exasperated look before disappearing into the kitchen.

Chloe nodded toward the kitchen. "That's my boyfriend. I know he acts like he finds me annoying, but he's actually obsessed with me."

Even in the brief moment she'd seen him, Teddy could tell that. It was in the way he looked at Chloe, like she was all that he could see and all that he cared about. Richard had never looked at Teddy like that. But Everett did.

"Listen," Chloe said, standing up. "We may not know each other well, on account of we just met, but I can already tell you deserve good things. I mean, look at you: all cute in your dress with your adorable haircut. You look like you're about to burst into song or convene with some woodland creatures or something."

"You're not the first person to say that," Teddy said.

"You should go for what you want, but whatever it is—a job, a business, a guy, a passion, whatever—you should make sure it's what *you* want, not what someone else wants for you."

Chloe walked over to the kitchen, grabbed a plate, and plunked a slice of pie in front of Teddy. "Here. Chocolate pie to go with your hibiscus tea."

"Thank you," Teddy said, genuinely touched. "And thank you for talking to me for so long."

Chloe waved her off. "I work here precisely so I can do things like have extended conversations with customers about their personal dilemmas. Anyway, enjoy your pie!"

After Chloe was back in the kitchen, Teddy didn't bother opening her laptop again. Instead, she took a bite of her pie, which was quite possibly the best pie she'd ever had in her life. *And to think,* Teddy marveled, *I never even would have had this—the pie or the conversation—if I'd been too scared to be by myself.*

When she was finished eating, she left her money on the table and packed up. She waved to Chloe, who was now at the hostess stand, as she left.

"Godspeed, young traveler!" Gary said from his corner table, and Teddy couldn't help but smile as she walked out the door and along the brick sidewalk. Okay, so she still didn't know exactly what to do about taking over Colossal Toys. After a lifetime of ignoring her own feelings, she needed more than one encouraging conversation to make such a big decision. But she'd been honest with someone, and she'd been at least a little bit bold. But even better? She'd gone to a new restaurant all by herself, and she'd had a wonderful time. *Eat at a restaurant by myself and have an emotionally vulnerable conversation with a complete stranger?* Check and check.

44

Dear Teddy,

I know we just hung out yesterday, and that this is scandalously late notice, but what are you doing tonight? I won't suggest going to the zoo again, but perhaps we could recreate our actions from the zoo in various locations around the city. A PG-13 tour of Columbus, if you will.

To be honest, I wouldn't be upset if it veered into a hard-R-rated tour of Columbus, but I think that would rule out a lot of family-friendly locales.

Hopefully,
Everett

. . . . . . .

Dear Everett,

Could we ever really re-create the romantic magic of the reptile house in any other setting? It's worth finding out. Alas,

I'm having dinner at my mom's tonight. Trust me, I'd much rather be hanging out with you, on a Columbus tour of any rating. Although the fact that I have plans might be for the best. An R-rated tour sounds like the kind of thing that could get your show canceled.

Concerned about your career,
Teddy

. . . . . . . .

Dear Teddy,

You make a good point.

Enjoy dinner at your mom's!

See you soon,
Everett

## 45

TYPICALLY, DINNER AT HER MOTHER'S HOUSE FILLED TEDDY with a cocktail shaker's worth of contradictory feelings: love, resentment, shame, guilt. But tonight, as she climbed the wooden stairs of the porch, she hummed "Almost like Being in Love" to herself. Today, she was a straight shot of one feeling and one feeling only: she was completely and utterly smitten.

Just thinking about Everett now made Teddy want to swoon, literally. She wanted to pretend her mom's porch swing was a fainting couch and flop onto it, holding a hand to her forehead, and then ask someone to bring her a glass of water and gently fan her face. But she knew she couldn't share the details of her newfound romantic relationship with her family. It probably wasn't in her mother's detailed plans for her.

Instead, she knocked and walked on in.

"Why are you whistling?" asked Emma, who was walking down the stairs.

"Am I?" Teddy grinned. "I didn't know. Because I'm happy, I guess."

Emma studied her. "When I'm happy," she said, "I like to scream."

Teddy nodded. "That's certainly one way to handle it."

Emma sighed the heavy sigh of a small child. "Mom says don't. She said the neighbors will worry."

"Your mom might have a point," Teddy agreed. "Screaming does tend to upset people."

Emma hopped down the last few stairs. "Grandma made enchiladas. I don't like enchiladas. Once Liam ate too much of them and then he threw up on the rug in the hallway and Daddy had to clean it up. Also once I threw up after I ate too many Popsicles and the throw-up was bright blue."

"Wow," Teddy said. "I can see why that might put you off enchiladas for a while."

Teddy was learning, through her niece and nephew, that the best way to talk to children was often to step back and let them steer, while occasionally asking a question or two.

"Come on," Emma said, grabbing Teddy's hand. "I got a new pony."

"Okay!" Teddy let Emma drag her into the living room, where, true to her word, there was a glittery pink pony next to all of Emma's other ponies.

Teddy sat down on the floor, tucking her feet underneath her. "Is this a unicorn?"

"No," Emma said, squinting at her. "It doesn't have a horn. See? Unicorns have horns."

"Ah, right," Teddy said. "I don't know how I forgot that. I'm pretty silly, I guess."

"You *are* silly," Emma muttered, now focused on combing her horse's hair.

"You're here!" Teddy's mother emerged from the kitchen, drying her hands on a dish towel. "I like your dress. You hungry?"

"Literally always," Teddy said.

When all of them were seated around the table, Teddy noticed

that her sister kept staring at her. After her fifth time looking up and meeting her eyes, Teddy asked, "What?"

"Something's different about you," Sophia said, eyes narrowed.

"I have a new lipstick," Teddy said, taking a bite. "Berry Crush."

"You look nice in berry shades," her mother said. "Not me. They make the veins in my face visible. I put on a berry lipstick, and boom, my face looks all blue. How are the enchiladas?"

"They're great, and I don't think that's true," Teddy said.

"Craig," Sophia said, "don't you think there's something different about Teddy?"

"Make sure you take some with you," her mother said. "I'll never eat all these enchiladas by myself."

Craig stopped shoveling enchiladas in his mouth long enough to peer over at Teddy. "The, uh . . . the, um . . . Is your hair a different color?"

"No, Craig," Teddy said, suppressing a smile. "My hair is the same color it's been since I was born."

"I mean, like"—Sophia waved her hand, frustrated—"your attitude. You're sitting up straight and smiling."

"She's whistling," Emma said. "I wish I could whistle. I can only scream."

"No screaming at the table," Craig and Sophia said at the same time.

"Are you on a new supplement or something?" Sophia asked once it was clear that Emma wasn't about to start screaming. "Vitamin D? I hear it's great for you."

"Um . . ." Teddy looked around the table. Her mother and Sophia were staring at her. Liam was picking his nose. Emma was hiding tomatoes under a napkin. Craig was eating as if someone might pull his plate away at any moment.

Of course she was different. She felt different. She'd kissed Everett

St. James multiple times, once near dangerous reptiles, and now all she could think about was kissing him again.

But she didn't want to tell her family that. It all felt too private. So instead, she found unexpected words coming out of her mouth.

"Well, actually . . . I'm taking over Colossal Toys. Josie's retiring and she wants me to be the new owner."

Her mother put down her fork and stared, openmouthed. "Teddy! This is great news!"

"Wow," Sophia said, but she didn't sound excited. She stared at Teddy as if she could read her thoughts.

"It is great news," Teddy said, looking at Sophia.

"This is amazing," her mother said, looking at Teddy as if she'd just announced she was the recipient of a MacArthur Fellowship. "Teddy, I'm so proud of you for stepping up and taking over."

"Yeah, well." Teddy twirled her fork in the air and lightly said, "I guess I am pretty amazing."

Her mother shook her head in wonder. "Look at my girls. All grown-up and taking over the world. A lawyer and a business owner. You know, when you're a single parent, sometimes you worry . . ."

Teddy's mom paused, dabbing at her eyes with her napkin. *Oh, no,* Teddy thought. Her mother was one of those people who rarely slowed down, but if she ever had the opportunity to think for a moment and get in her feelings (like if, for example, she heard a Mariah Carey song on the local easy-listening radio station), she could have a weepy sob fest with the best of them. And Teddy was afraid one of them was coming on right now.

"You worry that you can't help your kids all on your own. And it's hard to do it alone. I hope the two of you never have to find out."

Teddy's mother shot a glance at Sophia, who frowned. "I'm pretty sure Craig's not going anywhere. Craig, are you planning on leaving the family?"

"Nope!" Craig said cheerfully through a mouthful of rice. Honestly, Teddy admired Craig's ability to take her family's conversations in stride. Perhaps she should strive to be so unbothered.

Teddy's mom turned to look back at her, and Teddy waited a moment before realizing what her mother was asking. "No, Mom, I don't have immediate plans to become a single parent. I'm not pregnant. Look at me. I'm drinking wine."

"You've had, like, two sips," Craig said. "Pretty sure pregnant people can have that much."

"How would you know, Craig?" Teddy asked.

He shrugged. "I read a headline. I don't know. Don't quote me on it."

"I won't," Teddy muttered, then tipped her glass back to take a dramatic swig while staring at him.

"All I'm saying," her mother continued, "is that there are a lot of people in the world who will make a single mom feel like she's doing something wrong or like she's already screwed up before she's even begun. But you two are proof that I did an okay job. My two girls, taking over the world."

Teddy smiled with her lips closed. It was hard to muster a real smile when what she'd told her mother was a lie. Well, not necessarily a lie. She *might* take over the shop; after all, she loved Josie, and she wanted to make her happy. But did she really want to run a vintage toy store for the foreseeable future?

She wasn't so sure.

But it had taken only one sentence to make her mother happy, so she was glad she'd said it. And she could still do it! Maybe. Probably. She'd talk to Josie about it soon.

"A toast," Teddy's mother said. "To my two beautiful, amazing, successful daughters. Don't forget to take some food home with you."

They all raised their wineglasses (except for the kids, who raised their juice cups), and Teddy smiled as she tried to ignore the feeling in the pit of her stomach that something was deeply, deeply wrong.

## 46

"WHAT DO YOU THINK OF THIS?" EVERETT ASKED JEREMY, holding up a puppet.

Jeremy squinted. "Needs something."

This was why Everett loved working with Jeremy; Everett had known him for so long and they'd worked together on so many things that Jeremy didn't feel the need to sugarcoat his thoughts. If Jeremy thought what Everett was working on wasn't good enough, he'd tell him, not give him the news in a compliment sandwich.

"But what?" Everett asked, growing frustrated. "I don't like the part of having an idea that involves working on the wrong thing until a good idea deigns to appear. Why do I have to keep trying out new ways to make this puppet look right? Why can't I find out be- - fore cycling through five hundred incorrect options?"

"You know what you could do," Jeremy said. "You could . . . go with it. Accept that puppet as it is. Done is better than perfect."

They laughed. Both of them knew that Everett's philosophy was "it's not done *until* it's perfect."

"Do you think it needs different hair? Should I make the eyes farther apart?" Everett held the puppet out and stared at her.

"You need something, but I'm not sure what. I'll know it when I see it," Jeremy said.

"Same here," Everett said with a sigh. "Well, thanks for the help."

"Anytime," Jeremy said, and walked out of the office with a wave.

Everett stared deep into the puppet's unblinking eyes. "What do you need?" he asked. "What will make you feel real?"

He moved the puppet's mouth, and in a garish, high-pitched voice, he squeaked, "A sooouuuullllll!"

He leaned back in his chair, staring at the ceiling. "I'm losing it."

"Yep."

He spun his chair around to see Astrid leaning in the doorway.

"How do you always sneak up on me?" he asked. "You must have the quietest shoes in the world. Your footfalls are silent."

"Yes, I buy my shoes specifically for the purpose of surprising you," she said. "Have a minute?"

"For you, I have as many as five."

"Great. Listen, I heard from the Imagination Network."

Everett sat up straight.

"They want to fly us out to New York in two weeks," she said. "To tour the studio and meet with the president and the VP."

Everett's mouth dropped open. "Are you . . . are you kidding?"

"No. I already hit my joke allotment for the year," Astrid said, looking down at her clipboard and marking something. Everett could only imagine that she'd checked "give Everett news that will completely change his life" off her list.

Everett sat back and ran a hand through his hair. "I can't believe this. Our show could be with the Imagination Network. We could be working in New York, Astrid!"

"Well, *you* could," Astrid said, scribbling something on her clipboard.

"Wait, what?" Everett asked. "You're not coming with me?"

"In two weeks? Of course." She crossed the room and sat down in the chair across from him. "But if the show gets picked up? Well, my contract is here with the station."

"But you wouldn't want to get a new job?" Everett asked. "I know they'd want you with me. You're essential to the show!"

"Thank you for recognizing my brilliance, but I work on other shows here, Ev. You know that. And do you expect me to move my partner and my kid to New York for a new job?"

Everett stared at her.

"Okay." She smiled. "So you do expect that. Not everyone's like you, Everett. You know that, right?"

"What do you mean, not everyone's like me?" he asked.

"I mean not everyone puts work first, and second, and third with the rest of their life a distant hundred-and-fiftieth place. I know that this is all you care about, but it's not all *I* care about. I love the show, and I love my job, and I suppose that, in some strange way, I love you, too. But I have my own life."

"This isn't all I care about," Everett said. "I care about work a perfectly normal amount."

Astrid nodded. "Sure. But someday I hope you figure out that just because your name's in the title, that doesn't mean the show has to be your whole life."

She got up and walked toward the door. "Just be ready for the meeting. I know you will."

"I sure will," Everett muttered as Astrid walked away (or at least he assumed she did; as usual, he couldn't hear her footsteps).

He pulled out his phone and sent an SOS text to Jeremy, who showed up about ten seconds later. "Did you figure out the puppet?" Jeremy asked, sitting down.

"This isn't about the puppet," Everett said quickly. "Do I only talk about puppets?"

Jeremy frowned. "Well . . . define 'only.'"

"We talk about life sometimes! Don't we? Didn't we recently talk about what we had for dinner last night?"

Jeremy nodded slowly. "Can I ask where this is going?"

Everett leaned forward and cradled his head in his hands. "Am I a bad friend?"

"No! Do you remember the time the station wanted to cut my salary and not yours? You threatened to quit unless they promised not to pay me less," Jeremy said. "That was being a good friend. Or what about the time you came to my daughter's birthday party in character and Marzipan attacked one of your puppets? You didn't even get mad."

"Marzipan is surprisingly vicious for her size," Everett said, referring to Jeremy's Chihuahua. In fact, the puppet had been on his hand when Marzipan attacked and it had been a real beast to clean blood out of the felt, but he hadn't mentioned that to Jeremy.

"I know you care about our friendship in your own way," Jeremy said.

Everett paused. "In my own way?"

Jeremy thought for a moment as if choosing his words. "You're . . . focused on your work. Which is good. The show wouldn't be what it is if you didn't care about it so much."

"But do I care about anything else?" Everett asked. "Does everyone else think I'm some sort of workaholic robot who doesn't invest in human relationships?"

"No one thinks that," Jeremy reassured him. "But some people do think you live in the studio. The other day, an intern asked me if you slept on the couch."

"Why would I sleep on the couch? I have a home!" Everett said.

"But you're here a lot," Jeremy said. "You're here when people come in, and you're here when they leave."

"My name is in the title!" Everett sat back in his chair so hard that it rolled across the floor and bumped into a file cabinet. "I have to work this hard because if it's shitty, it has my name on it!"

"Is this a random outburst? A midlife crisis?"

"I'm not midlife," Everett said.

"Any one of us could be midlife," Jeremy pointed out. "We don't know."

"Okay, so I haven't mentioned this yet because I didn't know if anything was going to happen, but . . . the Imagination Network is interested in the show, and Astrid and I are gonna fly to their studio to meet with the big shots."

Jeremy raised his eyebrows. "So what would that mean?"

"Well, if it goes well . . . they want to buy the show. Which would mean we'd be working at their studio in the city."

"Hmm."

"So . . . what do you think about that? You'd come with me, right?" Everett asked, leaning forward on his elbows.

"Well . . . ," Jeremy started, "it's not that I don't want to, Ev. You know I love the show. But my kids are in school here, and Tess's parents are getting older and they need us around. Also I've got that huge aquarium. You think it's easy to move saltwater fish? Because let me tell you, it is not. They're easily stressed."

"But . . . you've been with me from the beginning. I know it's my name, but this is *our* show."

"I know," Jeremy said. "And if the show was here . . . well, I'd keep working on *Everett's Place* until I die. You'd have to bury me in the studio."

"Seems like your family might have some objections to that," Everett muttered.

"But if the show ends up leaving, I don't think I could come with it. I'm sorry. Hopefully I'll be able to get a job on another show at the station," Jeremy said, concern flickering across his face for just a moment.

Everett's eyes widened. "You think I could leave you here without a job? No way. I can't imagine doing the show without you. Without you to give him his sassy personality, Larry the Llama would be a shell of himself. What, am I supposed to work with some other puppeteer? Am I supposed to have a conversation with someone else's hand shoved up Larry? It's not right."

Jeremy shook his head. "You don't need to worry about me, Ev. Do I wish things could go on the way they are forever? Sure. But you have to think about what's best for the show. Maybe it's just the end of an era."

"No." Everett pointed at him. "Not yet. We don't know what the Imagination Network is gonna say. Maybe they'll meet us and decide to pass."

"Nah," Jeremy said with a smile that looked more sad than happy. "They're not gonna pass. No one ever passes on your ideas."

"But I don't want to do this show without you!" Everett said, starting to feel a little frantic. "Maybe you could convince your entire family to move. There's gotta be a safe way to move that fish tank. Money is no object. We could do that thing where we lift up your house and put it on a truck and move it, like in *The Little House*. That sounds feasible, right?"

"Ev." Jeremy shook his head, smiling. "See? You are a good friend. Really. And I know that however things end up, you'll make a good show. You always do."

Jeremy patted him on the head before he left, which made Everett feel a little like a confused and petulant baby. Was it really so wrong to want his friends to make the show their number one priority, too?

Well, okay, so he knew it was. He knew he was being unreasonable, but that didn't change the way he felt. That was the annoying thing about feelings: just because you accepted them, it didn't mean they went away. They were still *there*, clouding his judgment and making him feel irrational.

He put his hand back in the new puppet and held it up. "What should I do?" he asked, but the puppet didn't answer, because she wasn't anybody yet.

He knew that other people didn't understand what he was waiting on. They didn't get why he couldn't glue some eyes on a piece of felt and consider the job done. But it wasn't like that; he'd never worked like that, and he didn't *want* to. He needed the puppet to feel real, to seem like it was a creature outside of himself, to look like a foreign object, not something that came from his own mind and hands. He couldn't fake the element of surprise when he talked to the puppets on camera; he needed to be genuinely surprised, as if he were talking to someone who might say something he didn't expect, not just himself or Jeremy saying the lines he'd already written.

"Half-assing it" simply wasn't part of his vocabulary. Kids would spend their entire lives encountering adults who were half-assing jobs that deserved their full attention. He wasn't going to be another one. After all, didn't he always tell kids that all they had to do was try their best and be kind? What sort of an example would he be if he wasn't giving it his all?

He sighed. Maybe the puppet needed a new nose. Or maybe he'd move the eyes again. Something had to work.

But for the first time he could remember, Everett didn't want to keep working until the middle of the night until he figured it out. He didn't want to sit here by himself and stare at a soulless puppet. He wanted to see another person.

He wanted to see Teddy.

47

THE OPENING NOTES OF "CHRISTMAS WRAPPING" BY THE WAIT-resses started to play, and Teddy looked toward the speakers in confusion.

"Josie?" she called over the sound of jingle bells. "Have we time traveled?"

"What?" Josie asked, poking her head around an aisle, where she was organizing some action figures.

Teddy pointed to the speaker. "The Christmas music. You never start this early. It's not Thanksgiving yet."

Josie walked to the counter and sighed. "Teddy. Darling. I made the mistake of turning on the news today. Have you ever watched cable news?"

Teddy shook her head. "That's what the Internet is for. I get notifications on my phone if something important happens."

"Well, don't start watching it now. Because five minutes of twenty-four-seven news coverage will convince even an optimist like me that the world is in the shitter. It's a mess out there, apparently," Josie said, pointing toward the street as if danger lurked right outside the shop door. "And now I can't think about anything other than the fact that the world is full of sad, heartbroken, and lonely people. It's enough to really bring a person down. I had to turn to

Christmas music to make myself feel better, because Christmas music makes *everyone* feel better."

Teddy tilted her head. "I mean, it certainly makes me feel better. I love this song. But that can't be true for everyone. What about people who don't celebrate Christmas? Or people who get mad about Christmas music being played too early? Carlos?"

He looked up from his comic.

"Your thoughts on Christmas music?" Teddy asked.

"I listen to it on December twenty-fifth," he said, then returned his gaze to his comic.

Teddy and Josie looked at each other, mouths agape. "There's a wealth of beautiful, joyous, jingle-bell-filled music out there and you restrict your listening to *one day*?" Josie asked, incredulous.

Carlos nodded without looking up.

Teddy shook her head. "That feels like a personal insult to Mariah Carey."

"Sorry, sugar, but I'm gonna keep playing it in the store whenever the spirit moves me," Josie said to Carlos.

He shrugged, seeming genuinely unbothered. "Your store, your rules."

Teddy's phone buzzed just as a customer walked in, and she checked it as Josie greeted them.

I know text messages are a callous, unromantic, and frankly just plain boring medium. But I didn't want to risk you not seeing an email in time. When do you get off work? Want to take a walk?

Teddy smiled. *Twenty minutes and yes*, she texted back.

The door swung open again and Everett walked in.

Teddy stood up straight. "That was fast."

"Yeah." Everett ran a hand through his hair, leaving it standing straight up. "I was in the neighborhood. Full disclosure, I was outside when I texted and—I don't know—I didn't want to wait. But now that I'm in here, I can see that that was the wrong impulse. Uh, Josie? Anything I can help out with? Anything need . . . dusting?"

He turned to Josie, who was staring at him with an amused expression. "You want to dust?"

"I'm here for the next twenty minutes. I might as well make myself useful," Everett said.

"Have you met Carlos?" Josie asked, ushering Everett toward the counter.

"Not officially, and only in costume," Everett said, holding out his hand.

"Nice to meet you," Carlos said politely, shaking Everett's hand before returning to his book.

"Don't bother him when he's reading," Josie stage-whispered. "You'll learn. Anyway, you two don't need to hang around here. We're almost closed, anyway."

"Josie, you're a good woman," Everett said, then turned to Teddy. She couldn't miss the way his eyes changed when they were on her; they were softer and brighter in a way that made her entire body feel warm and cold at the same time. She blushed.

"Ready?" Everett asked, and she could only hope he couldn't read her thoughts.

Josie might have been right. In fact, she certainly was. The world was full of sad, heartbroken, and lonely people. Pain was everywhere. But at that moment, as Christmas music played in November and Everett St. James smiled at her, Teddy didn't feel even the slightest bit sad, heartbroken, or lonely. She felt happy and hopeful and whole. *The world is definitely not in the shitter,* she thought to herself as she smiled.

"SO WHERE ARE we going?" Teddy asked as they walked down the sidewalk, pulling her purple peacoat tighter against the wind. She regretted her hat choice, a little black beret-type thing that had feathers sticking out of it. It had seemed charming and chic when she saw it in the store, and Eleanor and Kirsten had been very encouraging, but now that she was wearing it out with a man, she felt insecure. Perhaps plumage didn't belong on dates, but it was too late now.

Everett smiled crookedly. "That's the beauty of a walk, isn't it? You don't have to *go* anywhere. You get to enjoy each other's company."

Teddy couldn't argue with that, as she was presently enjoying Everett's company and the olive green military-style jacket he was wearing. The jacket, combined with the slightest bit of scruff on his chin (he was always clean-shaven on the show), made him look both familiar and excitingly foreign, like walking into your own living room to find the furniture rearranged.

They came to a crosswalk. "Let's cross here," Everett said as he took Teddy's hand. He nodded toward their entwined fingers. "Safety first."

"Right." Teddy swallowed. "The buddy system. Without someone holding me back, I just might run into traffic."

"You look like a daredevil," Everett said, and Teddy stifled a laugh.

"What?" Everett asked as the white WALK sign flashed and they darted across the street.

"I'm many things," Teddy said as they stepped up onto the sidewalk. "But a daredevil isn't one of them. Not now, anyway. I was quite a brave little child, once upon a time."

Teddy winced. Babbling. Word vomit. Verbal diarrhea. Whatever disgusting euphemism you wanted to use, that was what was currently pouring out of her mouth.

"So what changed?" Everett asked as they walked past town houses, away from High Street.

"I don't know. I did, I guess. You get older and figure out that taking a chance can lead to getting hurt or hurting someone else." She looked at Everett. "Or maybe you didn't have that experience."

"I think you seem pretty brave," Everett said. "It was brave to send me an email, right?"

"Is it brave or is it weird to send an email about my personal problems to the host of a children's television show?"

"Well, either way, weird or brave"—Everett squeezed her hand—"I'm glad you did it."

"Me, too," Teddy said quietly, and then she noticed that they were walking into Goodale Park.

"I love this park," she said. "Sometimes Josie and I have lunch or ice cream in front of the fountain."

"My parents live right over there," Everett said, pointing in their general direction. "I grew up basically thinking this was my yard. And then when I got older, this is where I took Gretel for walks when she was fussy. Just popped her into that stroller and walked her until she fell asleep."

Teddy couldn't help smiling at the thought of Everett pushing a stroller. "It's no wonder you're good with kids. You had a lot of practice."

"Yes and no. In a lot of ways, Gretel was never really a kid, you know?" He appeared to think for a moment. "Or I guess she's a kid on the inside, but she's always done a better job of hiding it than most kids."

"I can see that," Teddy said as a little boy on a scooter stopped right in front of them.

"Are you Everett?" he asked.

Everett smiled, and Teddy was pleased to see once again that his professional smile looked just like his personal smile. Everett on

TV was the same person as Everett in real life, because Everett only knew how to be himself. He wasn't trying to impress anyone, and he wasn't flexing in front of Teddy, making sure she knew how important he was, the way Richard had when he was with his doctor friends.

"I am! What's your name?" Everett asked, getting down on one knee.

"Nathan," said the kid. "I didn't know you came to the park. I thought you stayed in your house on the TV."

Everett didn't even laugh; instead, he nodded and said, "I love coming to the park! The house you see on the television is just my TV house, where we can all hang out during the show. I live in a real home, just like you."

Nathan nodded, and that was when Teddy noticed the visibly flustered woman standing behind him.

"Oh, wow, this is . . . like a celebrity sighting!" she said with a laugh. "We watch your show every day!"

"Thank you!" Everett said, standing up. "It's so nice to meet you both!"

"Oh," the mom said with a shocked exhalation, "you are . . . tall. You can't tell that on TV."

"Nathan," Everett said, focusing on the boy, "I'm glad you're wearing a helmet on your scooter. Gotta keep that big brain safe, right?"

"That's what Mom says," Nathan agreed.

"Well, your mom's a smart woman," Everett said, and Teddy could swear the woman looked like she was about to faint.

"Okay," Nathan said, losing interest. "We're gonna go get hot chocolate. I'll see you in your TV house."

"Bye, Nathan!" Everett said, waving as the boy scooted away. He nodded at Nathan's mom, who tucked her hair behind her ears and stealthily looked Everett up and down.

"Uh, wow," Teddy said once they were out of earshot.

"What?" Everett asked, taking her hand again.

"I never thought I'd see a message board mom come to life," Teddy said, shaking her head in wonder.

Everett frowned. "Really? All she said was that I was tall. That's an indisputable fact."

"It was the way she said it," Teddy said. "There was a lot of subtext in that indisputable fact. What she said was 'You're tall,' but the unspoken part was 'like a tree I'd love to climb.'"

Everett threw his head back and laughed, that unselfconscious, unbridled laugh that made Teddy's whole body shimmer like a disco ball. "That was not what I heard. I think this one might be on you. You might just have an incredibly dirty mind, assigning sexual-tree subtext to a woman who was simply noting my height."

Teddy shrugged. "All I'm saying is, maybe next time you ought to play to your mom audience a bit more when you meet a fan. Shake her hand. Compliment her hair. Give her one of those Everett St. James smiles."

They stopped walking and sat down on a bench by the pond, where they could watch the elephants on the fountain shoot water out of their trunks. "Teddy, are you suggesting that my success is merely a product of my devastating good looks and not a combination of talent and hard work?"

"Yes." Teddy nodded. "You're all style, no substance. But what can I say? It makes me feel good to have some eye candy on my arm."

Everett laughed.

"Okay, can I be serious for a second?" Teddy asked.

"Thank you for admitting you weren't being serious before," Everett said. "I think my feelings were about to get hurt."

"How often does that happen?"

"You mean, getting recognized?"

Teddy nodded.

Everett shook his head. "Not every day or anything. Most people I run into over the course of the day don't watch local children's television, you know? But every once in a while, a kid knows who I am."

"Wow," Teddy said. "That must make you feel amazing, to have someone run up to you just to tell you that you're awesome."

Everett shook his head. "Believe it or not, children usually don't tell me I'm awesome. Most of the time they want to tell me long, involved stories about their pets or their imaginary friends. And anyway, I don't want them to tell me I'm awesome. That's not the point of doing the show."

"What is the point of doing the show, then?" Teddy asked.

"I think . . . ," Everett said, staring at the water. "I think we all have a calling. I know that sounds like I'm speaking from a spiritual place, and you can look at it that way, but that's not what I mean. I just think that all of us have a way we can best help the world, you know? Everyone has a gift. And as much as I might wish I could be—I don't know—a doctor who saves lives, the truth is that I'd be a pretty shitty doctor. I don't like blood and I don't like hospitals and I can get distracted, so I'd probably take out the wrong organ when doing an appendectomy."

Teddy laughed.

"But I *am* good with kids, and I'm good at being on television, and when I do those things, I can help the most people. For whatever reason, I can talk to kids and they listen to me. I can help kids understand their feelings and try to figure out what to do with them. I don't want to sound like I think my work is any more important than what other people do, because it's not. But it's *my* work, and it's all I can do, so I just . . . I don't know. I just do it. I guess that's the whole point."

Teddy watched him watching the fountain and thought about the nonchalant way he'd talked about his talents. The way he'd said

"I'm good at being on television" and managed not to make it sound like he was bragging . . . because he wasn't. It wasn't a measure of his importance or his worth, the way Richard used his career to justify everything he did and the way he treated other people.

Everett turned to look at Teddy and laughed. "Oh, no. Why are you looking at me like that? Am I being insufferably pretentious over here, talking about my *work*? You can tell me to shut up. Just say, 'Everett, please stop—'"

Teddy leaned over and pressed her mouth into his.

"Okay, this works, too," Everett muttered, pulling her to him.

Teddy put her hands on his face, feeling his warm skin under her fingers as the wind blew and cold air swirled around them. *We are in public,* she reminded her logical brain, but her logical brain responded with an out-of-office message. Her libido was steering the ship now, and it had charted a course for the land of public indecency.

She felt Everett's hand move farther up her thigh and her logical brain stepped back into the office. There could be viewers around. Children. Anyone.

"Wait. Stop," Teddy said, breathing hard.

Everett pulled back. "You're right. We're on a bench in a public park. We should stop."

"Can we go to your place?" Teddy asked, her hands still on his cheeks.

Everett blinked a few times. "I mean . . . yes. Yes, we absolutely can."

Teddy paused for a moment, trying to remember dating advice she'd read in an ancient issue of *Cosmo* when she was in high school and trying to act more like a normal girl. Most of it had been sex tips that were supremely irrelevant to her life back then, but there was one piece of advice she remembered: don't sleep with a man too soon.

"We can play Candy Land," she said forcefully.

Everett paused. "Is that . . . a euphemism? Because I don't understand it. Can I look it up on Urban Dictionary before I agree to anything?"

Teddy laughed. "The board game. I just bought it for my niece and nephew and it's in my car. I thought maybe we could give it a test drive."

"You know, I really like that you didn't suggest we watch a movie or have a drink. That's what everyone else would do. Let's play a childhood board game. Why the hell not?" He leaned forward and brushed the feathers on her hat. "I like this hat, too. It's cute."

"You don't think I look like a bird?" Teddy asked.

Everett thought about it for a moment. "Maybe a very sexy bird."

"I don't think birds can be sexy," Teddy said, standing up.

"I don't know. You ever see a flamingo? Legs for days," Everett said, grabbing her hand. "Let's go play some Candy Land."

## 48

AS IT TURNED OUT, CANDY LAND WASN'T EXACTLY THE THRILL-a-minute ride Teddy remembered from childhood. In fact, it could be more accurately described as boring.

But it could also be, she discovered, a hotbed of sexual tension, although that might have had more to do with who she was playing it with and less to do with the Crooked Old Peanut Brittle House.

"This is great, actually," Everett said, drawing a red card and moving his gingerbread man. "Damn. I'm stuck in a cherry pitfall until I draw another red."

Teddy pressed her lips together. Everett's dedication to playing Candy Land was admirable, and it made her like him more. But she was much more interested in studying the lines of his face than the moves on the board.

"What?" he asked, looking up. "It's your turn, and if you're trying to psych me out by giving me bedroom eyes, you're going to lose. I have an amazing poker face, and you'll never figure out my strategy."

Teddy laughed. "There is no strategy in Candy Land. It's all luck."

Everett cracked his knuckles. "That's what you think."

"Do you have any snacks?" Teddy asked. "I'm starving."

"This seems like a strategy to avoid losing to me, but I'm hungry, too, so okay," Everett said, standing up and walking to the kitchen. "Where do you stand on Bagel Bites?"

"It's a contentious issue, but I'm staunchly pro," Teddy said, following him into the kitchen.

"Great," Everett said, pulling them out of the freezer and putting them on a pan. "Because that's about the only food I have here."

Teddy looked around the kitchen. "I take it you don't cook a lot," Teddy said, noting the absence of any sort of equipment or stubborn tomato sauce stains on the counter. She also noticed that Everett hadn't been kidding earlier about his place being basic. Teddy looked over the half wall into the living room and saw a couch, a chair, curtains—all of the basic things a person needed to exist in a space. There was artwork on the walls—paintings that looked like they probably had some personal meaning, a bulletin board with all sorts of clippings tacked on—and a full bookshelf in the corner, but there wasn't a lot of *stuff*.

Everett smiled wryly. "The thing is, I like cooking. And I love eating. But I don't end up having a lot of time for either."

"You don't end up having a lot of time for eating?" Teddy asked. "I'm not sure I understand."

Everett leaned against the counter. "You know when you're really lost in work and you forget to eat two meals in a row?"

"No," Teddy said slowly. "That has never in my life happened. I can't even imagine a situation in which my growling stomach wouldn't be my number one priority."

As if it had been waiting for a sign to make its presence known, Teddy's stomach growled so loudly that Everett's eyes widened.

"See?" Teddy pointed to her stomach. "She's not some retiring wallflower. She makes her needs known."

"Okay, new plan," Everett said, pulling his phone out of his pocket. "That aggressive stomach growling means you're too hun-

gry for mere Bagel Bites. They're just the appetizers now. I'm ordering pizza."

"A pizza-based appetizer and a pizza main course? I like the
way you think," Teddy said, nodding approvingly.

They ordered an almond pesto pizza and a fennel sausage pizza
from Harvest Pizzeria, and by the time they arrived, Teddy had already had one glass of wine on an empty stomach and was feeling
pleasantly loose-limbed. She loaded up her plate and sat on one end
of the couch, while Everett sat on the other. She crossed her legs
and faced him, propping her plate on her lap.

"So," she said, taking a bite. "Oh, geez, this is good. So what
made you decide to get into puppets?"

Everett winced, chewed, and swallowed. "When you say it that
way—*into puppets*—it sounds like a fetish."

Teddy laughed. "Okay. Uh . . . what prompted your interest in
puppetry?"

"Better. I guess . . . television. Jim Henson. I was obsessed with
the Muppets as a kid, at the way he could use these sometimes goofy-
looking animals to relay complex things. The way they seemed human, even though I logically knew they weren't. And Mr. Rogers,
who was weird in a different way, but weird all the same. That bra-
zen, open, earnest trust and love of children? The ability to talk to
them and relate to them on their level, the way he could use puppets
to explain concepts like divorce and war, all while never talking
down to kids or dismissing their feelings? That was what I admired."

Teddy stared at him, then grabbed another piece of pizza. Two
feelings fought each other to the death inside of her. First was her
sheer attraction to Everett and the way he lit up when he talked
about feelings in a way that no man in her life ever had—not her
dad, wherever he was. Certainly not Richard. None of her teachers
or relatives, all of them models of male stoicism who thought that
admitting a feeling was the same thing as admitting failure.

But then there was another, less admirable feeling, one snaking its way through her guts. Jealousy that Everett had always known what he wanted to do, that he'd had a clear path since he was a child. Well, maybe not a clear path—he'd had to whack away some overgrown brush to get to his destination, but at least he knew a path was there. Teddy felt like she'd been born in the middle of a forest, nothing but trees everywhere blocking out the light, stumbling around and trying to figure out where to go.

"What's that like?" she asked softly. "Always knowing what you want to do. Having a passion."

"I don't know," Everett said simply. "This is the only way I've ever been."

Teddy sighed. "I wish I was like that. I wish I had neon lights and a big blinking arrow pointing toward my life's purpose."

Everett smiled and put his pizza plate on the coffee table. "But isn't this more exciting?"

Teddy blinked. "In what way?"

"Well, for us freaks who've been pursuing the same thing since infancy, there isn't any room for exploration. I always knew I wanted to be a puppeteer, and I wanted my own show. So my whole life was dedicated to that, and either I succeeded or I failed. With you . . . well, every new thing you try can be a success, you know? Who's to say what's a failure?"

Teddy smiled. "That's a nice way of thinking about it. But what do you mean, no room for exploration?"

Everett leaned back and looked at the ceiling. "This sounds ungrateful. And maybe a little pretentious. Okay?"

"Okay," Teddy said slowly.

"I've never tried anything else," Everett said. "This has always been what I'm good at, so this is always what I've done. And I worked and worked for this, every step leading me toward my own show, and then when I got it, toward making the show the best thing it could be, the ideal version that was in my head. But now that I have it . . . where do I go? I got exactly what I wanted, but I have this strange, empty feeling inside me, like this isn't enough, but I don't know why."

Teddy chewed thoughtfully. "What would be bigger than having your own show?"

"Well," Everett said, crossing his arms behind his head. "Having my own *national* show. I have a meeting with the Imagination Network coming up."

When Teddy kept chewing without reacting, he smiled. "I always forget that not everyone is obsessed with the same things I'm obsessed with. They're basically the biggest possible deal when it comes to children's entertainment. Think Disney."

Teddy nodded. "Yes. Disney. That name, I know. So do you want to make your show with them?"

Everett paused, his brow knitted. "Well, yeah. I mean, doesn't everyone?"

"I'm not the person to ask."

"I can't really go anywhere else from here. There's no higher place to take the show than the Imagination Network."

"What if," Teddy said, extending her arm, "instead of going vertically . . . you explore laterally."

Now it was Everett's turn to stare at her.

"I'm sorry." She grimaced. "I had one glass of wine and I'm giving out unsolicited, unqualified advice."

"No." Everett turned to fully face her. "That's . . . no one's ever suggested that to me before. What do you mean, explore laterally?"

"Maybe instead of trying to make the show *bigger*, you could . . . explore other things, you know?" As Everett stared at her, she started to think that maybe she'd said the wrong thing.

"I mean, I'm drunk," Teddy said, even though she wasn't. Instead, she felt a familiar sense of shame creeping over her. This was the part where Richard—she meant Everett—would tell her that she didn't know what she was talking about. That she couldn't possibly give him advice on being a doctor—er, having a television show—when she worked retail. What would she know?

She opened her mouth to apologize again, but Everett was moving on. He didn't seem offended in the least that she'd given him career advice. In fact, he seemed excited.

"Can I show you something?" he asked as he stood up, holding his hand out to her.

Teddy let him pull her off the sofa and followed him into his bedroom, which was relatively sparse aside from the desk in the corner. Her feet tapped along the hardwood floor as she looked around. He let go of her hand to grab something off his desk, and then held up a puppet.

"This is what I've been working on," he said.

Teddy tilted her head. "A puppet," she stated.

"Correct," Everett said. "But it isn't finished. I've spent weeks trying to give this thing a genuine personality, and I can't do it."

"What do you mean, a genuine personality?" Teddy asked as she sat down on the bed, which felt a little bit forward but he was the one who'd brought her in here (and anyway, they both knew that Candy Land was functioning as board-game-based foreplay). She looked around his room again as he sat down beside her; it was clean, with dark green walls, a plush comforter, and even throw pillows.

"Wait," she said. "You have throw pillows. Did you pick those out yourself?"

Everett laughed. "I went to the store, looked at a display bed, and said 'I'll take that whole setup, please.' Home décor is another one of those things I don't have much time for."

Teddy smiled. "Okay, so back to what I asked before. How can a puppet have a genuine personality? Don't *you* give it a personality?"

"That's what a lot of people think," Everett said, "but that's never been the way ideas work for me. I can't will them to happen. I just have to keep working and eventually, if I try enough things, something will come to me. It's like magic."

"Magic that involves you working very hard and trying lots of things," Teddy corrected. "That kind of sounds like . . . work."

Everett smiled. "Right. But it doesn't always look that way on the outside, you know?"

Teddy sighed. "I wish I had what you were talking about earlier. A calling. Something that I love enough to keep working on it until I get a breakthrough. Something that feels like magic, even if it isn't."

"You'll find it," Everett said. "Or maybe it's not one thing for you—why limit yourself? Maybe there are tons of things out there that you love to do. A calling isn't always your job, you know. Maybe life itself is what feels like magic." He paused, looked away, and then looked back and met her eyes. "I can definitely say that my life feels a little bit more magic when you're in it."

Perhaps it went without saying that no one had ever told Teddy anything like that before. She'd spent most of her life feeling like she was objectively unmagical and now, hearing Everett say this, it was like a balloon was inflating in her chest.

"Magic?" she asked softly.

"Yeah, Teddy," Everett said, his eyes moving to her lips. "You're magic."

Teddy could have justified this as doing something that scared her, could have pretended that closing the space between her and Everett and grabbing his face with both of her hands as she kissed him was something that required bravery. But it wasn't. Kissing Everett in that moment and letting him roll her back onto his bed was the most natural, comfortable thing she'd ever done. It didn't feel scary in the least.

———————

WHEN TEDDY OPENED her eyes the next morning, it took her a moment to realize that she wasn't in the closet at her apartment listening to the sounds of Kirsten and the Viking talking over breakfast or Eleanor singing in the shower. She was in Everett St. James's bed, snuggled—*snuggled!*—against him like they were two bears in hibernation.

But she couldn't hibernate forever. Luckily, she'd remembered to check her phone before she fell asleep the night before. Kirsten and Eleanor had sent her numerous frantic texts asking if she'd been abducted, but once she told them she was spending the night at Everett's, they'd switched to sending various sexually suggestive emojis and gifs. But even if her best friends were no longer worried about her, she had places to be, and surely Everett had things to do that didn't involve her. So she got up, pulling her clothes on as quietly as she could.

"Where are you going?" Everett muttered without opening his eyes. "It's early."

Teddy stopped, her hands frozen on the buttons of her shirt. "I was going to make you breakfast."

"Come here," Everett said, pulling on her arm. "Why did you put clothes on?"

She smiled and sat down on the bed. "Don't you have things to do today?"

"All I wanna do is spend time with you," Everett said, lifting the blankets and pulling Teddy under them. She let out a happy shriek, then situated herself under his arm.

He wrapped his fingers in hers and she stared at their hands, his so much larger than hers. These hands that did such amazing things and entertained so many people were now holding hers. She couldn't believe it.

"What do you want for breakfast?" he asked, depositing the words directly into her ear. "I'm not letting you get up and cook for me. And also there's nothing in the fridge, so your options are very limited. We don't even have any more Bagel Bites."

"Damn. They're my favorite breakfast." Teddy thought about it for a moment. "You know what I would really love right now?"

Everett groaned. "Please don't say pancakes. Because I'll do it, but I think my flour may have expired several years ago."

"A bacon, egg, and cheese biscuit from McDonald's," Teddy said.

She felt his lips form a smile against her skin, and she memorized that feeling. He kissed her shoulder softly. "Let's hit the drive-thru, Theodora Phillips," Everett said, and those became the most beautiful words she'd ever heard.

AS THEY ATE their sandwiches in the parking lot (because everyone knows that fast food is only good if eaten immediately), Teddy had an idea.

"I want to do something for Eleanor and Kirsten," she said as she chewed. "They've been such good friends, and I've been extremely needy. And also before I texted them last night to let them know I was staying at your place, they were fully convinced I'd disappeared and were about to call the police. I feel bad about worrying them."

"I don't think you're needy," Everett said, taking a bite of his hash brown.

"Maybe not to you," Teddy said. "But I showed up on their doorstep crying and homeless. I literally *needed* a place to live. I thought maybe I could plan them a special themed movie night, but . . . do you think we could do it at your place?"

Everett stopped chewing and smiled at her. "Are you asking me to . . . meet your friends?"

Teddy inspected her coffee. "I suppose I am."

"Wow," Everett said, looking out at the parking lot. "Big step. I guess you must really like me, huh?"

"Please stop," Teddy muttered, trying not to smile.

"I mean, I assume you don't let just anyone meet your friends, so you must think I'm pretty great."

"I rescind my question."

"You're obsessed with me."

They smiled at each other.

"Yes," Everett said. "Movie night at my place. I can't wait to meet . . . What are their names, again? Karen and Donna?"

Teddy sighed.

"Kirsten and Eleanor. I'm kidding," Everett said. "It's really nice that you want to do something for them."

"Well, *they're* really nice. They're kind of the best. The least I can do is plan a themed movie night and dinner for them."

"Wait," Everett said with his mouth full. "This is a dinner and it has a theme? What's the movie?"

Teddy smiled. "Have you ever heard of a film called *Blood Sacrifice*?"

## 49

"I NEED SOMEONE TALL TO HANG THIS SKELETON UP."

Everett looked at Teddy as he taped paper bats to the living room wall. "Well, today's your lucky day, because I'm tall and I live to hang leftover Halloween decorations in my apartment."

Teddy handed him the skeleton and gave him a kiss. "I hope they like it."

"Of course they're going to like it. It looks like we're throwing an extremely late Halloween party in here." He stood back and admired the skeleton that now hung on the coat closet door. "He looks like a Stanley, right?"

Teddy pulled a giant tangled spiderweb out of a box. "I know they'll like it no matter what. They're not exactly complainers. But I'm worried the decorations aren't realistic enough. I thought about trying to re-create bloody entrails, but that seemed too difficult."

Everett laughed, but then Teddy shot him a horrified look and he realized she was serious. She was literally wringing her hands. "Whoa, whoa, whoa," Everett said. "You planned a perfectly spooky movie night and your friends are going to love it. Did I tell you that lasagna is my favorite food?"

"You've said, like, fifteen different things are your favorite food since we met," Teddy said, rubbing a hand across her forehead. "I'm starting to think that your favorite food is 'food.'"

"Yes," Everett said. "But lasagna is especially good. Oh! I forgot to tell you."

He opened the oven, where he'd shoved a loaf of bread in beside the lasagna. "I made garlic bread! I mean, I bought garlic bread, and then I opened the bag and put it in the oven, and that's basically making it, right? I thought it fit the vampire theme."

Teddy looked at him blankly.

"You know," Everett continued. "Because of the garlic?"

"What do vampires have to do with anything?" Teddy said, adjusting the spiderweb on the couch.

"Because of the movie!" Everett said.

Teddy shook her head. "There are no vampires in *Blood Sacrifice*."

"Then what is this movie about?" Everett shouted, exasperated.

Teddy giggled, then full-on laughed, and then couldn't stop laughing. "A lot of blood. And a lot of sacrifice," she said through her laughter.

## 50

"WHAT'S SO FUNNY?" EVERETT ASKED, A DISH TOWEL IN ONE hand and his other hand on his hip. Teddy stopped laughing and took in the scene: Everett in the kitchen, entirely too big for that tiny space. Everett looking at her, a half smile on his face. Everett preparing garlic bread for her friends, whom he was willingly hanging out with.

She just wanted this night to go well. She wanted it to be *perfect*.

"*You're* funny," she said, walking behind the counter and giving him a kiss. "And you're sweet. Thanks for making me feel less nervous."

"Again, I don't think you have anything to be nervous about. They're your friends! But I'll accept this all the same," Everett said, squeezing her hips.

The doorbell rang, and Teddy's heartbeat quickened.

"Let me get that," Everett said, and strode past Teddy before she could stop him.

She watched, frozen, as Everett opened the door. Would this be like it had been with Richard? She didn't think Everett would be condescending and borderline rude, but you never knew. Maybe she was simply drunk on love and unwilling to see his flaws.

As Everett greeted her friends and Kirsten gave him air-kisses on both cheeks, Teddy walked toward them.

*"Très dramatique!"* Kirsten said, gesturing to the decorations as Eleanor hugged Everett. And then she leaned toward Teddy and stage-whispered, "Oh, I like this guy."

Teddy immediately blushed, because Kirsten's whispers were about as loud as anyone else's regular speech. But when she glanced at Everett, he was looking right at her. He wiggled his eyebrows, then pointed to himself and gave a thumbs-up.

"Let me take your coats!" Teddy said brightly. "And then you can have a seat at the table!"

EVERYONE LOVED DINNER. Eleanor and Kirsten had oohed and aahed appreciatively when Teddy explained that the lasagna was supposed to symbolize the oozing blood they would later see in the film.

"Love this dedication to a theme," Kirsten said as she took a sip of wine.

And now they were set up in front of the television, Eleanor and Kirsten on the sofa and Teddy and Everett smooshed into the over-sized armchair. As the opening credits played over sinister music, Everett whispered, "So wait. . . . How scary is this, exactly?"

"I guess it depends on what scares you," Teddy whispered back.

Everett frowned. "You already mentioned bloody entrails, and while before tonight I wouldn't put those on a list of fears, I've gotta say, they're up there now."

Teddy winced. "Then this might be a difficult watch for you. How do you feel about eyeballs popping out of heads?"

"Not good!" Everett said loudly.

"Hey, lovebirds," Kirsten said, throwing a gummy skull at them (Teddy had taken some of the leftover Halloween-themed candy from Colossal Toys), "I can't even hear the blood or the sacrifice over your romantic mutterings."

"This is not romantic," Everett said, pointing at Teddy. "She told me an eyeball is going to pop out of someone's head."

"Spoilers!" Eleanor shouted, putting her hands over her ears.

"No, I didn't. I said 'eyeballs,' plural," Teddy corrected.

"Oh, I like how they made the title look like dripping blood," Kirsten said, pointing to the screen.

"It's the attention to detail that makes this a classic," Eleanor agreed.

Everett shook with laughter. "Your friends are great," he whispered.

Teddy exhaled and, for the first time that night, let herself relax (or as much as one could relax while watching a blood-splatter-filled movie). She rested her head on Everett's shoulder as he put his arm around her, and then she caught Eleanor's eye. Eleanor winked and went back to watching the movie.

This was all okay, she realized. Everett wasn't Richard, and she could be with him while still having her own dreams. She had friends and her own life, and she might not fully know what she wanted to do with it yet, but she was starting to feel happy.

Eleanor and Kirsten screamed as someone on-screen brandished a knife, and Everett looked down at Teddy.

"Why are you smiling? Do you love this?" he asked, laughing.

"Yeah," Teddy said. "I kind of do."

## 51

THE NEXT EVENING, TEDDY FOUND HERSELF THINKING ABOUT Everett's puppet dilemma. But even more than that, she found herself thinking about something she could do to solve it. And so she sat down in front of the sewing machine, googling things as she went along, making a wardrobe fit for a puppet.

"You know," Eleanor said after Teddy explained what she was doing, "it isn't your job to fix this for him."

"I know," Teddy said, frowning as the machine jammed. "Come on, Scott."

"Kirsten and I love Everett, and he's not Richard. He's, like, the anti-Richard. Richard was cold and boring and pretentious and—"

"Okay, I get it. Everyone in my life hated Richard," Teddy said with a small laugh. "I promise, you don't have to remind me anymore."

"All I'm saying is, Everett didn't *ask* you to do this. He's not expecting you to drop everything to solve his problems."

Teddy opened the top of the machine, moved the thread around a bit, and shut the top again. "I know that," she said as the machine started. "But . . . I'm actually enjoying this. Is that weird?"

Eleanor smiled. "No! It's great. You deserve to do something fun. Just . . . make sure it's really for you, okay?"

"It is!" Teddy said a bit defensively, and Eleanor left it there. But hours later, when Teddy was standing in front of Everett's door with a puppet-sized dress in her hands, she started to wonder if Eleanor was right. Was she doing it again? Was she melding her life to someone else's, letting someone else's passion take over her own?

But then Everett opened the door, and seeing his confused face break into a smile forced all other thoughts from her head.

"Oh, man, am I glad to see you," he said as she stepped inside. "You want something to drink?"

She shook her head as she sat down on the couch. "So . . . I brought something. It's for the puppet."

Everett's eyebrows rose as he sat down beside her.

"I hope it's not overstepping any boundaries, and if you don't like it, I won't be offended. It's just something I put together. . . ."

"Let me see it," Everett said.

Teddy pulled the dress out of the bag. "It's a puppet dress. When you were telling me she didn't have a personality, I started thinking about how I felt so much more like *I* had a personality when I started wearing what I wanted. So maybe you can kind of . . . build her personality from the outside in."

Everett held the dress in his hands, not saying anything.

"It's okay that you don't like it," Teddy said in a rush. "It was a silly idea, anyway. I don't know anything about puppets or making one, and I don't know why I—"

"Teddy," Everett said, looking up at her, "this is amazing."

Teddy paused. "It is?"

"Hold on." Everett got up, went into his room, and came back holding the puppet. He pulled the dress on it and held it up. "Look at this! Look at how perfect she looks! Her name is Bernadette, right? She's definitely a Bernadette."

Teddy slumped with relief. "So . . . you like it?"

"I love it," Everett said, leaning over and kissing her hard. "I can't believe you did this."

"Well, I learned to sew in class, and it's been one of the things I really enjoy doing. . . ."

"Wait." Everett looked at her. "Maybe this is it."

"What do you mean, 'it'?"

"Maybe this is your thing. Your passion."

"Making dresses for puppets?" Teddy asked.

"No." Everett smiled. "Design. You should work on the show! You could work on puppet design, set design . . . I mean, clearly this was such a good idea . . ."

He kept talking, but Teddy tuned out. Working with Everett? Being his employee?

"No," she said suddenly.

Everett stopped in the middle of a sentence, his mouth open.

"I don't want to work for you," she said.

"It's not really *for* me," Everett explained. "I know my name is in the title, but we all work together. It'd be more like working for the *show*. . . ."

"No, Everett," Teddy said again, more firmly, "I don't want to do what you're doing."

Everett's brows crinkled. "Why not?"

"Because I . . . I need my own thing!" Teddy said, exasperated. "I spent years being steamrolled by my boyfriend's passion. Everything I did was in service of Richard and his big important job as a doctor. I didn't do anything for me or find anything out about myself and I don't want to do that again. The entire point of Teddy Time was to figure out who I am, not leap into my next boyfriend's dream. Do you get it?"

"I'm sorry," Everett said, putting Bernadette on the ground. "Did you say I was your boyfriend?"

"Shit," Teddy muttered. "Didn't mean to say that part out loud."

"So am I, then?" Everett asked, leaning forward. "Your boyfriend?"

"I guess that depends," Teddy said lightly.

"On what?" Everett asked, so close their lips were almost touching.

"On whether or not you're asking me to be your girlfriend," Teddy said.

Everett kissed her, holding her face in both his hands. "Teddy, will you do me the honor of being my girlfriend and accepting all responsibilities contained therein, including but not limited to (a) spending time with me and (b) that's pretty much it?"

"Where do I sign?" Teddy smiled and kissed Everett again. "Yes. I'll be your girlfriend."

"Glad that's settled," Everett said. He kept one arm around her as he said, "It's okay. You don't want to work for the show. I get it."

Teddy frowned. "Do you?"

Everett shrugged. "I think it would be great, but if you don't want to do it, you don't want to do it. I'm not going to be upset or try to convince you."

Teddy smiled in relief, even if part of her wasn't sure Everett completely understood what she was saying. "I didn't even tell you, I might have actually figured out what I want to do with my life. Josie wants me to take over Colossal Toys. I could be a business owner!"

"Wow," Everett said, eyes wide. "That's a big deal. Do you want to run the store?"

Teddy shifted uncomfortably. "Well, I don't know. Honestly, owning a business doesn't sound like much fun, but jobs aren't always fun, are they? I mean, you're following your dream and it still involves a lot of work, right?"

"Well." Everett nodded. "Yeah. No job is enjoyable all of the time."

"Exactly," Teddy said, reassured. "I don't even know if I want to do it yet. But this might be my thing! My passion!"

Everett leaned forward and kissed her again. "Then I'm happy for you. Congratulations."

Teddy smiled. "Thanks, boyfriend."

"You're very welcome, girlfriend."

"Well, since we now have this official designation, it seems only right that we celebrate," Teddy said.

Everett tucked her hair behind her ear. "Oh, yeah? And how would we do that?"

Teddy smiled. "Oh, I can think of a few ways."


**WHEN TEDDY WAS** about to leave, she finally asked Everett the question she was dreading. "Oh, um . . . wouldyoumaybewanttogoto dinneratmymom'shouse?"

Everett paused. "Were those . . . words?"

Teddy took a deep breath. "Would you like to go to dinner at my mom's house tomorrow? With me?"

Everett smiled. "Would be kinda strange if I went without you."

"Just answer the question," Teddy said with a straight face.

"Of course!" Everett put his hands on her shoulders. "Who wouldn't want to hang out with your family?"

After Teddy was silent for a few moments, Everett said, "Oh."

"Not that I want to talk about him anymore, but Richard always had some excuse for why he couldn't come see my family. It was . . . well, it was embarrassing, you know? To constantly have to tell them why he wasn't there."

"I'm sorry." Everett wrapped her in a hug and said into her hair, "You tell me the time and I'll be there."

"Yeah?" Teddy smiled.

"Of course." Everett kissed her on the forehead, and Teddy couldn't remember the last time she'd felt so safe, so secure, so . . . well, so loved. As she felt the rise and fall of Everett's chest under her cheek, she realized that she couldn't imagine being happier, and this was all because she'd done the things that scared her. Because she'd taken a chance, she'd emailed Everett, she'd agreed to go out with him even though she was terrified.

It turned out that taking control of your own life was actually kind of amazing.

**52**

Dear Teddy,

I forgot to clarify: what should I wear to dinner tomorrow? Is this formal? Semiformal? Beachy casual (a real description from a wedding invitation I once received)?

Beachily,
Everett

. . . . . . . .

Dear Everett,

Yes, beachy casual.

Thanks for asking,
Teddy

Dear Teddy,

Okay, seriously, I know that dinner at your mother's house in
Ohio in November doesn't have a "beachy casual" dress code
but now I'm worried. Am I going to look bad if I don't show
up in a Hawaiian shirt and board shorts?

Getting my feet flip-flop ready,
Everett

. . . . . . . .

Dear Everett,

Frankly, I'm concerned that you own board shorts.

No dress code. Wear whatever you want. Everyone's going to
love you.

See you tomorrow,
Teddy

## 53

THE NEXT MORNING, ASTRID TEXTED EVERETT TO TELL HIM
that their meeting with the Imagination Network had been bumped
up, so now he had even less time to prepare. Everett wasn't one to
panic (he was more the silent-stress type), but he found himself
pacing his apartment, tugging on his hair. He had zero idea what
he was actually going to say to these people. How could he possibly
convince them that his show belonged at their studio? He knew in
his heart that it did, but knowing things wasn't ever a problem for
him. Translating what was going on in his head into something
that the outside world could understand . . . well, that was the hard
part.

*I'll be ready,* he texted Astrid.

*This is just a meeting!!!* she texted back. *Don't go overboard on this. If
you show up looking sleep-deprived and unshowered it will NOT be good for us.
Get some rest.*

Okay, so Astrid knew him. But if she knew him so well, then she
had to understand that "being chill" wasn't his style. That wasn't
the way he worked, and it never would be.

Everett sat down, grabbed a notebook, and started writing. He
worked so hard, in fact, that he didn't glance at his phone even
once.

## 54

TEDDY'S EYES KEPT BOUNCING TO THE GIANT DECORATIVE clock on the wall. It was one of those things that looked like an antique even though it had been purchased at HomeGoods in 2012.

"Let's eat," she said in a burst. "I don't think he's coming."

"Maybe he's running behind," her mom said. "He might be stuck at work."

Craig stopped, his fork halfway to his mouth. "Oh, were we waiting?"

"Craig," Sophia groaned, "did you not notice that none of us were eating?"

"No, Craig has the right idea," Teddy said, heaping a spoonful of macaroni and cheese on her plate. "We're eating. Everyone's eating."

"Mom says we're in charge of our own bodies and our own tummies and we don't have to eat anything we don't want to," Emma said, staring at Teddy with big eyes.

"Your mom's right," Teddy said, giving Emma a spoonful of macaroni. "But you love macaroni and cheese, right?"

Emma nodded.

"Okay, then," Teddy said, passing the bowl to Sophia, who tried to catch her eye.

Now everyone thought she was a liar. Her family likely assumed she'd had some sort of breakdown after Richard dumped her that caused her to create a fantasy relationship with a television host. Which might have been exactly what happened, because Everett, her supposed boyfriend, should have been there and he wasn't, which could mean that she'd made the whole thing up.

She discreetly pulled her phone out under the table. *Hey, where are you?* she tapped out.

"No phones at the table," Emma said. "That's what we always tell Mommy."

"Well, Mommy has a job to do, and sometimes bosses don't respect Mommy's personal time," Sophia said crisply. "But you're right, sweetie."

What Teddy wanted to ask Everett was *Hey, what the hell is UP?* but she didn't text that. Although being mad was an unusual and uncomfortable feeling for her, it was a bit of a relief to feel anger instead of fear. Invigorated, she took a too-large bite of mac and cheese.

They got through dinner by listening to Craig tell a story about how he'd discovered a kitten under the hood of a 2012 Honda Civic and had spent most of his day attempting to rehome it. Teddy suspected he was talking so much to take the attention off her and make the meal less awkward, which she appreciated, but she was still eager to get out of there. As soon as she'd carried her dishes to the sink, she said her goodbyes and headed out to her car.

As she was opening her car door, she heard, "Hey!"

She turned to see Sophia pulling her coat on as she walked down the porch steps, the front door swinging shut behind her.

"Did I forget something?" Teddy asked.

"No, I wanted to talk to you," Sophia said.

"You did?"

Sophia rolled her eyes. "Don't sound so shocked."

"We just . . . We don't . . ."

"We don't talk a lot. I get it. But I wanted to ask you something. . . . Are you really going to take over the toy store?" Sophia stared at her with her arms crossed.

Teddy crossed her arms, too, even though she knew it was combative body language; right now she needed the armor. "Yes. Why?"

"Why?"

It took Teddy a moment to realize that Sophia was asking a separate question, not mimicking her like a petulant child. "Because I want to."

"Are you sure that's a good idea?" Sophia asked, tilting her head. "Because—"

"Sophia!" Teddy practically shouted, then lowered her voice because she didn't want the entire neighborhood to hear. "What the hell are you doing? We've barely had a real conversation since you went to college. You left me at home alone. And now you want to give me sisterly advice?"

Sophia's eyes widened. "I didn't *leave you alone*. I was a kid and I went to school."

"I don't need your help. Not now—it's too late. Not everyone has known what they wanted to do for their entire lives. Some of us have to figure it out, and it sucks. Sorry I haven't wanted to be a lawyer since birth. Maybe I need to pick something and go with it and see what happens. At least I'm trying!"

She got into the car and slammed the door, pulling out of the driveway and barely glancing back at Sophia's openmouthed stare.

Teddy tried to remember the last time she'd yelled at Sophia. Maybe never. When Sophia had gone to college and become a lawyer and married Craig, Teddy had never once yelled at her for forgetting that she even had a little sister. But letting her feelings out now felt surprisingly okay. All of the resentment toward Sophia for being the "perfect" one, all of the sadness Teddy held over their relationship . . . it had all exploded back there in the driveway. She felt like she was flying, like she was going over a waterfall, like she was on fire . . . but in a good way.

She flipped on her turn signal and headed to Everett's.

## 55

EVERETT BARELY HEARD THE FIRST KNOCK ON THE DOOR. OR the second. But by the third, he realized that the knock was real, outside of him, not in his head. And it wasn't stopping. He stood up, sketches sliding off his lap, and walked to the door. The knocking kept going, loud and persistent.

He swung open the door and found Teddy, her fist poised to knock again.

"Hi!" he said. "What a nice surprise to see you!"

"Is it?" she asked, lips pursed. "Is it a surprise?"

This felt like a trick question, but he wasn't sure why, so he answered, "Yes."

"Okay, then," she said, brushing past him and into the apartment. "In that case, I must've imagined that we had plans tonight."

Everett shut the door. "We . . . Oh, no."

"'Oh, no' is right," Teddy said, turning to face him. "You were supposed to be at my mom's house for dinner."

"I was supposed to be at your mom's house for dinner," Everett said, raking his hands through his hair. "I was. Oh, shit."

"I had to sit there as everyone stared at me and wondered where you were. Except for my sister's husband, Craig, who was eating mac and cheese like nothing was wrong, which is a very Craig thing to do

but you wouldn't know because YOU HAVEN'T MET CRAIG!"
Teddy took in a deep breath. "Oh, I don't like this. I don't like sounding like this or yelling at you."

"Hey." Everett crossed the room and put his hands on her
shoulders, peering down into her face. "You're allowed to be angry.
I fucked up. I was supposed to be there, and I wasn't, and I'm so, so
sorry."

"You are?" Teddy asked in a small voice.

"Yes, Teddy! I can't even tell you how sorry I am. You can be as
mad at me as you want. Yell at me. Break a lamp. Here." He flexed
his arm. "Punch me on the biceps."

Teddy bit her lip. "That would hurt my hand more than it would
hurt your arm."

"You can try it," Everett said. "I deserve it."

Teddy sighed. "Just seeing you makes me less mad, but I was *so*
mad, Everett. I yelled at my sister. The entire drive over here, I was
coming up with all these terrible things I was going to say to you,
and I'm not the kind of person who comes up with angry monologues."

"Well." Everett put his arm down. "Maybe you should be. It's
probably too soon for me to say this, since I haven't even started
making it up to you, but it's kind of nice to see you angry."

"What?"

Everett wrapped her up in his huge arms. "I like seeing your
emotions. It makes me feel like I know who you are inside, you
know? I don't want to see only the put-together, sweet, pretty parts
of you that the rest of the world gets to see. I want all of it, even the
angry, ugly parts. Even when it's directed at me."

Everett could feel Teddy swallow against his chest.

"But you're not ugly when you're mad," he said into her ear.
"You're actually kinda hot."

She laughed and pulled back. "I hate you."

"You don't!" Everett said. "And I promise, you tell me when the next dinner at your mom's house is, and I'll be there with bells on. Not literally, unless you want me to wear them as a form of atonement, and in that case, bells it is."

"Okay." Teddy took a deep breath and nodded. "So . . . you were working?"

Everett groaned. "Yeah. The meeting in New York got bumped up, so I was trying to get ready for it and completely lost track of time. You want something to drink?"

Teddy shook her head and sat down on the sofa.

Everett sat down beside her. "It's, like, I can't stop thinking about it. I can't turn my brain off. All I'm thinking about is if the Imagination Network is gonna like the show."

"Wait," Teddy said. "The Imagination Network is in New York? That's the meeting you're going to?"

Everett nodded.

"The Imagination Network that wants to buy your show?"

"Well, that's the hope, anyway," Everett said, taking a sip of the now-warm beer on his coffee table. "We'll see what happens."

"I didn't know . . . I wasn't . . . ," Teddy started. "So the Imagination Network is *in New York*?"

Everett knew he was missing something, but he wasn't sure what. "That's correct."

"So if they bought your show, you would . . ."

"Move to New York," Everett completed her sentence.

Teddy eyes widened. "Were you planning on telling me that you're moving to another state?"

"*Hopefully* moving to another state," Everett corrected, then realized that was the wrong thing to say. "I thought you knew."

"How could I have known that?" Teddy asked, her voice growing louder. "I'm sorry I don't know the location of every children's entertainment company."

"Is that . . . a problem?" Everett asked.

"Uh, yeah, Everett," Teddy said. "It's almost a nine-hour drive."

"Much shorter by plane," he pointed out.

"Oh, my God," Teddy said, folding herself in half so she was talking to her knees. "You missed dinner. You're moving. All because of your job. I've been here before, and I know how this ends."

"What are you talking about?" Everett asked. "And also what are you saying? Your voice is very muffled."

Teddy sat up. "I've already dated one guy who treated me like garbage because all he cared about was his job and the prestige of it. And Richard *dumped* me, Everett, after I spent years bending over backward to help him follow his dream."

"Hey, I have zero intentions of dumping you," Everett said. "That's the furthest thing from my mind, trust me."

"How are we going to stay together if we're in different states?" Teddy asked, dragging her hands over her face.

"We don't have to be in different states," Everett said slowly. "You can come with me."

Teddy dropped her hands into her lap and sat completely still. "You think I should move to New York with you?"

"Yes!" Everett grabbed her hands and smiled. "Think about how great it would be. I'm sure we can find you a job on the show—"

"No."

"No what?" Everett asked.

"No!" Teddy said louder, standing up. "I'm not doing that. I want to visit New York, but I mean *visit*. On my own terms. And I don't want to work for you, Everett. I already told you that."

"Okay, again, it's not really working for *me*," Everett said, standing up to face Teddy.

"And anyway, I'm taking over Colossal Toys, remember? How am I supposed to run a toy store in Columbus if I'm in New York?"

"You decided to take over?" Everett raised his eyebrows. "You never told me that was for certain."

"Don't sound so incredulous! Do you think I can't own a business?"

Everett held up his hands. "Whoa. That is not what I said. I think you can do anything, Teddy. Of course you can own a business if you want to, but you didn't sound remotely excited when you told me about it. In fact, you kinda sounded like you wanted me to talk you out of it. You've spent a lot of time telling me that you wanted to discover what you're passionate about, and not once did you mention small-business ownership or vintage toys."

"Well, maybe you don't know me that well after all. I am *just* starting to get my life back. I don't want to give it away to someone," Teddy said.

Everett looked down at her hands, curled up into fists. "What do you mean . . . you don't want to give it away to someone?" he asked slowly.

"I mean." Teddy exhaled, looking everywhere in the room except Everett's face. "I . . . I like you, Everett. I like everything about you, and I like that you care about your job and that you're good at it. But I can't be a sidekick to your dream. I need to find my own."

"You *will* find your own!" Everett said, stepping toward her, but Teddy stepped back, finally meeting his eyes.

"Look at us already," she said. "We've been together in person for, what, a few weeks?"

"Thirty-seven days since your first email, which was the moment I fell in love with you, if I'm being honest. That's the moment I knew you were the girl for me, and I don't need any more time to know how I feel."

Teddy bit her lip and one treacherous tear slowly rolled down her face. "I can't be the girl for someone else. I have to be my own girl."

Everett shoved his hands in his pockets. He felt precariously close to tears himself. "What are you saying, Theodora?"

She winced. "I think . . . I think we want different things, Everett. It doesn't matter how much we like each other. It isn't going to work. What are you going to do, give up your show?"

"Do you want me to?" he asked, an edge to his voice.

"No!" Teddy practically shouted, and her voice cracked on the word. "I don't want you to give up anything that makes you *you*. That's what I *like* about you."

"Then what are we supposed to do?"

"I think." She took a deep breath. "I think you should go to New York, and you should be fabulously successful as a nationally syndicated children's television host, and you should be happy that you get to spend all your time working at a job you love. And I should stay here in Ohio and figure out my own life by myself."

"You think we should break up," Everett said flatly.

"That's another way to put it."

"No," Everett said. "Nope. I don't accept this. We're not breaking up."

"Well, unfortunately you aren't the only one who has a say in this," Teddy said, a hint of steel in her voice.

And Everett, as much as he wanted to beg and plead and kiss her until she changed her mind and agreed with him—and he was sure she would do it, if only for a little while, if only until the next day—couldn't make her doubt herself again. He couldn't be another man who kept her from doing what she wanted.

"Okay," he said. "But you're wrong."

Teddy's brow furrowed. "About what?"

"I don't like you, Teddy," Everett said, taking in every detail of her face. The almost eerie wideness of her eyes. The angles of her high cheeks, slightly flushed. The way her tiny ears poked through her hair. "I've never liked you. I'm in love with you, and I have been since the beginning."

Teddy shook her head as the tears on her cheeks sparkled. "Don't say that."

"I'm not going to stop you from doing what you want, but I'm not going to lie to you, either. I love you, Theodora Phillips. And I think you love me, too."

Teddy smiled at him as she cried, looking like one of those thunderstorms that happened while the sun was shining. He didn't understand how she could make him feel like this: the pure joy of seeing her mixed with the agony of knowing she was leaving.

She walked toward the door. "I have to go."

"Teddy . . . ," he said as she opened the door.

"Good luck at your meeting. I know they'll love you. Everyone does." She smiled and quietly shut the door behind her.

Everett stared at the door until he realized she wasn't coming back. "Everyone except you," he said to the empty room.

## 56

TEDDY DROVE UNTIL TEARS BLURRED HER VISION SO MUCH that she didn't feel safe, so she pulled into a parking lot to get herself together. But then she didn't feel like getting herself together, so she screamed, closing her eyes and stretching her mouth open as far as it could go.

All she wanted to do was go back to Everett's apartment and kiss him and forget all about this. She didn't want to think about the fact that he was leaving. She wanted to live in a beautiful fantasyland where Everett's job still existed, but as an abstraction that didn't affect her happiness in any way.

But that wasn't real life, unfortunately. She hit the steering wheel, hard. "Ouch," she muttered. This was why she didn't dramatically hit things: because it hurt, and also no one was around to see it. She stared out at the parking lot. The potholes full of rainwater and dead leaves weren't exactly an inspiring sight.

Her phone rang, and her stomach felt like a roller coaster at the top of a big hill, floating and waiting to drop. She checked the screen. Richard.

"Oh," she said, both relieved and disappointed that it wasn't Everett.

She blew her nose, then answered. "Hello?"

"Hey, babe," Richard said, "how's it going?"

"Um." Teddy considered telling Richard the truth for a moment, then quickly decided against it. "Fine. Things are fine."

After Richard didn't say anything, she asked, "And how are you?"

"Well." Richard exhaled into the phone. "I miss you. The town house isn't the same without you."

Teddy pulled the phone away from her ear, stared at it for a moment, then brought it back to her ear. "Excuse me?"

Richard laughed, which made her feel prickly and irritated for reasons she couldn't fully articulate. "Are you surprised? I miss you!"

"But don't you have a girlfriend?" she asked sharply.

"I . . . What? How do you know that?"

Teddy sighed. At another time, she would've been mortified that she had spied on Richard. But right now she felt so low that it didn't matter.

"I hid behind a garbage can and saw you at HighBall. *Whatever*," she said. "Who cares how I know? I don't think she'd be happy that you're calling me."

"We're not together anymore," Richard said as if this made it all better.

"Oh, so you're calling me because you're single now, and you need someone to make your dinner?" Teddy asked loudly.

"No, I—"

"I'm not in the mood for explanations right now, Richard. I mean it. I don't give a shit why you think you miss me. I want you to stop calling me, and go—I don't know—go fuck yourself! Oh, and stop calling me babe. Sometimes I think you don't even know my real name."

She pressed the END CALL button and barked out a loud laugh to herself. Never in her life had she said anything like that to an-

other person, but she supposed there was a first time for everything.

The smile on her face faded as she remembered Everett. But
then, as she looked around, she realized that the parking lot she was
in belonged to a Taco Bell.

"Oh, hell yes," she whispered as she started the car and pulled
into the drive-thru. She might have been feeling the lowest she'd
ever felt, but at least the universe was providing for her when it
came to Crunchwrap Supremes.

**"DON'T GET ME** wrong. I'm happy that you brought home enough
Taco Bell to feed a small, bean-loving army, but . . . are you okay?"
Kirsten asked, squinting at her.

"Your mascara is . . . Well, it's everywhere," Eleanor said, gesturing toward her face. "I think some ended up on your neck."

"I am *not* okay," Teddy said. "In fact, you might say I'm terrible.
Everett is moving to New York, and we broke up."

"New York, New York?" Kirsten asked.

"Well, it's certainly not New York, Ohio," Teddy said, shoving
a Cinnamon Twist into her mouth.

"And he broke up with you?" Eleanor asked, grabbing a Cinnamon Twist of her own (Teddy had bought two servings for each
of them, figuring they were mostly air).

Teddy shrugged. "I broke up with him. Same diff. I mean,
what else were we going to do? Date long-distance? I'm a grown
woman, not a lovelorn teenager who met a boyfriend at summer
camp."

Kirsten picked up Teddy's cup and sniffed it. "Is this Mountain
Dew Baja Blast spiked with something? Because you are acting . . ."

"Unhinged," Eleanor said. "And I mean that with love."

"I'm completely hinged," Teddy said with her mouth full. "But I can't do that. I can't give up everything to be with another guy. I did that once and it didn't work out well, and just because Everett is smart and sweet and sexy doesn't mean anything. I thought Richard was pretty great when we started dating, too."

"Mmmm, did you, though?" Eleanor asked thoughtfully. "Granted, I wasn't there, but did you really see him and think, 'Ah, yes, this man is sweet and smart and sexy'? Or did you have low self-esteem?"

"Damn," Kirsten muttered, taking a noisy drink through her straw.

"Oh, speaking of Richard!" Teddy's eyes widened. "He called me and said he dumped his superhero girlfriend and he misses me!"

"Oh, no," Kirsten said. "What did you do?"

"I told him to go fuck himself!" Teddy said with a cackle. "Oh, I'm eating too much. I'm gonna feel this tomorrow."

"Please slow down," Eleanor muttered. "This place only has one bathroom."

"He *should* go fuck himself," Kirsten agreed. "Honestly, that's too good a fate for him. So did he want you back?"

Teddy snorted. "Who knows? Richard's problems are no longer my problems."

Kirsten leaned forward to give her a high five.

"Okay, but back to the whole 'you just dumped Everett, who I'm pretty sure was the love of your life as recently as this morning' situation," Eleanor said. "Wow, these Cinnamon Twists are delightful."

"Sometimes simplicity is delicious," Teddy said.

Eleanor shook her head. "Let's not change the subject. Are you sure you're fine with this? Because you're acting very . . . upbeat."

Teddy shook her head. "I'm not thinking about it because I don't want to have a complete mental and emotional breakdown. I want to let this Cheesy Gordita Crunch cure my ills."

"Seriously, you bought *so* much Taco Bell," Eleanor said. "This is, like, the entire menu."

"Soft tacos will fill the void," Teddy said with her mouth full.

"Honey, we love you," Kirsten said, leaning forward. "And that's why we don't want you to wake up tomorrow full of regret and questionable beef. Are you sure this is what you want?"

Teddy sighed and slumped over. "It's not what I want. It's not what I want at all. But it's what I've got. Everett's leaving, and I can't go with him. I have to make my own life, one that has nothing to do with some guy's big dreams. I can't be a sidekick again, not after all the work I've been doing."

Eleanor slid over to put an arm around her. "Okay, sweetie. That sounds good. But know that anytime you want to talk or cry or have a pajama-movie night, we're here."

"And so is the ice cream freezer," Kirsten reminded her. "It's always stocked and waiting."

Teddy looked at the half-eaten Taco Bell feast on the coffee table, and suddenly, it didn't look so appealing anymore. Tears sprang to her eyes. "I think my Richard-fueled anger is starting to wear off," she said softly.

"So what you're gonna do is go get in your jammies," Eleanor said in her teacher voice, taking charge. "And we're going to watch an Alfred Hitchcock movie that will make you think, 'Well, at least I'm not mixed up in THAT situation,' while you drink a cup of Sleepytime tea. And then we're going to tuck you in and you're going to go to sleep."

"I may fall asleep during the movie," Teddy said.

"Perfectly acceptable," Kirsten said. "Happens to the best of us. Most movies are too damn long, in my opinion."

"Hear, hear," Eleanor said.

Teddy sat up straight and blinked her tears away. "Wait. I just had an idea. Instead of a movie . . . are you guys up for a little light vandalism?"

**57**

"THE CASHIER AT WALGREENS TOTALLY KNEW WHAT WE WERE up to," Eleanor said.

"What? Probably lots of people buy several packs of toilet paper and nothing else," Teddy said. "Maybe we're having massive intestinal distress. That's normal."

"Yeah, maybe we're three sexy, diarrhea-prone ladies ready to take on the night," Kirsten said, and Eleanor wrinkled her nose.

"Well, this is it," Teddy said, parking across the street from the town house. "Are you guys sure you want in on this? I won't be offended if you want to bail."

"Teddy," Eleanor said from the backseat, "what kind of friends would we be if we made you toilet-paper your ex-boyfriend's house by yourself?"

"We're with you in your time of need," Kirsten said, then ripped open one of the packages of toilet paper. "Let's do this."

Teddy had never toilet-papered someone before, so she was surprised to discover that it was actually, well, kind of fun. Unfortunately, Richard had only one small tree in his front yard, but the three of them used as much toilet paper as they could covering each of its branches.

"Am I wrong, or is this beautiful? I mean, it's art," Kirsten said, standing back and admiring their handiwork with her hands on her hips.

"I think you might be right," Eleanor said. "Frankly, Richard is lucky we toilet-papered him. We improved the look of the place."

Teddy sniffled.

"Oh, no, Teddy," Eleanor said, "are you okay?"

"It just hit me," Teddy said. "I broke up with Everett. And he's leaving."

"Okay," Eleanor said. "Back in the car. Wow, we did not use much of that toilet paper."

"It's possible we overbought," Kirsten said, picking up the unopened packages. "I've never seen anyone cry while toilet-papering."

"There's a first time for everything." Teddy used some of her roll to wipe her nose.

After they got in the car, she took one last look at Richard's place. The dangling toilet paper blew around in the wind, ghostlike. Kirsten was right—it *was* kind of beautiful. And it had taken Teddy's mind off Everett for a few moments.

But as they drove back to their place, she couldn't help but wonder what he was doing.

## 58

EVERETT SPENT THE NEXT FEW DAYS IN A FOG. HE FELT LIKE all voices were coming to him through a long tunnel, bouncing off the walls and echoing before they hit his ears. Astrid and Jeremy asked him if he was okay, and he nodded and smiled every time. There was no way he could explain to them what had happened or, more than that, how he felt.

"So when are you bringing your Internet girlfriend over?" Natalie asked during their weekly brunch date. She'd made pancakes, Everett's favorite, but they had no flavor as he shoveled them in his mouth.

"We broke up," Everett said, taking another bite.

Natalie put down her fork. "What? You broke up with her?"

Everett looked back at her, his eyes wide. "In what world would I break up with her, Nat? She's perfect. She dumped me."

"She dumped you?"

"Okay," Everett said, rubbing a hand over his face. "Can you please stop repeating every traumatic thing I tell you? That would be great."

"I'm shocked, that's all," Natalie said, still eating. Everett was glad at least someone still had an appetite. "I thought you guys were, like, made in the stars. Made for each other? Written in the stars? Both of those. I thought it was email fate or whatever."

"Yeah, well." Everett shrugged. "Apparently not."

"Dude, no wonder you came in here looking like a linebacker who lost a game. Does that analogy make sense? I mean, you looked like a big guy who was sad."

Everett pointed to himself. "As far as I'm concerned, that analogy is perfect. I'm a big guy and I'm sad."

"Ev, I'm sorry." Natalie reached out and put her hand over his. "Breakups suck. What happened?"

"Well, you know I'm trying to sell the show to the Imagination Network," Everett said, and Natalie nodded. "That will involve moving to New York, and Teddy doesn't want to come with me. She wants to—I don't know—figure out her own life. Without me."

Natalie rolled her eyes. "You can't blame her for not wanting to move to New York with you."

"I don't blame her for anything!" Everett almost shouted.

Lillian poked her head out of her and Natalie's bedroom.

"Everything's fine." Natalie waved her off.

"I'm just going through a crushing heartbreak," Everett said. "Nothing to worry about."

"Okay!" Lillian gave them a thumbs-up and shut the door.

"I don't blame her," Everett said more quietly. "But that doesn't mean I agree with her. I think we could work it out. Somehow."

"So how do you feel about moving?" Natalie asked, pouring more syrup on her pancakes.

"What do you mean, how do I feel about it?" Everett asked. "I've been wanting this since I was a little kid. It's good for the show."

"Well . . . ," Natalie said, drawing out the word.

"Oh, no," Everett groaned. "That's the tone of voice you use when you're about to give unsolicited advice."

"That's the only kind I can give you. You never solicit my advice, even though it's impeccable. All I'm saying is . . . so what if you've wanted it since you were a little kid? Sometimes what you want can change."

"I'm not going to quit my job," Everett said testily.

"I'm not suggesting that. Frankly, you're not qualified for anything else. But think about how you were so set on going away to college. Remember that? You had all these big dreams and plans about how you were going to live in a cheap apartment and eat nothing but dented cans of green beans you got on sale to save money, and you were going to spend all your time learning about puppetry."

He knew that was what he'd wanted when he was a teenager, but it all seemed so distant now. "Yeah, but then Gretel was born and I stayed home and it was great. I wouldn't be doing all the things I'm doing now if I'd gone away. It all worked out for the best."

"Exactly." Natalie gave him a long look. "You changed your plans because of someone you loved. And now you don't even care about that other thing you almost did."

"I don't really know how that's relevant," Everett said, taking another bite of pancakes. They were starting to taste a little more like food instead of cardboard.

"Work isn't everything, you know," Natalie said. "Not everyone's going to be as forgiving as me."

"What's that supposed to mean?"

"Ev." Natalie sighed. "Come on. How many times have we talked about how you let work take over everything? You can't expect everyone to constantly forgive you for forgetting things or missing their calls because you're 'inspired.'"

"My job depends on inspiration!" Everett said. "Sure, this sounds trite, but the show doesn't make itself! Someone has to have the ideas and do the work to make them reality. And that someone is *me*. And if I'm not thinking about it all the time and working on it all the time, it doesn't happen. The show needs one hundred percent of me."

"I know your work matters," Natalie said, holding her hands up. "No one's suggesting that it doesn't. But the people who love you matter, too. And if you keep blowing everyone off to give one hundred percent of yourself to work, someday you're gonna wake up and no one will be there anymore. Maybe you need to learn how to give work fifty percent and the rest of your life the other fifty percent."

Everett frowned. "What about seventy/thirty?"

Natalie raised her eyebrows. "I'm not the one you need to negotiate with. And here's another question: is this the first time someone's ever turned you down?"

"Um, no. I've faced plenty of rejection in my life. Did you forget about Elissa? She broke up with me and now she's married with a baby. I'd say that's a pretty clear rejection."

Natalie shook her head. "But you didn't love Elissa."

"I loved her!" Everett protested.

"Not like this. I have never, ever seen you like this about anyone . . . or anything, except for work. It's honestly unsettling seeing you so lovelorn."

Everett stared at his pancakes.

"Everett." Natalie leaned forward. "This is the last bit of unsolicited advice I'm going to give you, okay? Take some time to think about what you really want. Not what you wanted five or ten years ago, and not what you think you're supposed to want, but what *you* want."

"Thank you," Everett said. "I know you're saying all this because we're best friends and I love you for it, but also I do want to crawl out of my skin whenever you give me unasked-for advice."

"I'm going to stab you in the hand with this fork if you don't start acting more grateful," Natalie said calmly.

Everett smiled. He still wasn't really sure what Natalie was talking about, but he had friends and a job he loved. He might not have a successful relationship, but two out of three weren't bad. Or at least that was what he'd tell himself.

59

Dear Teddy,

I miss you. Can we talk?

Everett

. . . . . . . . .

Dear Everett,

I think it's for the best if we don't.

Teddy

# 60

NOW TEDDY UNDERSTOOD WHY PEOPLE HAD HOBBIES—THEY gave you something to pour yourself into when you otherwise felt too miserable to function. She could think about her life, or she could knit while watching a Rock Hudson marathon on Turner Classic Movies.

This explanation wasn't exactly comforting to Eleanor and Kirsten, who both kept checking in on her, but now Eleanor was at work and Kirsten was doing a consultation with a client, so Teddy was free to lounge on the couch without their worried faces occasionally appearing in front of her. Of course she knew they meant well, but what did they want her to do? Get up and perform one of the dance numbers from *Singin' in the Rain*? She felt like a piece of hot garbage and she intended to stay on this couch all day, making a wonky scarf (she'd learned knitting from a YouTube tutorial, but her skills left much to be desired) and admiring Rock Hudson's glorious chin while taking advantage of all that the ice cream freezer had to offer.

She'd made it through *Pillow Talk* and was on to *All That Heaven Allows* when the doorbell rang. Teddy frowned as her knitting needles stilled. Perhaps it was a delivery person. But then the doorbell rang again, and again, and someone started knocking.

"Okay, all right, I get the point!" she said, standing up and crossing the room. She yanked open the front door and came face-to-face with her sister.

"Sophia?" she asked.

Sophia's eyes widened. "Whoa."

Teddy self-consciously touched her hair, which she realized had come halfway out of her bun. It was hard to make a bun with a bob—it required a lot of bobby pins. "I don't look that bad."

Sophia squinted at her. "Why are you wearing my junior high softball T-shirt? How did you even get that?"

Teddy crossed her arms over her chest. "Anything you didn't take with you when you went to college was fair game. I've had it for years and it's mine now. Don't judge my wardrobe. And anyway, shouldn't you be at work?"

Sophia shook her head. "I took some time off. Do you want to take a walk?"

Teddy looked behind her at the television, where Rock Hudson was wearing flannel. Then she looked down at her T-shirt and sweatpants and sighed. "Let me put the ice cream back in the freezer."

TEDDY DID FEEL better once she combed her hair, threw a coat on over her ensemble, and got out in the fresh air. It was cold, but the sunshine made her feel at least somewhat human. But as she and Sophia walked down the sidewalk, she grew more and more confused.

"What's going on?" Teddy finally asked. "I can count on no fingers the number of times you've come over here to take a walk with me."

"I wanted to apologize."

Teddy stopped walking. "For what?"

"Don't be dramatic. Come on."

They kept walking in silence for a moment, and then Sophia said, "We were friends once, right?"

Sophia suddenly looked at her with so much energy that Teddy almost shrank away, but instead she looked back. "Yeah. Yeah, when we were kids."

Sophia nodded. "We were."

Teddy smiled, despite herself. "It was basically me and you against the world, right? After Dad left and Mom had to work so much."

Sophia let out a tiny laugh. "Yeah. Well, it was me attempting to run a household and you shutting out the world with books."

Teddy kept walking, watching her boots step over the cracks on the sidewalk.

"I don't resent Mom for working so much—she didn't really have a choice, you know? But sometimes I got tired of being the one who made dinner every night. The one who forged Mom's signature on your permission slips. The one who calmed you down when you had nightmares. Sometimes . . . well, sometimes I just wanted to be sixteen."

Teddy frowned. "I thought you were the coolest girl in the world back then. I wanted to be you."

Sophia smiled skeptically. "Yeah? God, I didn't even want to be myself. I wanted to have no responsibility, for even one day. And then when I went to college, it was like I got my wish. Sure, there was homework and exams and all that stuff, but I didn't have to worry about making sure we sent in a check to the electric company. My roommate always complained about doing her own laundry, but I was, like, *stoked* that I didn't have to do laundry for a family of three."

Teddy didn't say anything, and Sophia continued.

"It's not that I didn't want to come home more often. I wanted to see you. But every time I planned a weekend home, I started feeling all heavy and stressed out, because I knew if there was anything wrong at home, I'd be the one to take care of it."

"You could've told me that," Teddy said softly.

"I'm sorry, okay?" Sophia said forcefully. "I'm sorry I'm a shitty sister. I'm sorry we don't have a relationship now and it's my fault."

Teddy thought about Sophia's words for a moment. What she wanted to say was a bit of a risk, and it definitely scared her, so she opened her mouth and let the words come out. "Maybe we can try to have a relationship now."

Sophia raised her eyebrows. "Yeah?" she asked hopefully.

Teddy nodded.

Sophia exhaled. "Great, because in that case I want to tell you that you're making a huge mistake."

Teddy frowned. "*This* is the relationship? You criticizing me? I thought maybe we'd go get a pedicure together or something."

Sophia shoved her hands in her coat pockets and stared straight ahead. "Don't get a job you don't love to make someone else happy."

Teddy couldn't help herself; she laughed out loud. "Not all of us are like you, Sophia. You've been the golden child, the 'most likely to succeed' Phillips sister your whole life, while I've been—I don't know—'most likely to blend into the background.' Some of us didn't pop out of the womb wanting to be lawyers."

"I don't want to be a lawyer!" Sophia said so loudly that a man walking his dog across the street stopped and stared. Sophia waved at him and muttered, "Mind your own business."

"You're being ridiculous," Teddy said. "You've wanted to be a lawyer since we were kids. You've always been so good at arguing."

"No, *Mom* wanted me to be a lawyer," Sophia corrected her. "Don't you remember what it was like after Dad left? Mom became a walking copy of whatever the nineties equivalent of *Lean In* was. She was always, like, researching colleges and buying me SAT prep software programs and talking about my big future as a powerful lawyer and it was . . . I don't know. I didn't realize I could want anything else, you know?"

Teddy nodded. They turned toward Grandview Avenue. Teddy crossed her arms and smiled at someone walking a greyhound.

"I remember what you were like when you were a little kid," Sophia said as they walked past a hair salon. "You had so much energy, and you didn't care what anyone thought. I was miserably full of hormones and I so admired that about you. It was like you weren't concerned with impressing anyone; you were just yourself. You were . . ."

"Hell on wheels," Teddy said quietly.

Sophia smiled. "Yeah, basically. But then, after Dad left, you changed."

Teddy thought about it for a moment. "I don't think you can be hell on wheels forever."

"Maybe we should try, though," Sophia said. "I wish I had a little bit of that young Teddy spirit."

Teddy frowned. "So do you really not want to be a lawyer? Seriously?"

Sophia shook her head vigorously. "No. Craig keeps telling me I should quit and go back to school, that we have money saved up. He always says you shouldn't spend your life following someone else's dream."

"Craig said that, huh?" Teddy asked, nodding slowly. Apparently he held hidden depths when he wasn't shoveling food into his mouth. "So what do you want to do?"

"I want to be a teacher," Sophia said. "A high school teacher. Is that ridiculous?"

Teddy smiled. "No, Sophia. It's not ridiculous at all."

Sophia sighed. "You don't want to run a toy store, do you? I've never once heard you say that was your dream."

Teddy could feel herself getting defensive, but willed herself to push her shoulders down and take a deep breath. "Maybe life isn't always about dreams, though. Maybe it's about making the best of what's in front of you."

Sophia chewed on her lip. "Yeah. You're right; sometimes it is. But I don't think that's the situation you're in, and I don't think you want to do this. Rarely is there a situation where your only choice is to run a vintage toy store."

Despite herself, Teddy smiled. "Well, thanks for the advice."

Sophia groaned. "I'm sorry. I'm being annoying. It's just . . . I care about you, okay? And while I'm on a roll . . . what happened to that guy?"

"Everett?" Teddy asked. "Well . . . I kind of broke up with him."

Sophia frowned. "Why?"

Teddy sighed. "He has a big life, you know? Big dreams. Big goals. And I don't know if I can handle that again. I don't want to lose myself in someone else."

Sophia thought about it for so long that Teddy thought she wasn't going to respond, but then she said, "Yeah, but you only lost yourself in Richard because he sucked. When it's really love, you don't have to lose yourself. Falling in love should make you *more* yourself."

"Maybe instead of becoming a teacher, you should start writing self-help books," Teddy joked, and Sophia elbowed her. But Teddy's mind snagged on her words. Was Sophia right? Was there a way she could be with Everett without losing herself in the process?

But then she realized where they were and stopped walking. "Did you see that we're right in front of Jeni's?"

Sophia glanced up at the sign and her face looked exactly the same as it had when they were kids and she saw ice cream. "Well, we have to go in, right?"

Teddy nodded. "I don't see any other option."

AFTER SHE GOT back home, Teddy spent the rest of her afternoon cleaning up. She still needed to keep busy to avoid thinking about Everett, but luckily going through the boxes of clothes she had brought from the town house kept her occupied.

When her phone rang that evening, just as it was getting dark, she frowned. It was an unknown number, so she answered it, reasonably sure it wouldn't be Everett or Richard.

"Hello?"

"Hey, it's me."

Teddy paused for a moment, running through the list of male voices that could be calling her from a number she didn't recognize. "Um . . . I'm sorry, who is this?"

"Carlos!"

"Oh," Teddy said.

And then she realized that Carlos wasn't calling her to shoot the breeze, because he didn't shoot any breezes that weren't vintage toy related. "Carlos, what's wrong?"

"Josie's in the hospital," he said. "I'm here now. Can you—"

"I'm coming," Teddy said, then hung up.

## 61

AFTER CALLING CARLOS BACK TO GET DETAILS ABOUT WHICH hospital and how to find Josie (seriously, how did people in movies always end these conversations so dramatically? Didn't they need to clarify anything?), Teddy drove there in record time. She hadn't asked Carlos how Josie was doing—it seemed silly to waste time on the phone when Josie needed her now—and when she burst into the room to see Carlos sitting at her bedside, Josie laughing and talking, relief hit her so hard that she thought she might cry.

"Josie!" she croaked, unable to think of anything else to say.

Carlos stood up and gave Josie a kiss on the forehead. "Since you have company, I'll be getting home."

"Thank you for coming here, sweetheart," Josie said with a gentle smile, her voice slightly hoarse.

Carlos nodded, then gave Teddy a hug. She froze, then relaxed into it and hugged him back. "I'm glad you're here with her," he said, meeting her eyes, before he left.

Teddy watched him go, shocked.

"He might not have much to say most of the time," Josie said, prompting Teddy to turn around. "But he knows what to say when it matters."

"Josie, what happened?" Teddy asked, sitting down on the chair at Josie's bedside.

Josie rolled her eyes. "It's stupid. A heart attack."

Teddy opened her mouth and Josie held up a hand. "A minor one. Very minor. The most minor thing that could be considered a heart attack, really. I'm perfectly fine."

"Perfectly fine people don't have heart attacks," Teddy insisted.

Josie sighed. "I'm seventy years old. If a minor heart attack is the worst thing to happen to me, I feel pretty lucky."

Teddy swallowed, looking at her hands. "I don't want anything to happen to you."

"Honey." Josie reached out and grabbed Teddy's hands, then waited until Teddy met her eyes. "I've had a good long life."

"Stop it!" Teddy said, tears springing to her eyes. "What are you saying?"

"Oh, shut up and listen," Josie said. "I was so lucky to meet John, and you know we never had children."

Teddy nodded. Josie had had such a packed-full schedule that Teddy always assumed she'd never wanted kids, that taking care of someone else would have slowed her down.

"We tried. For a long time. And when it became clear that it wasn't gonna happen for us . . . well, I figured maybe it wasn't meant to be. John and I always loved spending time together, just the two of us, and we thought it might be for the best. We could be together, uninterrupted. We could travel."

Josie sighed. "But of course, we didn't travel. John opened the store, and that was that. We spent all our time working. And after he passed away, I guess part of me wondered . . . well, if maybe I'd made a mistake. If I should've figured out why we couldn't get pregnant, seen if doctors could've helped us. Or looked into adoption. Had a family another way."

"Oh, Josie," Teddy murmured, squeezing her hands. "I didn't know. . . ."

Josie shook her head quickly. "This isn't a sob story, sweetie. That's just what life is. Even if you're happy with the path you went down, part of you always wonders what was on that other road you passed a few miles back. That doesn't mean it's some grand tragedy. But it's a loss all the same."

Teddy pressed her lips together.

"But then." Josie smiled. "I met you. And from the moment you walked in the store, with that shy smile and your bright eyes, I thought, 'Oh, this is my daughter.'"

Teddy wiped away a tear and nodded.

Josie squeezed her hand. "You're my family, Teddy. And, honey, I'm so proud of you."

"I want to take over the store," Teddy said suddenly, her conversation with Sophia and all thoughts about how she didn't really want to do it flying out of her head. "I know I can do it. I—"

"No." Josie shook her head. "I've been thinking about it, and I can't let you do that."

Teddy felt the breath go out of her. "But . . . you said . . ."

"I love you so much that I can't let you run the store," Josie said.

Teddy sat in silence as the machines beeped. She heard people bustling down the hall, carts moving, and shoes squeaking. "Help me out here, because I don't understand."

"Do you really want to run the store?" Josie narrowed her eyes.

"Yes!" Teddy yelped.

"Does running a vintage toy store light you up? Is it your passion? Way down deep in your heart, is it what you've dreamed of?"

Teddy took a deep breath. "Well. No. But it's yours, and—"

"And I never wanted it in the first place," Josie said, cutting her off. "This was John's dream, and I spent years filling up the rest of my time with *my* dreams. I'm not going to let you do the same thing. I've seen the way you've been lately. Trying new things, spending time with that exciting new boy . . ."

Teddy shook her head. "We're not—he's not—"

Josie held up a hand. "Don't bother explaining—the man's perfect for you. But the store . . . I'm going to ask Carlos to take it over. I should've done that in the first place. That man lives and breathes toys, and I don't know why I worried he was too young. I think I was blinded by how much I love you and how much I wish that was the story: a woman passing down a beloved business to a girl who loves it just as much. But maybe the real story is 'a woman is glad to get rid of a business she never cared for all that much, and a guy is going to do an amazing job running it.'"

"But, Josie . . . what am I going to do?" Teddy croaked. It wasn't that Teddy didn't think Carlos should take over the shop—he deserved it, and he'd be better at it than she would've been. But now it felt like she truly had nothing certain in her future, nothing she could count on.

Josie smiled at her, and even though she was lying in a hospital bed, Teddy felt, as she always did, that Josie was looking down on her with love, like a mother cradling a baby.

"That's the great news. You've got your whole life to figure that out." She laughed. "Look at me. I'm seventy and I still don't know."

Teddy attempted to laugh and managed a snot-filled chuckle.

"You're gonna be fine," Josie said, a certainty in her voice that Teddy wished she felt.

"I hope you're right," she said. "But about the guy . . . I think you're wrong there. I'm worried I'm getting into another Richard situation. Another relationship where a man will take over my life, swallow up all of me and my wants and my needs. How do I know I'm not going to do that again?"

"Have you talked to him about it?" Josie asked, her voice gentle.

Teddy shrugged. "Sort of."

Josie sighed, long and ragged. "Don't be ridiculous. You've gotta have a conversation. Tell him everything about how you feel and give him a chance to tell you what he's feeling. Don't run away when it gets hard, because let me tell you—if you're with someone for their whole life, things are gonna get hard. They're gonna get hard in ways you can't even imagine. The only chance you have of making it work is by opening up your mouth and saying what you're feeling."

Teddy let out a strangled sob-laugh. "There are so many things in the way. I know people always say love conquers all, but I don't know if I believe that."

"That's bullshit," Josie said. "Love doesn't conquer all. But when it's real, when both of you feel it, it can conquer a whole hell of a lot."

Before Teddy could tell Josie all the myriad ways she was wrong and would never understand the particular complexities of her relationship (or nonrelationship, to be more accurate) with Everett, she heard a rap on the door.

"Mind if I come in?" A nurse walked in and checked one of the machines attached to Josie.

"Think I'll make it through the night?" Josie asked.

The nurse gave them a closed-mouth smile. "I think you're gonna be okay." She turned to Teddy. "You two related?"

Teddy opened her mouth, but Josie spoke before she could. "This is my daughter," she said, squeezing Teddy's hand again.

"I can tell," the nurse said with a nod. "She's got your smile."

Teddy knew that was impossible; she didn't have Josie's megawatt, room-brightening, day-making smile. The nurse was being nice to her because she had eye makeup all over her face. But in that moment, in the hospital room made cozy by Josie's presence, she was willing to believe it.

After the nurse left, Teddy went to find Josie's requested snack (Doritos, which seemed like an incredibly unhealthy choice, but Teddy wasn't in a position to judge). And then she sat there, holding Josie's hand, until Josie finally fell asleep.

## 62

EVERETT COULDN'T FOCUS AS HE PACKED FOR NEW YORK. AS he paced around the airport. As he sat beside Astrid on the flight. The meeting was a blur—he talked about the show and its purpose, and he knew everyone in the meeting loved everything he was saying, even if he could barely remember their names when he shook their hands.

On the sidewalk outside the Imagination Network building, Astrid ran through what had just happened.

"That was a good meeting," she said.

"Yeah," Everett said, stunned.

"A *really* good meeting."

"Yeah," he repeated.

"Everett, this is . . . happening. The show. The Imagination Network." She leaned in and stared at him. "Why don't you look excited?"

Everett shook his head and rubbed his hands over his face. "I'm excited. Really. I just . . ."

He thought about what Natalie had said, about how there had to be more to life than work, about how maybe he could give work 50 percent instead of 100 percent. He hadn't really understood her at the time, but now . . .

He thought about Astrid and Jeremy, how he'd been working with them for so long and how he'd be working with all-new people when the show was in New York. He thought about Jeremy working on some other show if he wasn't around. He thought about Gretel and the way he'd changed his life to stay home with her once before, the way she'd cried and hugged him when she said she didn't want him to move. He thought about his parents and how, as the saying goes, they weren't getting any younger.

He thought about all the kids he could reach with a national show. All of the families he could influence, the emails he could answer, the feelings he could explain.

And then he thought about Teddy. Her laugh and her smile and *her*. The way that if he really did this, if he really moved, he didn't know if things between them could ever be fixed.

"Hey, Astrid," he said, suddenly calm, "do you think we can go back up there? I have something I need to ask them."

## 63

THE NEXT EVENING, TEDDY WAS WORKING AT THE STORE. JOSIE was at home and recovering, which mostly meant a lot of grumbling whenever Teddy or Carlos reminded her that she needed to rest. Cold rain poured down outside, plastering the dead leaves onto the sidewalk and making Colossal Toys seem that much cozier. Thanksgiving was in a couple of days, and the holiday break combined with the bad weather meant that the shop was empty as Carlos restocked shelves and Teddy stared out the front windows from her place behind the cash register.

Normally, with no one to help and Carlos preoccupied, she would pull up an episode of *Everett's Place*, but obviously that wasn't a comfort for her anymore. That might've been the worst part of this whole situation—that her ultimate security blanket was now gone forever.

Or maybe it was that Everett had become her human security blanket, and now he was gone, too.

A man who looked like Richard cupped his hands around his face and peered into the shop. Teddy smiled thinking about how strange it would have been if Richard ever showed up at Colossal Toys, then stood up straight when the man walked in and she realized he *was* Richard.

"I see a smile on your face!" he said. "That has to be a good sign!"

Teddy frowned. "What are you doing here?"

Richard looked flustered, as if he'd expected a different response. "I came to see you. What else would I be doing here?"

"But you've never come to the shop," Teddy said, confused. "Not when we were together. Not even when I asked you to. You said there was nothing here an adult man should ever need to buy."

Teddy heard Carlos drop a box and curse quietly, but she kept her eyes on Richard.

Richard sighed. "Well . . . I was wrong. What else do you want me to say? I came to see you because I didn't want to leave things the way we left them after our phone call. And also my doorbell camera saw you toilet-papering the town house."

Teddy paled. She'd forgotten about the doorbell camera.

"Don't worry. I'm not mad," Richard said, smiling magnanimously. "I paid the neighbor's kid to clean it up. And I know it wasn't your idea."

"How do you know that?" Teddy asked.

"I should've asked your friends to come clean it up," Richard muttered.

"It *was* my idea," Teddy said so loudly that she was practically shouting.

"What?"

"I instigated the toilet-papering," Teddy said. "And I'm not sorry. We all agreed it was an improvement. Why are you here, Richard? Are you hungry? Because this street is lined with restaurants and I'm happy to give you a recommendation. Go get some chicken fingers at Raising Cane's. I *know* you like chicken fingers."

"I didn't come here to argue, Teddy," Richard said. "I came here to tell you that I love you."

Teddy stared at Richard, the silence between them growing into something so awkward that it was no longer even awkward any-more. And that was when the door burst open.

"I ran here," Everett said, out of breath and dripping wet. "From the parking garage. Do you know how hard it is to find parking around here? I mean, of course you know. But I'm here and I wanted to tell you . . . Oh, I'm sorry. Am I interrupting some-thing?"

Teddy's shock at seeing Everett was quickly overrun by her shock at seeing Richard and Everett standing directly beside each other, a situation she had never expected to happen. She realized that neither knew who the other was—Everett had never seen a picture of Richard, and Richard didn't know she'd dated anyone since they'd broken up.

"What are you doing here?" she asked, but her voice didn't sound anything like it had when she had asked Richard the same thing. Gone were the sharpness, the annoyance . . . Now, the words barely came out in a whisper. The moment she saw Everett, before his pres-ence had fully registered, she'd already felt like she was floating, the same way she always did when she saw him.

"We're kind of in the middle of something," Richard cut in, look-ing Everett up and down with a scowl. "If you don't mind."

Everett narrowed his eyes. "Wait. Is this . . . ?" He looked at Teddy for confirmation.

"Richard, Everett. Everett, Richard," Teddy said.

"Oh, bud," Everett said, "you should really not be here right now. What, did you remember something shitty you forgot to say when you and Teddy were dating?"

"And who are you?" Richard asked.

"I'm Everett St. James and I'm in love with Teddy. And I came here to talk to her, not deal with some bro in . . . in . . . *loafers*," Ev-erett said in disgust.

Richard pushed his shoulders back and stared up at Everett, his mouth arranged in what Teddy thought was supposed to be a snarl. "Excuse me? I don't really think you should be criticizing someone else's clothing. You're wearing a soaking-wet cardigan."

"Okay, once again, I ran here *in the rain*. How are you not wet? Did someone drop you off at the door?"

"No," Richard sneered. "I have an umbrella. Ever heard of them?"

"I happened to forget my— Why am I talking to you?" Everett shook his head. "I came here to talk to Teddy."

Richard reached behind the counter and grabbed Teddy's arm. "She doesn't want to talk to you. I don't even know who you are and I can tell that she doesn't."

"Richard," Teddy said, her voice a warning as she tried to pull away from his grip. But even from the other side of the counter, he was surprisingly strong. "Richard, let go of me."

"Let go of her," Everett said, his voice edged with steel.

"Mind your own business, dude," Richard said. "I don't know what claim you think you have on her, but Teddy needs me. Look at what she's doing without me . . . still working here and toilet-papering my house with a bunch of losers. Teddy can't do anything without me!"

And that was when Everett punched Richard in the face.

## 64

"EVERETT!" TEDDY SCREAMED. "YOUR HAND!"

"Oh, my God," Everett moaned, looking at his hand. What had he been thinking? How the hell was he supposed to hold a puppet if he broke a finger? "My hand."

"What the fuck?" Richard said, holding his face. "I think you knocked out a tooth. I'm bleeding."

"All right! That's it!" Carlos shouted, walking between the men and Teddy. He pointed to Teddy. "You, in the back room. And both of you." He pointed toward Richard and Everett. "Out of the store! Now!"

Carlos walked behind the two of them, as if he was afraid they wouldn't really leave.

On the sidewalk, he crossed his arms and stared at them like he was their disappointed father. "Richard, you're officially banned from the store. Which should be fine with you, since I heard there's nothing in there an adult man needs."

Richard scowled.

"Everett, you can come back tomorrow. You know, as long as Teddy says you can. Hope your hand's okay."

With a wave, he shut the door, leaving the two of them standing in the rain on the sidewalk. They stared at each other.

"I'm, uh . . . I'm sorry I punched you," he said.

"You're a real dick. You know that?" Richard said, wincing as he touched his face.

Everett lifted a shoulder. "That's actually not the consensus among people who know me. In fact, I'd say *you're* more of a dick. That's why people call you Rick the Dick."

Richard looked at him. "Who calls me that?"

Everett gestured vaguely toward the street. "Everyone."

"You're lucky that guy broke things up," Richard muttered. "Because you don't want to know what would've happened if I hit you back."

"Oh, I am not concerned," Everett said lightly. "Because here's the thing, *Rick*. I don't even believe in violence. I work with kids. Do you know that? I spend all day talking about how we need to use our words instead of our fists, and I believe that. Before tonight, I'd never hit another person in my entire life. I don't even kill spiders; I put them in a cup and then release them outside. But there's something about your face, specifically, that makes me want to hit you. And let me tell you something."

He took a couple of steps until he was directly in front of Richard. He had to lean down to meet Richard's eyes, and when he was an inch away from the other man's face, so close that he could see a zit forming on Richard's nose, he said, "If you ever lay a hand on her again—if you ever *contact* her—I will find out, wherever I am. And I will find you, and I will destroy you."

Richard backed up and shook his head. "Who are you even?"

Everett started walking toward the parking garage without answering. But then he turned around, threw his hands in the air, and shouted, "I'm Everett St. Fucking James, you dick."

# 65

TEDDY SAT IN THE BACK ROOM, BREATHING HARD. STUNNED into compliance, she'd followed Carlos's command without thinking, but now that she had a moment of quiet, everything that had happened finally sank in. Richard and Everett had both come to the store, and they had both declared their love for her. And then *Everett had punched Richard in the face.*

Teddy heard the sound of the shop door opening and closing. And then a small knock, and Carlos poked his head in.

"Can I come in?" he asked softly.

Teddy nodded.

"Sorry I was so bossy," he said. "But we can't have fistfights in the store. It's bad for business."

Teddy smiled weakly and wiped away a tear. She hadn't realized she was crying. "Thank you. Richard was . . . I didn't know he . . . I mean, he's never been like that before."

"He seems like a huge douchebag."

Teddy barked out a laugh, shocked. "That's a good way to put it."

She and Carlos looked at each other for a moment, and then he said, "Thanks for always trying to talk to me."

Teddy frowned. "You're welcome, I guess. But it's not a chore,

Carlos. I like talking to you! I don't want you to feel like you can't be yourself here."

Carlos looked at his shoes. "I can tell you're making an effort. It's just . . . conversations are hard for me. I'm bad at small talk. But toys? I understand toys."

Teddy smiled at him. "You're going to be a great owner."

He nodded. "I know. Why don't you take the rest of the night off?"

Teddy started to protest, but then she realized that she didn't think she could go back to work. Seeing Richard had been unpleasant, but seeing Everett . . . Well, she felt like she'd run a marathon and now needed someone to dump a cooler of Gatorade on her.

She'd been thinking about Sophia's words for days. About how falling in love didn't necessarily mean losing herself. And she thought about what Josie had said in the hospital: *If you're with someone for their whole life, things are gonna get hard. They're gonna get hard in ways you can't even imagine. The only chance you have of making it work is by opening up your mouth and saying what you're feeling.*

Maybe she didn't know what would happen if she talked to Everett, but she knew one thing: she didn't want to end things without telling him how she felt.

Teddy said goodbye to Carlos and ran to her car in the parking lot behind the shop, fat raindrops pelting her on the head. She got into her car, shook herself off, and started to text Everett, wincing when she saw that her last text to him had been from dinner at her mom's house.

But then she realized that texts weren't really their medium, anyway. She opened her email and started typing.

66

HALF AN HOUR LATER, TEDDY STOOD AT THE BACK DOOR OF the station, hunched under the awning but still somehow getting wet. She texted Everett, *Where are you? Please say you're at the station.*

About two seconds later, he pushed open the heavy door to let her in.

"If you came here to yell at me for coming to your place of business and punching your ex-boyfriend, that's fair. Not my finest hour, and I apologize," Everett said as the door swung shut behind them.

"No, I . . . Can we talk?" Teddy asked.

Everett's eyes widened and he nodded. Teddy heard a squeaking noise coming down the hallway as a man pushing a bucket came into view.

"Hey, Tom," Everett said with a wave.

Tom said, "Weird date spot," then kept on moving.

"Sorry," Everett said, leading her toward the set and taking her wet coat. He gestured toward the sofa as he flicked on a light. "Would you like to have a seat?"

Only the light directly above the sofa was on, making Teddy feel like she was part of a bizarre play, but she took a seat, anyway. She wished her hair wasn't soaking wet and plastered to her head. When

Everett sat down across from her, the shock of his nearness was almost too much to handle, but she made herself form words.

"This isn't about earlier tonight. Although, yes, I would prefer you didn't punch people in the face, but Richard . . . well, Richard may have deserved it."

"I'm glad we agree on that," Everett said.

Teddy took a deep breath. "Have you checked your email?"

Everett stared at her for a moment, then said, "Actually, I'm trying a new thing where I spend my evenings not thinking about work, so . . . no. I know I'm *at* work, which may contradict what I said, but I was planning on asking Tom if he wanted to go get a drink when he was done. Why? Did you send me something?"

"Yes." Teddy nodded quickly.

"I was joking," Everett said, grabbing his phone. "Did you really email me and then drive here to make sure I got the email?"

"That's exactly what I did," Teddy said. "I sent you an email, but I decided I couldn't wait to see you, so . . . can you read it?"

"Right now?" Everett asked, finger poised over his phone screen. "While you watch me?"

Teddy nodded again.

Everett bit back a smile. "Right. Okay. This is kinda weird, but I like it."

Teddy watched him read, although of course she knew what she'd written.

Dear Everett,

You once told me that nothing I ever said could come out wrong, and while it means a lot to me that you said so, I don't really believe that. Sometimes it seems that all my words come out wrong, like they're getting jumbled in the time it takes them to get from my brain to my mouth. But this? Well, we met through email, and that's how we got to know each other, and I think I might be able to actually say what I mean here.

I told you we shouldn't be together because I didn't want to move and I didn't want you to give up on your dream. And that's all still true—I want to live here, in the same city as my friends and my family (who I'm starting to be a little bit more honest with, actually), and I certainly don't want you to ever stop doing the show.

But I forgot about something pretty important. I'm in love with you, Everett. I'm in love with everything about you, and the way I feel when you're around, and the way you light up every room and situation and make it better. I'm in love with the way you listen to me and make me feel like I matter.

You were right about Colossal Toys. I didn't want to run it, so I'm not going to. I don't know what I'll do instead, but I know I'll figure it out. Thank you for trusting me before I trusted myself.

I know you're not going to stay here, and I'm not going with you, but someone pretty important to me told me that while love doesn't conquer all, it can still conquer a whole hell of a lot. So maybe it will be hard and messy, but that doesn't mean we can't try to conquer it together. I can't think of anyone else I'd want to conquer it with.

I love you.

Theodora

Teddy watched his face the entire time he read, her eyes on his eyes as they moved across his phone. And then, when he started typing, she leaned forward, trying to see what was on his screen.

Her phone dinged. "You should check your email," he said, his face blank.

Teddy held her breath as she pulled her phone out of her bag. Her hands shaking, she opened her email and read three words on the screen.

**I'm not moving.**

She dropped her phone in her lap and looked at Everett. "What?"

He smiled. "I'm not going to New York. I'm staying here."

Teddy's mouth dropped open. "Everett, what happened? You didn't tell them no, did you? Did they tell *you* no?"

Everett shook his head. "I spent so long thinking that the only way forward was up, you know? That if I followed this path with the show, I'd be happy. More prestige, more acclaim, more viewers. And then I realized . . . I love my job. But I don't want my job to be my life. I don't want to give up time with my friends, or my sister, or my parents because of work." He swallowed. "And I don't want to give up time with you."

"So did you quit your show?" Teddy asked, looking confused. "Because I can't imagine you without this show."

"No, I asked the Imagination Network if we could work with them, but keep filming here. I told them that being here, on this set, in this city, was integral to the soul of the show, and they thought so, too. So I'll get to keep my producer, my crew, my sofa . . ." He paused, meeting her eyes, looking almost shy. "And I hope I get to keep you, too, Teddy."

"So," she said in a small voice, afraid to speak too loud in case she scared her happiness away, "you're staying in Columbus."

He nodded. "Probably have to take semifrequent trips to New York, but yes, I'm staying right here."

Teddy blinked. This seemed too good to be true, that she was suddenly getting exactly what she wanted. There had to be some catch, some trapdoor waiting for her to step on it.

But also . . . maybe she was being ridiculous. Joy was in front of her, and maybe she shouldn't question it or analyze it to death or waste her time worrying about when the other shoe might drop. Maybe she should just appreciate what she had while she had it.

Teddy got up and then sat down on Everett's lap, wrapping her arms around his neck. "I'm so glad you're staying here," she said, trying not to cry.

"Hey," Everett said, wiping a tear off her face with his thumb. "What was it you said in your email?"

"Which part?" Teddy asked, wishing Everett would stop talking so she could kiss him. "I wrote it pretty fast in my car. I was kind of rambling."

"The part about how you love me," Everett said. "Is that true, or did you add it in there for dramatic effect?"

Teddy smiled. "It's true," she said. "I love you, Everett St. James. I knew I loved you on our very first date."

"Well, I have you beat," Everett said, kissing her neck. "Because I knew I loved you from your very first email. Maybe I didn't think those words, but I knew you were special, and I knew I wanted to meet you. I love you, Theodora Phillips."

Teddy grabbed his face and kissed him, hard. "You promise you're not leaving?"

"Promise," Everett said. "I have way too much to stay here for. And I'm never, ever forgetting plans with you again, okay? I don't want work to be my life anymore. I want my life to be my life."

Teddy smiled and kissed him.

He lifted her off his lap and stood up. "What's happening?" Teddy asked, standing up.

"Let's go home," Everett said. "We need to stop making out on the studio couch. It's been around awhile, and also Tom is out there and he's an incorrigible gossip."

Teddy smiled as Everett held out a hand. And as she took it, letting his big fingers wrap around hers, she knew this didn't solve all her problems. She was still a work in progress, still a blank canvas. But now she knew she didn't have to fill that canvas alone.

"Let's go home," she said. He kissed her on the forehead and Teddy knew that, even if she couldn't plan out her whole future, she could figure out her entire life this way: taking one step at a time with Everett St. James by her side.

# Epilogue

JOSIE'S SMALL BACKYARD WAS BEAUTIFUL IN EVERY SEASON, but in early August, with the echinacea slowly swaying in the wind and her huge outdoor table illuminated by twinkle lights in the dusk, it was Teddy's favorite place on Earth.

And right now, with everyone she loved crowded around that table, she didn't think it was possible to be happier. Kirsten and Eleanor had organized a birthday dinner for her, with Josie providing the food. Teddy's plate was heaped high with corn, tomato-and-orzo salad, and perfectly grilled chicken pieces, and she was already eyeing the huge chocolate sheet cake in the center of the table. Also, she was slightly tipsy on Josie's signature sangria, which probably should've come with some sort of warning.

Teddy looked around the table, at her mother, Sophia, and Craig (who was, naturally, gnawing on a chicken leg). The Viking was talking to Carlos and his girlfriend, presumably about toys. Natalie and Lillian were laughing at whatever Josie was saying, Kirsten and Eleanor were whispering about something, and Sophia and Craig's kids were running around and throwing tennis balls to Josie's dogs. Even Everett's family was there, and Everett's coworkers, Jeremy and Astrid, whom she'd become friends with over the past year.

It was perfect, made more so because Everett was right beside her, holding her hand the whole time even though it made the process of eating grilled chicken significantly more difficult. She looked over to smile at him, only to see him mouthing something to Kirsten.

"What are you saying?" she asked, narrowing her eyes. "Are you planning something?"

Everett widened his eyes. "What?"

"Is this going to be one of those situations like at a restaurant where you tell the waitstaff it's my birthday and everyone has to come out and sing an awkward song? Because there aren't any servers here, and I'm sure Josie would be happy to sing, but it's gonna be uncomfortable."

Everett leaned in and kissed her cheek. "All will be revealed."

Teddy heard the telltale clink of flatware on a wineglass and turned to see Kirsten and Eleanor standing up, getting everyone's attention.

Everyone quieted down as Kirsten said, "Hello, friends, family, and lovers of Teddy Phillips!"

"Just the one lover but okay," Everett muttered in Teddy's ear.

"Thank you all so much for being here to celebrate the birth of one of our absolute favorite people," Kirsten said.

"And thank you so much to Josie for hosting us and providing a truly stellar dinner," Eleanor said, leading everyone in a round of applause. Josie did a dramatic bow, complete with hand flourishes.

"Teddy, you know we love you, but we wanted to take a moment to tell you, with God and this lethal sangria as our witnesses, that we're so happy you moved in with us last year, and we can't imagine our lives without you. Happy birthday!" Kirsten said with a smile.

"Cheers to Teddy!" Eleanor shouted, lifting her glass.

"Oh, no," Teddy said to Everett, dabbing at her eyes with her napkin. "I'm gonna cry."

"And now," Kirsten said, "I believe one Everett St. James would like the floor."

Teddy whipped her head toward him as he stood up, not looking at her. Everett didn't often get anxious—after all, he was used to people looking at him—but as he crossed and uncrossed his arms, Teddy realized he was nervous.

"So, uh," he started, one hand rubbing the back of his neck, "hi, everyone. Most of you know me as Teddy's boyfriend, and I wanted to say a few words about her on her birthday. Teddy changed my life when she . . . when we . . . uh . . ."

Everett looked at her, looked away, and sighed. "Okay, I can't do this. Hold on. I've gotta . . ."

He fumbled in his pocket, then pulled out his phone. Teddy watched in confusion as he typed something out, and then she felt her own phone buzz in her lap.

She picked it up. *One new email from Everett St. James.*

"Did you just . . . ?" she started.

"Can you read it?" he asked quickly.

Teddy opened her email and everything went quiet. She could no longer hear the dogs barking or the kids' happy screeches or Natalie asking, "What are you guys doing?" All that mattered to her were the words on her phone.

Dear Theodora,

Will you marry me?

Very sincerely yours,
Everett

She stood up, knocking over her chair. "Oh, God, sorry. I mean . . . yes. Yes. Yes, Everett!"

She jumped onto him and he picked her up, her lips pressed onto his and her arms around his neck.

"I love you so much," he said into her mouth, and she smiled back.

"What exactly is happening here?" Josie asked.

"They're engaged!" Kirsten and Eleanor shouted in unison, and then everyone lost it. Soon they were all cheering and shrieking and crushing Teddy in hugs. Craig shook Everett's hand and said, "Welcome to the family. Gimme a call if you ever need any tips." Teddy's mother started crying. Even Josie's dogs, confused by the commotion, jumped on Teddy as if they were trying to give her a hug in their own way.

Amid the chaos and the yelling and barking, Teddy felt a hand grab on to hers, and she looked back to see Everett talking intently to Craig as he squeezed her hand. She couldn't believe that less than a year ago, she'd been miserable, shrinking herself to fit into someone else's life and someone else's idea of who she should be. Now nearly everything about her life was different. She lived with Eleanor and Kirsten in the most colorful, warmest home she could imagine. Her mother was actually working on figuring out her own life instead of Teddy's. Sophia had quit her job months ago and was now back in school. On evenings and weekends, Everett spent time with Teddy instead of working, and sometimes they even watched bad reality TV and ate takeout with Natalie and Lillian. Carlos ran Colossal Toys, although Teddy didn't work there anymore. Now she had a job at the sewing shop, and she was happy even though she didn't know if she'd stay there forever. Maybe she'd always love it, or maybe she'd find something else she loved more. Because that was what life was all about, right? Trying new things, discovering what you loved and hated, exploring all of your major and minor passions? Maybe she wouldn't ever find one big thing that lit her up;

maybe it was enough to be constantly discovering a million little things that made life worth living.

Everett met her eye and smiled, and as Teddy smiled back, she knew. Loving someone and being loved back, getting the chance to wake up every morning and uncover new passions, deciding on her own what her life would be . . .

It was more than enough. It was everything.

# Acknowledgments

I'm so grateful for the long list of people who made this book what it is. First and foremost, thank you to my amazing editor, Cindy Hwang. I still can't believe that I'm lucky enough to work with you. Thank you for understanding this book and for calling it "hot Mister Rogers."

Thank you to my agent Stephen Barbara for always advocating for my books and for asking a question I'll be pondering for the rest of my life: was Mister Rogers hot?

Thank you to everyone at Berkley, including Brittanie Black, Diana Franco, Tara O'Connor, Fareeda Bullert, Elisha Katz, and Angela Kim. It's a wonderful feeling to know that my books are in such great hands.

Thank you to Rita Frangie and Farjana Yasmin for an absolutely perfect cover. You captured Teddy and Everett down to the smallest details. I know I say this every time, but I think this is the best cover yet.

Thank you to COSI for hosting a Jim Henson exhibit in 2019. It reminded me of the importance of creativity, originality, and beauty, and also made me think that the world needs more romances about puppeteers.

Thank you to all the picture book authors and illustrators who made videos during the pandemic for a) entertaining my child and b) helping me understand Everett a little better.

So many thanks to Lauren Dlugosz Rochford and Emily Adrian for reading my words and encouraging me to keep going.

Thank you to Mary Schmich, who was most likely the person who actually said, "Do one thing every day that scares you." Sorry so many people, including my fictional characters, misattribute your words to Eleanor Roosevelt.

Thank you to the librarians who read and recommend my books, and extra thanks for doing your jobs so well during such a difficult time.

A massive thank-you to all the bookstores and booksellers who've supported me and my books. Extra special shout-outs to Annie at The Bookshelf, Carl at Fountain Bookstore, Paul at Silver Unicorn, Anna and Amanda at One More Page, Kate and Beth at Bookmarks, Kim at Joseph-Beth, Chelsea and Vanessa at Wheatberry, Kim at Read It Again, and everyone at The Book Loft and Cover to Cover. Thank you for letting me take part in virtual events, putting my books on your Best Of lists, making my books your staff recommendations, and/or being amazing in general. This is a rough time to release a book, sell books, or be a human, and I get genuinely tearful when I think about the support and warmth you've shown me.

My family kept me relatively sane while I wrote a book during a pandemic. Thank you to Harry for always encouraging me to take a break, and thank you to Hollis for the in-depth LEGO knowledge this book needed.

And finally, thank you to everyone who reads my books and recommends them to their family and friends. Thank you to the book bloggers and the bookstagrammers and anyone who has ever sent me a kind message or email. I enjoy the process of writing, but the real reason I write is because I love to connect with readers. I couldn't do this without you, and I wouldn't want to.

# VERY
# SINCERELY
# YOURS

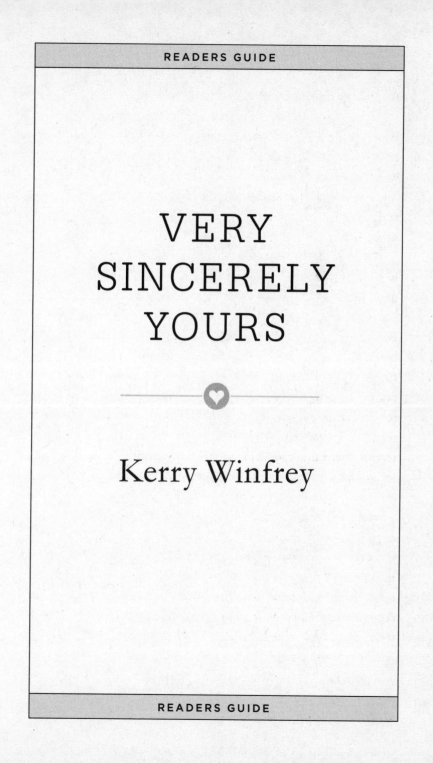

## Kerry Winfrey

# Questions for Discussion

1. Everett has always known what he wants to do with his life, while Teddy has never identified what she's passionate about. Do you relate more to Everett or Teddy?

2. Teddy decides to do one thing every day that scares her. What kind of things have you done that scared you? Did you end up enjoying them?

3. Getting dumped by Richard pushes Teddy to make some big changes in her life. Do you think she would have made these changes if Richard hadn't broken up with her? Have you ever gone through a seemingly negative experience that changed your life for the better?

4. Teddy and Everett get to know each other via email before they meet in person. Have you ever started a relationship with someone online? What do you think the benefits are of getting to know someone this way?

5. If you were in Everett's position and had a chance to go to New York for a job like his, would you have gone? What might change your mind?

6. Teddy finds comfort in watching *Everett's Place*, even if she isn't the target audience. Do you have a show, film, or book that's a metaphorical security blanket? Would you ever want to meet the creator?

7. Everett and Teddy had very different childhoods. How did their backgrounds and families affect their confidence in their own abilities and their determination to follow their dreams?

8. How do Everett and Teddy change each other's trajectories? What do you think the future holds for their relationship?

Keep reading for an excerpt from
Kerry Winfrey's next novel . . .

# JUST ANOTHER
# LOVE SONG

*Coming soon from Jove!*

I'VE IMAGINED RUNNING INTO HANK TILLMAN ROUGHLY ONE million times since we graduated from high school fifteen years ago. Maybe he'd see me walking my Great Dane, Toby, down Main Street, my hair blowing in the wind in a casual-yet-gorgeous way, and he'd be rendered speechless by my beauty. Maybe he'd see me at work and be impressed that Sandy Macintosh had grown into a competent, successful, but (most important) extremely sexy business owner. Or maybe he'd see me attempting to play basketball with my best friend Honey's three kids, and he'd be mesmerized by my athletic prowess and ease with children (forget the fact that I can't make a basket to save my own damn life, and that Honey's six-year-old, Lydia, makes fun of me every time we play because she's a bad sport).

But never, in any of my wild imaginings, did I picture our reunion happening in the soda aisle of Tillman's Grocery, with me covered in dirt, my hair twisted into a messy, lopsided bun, as the Santana and Rob Thomas song "Smooth" played softly through the grocery store speakers.

"Hey, Sandy," he says casually, as if we see each other every day, instead of our reality, which is that the last time I saw his face in

person was right after I kissed him goodbye and he went off to
college.

And what a face it was . . . and *is*. I allow my eyes a moment to
roam over him, to take in the lines that weren't there fifteen years
ago, the crease of his forehead and the crinkles by his eyes. The way
his nose is just the slightest bit crooked because he broke it at football practice freshman year, when he was the only freshman to
make the varsity team. Those eyelashes that made me jealous, because they were longer than any boy's really had to be and mine
were always so short and stubby. I have the desire to reach my hand
out and touch his face, to run my fingers over the topography there
and see what's changed.

His eyes dart over my face, like he's doing the same thing, and I
look away quickly. I'm covered in dirt because, well, I've been in the
dirt all day, installing a new garden for a client. I ran to the store
because my employee, Marcia, has a monstrous Diet Coke addiction and gets twitchy if I don't keep the mini fridge at the greenhouse stocked.

I try not to wonder what he thinks of how I've changed over the
past fifteen years. Because, after all, this is probably the first time
he's seen me. I use social media just like anyone else, but mostly to
keep up with everyone who moved out of Baileyville, or to like the
constant stream of kid photos that Honey posts. I keep my personal
updates to generic sunrises, and my business account is nothing but
pictures of gardens and flowers. My online presence is negligible,
just the way I like it.

But I've had plenty of opportunities to see Hank, of course.
Album covers. A recording of Austin City Limits on PBS. A magazine article here and there. Because Hank Tillman became what he
always said he'd be: a musician.

I try not to look at that stuff, because I try not to live in the past, try not to think about all the things I said I'd be back then, back when we were seventeen and stupid and so, so in love.

"Hey, Hank," I almost whisper, willing myself to look anywhere but at him. I glance at the root beer, the orange soda, but I look back at him as he sticks his hands in his pockets. My eyes dart to his arms sticking out below the rolled-up sleeves of his faded red flannel shirt. They're tanned and rough, like he's spent the entire summer, his entire life, outside.

I hate this, hate that he's somehow become even more handsome and that I know all these details about him down in my bones, like they're a part of me, like I'll never be rid of him no matter how hard I try. *He moved on,* I remind myself. *He left town and he left you and you did just fine for yourself, didn't you? You own a business. You have a house. You have employees and a dog and a front porch and a very expensive espresso machine.*

I know I should be an adult here, make polite conversation, ask him why he's back in town . . . but every cell in my body is screaming, *Get out of this store now!* I attempt to walk past him, but my bare arm brushes against his bare arm and I gasp. It's been so long since the last time I touched him, and it's pathetic the way that grazing his arm brings me right back to being seventeen and in love, the radio playing in his truck, the windows open and the breeze warm as we drove the winding back roads of Baileyville.

The case of Diet Coke slips out of my hand and crashes onto my toes. "Shit," I mutter as I bend down to pick it up.

"Are you okay?" Hank asks, reaching out to help, but I just nod quickly.

"I'm fine!" I say, pretending that it doesn't feel like one of my toes is on fire. "I gotta go!"

I turn around, attempting to make my way to the cash register as quickly as I can. From now on I will not enable Marcia's addiction; trying to be a good boss only injures my foot and makes me run into my first love.

"Sandy . . . ," he says, and I turn around. Our eyes meet, and I see it all for just a moment, a flash of everything we went through when we were just kids. Passing notes in class. Promising everything. Kissing in his parents' barn. Never dreaming that things would end up this way.

"It's good to see you," he finishes. I nod, not trusting myself to speak. Because what could I say? *Well, it's not good to see you, Hank, because I like to pretend you don't exist.*

Instead, I just hobble to the register.

MARCIA CLAPS WHEN I walk in the door, holding the box of Diet Coke aloft. "Thank you so much, and wait, are you *limping*?"

"I think I broke my toe when I dropped this case of poison liquid on my foot," I say, handing it to her. "I'll take over the register if you can go put this in the fridge."

"My hero," she says, hugging the box.

"You need help," I tell her.

"And you need medical attention," she says before heading to the break room.

I smile and roll my eyes, then lean over the counter and take a look around me. The interior of my greenhouse, Country Colors, isn't huge—this room, with the register, is fully enclosed and full of garden tools, indoor plants, and lawn decorations. But the double doors open into the greenhouse proper, where we keep the plants. Not that we have many customers right now, because it's July. Everything's planted, and as the saying goes, the corn should already be knee-high. There's still plenty of gardening to be done, of course, but people have their eyes on harvest, not putting new

EXCERPT FROM *JUST ANOTHER LOVE SONG*     367

plants in the ground, so we're in a bit of a slow period until things pick up for the pumpkins and mums in September.

*This is mine,* I remind myself. Country Colors was tiny when I started working here in college, just looking for any job in a town where there weren't many employment opportunities. At the time, I was depressed and anxious, feeling like I'd been left behind by the friends who'd gone away to school while I stayed in place, attending Baileyvillle Community College. I'd dreamed of being an artist, but BCC didn't even have art classes. I majored in marketing, which my mom insisted was very creative and basically the same thing as painting. She's always known how to put a positive spin on things, my mom.

But what started as a way to make a few bucks grew (pun intended) into something so much more. Unlike marketing, gardening actually *was* creative. Planting things and watching them grow was rewarding in a way that little else in my life was, and more than that, it was unpredictable. Flowers, as it turned out, had minds of their own.

Soon, I was spending all my free time at the greenhouse, and when my boss retired, she asked me if I wanted to take over. And so Country Colors became mine—my sanctuary, my second home, my new dream. Did I still miss art, the feeling of paint under my fingernails? Sure, but now I had dirt under my fingernails. Maybe the dream hadn't changed so much as the medium did.

I'm happy with the way things turned out. Really, I am. If only Hank Tillman hadn't showed up to remind me of how different things could've been.

A bloodcurdling scream from Marcia jolts me out of my contemplation and I run into the break room, sure she's been hacked to bits by a serial killer who targets greenhouses (which sounds like the plot of one of the cozy mysteries my parents keep stocked in their B and B).

"What happened?" I ask as I burst into the room.

Marcia is standing still, Diet Coke dripping off her face. She looks at me, her eyes wide in shock.

"Oh," I say. "I should've warned you not to open it yet. I guess it got kind of shaken up when I dropped it."

She slowly smiles. "This is disgusting."

"You look very sticky," I agree. "Why don't you go home and get cleaned up? I think I can handle it here until close."

"Fantastic," she says. "That shaken-up can of Diet Coke was a blessing, not a curse, because tonight's my and Aimee's anniversary."

I swat her on the arm, which was a bad idea, because that's also covered in soda. "You should've told me! I would've let you leave early, anyway."

She shrugs, and I smile as I think about her wedding to Aimee three years ago. It happened in her backyard, under an arbor covered in pink climbing roses, with the reverend from the Baileyville Unitarian Universalist church marrying them. We all blew bubbles at the end as they got on a tandem bike and rode to their reception in the park.

As I watch Marcia now, humming happily to herself as she attempts to dry off her shirt with paper towels, a pang of longing hits me. It's not that I want what she has, exactly. . . . It's that I want to even know what it's like, to have someone waiting at home, someone I can't wait to see. I'm happy with my life—my job, my friends, my home—but it would be nice, wouldn't it, to have another person to share it all with?

Dating isn't exactly easy in a small town, though. Apps have a very different vibe when everyone on them is someone you went to kindergarten with (or, in one case, is your recently divorced kindergarten teacher who wants to "get back out there").

"Okay, I'm headed home," Marcia says, tossing the soda-soaked paper towel into the trash.

"Happy anniversary," I call after her, and she shoots me a quick smile as she hurries out to her car.

I head back up to the register and look out over the shop once more. And although I don't want to, I find myself wondering again what, exactly, Hank Tillman is doing back in Baileyville.

Photo by Alex Winfrey

**Kerry Winfrey** writes romantic comedies for adults and teens. She is the author of *Love and Other Alien Experiences*, *Things Jolie Needs to Do Before She Bites It*, *Waiting for Tom Hanks*, and *Not Like the Movies*. When she's not writing, she's likely baking yet another pie or watching far too many romantic comedies. She lives with her husband, son, and dog in the middle of Ohio.

CONNECT ONLINE

🐦 @KerryAnn
📷 @KerryWinfrey
ayearofromcoms.tumblr.com

Ready to find
your next great read?

Let us help.

**Visit prh.com/nextread**